"In the mood for sweet and sexy?"
(*USA Today*) Then discover the novels of

Carrie Lofty

and enjoy "romance with sizzle" *(Coffee Time Romance)* and "a sensual journey" (*Australian Romance Readers Association*) in book after book!

Praise for Carrie Lofty and her award-winning fiction

"Lofty shows us a world filled with courage, hope, and the limitless possibilities of love."

—*Fresh Fiction*

"Richly nuanced characters come together brilliantly."

—*The Chicago Tribune*

"The fireworks are zingy hot, the dialogue deliciously cutting."

—*Drey's Library*

"Exquisite sensuality."

—*The Romanceaholic*

"She paints a picture rich with emotion, struggle, and passion."

—*Smexybooks*

"Lofty's prose is exquisite, her characters are extremely likable and genuine. . . ."

—*The Romance Dish*

"Hot and passionate with sizzling chemistry. . . ."

—*Book Lovers Inc.*

"Watch Lofty's star rise."

—*RT Book Reviews*

BLUE NOTES

CARRIE LOFTY

G

GALLERY BOOKS

NEW YORK   LONDON   TORONTO   SYDNEY   NEW DELHI

G

Gallery Books
A Division of Simon & Schuster, Inc.
1230 Avenue of the Americas
New York, NY 10020

First Gallery Books trade paperback edition May 2014

GALLERY BOOKS and colophon are registered trademarks of Simon & Schuster, Inc.

For information about special discounts for bulk purchases, please contact Simon & Schuster Special Sales at 1-866-506-1949 or business@simonandschuster.com.

The Simon & Schuster Speakers Bureau can bring authors to your live event. For more information or to book an event contact the Simon & Schuster Speakers Bureau at 1-866-248-3049 or visit our website at www.simonspeakers.com.

Interior design by Jaime Putorti

Manufactured in the United States of America
10 9 8 7 6 5 4 3 2

Library of Congress Cataloging-in-Publication Data

Lofty, Carrie, 1976–
  Blue notes : by Carrie Lofty.—First Gallery Books trade paperback edition.
      pages cm
  1. Women pianists—Fiction. 2. Billionaires—Fiction. 3. Friendship—Fiction.
  4. Psychological fiction. I. Title.
  PS3603.05475B58 2014
  813'.6—dc23
                          2013046835

ISBN 978-1-4767-0689-4
ISBN 978-1-4767-0691-7 (ebook)

*To Karen Hermanson Martin, for Cosmos,
cleaning up my nasty Mac'n'Cheese, poetry
readings, Mothra, midnight runs to the
Galley, MK and DM joint coping sessions,
and your enthusiasm for a poster of* The
Crow *and an X-Men bedspread that
helped launch one of the most important
friendships of my life.
I love you.*

BLUE NOTES

PROLOGUE

"Please continue, Miss Nyman."

I cringe at the name, because it isn't mine anymore. The judge keeps using it. I guess he has to. The foster parents I've been assigned by the State have agreed to become my permanent guardians if Dad is convicted. I've lived with them for seven months. It's not exactly witness protection, but we've already discussed changing my name and moving out of state. Right now, they're at a nearby hotel waiting for me.

I haven't been a nice kid in those seven months. In fact, I've been kind of a brat. Or depressed. Or screaming from nightmares. They've put up with a lot, including shuffling me back and forth to my shrink appointments. Three times a week is a lot, but I have lots to sort out. New guardians. Getting ready for a new life in Baton Rouge, where Clair's family lives.

Plus this trial.

I have to be nicer to Clair and John Chambers. They deserve better.

Sitting here on the witness stand, I make a promise to myself to be different from now on.

That's my future—the one I want to get to. Apparently Baton Rouge is hot and has a ton of bugs and some really nosy people, but it's a nice place to live. The Chamberses have picked out a small, pretty home near her parents'. But I don't care what the house is like. I'll have a bed with fresh sheets, hot meals, and two people across the hall who actually care about me.

And Clair's piano. Oh God, a real piano in the house where I'm going to live.

But first, Rosie Nyman, the girl I don't want to be anymore, has some cleaning up to do.

"I'm fifteen years old." Thank God my voice is steady. "My father is Greg Peter Nyman, and my mother was Jessica Lynn Nyman. She was murdered."

I don't look to where Dad is sitting with his defense guy. I can feel his glare, though. He's been staring at me since I stepped into the courtroom. He stared at me the same way during all the prelim stuff. "You won't go through with it, Rosie girl," he said once, before the guards hauled him away in manacles and handcuffs. "I'll find you if you do."

I'll find you if you do.

Those are words to keep a girl awake at night.

"Miss Nyman?" This from the prosecuting attorney. She's pretty and a total badass. Although nobody else would make the comparison, she reminds me of Clair. They're both tigers ready to maul the bad guys. In this case, the bad guy is my father. "When you say she was murdered, can you be more specific? Tell us what you saw on the night of May twelfth last year."

"We were squatting in a trailer outside Stockton. We'd only

been there a couple weeks since leaving Colorado. I didn't like it there."

"In Colorado?"

"Oh, sorry," I say, trying not to get flustered. "I didn't like it there either, but Stockton was worse. It was someone else's house, you know? Creepy. They had a fight about it."

"Your mother and father?"

I nod at the prosecutor. Her name is Ursula Lineski, which always makes me think of a Disney villain. It's backward, though, because she's on my side. "Yeah, they fought about how it was a shitty place to live. Oh, sorry." I look up at the judge, expecting lightning bolts to shoot from his eyes because I cussed in court. "I didn't mean to say that."

"Because it's not true?" he asks, almost fatherly—if "fatherly" means nice and reassuring. He looks like he could be Morgan Freeman's younger brother.

"No, sir. I just have trouble with using words I shouldn't. Sorry," I say again.

"I'd like to hear what you remember of the actual exchange." Ursula stands between me and my dad. I think it's on purpose, and I like her even more for it.

"Then I'll have to use those kind of words."

She smiles a little. "Just be as accurate as you can, Miss Nyman."

I inhale until I *know* my lungs are gonna pop. I want my fingers on ivory keys.

I clear my throat while tapping out "Für Elise" on my thigh. "Mom said, *You're a goddamn motherfucker for dragging us to this shithole.*" I'm telling the truth, and it's how I grew up thinking everybody talks, but I still blush. I can't look at Ursula or the judge. "Für Elise" is gone. I pick at a cuticle and watch the blood well under the ragged skin. "Dad said, *And you're an ungrateful bitch who won't shut up.* It kinda went on like that until Mom had had enough."

"How do you mean, had enough?" Ursula asks. She knows the answer, but the jurors need to hear it. They need to hear it from me. Mom was no saint—more like a shrieking devil—but I'm the only one left to speak for her.

"She threatened to call the cops. She'd done it before, so I didn't think anything about it. But they kept at it."

"Where were you at the time?"

"Behind this nasty recliner. I'd cleared away some old newspapers and used a blanket to make a—God, this sounds dumb. I made, like, a fort. You know, how little kids do?" I shrug. "Sometimes they'd fight and have sex. Or they'd get wasted. Or high—mostly high. Or Dad would hit her."

"Objection," calls my dad's attorney. "The defendant is not on trial for drug use or assault."

"The witness is establishing a pattern of behavior," Ursula counters. "This was her world, as much as their itinerant lifestyle."

"I'll allow it," the judge says. "But, Miss Nyman, please limit your remarks from now on to the events in question."

"Okay. Sorry."

"It's all right," Ursula says, her voice sorta hypnotic. She can be a tiger and a snake charmer. "Go on?"

"She kept at it, the threats. I never heard her make more than one or two—wait, that's the past. That night, she said she'd tell them about the meth in the trunk, and what he'd done in Colorado. I don't know what that was, but he got really mad. Now can I say he hit her?"

Ursula nodded.

"Yeah, I was watching from behind the recliner. He hit her in the stomach and punched her face. There was blood. She used a towel to wipe it off her nose. I know it's horrible and I shouldn't have thought it, but I hoped she'd fight back because then they'd take it out on each other." My chest clenches. "Not me."

"*Did* she fight back, Miss Nyman?" Ursula asked.

"No. She got all calm and quiet. *I'm going to the police, you prick*, she said. I knew she'd been popping oxy like candy. But she didn't sound high. She sounded like a regular person."

My definition of a regular person has changed a lot since being taken into State custody. Nice people live in this world. I like them, but I don't know how to relate to them.

"Dad freaked me out too, because he got calm and quiet like her. It was so weird. They just stared at each other." I exhale. "That's when Dad left. He slammed the door. I didn't see him again until he was arrested."

"What was he arrested for, Miss Nyman?" Ursula is pacing, but not in an agitated way. It's almost lulling. She never leaves an open line of sight between me and Dad.

"For killing her. It was the next day. There was so much blood. . . ."

Next thing I know, I start . . . *leaking*. I just can't hold it in. It's not crying. That means being all blubbery and sobby. The bailiff hands me a box of tissues and pours me some water. He's tall and stocky, like he could flip a semi. That's probably a good trait for a bailiff.

"I got off the school bus at the entrance to the trailer park, with the other kids." I want to say, *My folks were good at making sure I was legal and in school and not around to mess in their business*, but I don't. "Mom was dead on the kitchen floor."

I go on with the details, feeling swoony and out of body—kinda like I felt back then. It was almost eighteen months ago, but even on the stand, I know I won't ever forget what I saw. I think I have a lot more I'd like to forget than most people.

The cross examination is brutal. Ursula can't protect me anymore. The defense prick keeps moving out of the way. I think it's on purpose, to let Dad glare at me. I still don't look at him, but I bet he's smirking.

"Isn't it true, Miss Nyman, that in your statement to the police, you recalled signs of your mother having been under the influence of drugs?"

I nod. I don't say anything until he prods me. "Yes," I finally answer. "Needles and track marks."

"Can you be more specific?"

I glare. "Heroin. I think she'd cooked some heroin."

"And she was armed?"

"The police guys told everyone this stuff," I say.

"You're here because you were the first witness on the scene, Miss Nyman. Please answer." He has beady eyes and a mustache like something out of a '70s porno.

"A switchblade was on the floor near her right hand."

"Ah. So she fought back."

"I can't be sure of that, can I? Speculation."

The mustache makes his smile creepy, kinda like a clown. "You've been coached well." He stands with his hands behind his back and glances between me and my dad. "Miss Nyman, look at your father. Look at him."

I do. For the first time since I sat down, I *really* do. He's wearing a suit, with his hair clean and slicked back. He's had a shave. He's gained a healthy amount of weight, and his skin has a healthy glow. He was probably forced into detox. I can't remember seeing him seem so ordinary. Yet no amount of soap and scrubbing can change his face. I don't know if there's a hell, but his expression promises he'll do his best to send me there.

"As his only daughter, as his little girl, can you honestly say that you believe your father capable of murder? That he killed your mother?"

"Yes, sir," I say. "I can honestly say that."

His shoulders slump in resignation. Maybe he thought his last card was to appeal to me as a daughter. Or to let my dad's sneering, vicious glare scare me into silence.

Not a chance.

"No further questions, Your Honor."

The case is over. Putting a fifteen-year-old on the stand probably counts as cruelty to some, in light of how much evidence the police had. Ursula said she had a really good shot at first degree if I testified. Which meant he'd be put away forever. No chance of parole.

Instead, he's convicted of second degree murder and sentenced to twenty-five years.

There were mitigating circumstances—something about the switchblade and how Mom fought back. I don't catch more than every fourth word. All I know is that when the cops finally drop me off at the hotel, I don't flinch when Clair and John give me smothering hugs, something I'm still trying to get used to.

Now, Rosie Nyman is as dead and gone as my mom.

My name is Keeley Chambers.

~ ONE ~

*Y*ou're going to be a star.

That's what Clair, my foster mom, said whenever she stood on the stairs of our basement rec room, smiling, listening to me pounding and pounding. I've never told Clair how much I hated being surprised that way. How embarrassed I got. It's like when I was sixteen and the bathroom door at the movie theater wouldn't lock. I tried to keep it shut by putting one foot out. Not easy. Not dignified. I cringed the whole time. It definitely wasn't something I wanted a stranger to see. Some absentminded woman barged in anyway.

Insert mortification.

My music is . . . private. It's a hole in me where anyone can look inside. It's a damn bathroom door that won't lock. The keys aren't my friends when I'm so pent up. It's only afterward, when I write down what's flowed through me, that I feel in control again. The music doesn't own me then. I own it.

It's not that I don't think I'm good; it's being watched that gets me all sick inside. That's the real challenge. My profs at Tulane tell me I'll have to get over it one day. "One day" is coming soon. The winter recital is just over three months away. If I can't make myself heard there, I might as well call music my hobby and go home.

Not an option. I'm a junior now. This is *me*.

I never feel more secure than when I'm in a private rehearsal room, like the one in Dixon Hall. Living in New Orleans had been my dream for so long that I don't remember when or how it started. I'd wanted to smell the Garden District and walk the French Quarter. In spring, I want to find a place high above the glittering, cocktail soaked chaos of Mardi Gras. It's a city of mystery and romance, like a sultry smile that never fades.

New Orleans has secrets.

Maybe that's what sparked my fascination. I have secrets too.

I strip off my lightweight sweater. The rehearsal room is intentionally chilly. Serious practice gets hot real fast.

But I shed more than layers of clothing. When sitting on a piano bench, I can shake off emotional burdens—memories of my long gone parents and our lives on the run, knocking off liquor stores, cooking meth in the woods of a shady, scary as hell West Virginia commune, and even defrauding a securities company.

My tank top is so old that I remember Mom shoving it in her purse at a Walmart. *My girl needs clothes*, she'd said. *But we need to eat too.* Eat. Drain fifths of Jack in an evening. Forge IDs to buy more pseudoephedrine. You know, the basics of a life well lived.

The yellowed tank top is stretched to hell, leaving me free to move. It's probably another reason why I prefer privacy. No one wants to watch a maniac musician playing with the grace of someone tumbling down a flight of stairs.

I begin by touching Middle C. The key is sleek. Cool to the touch. Ready for me.

I shiver.

The only way to banish the cold is to light a match. I start an ivory bonfire.

What emerges is always a mystery, dictated by my mood. Today I'm nervous about meeting the freshman pianist I've been assigned to mentor. But my nerves melt away as I begin to play and play. Verbs chase the chords—verbs like flutter, dance, seduce, fling. *Murder.* I abuse the instrument. I abuse my ears, my hands, my upper back. I smash the rules of harmonics.

When I finish, I'm breathless and limp. My forehead falls forward and thunks on heated stripes of black and white. The bite of pain snaps me out of my trance. The keys become my friends again. I turn my head to the side and pet Middle C. No wonder I've developed this weird habit of apologizing to pianos.

Clair thinks I'll be a star. I think I'll be something like an art house curiosity. A cult following, perhaps? Or a hermit holed up in a closet-sized studio, freeing the knots in my guts, writing pretty music for other people to play. Let them be the stars. I can deal with that. Most people like music to be pretty, but I'm not the lullaby kind. Knowing that fits hand in glove with my shyness on stage. I don't want to perform in front of other people, and even if I did, they wouldn't want to listen.

God, I need a shower. Thumping out an original composition is as hard as a Piloxing class. No one thinks twice about taking a change of clothes to the gym. To the fine arts building, though? Yeah, right. I'm a wad of wet cotton balls held together by jeans and the light sweater I button over my morning-after tank top.

Not that I have personal experience with mornings after.

A tingle of fear rushes in at the idea, followed by my distrust of being impulsive. After all, Mom got pregnant at sixteen. Really bad choices followed. I could use all eighty-eight piano keys to count reasons why waiting is a bright idea. Plus . . . well, I'm not very good at trusting people. It took years for me to relax around Clair and John.

A boyfriend would be nice, though. Someone to talk and laugh with. Touch. Explore. Kinda . . . I don't know. Practice? I'm not the type to start without knowing where to put my hands. I'm used to knowing what to do with my hands.

The trek to my dorm awaits. I've done it only eight times since transferring from a Baton Rouge community college to Tulane. I don't know this campus well enough to get back the shortest way. I'm useless with maps. Even poking at my iPhone is useless. What seems so clear on a straight grid gets fuzzed out by the actual shapes of buildings and trees. I'm Dorothy trying to get to the Emerald City. Only, someone forgot to paint the sidewalks yellow.

I'll get faster. Or I'll get over the silly reflex that other students give a crap about how I look. They hurry past. A split second is all. If they're anywhere near as self-conscious as me, they're sure as hell not paying attention *to* me.

I load up my purple—I love purple—messenger bag with sheaves of notes. Then I pull out my iPod and adjust my earbuds. Forget classical when I'm "off duty." I search out Florence + the Machine. I like the songs of hers that no one wants to sing at karaoke. The good stuff. The stuff with soul so deep that I've developed a *really* unnatural relationship with her. She's simply Florence. "Goddess divine" works too.

Maybe I'm too into the music—mine and Florence and a bit of Zoltán Kodály, because I can never truly escape the classics. They overlap in some weird mash-up. Or maybe I'm too busy reading the hieroglyphics of my phone's tiny screen.

Or maybe it's nothing but a dumb thing the universe throws at me, just to be mean . . .

Because there's a man waiting outside the door.

First thing: chocolate. That's all I can think. I catch a glimpse of chocolate brown hair that's long enough to curl at his collar, but really neatly styled. The sunlight from a window at the end of the hallway makes the tips of those curls shine.

Second thing: an honest to goodness three piece suit. He sure isn't a student. He isn't one of the music profs either. They only dress up for performances. Normally they resemble me, half possessed and raggedy. This stranger looks like a full blown executive, but young enough to pull off posh guy trends straight out of *Details*. Coupled with that sunshine-touched hair, the suit makes him into a heady combination of young and mature.

Third thing: oh holy damn, he's ungodly handsome.

Air sucks up from my lungs and into my throat. Breathing, talking, even thinking—they crunch together like a car smashing into a concrete barrier.

I start with his eyebrows because they're a language all on their own. Something like surprise instantly changes into sobriety, and I can read it all across those expressive brows. They'd been lifted in an elegant arc that framed his face and gently furrowed his forehead. Now they flatten into a line that accentuates his sharp features.

I'm used to unmistakable sternness. I'm also used to sternness moving double quick to fury. Is this guy . . . calm? Assured? Detached? It's bugging the hell out of me because I can't read a thing. He stares at me with so much intensity. That doesn't help how stuck my breath still is.

"And I thought Katrina was a helluva storm," he says. "Do we really need more hurricanes in this town?"

He was listening?

I cringe, then my skin goes hot. Probably flaming red. To be so exposed to a drop-dead gorgeous guy—a man, really . . . Words fail. Brain cells fail. I stutter a meaningless sound.

I haven't been at a loss for words for years, not even when I gave testimony to the judge in San Joaquin. That had been a helluva lot scarier than getting attitude from a souped-up preppie.

He's still staring at me with that harsh but oddly unreadable expression. He's almost beautiful. His features are elegant, as if bred from perfect aristocratic lines. Cheekbones to die for. Lashes tipped with gold. Piercing, heart of a flame blue eyes.

Absolutely fathomless.

Then the strangest thing happens. My idiot brain remembers to act like a grown-up. "Where do you get off?" Okay, *sort of* grown-up.

His expression barely changes except that his eyebrows again lift into elegant arcs, but these are condescending. He's talking to an ant and wants me to know it. "Nowhere public."

It takes me a few seconds to catch the innuendo. I wind up even more embarrassed. I know the mechanics of a guy getting off, but that's where my knowledge ends. I want to find some snappy sexual retort that'd *really* shock him. . . .

Nope.

"I'm serious," I say, my anger rising. That's what my family does. *Did*. Confrontation means hackles up and voices raised. "Do you dress up and skulk around the music halls, waiting to insult someone?"

"I don't skulk." He waves a derisive hand toward the open door to my rehearsal room. "Whatever *that* was would've bent anyone's ear."

Speaking of ears and listening, his voice is *really* getting to me. It's refined but with that unmistakable New Orleans saunter. Down here people still believe in juju. Or pretend to. Where else can you openly carry voodoo dolls and tarot cards and be taken seriously? New Orleans tops the list. His voice *is* voodoo. I want to melt into it. Be hypnotized by it.

Instead, my pride gets the better of me.

"Maybe you shouldn't limit your *skulking* to this place." He scowls and seems surprised by my words. That gives me another kick of courage. "Why don't you head over to the art department and knock the wind out of someone else? 'Sorry, sugar, that color palette is an insult to my eyes.'"

His lips, which had been pressed tight and thin, relax a little. "I didn't call you 'sugar.'"

"Small favors."

"If I want to talk about how things look." He flashes his gaze up and down my body. It's definitely not appreciative. "You give me a lot to work with."

Talk about hitting a girl where she lives. Better yet, we've gathered a small crowd. Five or six students carrying different instrument cases stop to watch the drama. I would've, myself, had our places been reversed.

"I've been rehearsing for an hour," I say, proud that my words are steady and forceful. "You've been, what, primping for an hour? Give me that much time and I could look like a pretentious snob too."

He doesn't get mad. I don't know what to do with that. The way I was reared, a moment like this escalates to vicious levels— or worse than that, like when my mom threatened to turn state's evidence against my dad.

Instead, this guy seems amused. The relaxed lull of his lips has turned into a half smile that would outshine most *I'm really trying* smiles. "You really don't know who I am," he says with a chuckle nearly as hypnotic as his voice.

I'm burning from the skin inward, but I stand my ground. "What's so funny?"

"I'm not even sure myself. I appreciate the laugh, though."

It's not even his words that bug me. It's his tone and the way he's looking at me, like I was put on this earth to be his jester. I *so* want to hit him. A messenger bag can be turned into a weapon, right? I think the little crowd of onlookers wants it. I can feel expectation like a rising wind.

But I behave. I'm a living, breathing example of what amazing foster parents can do for a kid. Catfights are for girls on recess yards. I owe Clair and John better than that. They taught me that I owe *myself* better than that.

"Fine, be a jerk." I lift my chin and tug the strap of my bag. "Yeah, I'm loud and I'm a mess, but I'm damn good at what I do. You, however . . . You can get out of my way."

He steps dramatically back, even offering a condescending bow. "Like this, *sugar*?"

"Dick."

I turn away before I make a bigger scene. The impulse to run is *really* strong, but I'm okay. Right? Sure. No biggie. Just walk away as if I know where the hell I'm going. Which I don't. I'm blinking past a wash of red.

"Dead end that way," the stranger calls.

I come to an emergency door.

Screw it.

I slam the door's horizontal exit bar. It gives way. I let that *get out* impulse take over. I'm so wound up. I can't think of anything else. *Just get down the stairs and escape.*

As alarms ricochet through Dixon Hall, I really don't care.

~ TWO ~

"Did you hear something about the emergency alarm at the music building? Probably not the best for practicing!"

Great.

That's my roommate, Janissa Simons's, first question when I open our dorm door. She looks up from her vanity/desk combo. My side of the cramped room mirrors hers. I flop my bag on the floor and sprawl on my single bed. The western sun streams through the room's single wide window. It's bordered with thick, plain brown curtains that match the low, low carpeting. Instead of *Better Homes & Gardens*, we get the answer to that eternal admin question: *How many years can we accommodate sloppy coeds before we need to renovate?*

"Yeah, I heard it," I say, noting the cringe in my voice.

"I thought you'd be over there." Janissa smiles. "You look like it, anyway."

Great flicks through my brain again. I knew it. Apparently I don't just *play* like a hurricane. I wind up looking like I was caught in one, especially after running half blind past the great oaks of Newcomb Quad.

Funny, I didn't get lost. Propelled by instinct, I guess.

I wonder if our having known each other two weeks is enough for Janissa to pick up on my funky mood. "Gee, thanks. I didn't have time to stop by the salon on the way home."

She waves a hand. "Sorry, I didn't mean it that way. I wish I could get so worked up about anything."

Janissa's a chemistry major. *We speak a variant of math*, she'd said during our first day moving in. Technically that's true. Music theory involves a lot of math. So does chem.

It was enough for us to start up a quick, very necessary friendship. Geek Number One, meet Geek Number Two. She has the sleek hair of a starlet from the '40s, all auburn perfect. But she never styles it. Just lets it flop down her back. I suspect it's so long because she never makes time to get it cut. Doesn't matter. It's beautiful and so is she.

"Don't give me that," I say, grinning. "When you really get going, you wear pajama bottoms all weekend."

She grins in return. "Too true. Clean undies is about the best I can manage."

"My obsession is the piano. Yours is in your brain."

"Nah. You should've seen the time I lit an entire magnesium strip in my AP class."

"You're gonna have to explain that one."

She turns in her chair with a bright, animated gleam in her green eyes. "See, magnesium is a quick flash–burning metal. It's thin and can be cut in these long strips that get rolled up. So many uses."

I let that one slide, because as much as I like Janissa, I don't need to follow every detail to get a kick out of her stories. She's sweet, a year younger than me, short, with a ton of grace and a great figure. Like, D-cup hourglass great. Maybe guys don't swarm her because, pajama pants aside, she usually wears sweats and old T-shirts from when she played water polo in high school. She still swims every day, so she has great muscle tone too.

Not me. I have long fingers—the better to play piano with, said the big bad wolf. Everything about me is long and thin. Unless I'm sitting at a piano bench, I'm as graceful as a giraffe bending down in an attempt to drink.

That didn't stop my dad. It wasn't long after I hit puberty that he started talking about me "earning my keep." Circumstance meant I never got around to learning firsthand what he meant by that, but the words had been enough to turn my stomach to rancid meat.

"So," Janissa continues, "I needed an inch or so for a hypothesis about—" With another grin, she catches herself. "Doesn't matter. Anyway, I wondered what would happen if, well . . . if the whole roll caught fire."

"You daredevil," I tease.

"In this case, yeah. Magnesium burns *so* bright, you wouldn't believe it. I dropped it quick into a petri dish, which melted. I was at the back of the class and it just *glowed*. I couldn't look away. Just stared at how bright and big it was. My lab partner had been at the teacher's desk. She told me later that it'd looked like a flaming sunrise."

"And the teacher?"

Janissa laughs and tugs her hair back from her oval face. "Not amused. I got suspended for two days."

"You? A whole two days? No way."

She nods. "My parents sure as hell cared, but I didn't. One of the coolest things I've ever done, which, now that I think of it, is pretty sad."

"Not sad," I say. "Just proof of what I told you. You get worked up about your favorite things too."

"Whatever. I bet you've never done anything that stupid. And except for really needing a shower right now, you're always so put together."

So wrong on so many levels, I don't know where to start. So I don't.

But she's sweet to say I'm put together. That much is deeply ingrained. *Always look pretty*, Mom used to say. Not because she wanted a beauty queen for a daughter or anything, but because a tidy girl fits in at new schools. No threat that social services will come calling.

I wish I'd looked good for him.

Dammit. A dumb, stray thought about what I should've done or said when confronted by that arrogant bastard. Apparently I need to keep torturing myself over someone I'll never meet again.

I appreciate the laugh, though....

Sugar.

Still on the bed, I exhale quietly. My tension doesn't leave. Neither do the memories. Goose bumps cover my skin. "Sugar" could be such a cool endearment. He'd made it into a slur.

I prop myself on my elbows. "You wanna get dinner? I'll keel over if I don't eat soon."

"Can't." She glances at the digital clock on our minifridge/microwave combo. "I have thermodynamics in twenty."

Sure enough, a vibrating buzz shakes her phone on her desk. She has alarms for everything—as bad with time as I am with maps.

Janissa packs up and leaves with a wave and a smile. I'm left alone with my thoughts. Even my longed-for shower doesn't wash away the afternoon.

I can't get him off my mind.

My classes are over for the day. I call Clair, but I only get her voice mail. I try to keep my voice steady as I say a casual "Hi, I just miss you both." She'll probably hear through it. She always does.

So I need something else to do, like write down what I'd composed that afternoon—the hurricane session, apparently—and maybe watch *Say Yes to the Dress* while nursing a pint of Cherry Garcia.

Instead, I rummage through my desk to find the letter I've been ignoring all week. It bears the Tulane seal. I wear a ring with the same seal. It's given to juniors to wear upside down until graduation. I'm still getting used to wearing it.

The letter lists the name of my freshman mentee. Is that the right word? I'm her mentor. She must be my mentee. Too bad this girl, Adelaide Deschamps, will be at a complete loss with me as her guide. I wear a hefty, important ring, and *mentor* sounds so impressive, but I'm living in a dorm for the first time. Considering my ineptitude with maps, I can't even give directions for a damn. Two weeks on campus. Three weeks in town. No experience with guys or stability or telling the whole truth. My only friend so far is nearly as socially withdrawn as me.

What do I have to offer this poor girl?

At least Adelaide is a music major too—though musical theater, not composition like me.

I dial the number on the letter.

I'm not prepared for the blaring Dixieland that vomits out of my iPhone. I glare at it as if Steve Jobs himself were to blame for blowing up my eardrums.

"Hello?" The word is shouted. Of course it is.

"Adelaide?" I'm glad our room is empty because I need to shout in return. "I'm Keeley Chambers, your music department mentor."

"Yeah, I'm Adelaide."

That's it. No, *Glad to hear from you.* Or maybe, *I was hoping you'd call first because I was nervous too!* Just blaring Dixieland.

I want to hang up. This has already taken a lot more guts than I usually manage. *Stick with it*, my foster dad would say. Then again, my real dad used to say the same thing. But such a huge difference in meaning.

"I called to see when you can meet up," I say. "Get to know each other."

"Right, yeah. That's fine."

She sounds really young. A freshman, probably.

"This'll be good for both of us." I feel like I'm reading a script.

"Now's good," the girl shouts. "You know Yamatam's off South Carrollton?"

"Sure," I lie.

"Head on down. It'll be more fun here than at Dixon."

"What do you look like?"

"Doesn't really matter."

Now that I've adjusted to her blaring words, I can hear that she's a native of New Orleans, or at least Louisiana.

She might actually help *me* adjust to this place. I still feel disoriented here, a feeling that reminds me of the years I spent on the road with my folks. Dad would always make some joke about it—just another family adventure. *On the road again!* he'd sing, like Willie Nelson.

I caught on to that bullshit real early.

"Why wouldn't it matter?" I ask. "Appearance is kind of a big deal when meeting a stranger."

"If you can be here in an hour, I'll be the dynamic blonde onstage!"

Click.

The music is gone and so is the shouting girl. I'm still in my bathrobe, but she'll be onstage soon. I'm so curious.

I flip through my closet for something that's tidy and almost, nearly, could be if you squinted cool. I settle on a baby blue shelf bra tank top under a lightweight midnight blue linen blouse. Gold accented flip-flops and gold hoop earrings. Vintage looking jeans, a remnant from my freshman year, when Clair bought me a whole new wardrobe.

The bigger challenge still lies ahead: getting there. I really don't want to miss whatever performance Adelaide was talking about. That means getting there in—I check the clock on my desk—a half hour.

I Google Yamatam's, but it doesn't have a website. That means I have no way to check it out in advance—or to make sure my outfit won't be out of place. All I find is an address on Carrollton. Less than a mile away. Cool. I plug it into my iPhone and duplicate the directions on a Post-it.

We're talking *detailed* directions. No chancing this.

I take a deep breath.

Here goes.

~ THREE ~

The oppressive heat of Louisiana in September never fails to surprise me each time I step outside. I've been everywhere, but seriously, it's like walking into a wet nuclear blast that sits on my chest. I remember it being different in Chicago, when I was little. I don't know why, but I still miss winter, even the blizzards and the changing seasons, so hard. Southerners don't get it. I've given up trying to explain it to Clair and John.

Thankfully I find Yamatam's after backtracking only twice. It's an unmissable glowing inferno of people and music. I get in the *long* line like everyone else, glad to feel anonymous.

A guy is standing next to me. I get a whiff of cologne when the breeze shifts and wipes away the heavy humidity and the beer from inside the club. He smells amazing. I sneak a glance at his profile, trying to keep calm. Because he's hot. Incredible. Like, *please don't dribble on my shirt* perfect.

Wait. Hold up.

He's the guy.

The guy.

The one who ignited so many insane fireworks in my mind that I fled like a rabbit—a rabbit who can set off emergency exit alarms.

I pray. I usually don't. I gave up on that a long time ago, when the police never came any faster one way or the other. But I pray this guy doesn't recognize me. I battle a newly resurfaced faint or flight impulse so hard that my knees shake. At least the club's rhythmic thrumming gives me something to focus on. My knees can shake in time with Dixieland jazz.

Luckily he never looks my way. We reach the front of the line and he's ushered right in. My ID is scrutinized more closely. No surprise. I'm obviously a co-ed, while he exudes authority.

The big uniformed bouncer eyes me some more, then hands back my license. "Whatever," he mutters, and stamps the back of my hand. Ultraviolet ink equals legal permission to get hammered. Not that it matters to me. I haven't had a drink since I was a tween—sloe gin is a nasty bitch—and I never will again.

I follow gorgeous Mr. Arrogant up the steps to the club, which is above a resale instrument shop. The railing is sticky and rusted. I'm one step below him, slogging through the backlog that jams the stairwell. I wish a few people separated us. When did I become such a coward? You'd think staring my dad in the face and sending him to prison would've made me immune to fear.

Or maybe I'm going to be afraid forever.

I slide down the stairs and quietly slip behind a pair of very, very glitzy girls. I doubt I could ever pull off false eyelashes, midriff tops, and wedge sandals, but they wear the hell out of all three.

They only get cursory notice because the bulk of my attention is still on the stranger. He's got his hands in the pockets of his charcoal gray slacks. The fabric is pulled taut across his ass. I catch myself staring. Ugh, I'm hopeless. His back isn't much easier to ignore. He's seriously toned. A white button-down shows off the width and strength of his upper back, and rolled-up sleeves reveal toned forearms.

He's just so . . . *different.* Suave. Self-assured. He's fresh and actually handsome. Not just cute or hot. *Handsome.* I can't help but flash another glance up to where he still waits in line . . .

Right when he glances down at me.

Our eyes lock. That deep flame heart blue makes me shiver. I don't think I'll ever forget it. His expressive brows narrow, and his lips flatten. I decide to call that his stern face, since I recognize it now. I shouldn't be making mental notes on anything about him, but I can't help it. I'm terrified and excited at the same time. I want him to see me. *See* me, not examine me like some specimen in a jar. Maybe then I won't be so intimidated?

Then comes his smile. He clearly recognizes me too. *Oh my God, the smile is so much worse.* Or better? Mostly just devastating. It's slight, teasing, knowing. The surprise of it melts the remaining strength in my knees until I can't help imagining an impossible evening: I'd smile back, totally assured. I'd say something witty. He'd buy me a Diet Coke. He'd walk me back to my dorm. I'd be a wreck the whole time, wondering if he might kiss me at the door.

But after the kiss . . . I wouldn't have a clue about what to do. That'd be up to him. All him.

I grip the railing while my mind spins this useless, graceless waltz.

"Following me?"

His words are like a brick through a window. My stupid fantasy shatters. Yup, he still has the upper hand.

I shouldn't have been able to hear him over the music and the pair of girls that separate us. But I heard him perfectly. I can feel the words inside my skin. His tone, something between condescension and teasing, soaks into my bones, while he continues to assess me like I'm recovering from head trauma.

"A little obvious," I say, shouting more forcefully than the suave cool he'd used. "Yes, I'm following you. I'm totally a stalker."

If he keeps smiling at me like that, I can wait forever for his reply.

"You clench your teeth when you get angry," he adds casually. "It ruins the line of your lips."

Does he unnerve everyone like this? My face flares hot, and I've gone from skittish to angry in about five sentences.

"So when you said I wasn't much to look at—"

"I meant you gave me a lot to work with. Your lips being the best of it."

He says it so slyly that I find myself doubting what had passed between us. He couldn't have meant it in a positive way. I'd looked like hell, and he was doing some sneering, judgmental thing with his expression. He's smiling now, but nothing he's said feels like a true compliment.

If I were as talented with people as I am with the piano, I'd have come up with the perfect comeback, hitting that sweet spot between flirty and biting.

Instead I keep it simple.

"You're an asshole."

"Keep your opinion," he says. "A word of advice? Next time, turn left out of the rehearsal rooms. Setting off emergency alarms can get a little girl in trouble, especially if someone tattles. We wouldn't want that."

Oh, shit. Shit.

"*Little* girl? I'm twenty-one."

He looks me up and down again with an expression akin to pain or longing, as if he's lost huge chunks of his childhood too. But the shift is brief. He clamps it down. His smug, *don't give a damn* expression takes over. "Time doesn't make a person. Experience does."

"Then consider me about eighty years old, and don't ever call me 'little' again."

"How about 'sugar'? You've had a few hours to let that one sink in. Have you decided if it's off limits?" He hesitates with a new, unnerving curiosity in his gaze. Then he shrugs, back to acting as if I'm the least important creature on the planet. "Forget it."

He turns his back to me.

Just like that, he yanks his attention away—the attention I'd found so unnerving but now find myself craving.

That's when Mr. Stranger reaches back and takes my hand. In my fantasy, that would've been what I spent the whole evening working up to. Just touching him. Instead he makes the moves and I'm running to keep up. I can only hope my stamina holds out.

His hand is cool and smooth and makes the disorientation totally worthwhile. His fingers are even longer than mine. My hand in his makes me feel feminine and small, as if my troubles aren't all mine anymore. How can anyone do that?

The unbelievably hot, chocolate haired god of a man pulls me through the throngs and into the club . . . then lets go. He casually returns his hands to his pockets. "All right, I got you in. Now stop following me. If I want you, sugar, I'll come find you."

"You're an *arrogant* asshole."

"Yeah." His eyes are so very blue. They reflect the club's disorienting flash and dance of lights, gleaming, like I'm watching a kaleidoscope. "As for me coming to find you . . . you can't wait to see if I do."

"You think so?"

"Because now I've put the idea out there. You'll be looking for me all night."

I swallow. He could have any girl in this club, but he's zeroing in on me. "Why me?"

Did I say that out loud?

"You're dressed to blend in, not stand out. But at a nightclub, natural stands out. Does that make you plain or . . . intriguing? I'm hoping for mystery, Miss Fire Drill." He grins, and I want to claw his beautiful eyes out. "Or maybe to see how your lips look when you're not pissed off."

"Then don't piss me off."

His grin widens, revealing perfect teeth. A lot about him warrants the word "perfect," including a perfect movie star exit. He slides into a crowd large enough to field two opposing football teams *and* a marching band. I'm speechless. No one could expect otherwise. I become a tree or a part of the wall or a complete idiot, because I can't move. I watch his bright white shirt until I can't see him anymore.

His words are still ringing in my head.

You'll be looking for me all night.

My pulse is through the roof. My stomach is fluttery and won't settle. I'm curious, angry, and mortified . . . because I know he's right.

~ FOUR ~

During my trip to Never-Never Land, where a handsome stranger alternately bickers and flirts with me, the jazz band finishes its set. The loud, dissonant whir of the crowd is interrupted by the tinkle of a lone piano—the work of a girl with bright blonde curls. She's sitting on a bench onstage. Her back is enviably straight, completely at odds with her hippie meets Goth clothes. I could never pull off that look, ever, not with a hundred years of practice and a Mississippi bargeful of confidence.

She adjusts her mic.

That sound rouses me from my stupor and helps banish the confusion of the past few minutes . . . no, hours. Time to forget some unexpected playboy with a devastating smile and unnerving personality. I make myself use that word, "personality," because calling it "charisma" would make him irresistible.

I *will not* look around for him. Nope.

I rivet my attention to the young woman who'll look to me—a transfer on scholarship—to guide her through her first year in the music department. *Four semesters* at a satellite campus means I'm as clueless as she is, despite the fact that I'm a junior. Maybe more clueless, if I'm right in thinking her accent means she's native to New Orleans. One of my professors had mentioned her in passing, that she was the recipient of a music fellowship like mine. She has to be good. No university is in the habit of throwing money at students who aren't supergifted.

No way am I missing this. That means front row. I spot a lone chair between two couples—you know, that awkward place where a single person would have to sit and appear kinda desperate and alone because, hey, no date.

I scoot down the aisle and try to appear inconspicuous. Of course, I step on someone's foot, but I make it to my seat. The couple to my left will absolutely head to the nearest bed when they quit Yamatam's. The woman, wearing a camisole with a shelf bra that does little to conceal big boobs and perky nipples, is practically sitting in her date's lap. He's a total jock type, solid and tan. Why they're sitting in the front row baffles me. They don't fit with my idea of music aficionados. She slings her legs over the guy's lap and wraps her forearms around his neck.

I'm equal parts annoyed and envious.

With tons of willpower, I conquer the whitewater rush to scan the crowd for the provocative stranger. The last thing I want is to give him the satisfaction of making good on his assumption. I feel like he'd wait all evening to see the moment I give in and seek him out.

He's clearly used to being right, used to winning. That self-assurance had heated the air between us, and I'd wanted to be wrapped in his confidence as tightly as the couple next to me pressed limb to limb. Could my mysterious stranger, so sarcastic and intimidating, ever loosen up enough to let a girl drape across his body? Could *I*, in public no less?

And when did I decide on calling him *my* stranger?

He was a guy I'd never see again, because I'm not looking around. I'm not looking for him. Definitely not.

Turns out I don't need to.

"I'd like my seat, if you don't mind," comes that low, smooth New Orleans drawl.

I look up and catch my breath. His sharp, aristocratic features are easygoing, but a muscle at his jaw bunches with perfectly masculine power. His Caribbean clear eyes are pinned on the man currently covered by five and a half feet of double-D female.

"You're joking, right?" the jock asks.

"Not at all." He glances at me. "I plan to sit with my companion here."

His smile is slight, as if I know what the hell he's doing and I have his personal invitation to laugh along. I grip the metal folding chair and watch the drama with what must be a stupidly confused expression.

"Yeah, sure." The jock skims his hands down his date's sides, with his thumbs rubbing her nipples. "I'll get right on that."

That irresistible smile widens. I can't help but join him, although I hide my grin behind my fingers. I turn away, but it's just for show. There's no way I can take my eyes off him. I keep slipping him glances, and he keeps catching them.

"You're moving," he says quietly but firmly to the jock. "You just don't know it yet."

"Look, freak show, if you think I'm leaving my girl here with you, you're a whole ton of crazy."

"Forget him," the woman says, glaring up from under eye-lashes thick with blue mascara.

My stranger shrugs. It's a show of restrained tension—a hint of what he can do, what he's holding back—no matter his seemingly carefree demeanor.

"I didn't ask you to leave her or take her with you when you go. I want that seat, and that seat only." He leans over at the waist, nearly eye to eye with the couple. He's wearing the expression of a father who's nearly lost his patience and speaks to them just that way, parent to child. "Time to run along. You'll thank me after."

No way. No way will this bullshit work.

His stare hasn't wavered since locking eyes with the jock. They square off in silence. The jock has the advantage of probably forty pounds of free-weight muscle. But it doesn't matter. Amazingly, he's the one at the disadvantage and I can't figure out why. He blinks, defeated by steady, glacial blue confidence.

"Come on, Livvy," he says. "We don't need this crap."

He shifts so that Livvy can stand on her own. She's sputtering quiet profanity and tugging her skirt into place. The guy stands just as my stranger straightens to his full height—at least two inches taller. He looks so sleek compared to his bulkier opponent. I shiver thinking that, if forced, he'd be able to hold his own in any fight. Something about his posture. His fluid, powerful grace. I can't help but take him in from head to toe. He's treating me to the sweet privilege of another long, appreciative look, when I'd thought pride would keep me from soaking in him again.

He catches me in the act. He winks. My cheeks burst into flames, embarrassed like nobody's business. The humor in his smile takes on a sharper edge.

If I want you, I'll come find you.

Yeah, he found me. He'd won some weird duel between us. Or, he's in the process of winning.

He extends his hand to the jock. "No hard feelings. Go put two rounds on my tab," he says, handing the girl Livvy a business card fished out of his wallet. "Jude Villars."

Her eyes widen. "No way." Then she tosses her hair and puts on a defiant expression. "We have a lot of friends here, you know," she says, like a dare. "Could get expensive."

"Then the bartenders will be busy. Enjoy your night."

"Thanks." The jock stops mid-motion. Just as predicted, he'd thanked this man Jude for the trouble of vacating his own seat.

"Don't worry," Jude says. "I won't rub it in."

There's no huge change to his bright smile, except it suddenly seems dismissive—some change behind his eyes, where his interest winks out. He doesn't shove them aside. He doesn't gloat. He simply sits beside me with quiet nonchalance, as if the jock and his girl had never existed.

"And here we are again."

"We weren't here when we started," I say. I need water or something. The Sahara has nothing on my parched throat.

"But you must admit this is a vast improvement over the stairwell." Leaning back, he crosses his arms as if what he just did was perfectly normal human behavior. Our legs touch, shoved together by the narrow seating. If he wanted to move his thigh away from where it presses against mine, he would've done it by now. But he doesn't.

I need to take the offensive or I'll reveal what I know I am: a lamb to the slaughter, ready to walk to my doom for a bit of flirting. "Where do you get the nerve to make a scene like that?"

"Make a scene? Says you." He adds a quirking eyebrow to his smirk, which spikes my blush to inferno levels. "Besides, I have a reputation to live up to. Would you believe I've been told I'm an arrogant asshole?"

"Yes, I believe it."

"By some woman who has yet to introduce herself." He shakes his head in mock disappointment. "There's rude, and then there's *rude.*"

"My lack of an introduction compares to what you just did?"

"Yes." He crosses his arms and settles into the metal seat, appearing way too content with the world. "When company calls, you offer sweet tea. When it's raining, you share your umbrella. And when you're pursued by an intriguing man, you make pains to introduce yourself."

"I didn't get the handbook."

"I'd send you a copy, but exchanging email addresses looks like third base from here." He shrugs. "I suppose I could keep calling you 'Miss Fire Drill,' but it's such a mouthful."

"You can't keep from drawing the attention back to yourself, can you?"

"Busted. Now . . . your name."

"Keeley." It pops out. Honest to God, I can't help myself when he issues a command that strong. Maybe that's why he's sitting next to me and that jock will watch the show from the bar. "Can we be done now? I'm asking you. Please. You're not the one center stage. Let me watch her in peace."

"Her? Adelaide?"

I go still. There's genuine affection in his voice, and pride, and all of that is backed up by his widest smile yet—one he has

yet to shine at me. Big. Manic. Unabashed. It's a laugh without
sound. His smile is for Adelaide Deschamps.

I'd actually looked forward to sparring with him. I only realize it when he turns that carefree smile toward the young
woman at the piano. I'd been thinking him a sexy, astonishing
pest who'd acted like a polite caveman to sit beside me.

But he isn't here for me at all. I just happen to be in the front
row, right where he wants to be. For her.

"She can hold her own," he says. "How do you know her?"

"I don't." I'm proud of the detachment I force into my voice,
when all I want is to find the strength to be the first to pull my
thigh away. "I'm supposed to mentor her this year. I'd like to
know who I'm mentoring. What she can do."

Out of nowhere, Jude turns that ravishing smile on me. The
floor drops out from beneath my chair. I'm in free fall. It's more
devastating than staring into the sun; it's going blind and catching fire and being reborn. The only place I'm truly, securely
grounded is where our thighs still press together—so obvious, so
simple . . . and increasingly erotic.

"What she can do is take center stage and shake it like a Do-
berman with a bone. No one holds a candle. Although . . ." He
leans so close that I can smell his rich cologne. "Maybe this year
she'll meet her match."

~ FIVE ~

Adelaide Deschamps is a prodigy. She's the sort of performer who makes a girl doubt her own abilities—that girl being me, of course. I'm not used to that at all. Everyone is enraptured. And even though my welcome/unwelcome company is staring with obvious marvel and adoration, while his thigh is still confusingly pressed against mine, I'm enraptured too.

She's definitely classically trained. All those composers who bored me but inspired me to forge on with my own compositions—well, she probably knows each masterpiece forward and backward. But I'm surprised by how raw she is. It's like she skipped a few hundred steps, from "Chopsticks" to Chopin.

I don't know where her musical theater stuff is supposed to come in. There's none of the sorority don't give a damn nutso I'd heard over the phone. Seriously, she should be wearing a long formal black evening gown, performing at the Met. This eclectic crowd should be decked out in suits and fancy dresses, the kind I saw when Clair and John had taken me to the orchestra in

Baton Rouge. Once, we traveled all the way to Dallas when Joshua Bell was on tour. Sure, he isn't a piano player, only one of the best violinists of this century, but I had a major crush on him and they gave me the tickets for my sixteenth birthday.

My first birthday gift.

I remember hiding in my room, crying my damn eyes out after they told me we'd be seeing him perform. And I loved every minute of his astonishing show. Trying to soak it in. Knowing it wouldn't last forever.

This is one of those moments.

"She's so good."

The strange company I keep looks down at me. I can feel the weight of Jude's fire blue stare. It's easier to return that stare now. His nose is straight and a touch long, while his jaw is strong and defined. His lips are thin with an oh so kissable dip on the upper one. His eyes are narrowed, with those arching brows lifting and digging horizontal lines across his forehead. It's as if all his features decided to be horizontal or vertical. Little middle ground—just his cheekbones, carved into sharp but graceful slopes that angle toward a tiny pair of laugh lines at the corners of his mouth. His posture makes his neck seem longer, striped with strong tendons. The effect is predatory.

That's the look. *Predatory.*

It's not like it matters now. That's his girl onstage and he's a player and I'm that lamb braying for a quick death, not a slow bleed-out by humiliation.

I tear my gaze off his face, away from his bemused expression, his . . . ugh, just *him*.

Applause follows the apparent conclusion of Adelaide's recital. Only, she doesn't stop. She offers the crowd a quick nod before launching into a rip-roaring rendition of "If You Hadn't But You Did." Clair and John hired my high school music director to be my piano tutor, and she insisted on Broadway as well as the classics. She was weird and supercool. Horn-rimmed glasses and a slip showing—the goofy teacher everyone loved but didn't really get. She *adored* Broadway and made a solo pilgrimage every year to catch a show or two. The genre never clicked for me, but if anyone can change my mind, it's Adelaide Deschamps.

The mic isn't just for show. Her voice is Marilyn Monroe after sucking one little gulp of helium. She has the perfect blend of sexiness and playfulness. She hits the high notes, and she growls low, sultry notes as she accuses a phantom lover of cheating, all the time rollicking on the piano. She's two different people in one body—half master musician, half rockabilly sexpot.

I'm surprised when Jude's big hand finds my knee and gives it a squeeze. I'd been tapping my toes furiously, and our legs are still crammed together. I do the unthinkable. I pull his hand off my thigh—instantly noticing the lack of warmth—and go back to tapping my toes. I can't help it. The music is amazing.

I glance over to see if he shows any sign of being offended. Not a bit. That big, shark-wide grin is back, in profile, filled with teasing. He's toying with me to pass the time. I hate that.

Take me seriously or don't.

I shake off my annoyance. Adelaide doesn't play all hurricane-possessed like me. She's perfectly aware of every gesture. A slinky bit of side-eye. A beaming smile. A pause—then an exaggerated wink to add a touch of comedy to her sex appeal. Forget the Met. Her stage presence screams, *Doll me up and make me the next YouTube sensation.*

She's living art—consciously vampy and raunchy and complex and dramatic.

Her performance, plus Jude's totally surprising crash-bang into my life, makes me want to slip free of my skin.

When Adelaide finishes, she flips her shining curls over her shoulder with a dramatic flourish. She stands to receive a riot of clapping and shouts. Beaming, she dips a few curtsies more suited to a junior high kid making fun of the performance she's been forced to finish. Clown-like. She blows air kisses and wiggles her fingers at a few people.

Jude crosses his arms, which accentuates the striated muscles of forearms dusted with brown hair. His biceps pull against the material of his shirt. The fabric clings. I can barely keep from drooling. His brows are pulled down low. The set of his mouth says one thing: disappointment.

As the spotlight dims, Adelaide must see it too. She flips him the bird. Then it's back to smiles and honest to God giggles I can hear over the applause.

"Yes, she's very good," he says, almost too quietly to hear. "But she's a pain in the ass."

He turns to me and stares outright. I'm caught again. Lost again. His eyes are stormy and bright with emotion. With doubt? Hope?

Yeah, right.

"She's wild and takes everything for granted. Even what you just saw. Are you up to dealing with her?" He shakes his head in that gesture I don't like. Pity? Doubt? "Frankly, you're not the most resilient girl I've ever met."

Oh, how wrong you are.

"Is that why you're sitting with me? Checking me out?"

"Among other things," he says with a sharp grin.

"Does she practice?"

His eyes lose that scary intensity. He's about to tease me. How do I know that so quickly? I thought he was Fort Knox with me carrying only a tourist map. No way in.

"I bet you practice every day," he replies, dodging my question. It comes across as an accusation. "Yes."

"Like you did this morning?"

I look away, embarrassed all over again. He catches my chin, and our gazes smash together like speeding cars. He keeps doing that. Colliding with me. I can't tell if it's the best thing ever, or a force that'll bust me into a thousand pieces. All I know is that I can't stand how he's using all this magnetic, irresistible bullshit on me when his girlfriend is center stage.

He tightens his fingers in a silent prompt for an answer. "Yes," I say. "Like I did this morning."

"Can you do it again, or was that a onetime deal?"

"Of course I can do it again."

"Prove it," he says bluntly. "It's an open mic, Keeley. The next person up onstage is the next person to perform. Simple."

I start to tremble. "Do you mean *me*?"

"Why not?"

I can't answer. I blink past a surprising rush of tears. Suddenly I'm back in that damn courtroom, with a hundred pairs of eyes on me, hanging on every word. Some were sympathetic, like Ursula's and even the judge's. The reporters' were avaricious. The defense attorney may as well have been made of ice.

And Jude wants me to go through that again? Center of attention? It burned a scar onto my soul. How mortifying would it be to get onstage in front of all these people and just . . . *freeze*?

I don't duck in time to avoid a clue-by-four. The court-room . . . and the stage . . . and all eyes on me. I can't go through that again. It's only taken me, what, six years to figure that out, with this guy Jude watching me so expectantly?

"Keeley?"

"No way," I say. "And don't try the crap you pulled on that guy. I won't be bullied about this. You can't dare me."

"How can I resist? Hearing you through sound dampening walls wasn't enough. I want to *see* you too." He lets go of my chin, but doesn't let go of me—not emotionally, anyway. He strokes the backs of his knuckles against my cheek. "And a dare won't be necessary."

Jude says it with complete confidence. Oh, to have a tenth of his assurance. *I'd* be the one playing at the Met, wowing crowds with my own compositions. But I haven't played for anyone other than Clair and John, tutors, and profs. It's been years since I took the witness stand, but I can't imagine getting up in front of a crowd again. Little recitals and how I'd performed for a small panel of music administrators to earn my fellowship—those were low-key and necessary. This is huge and completely *un*necessary.

That doesn't keep me from wanting Jude to keep pushing. He stared at Adelaide with such entertained delight—until that confusing moment at the end when he seemed disappointed. I don't want to disappoint him. I *won't*.

Keep going. Don't stop. I want to play for you, but I don't know how.

I burn beneath the return of my blush. "If not a dare, then . . . what?"

His thumb lingers, slows, tracing my lower lip. "There it is," he says on a deep masculine sigh. A shiver of sexual awareness chills my skin, then sets me on fire. "You're confused and hope-ful. Not pissed off anymore. Your mouth is as beautiful as I knew it would be."

I swallow hard. What am I supposed to do with that other than mentally trip and never get up again?

I'm silently begging now. *Tell me more and I'll try to be-lieve it.*

"I can't follow Adelaide. She's . . . amazing."

"She's gifted at showmanship and artifice," Jude says. "I bet you're different. I want you to show this whole place. I want you to show me."

I don't reply. He keeps stealing my voice. I only have one left . . . and it's onstage.

It's a test. The whole night is a test. *How to survive a trial by spontaneous masculine overdrive.* Jude Villars—his eyes, his gor-geous face, those built arms, his man in a man's world way of dressing . . .

Show him what you can do.

Take him *by surprise.*

I take myself by surprise when I dig my fingers into his broadcloth collar. I drag him closer. The gap between our mouths isn't big. I could kiss him if I wanted. I want some re-venge for being emotionally tossed around. I want to break *him* into a thousand pieces.

"You think you've got it all figured out," I say. "You don't. Not about me."

The exhales between us are thick and hot. At least he's breathing as hard as I am. He chuckles softly. The sound, the secondhand feel of it, ricochets down my chest. I'm tinder catching fire. I can do anything.

"I wonder," he whispers, "have you ever kissed anyone as hard as you want to kiss me right now?"

I shove him away, but not before his words settle like lava behind my breastbone. I'm both molten and airy, and learning fast what it means to get really turned on. That's even more shocking than the idea of taking to the stage. No man has ever touched me with such knowing confidence. Brushing his thumb along my lower lip? He knows exactly what he's doing.

And I want more.

He's already made me angry. Now he's making me reckless. If that means going head to head with me makes him smile all wispy like he did at Adelaide, then bring it on. He's played with my brain all night. I can at least be memorable.

He stands when I do. I thought his height was a trick of perspective when he'd towered over the seated jock. No way. He's a good six feet, but I'm not letting him get away with talking down at the crown of my head. I tilt my chin. "Me and the piano. And you'll watch."

"I won't be able to take my eyes off you."

A thrill zings from head to toe before settling in my fingertips. Itching. Ready. "You better not."

People hoot when I approach the stage.

I'm not in court, but neither am I safe in a rehearsal room. I'm in a hot, colorful, loud, feverish club in New Orleans. And everyone in here expects to be entertained.

Can I give them that?

I shed my linen shirt. The upright piano is in surprisingly good condition. A spotlight turns the shiny brown surface into glass beneath the sun. It also has the welcome effect of blotting out the crowd.

When I sit on the bench and touch Middle C, I realize the truth of my words. *Me and the piano.* I pet the key, easing all other thoughts into a distant corner. They simply scatter, becoming air—the air that fills my lungs and gives me strength. Straightening my shoulders, my hands in place, I throw one last glance toward the obscured audience. I don't care what will burst out of my musical id, or what I'll look like afterward. No future now. Just the here and now and my music and Jude watching.

~ SIX ~

Most times, an improv crescendo is like a finish line I can't see until I'm right on top of it. Not tonight. I'm not so deep in the trance that usually comes with private sessions, but it hasn't affected what I'm creating. It's like I'm channeling from all the sources a rehearsal room can't provide.

I can see the crescendo a mile away. I already hear it in my head, even as my fingers rush and push to catch up. I can hear it—and it's perfect. Staggering. I almost back off and take a safer route, but I won't be able to live with myself if I start chickening out about composing.

So I barrel on, creating, navigating by touch and sound. At last, I reach the moment when I bring a dozen motifs together into a final, resonant chord.

I did it. Blame Jude or give me the credit, but I played until my heart beat outside my chest and everyone could watch.

They could see right inside me.

I'm dizzy. If I think too much about what I've just done, I'll go bonkers. How had I gotten from my dorm to here? From that front row seat to here? I'm shaking. I'm exhausted. At least I don't thunk my head on the keys as I come out of my near trance.

The club is utterly silent.

I don't dare turn my eyes to the glare of the spotlight. Instead I do as I always do. I whisper a breathless apology to the poor, abused upright. It held up under the pressure of my performance, but I may not. I wait to breathe, wait to hear anything after the lingering D minor and the drop dead quiet that followed.

I finally raise my head and turn. The spotlight is overwhelming. White. Glaring. I fight my reflexive squint. There's no way to grab a smidge of reaction, not by sight.

But then . . .

The applause is a hurricane loud enough to overwhelm my own. It hits me like a concussive wave, an earthquake, a tsunami—all those forces of nature. That applause is a match for my energy, with that energy pumped up two- and three- and fourfold. I finally have permission to breathe, but I can't. I inhale like sucking in salt water. I'm drowning in the unexpected. I'm sinking between the slats of the wooden floorboards and off on a long journey to the gulf.

Is that scary or thrilling?

Both.

Until right then, I hadn't thought about the plaster cast I've wrapped around myself since Mom's murder. I haven't just kept myself small—a girl hiding behind a recliner under a makeshift blanket fort. No, I've kept myself wound tight as a spring. Each nightmarish memory twisted the spring tighter, and tighter still. It's ready to snap.

What will I be if it does?

I rise to my feet. I offer a quivery bow, but there's a surprising part of me that isn't shaking at all. Down deep, it's like someone pulled that scared girl out from her fort, hauled her into an open field, handed her a pair of cymbals, and gave her permission to be *loud*.

The cheers keep coming. So does rush after rush of a single word.

Success.

I begin to walk toward the steps leading offstage when my treacherous, *really should be replaced* knees prove that I'm dissolving. Or snapping. Or being the bravest I've ever been. I must be a little bit brave, at least, because I'm not completely numb. I want to find a piece of paper and scribble notes—at the very least, the motif that sparked this whirlwind.

But my mind and my body have parted ways. I sort of . . . sag. The lights are bright and the handrail is hard to see.

He's there to make sure I don't fall.

What does it mean that I was hoping he would be? Jude tucks an arm under one of mine and supports my lower back. My mental protest says I don't want him to touch me, now that I'm all sweaty goo and raw, exposed nerves. My body fights back, insisting he's just what I need—strong and steady. I grip one wrist, which is surprisingly solid but soft to the touch because of a dusting of hair. He's wearing a wristwatch. In the age of smartphones, I can't remember the last time I saw a guy wearing a watch.

Won't falter. Won't let me go.

Only, he does. He really does. What had I been thinking? That he'd sweep me into his arms and kiss me in front of the whole club? In front of Adelaide? *Get off it, overactive imagination.* He finds a quiet corner that doesn't stay quiet for long as a jazzy trumpet quartet takes my place in front of the charged-up audience. I slouch against the cool wall. He's gone before I can protest.

Is that it? He did his good deed by bringing me into the spotlight. Now he's calling it a day?

It had been a good deed. As my breath returns, I'm still lightheaded. Exhilarated. I did that . . . that . . . *thing.* It felt amazing. Even the blue notes—those half steps between the half steps—rang true. Not sharps or flats, they exist like the vacuum of space, challenging musicians to push boundaries. Like I just did. And for the first time in a very long time, I didn't need anyone's approval. Not my music tutors' or professors'. Not my foster parents'. Not even the deafening din offered up by the clubgoers.

I take that back as Jude returns with two bottles of water.

I want *his* approval.

I'm sick. Deranged. Seriously desperate.

He doesn't say anything when he cracks the seal of one bottle and puts it into my hand. He even curls my fingers around the frigid plastic. I don't want to look down at my tank top. I don't want to see what damage my performance has done to my clothes. I'm still shaking, so I chalk it up to cold. Or shock. I briefly hand the bottle back, slip on my linen shirt, then take a long, unladylike swig.

When I finish, I undo my rubber band and go about trying to put my hair back into a ponytail, if not the neat bun I'd started with.

"Give me a minute." He runs his fingers through my hair. He even unsnarls a few of the inevitable tangles.

"A minute to . . . ?"

"Take it in."

"What, my hair?"

"Yes," he says soberly, softly. "And . . . all of you. I bet you don't have any idea how intense you look right now."

For a moment I don't move. I *can't* move. There's no defending against something so earnest, especially from a man who's teased and tested me all night; it doesn't fit with the pigeonhole I made for him just to keep sane. That pigeonhole is labeled "Player," which may or may not be an upgrade from "Arrogant Asshole."

"Quit."

"Why?"

"I don't need that fake stuff."

"Compliments? Attention?"

"All of that."

"I've never met a person who didn't secretly crave a little of both." He coils one long strand around his forefinger and gives it a little tug. His mouth is right beside my ear when he speaks again. "And life's too short to give attention to people who don't deserve it."

I snatch my hair free. Something snaps inside me. I've just come off a huge triumph, but it was goaded to life by this man and now it's being ruined by this man—mostly because he's saying all the right things . . . to the wrong girl.

"You walk around with so much . . . so much *confidence*. I bet everybody here wants you. I don't know why you're playing around with me, but I wish you'd stop."

"I'm not playing around. I'm talking. I happen to like talking to extraordinary women."

"Then go talk to Adelaide."

"I plan to," he says with a grin that makes me eager to eat out his heart. "But I have a confession."

Here it comes. He'll admit he's with Adelaide and the whole night has been a practical joke that'll splinter me into shards.

"Then confess."

"I wanted to see you play—what I missed earlier today, when all I could do was listen. But I also wanted to see you come down."

"Down?"

"Down from the sky."

The sky. Yeah, I was that high up. Saying so might have affirmed his near whimsical choice of words. I can't give that much away. I can't be that open. Not so soon. Not even when I suddenly imagine kissing his nape, right where his messy but not messy hair would meet the hot skin of his neck.

"Composing is like climbing until I can't see the ground anymore," I say, almost to myself, betrayed by my thoughts. My heart is beating so hard that it hurts. I want him to go. To stay. To kiss Adelaide right in front of me, to put me out of my misery.

Or to kiss *me*, which would be misery and ecstasy combined.

"Wait. Composing?" Apparently his features don't scrunch together when he's confused. They go placid and calm, with smooth lips and eyes shining like sapphires lit from within. "You threw that out to us on the fly?"

"Yeah."

He makes a noncommittal noise and doesn't take his eyes off me until I'm fidgety. I feel like a child who's been promoted to the grown-up table too early.

I want to scream: *What did you think?*

I don't scream, and he doesn't volunteer his opinion. He only urges me to take another drink.

"Adelaide knows when she's giving a good performance," he says, almost contemplative. I shake away a rush of envy at how much soft affection he gives her name. "You can see it on her smirking face when she finishes. She practically mocks the crowd for adoring her. It's a blessing or a failing. I haven't decided, and I've had years to try."

"You smirk too. I don't like it."

"Then maybe I'll make an effort not to. If . . ."

"What now? If I get onstage again?"

"No, if you leave your hair down for the rest of the night." He crosses his arms, cupping both elbows. I almost prefer his teasing to this deep assessment. "You're a lot to take in all at once, Keeley."

"*Me?* Go find a woman who can keep a rational thought in her head around you."

He only smiles. "I'd rather have another hour with you instead."

I pull my hair back and snap the rubber band into place. My ponytail is all that stands between me and the pull of his magnetic orbit.

"Then you shouldn't have started with me in the first place." I retrieve my water bottle. "I'm not someone you can learn in an hour. I'm surprised you think any woman is."

~ SEVEN ~

Have you ever had a crush on someone you've never talked to, but then you see that person in a crowd, and although he barely knows you exist, he smiles anyway? Maybe he's just being polite. Simple recognition. A shared humanity. I did that once with a cute librarian intern at the community college in Baton Rouge. He was tall and a bit hippie, but he had an incredibly inviting personality. I got the impression he was never unhappy. Probably untrue. Still, some people give off that vibe.

I saw him last summer at a little farmer's market. Just a glimpse. He smiled. I smiled back. I don't think he saw it when morning veggie shoppers swallowed him up.

I spent the next two hours shopping and talking to Clair, and I scarfed a heavenly cinnamon roll. My eyes, however . . . I kept a lookout for the librarian. Someday, I thought, I'll learn his name.

I never did. And I didn't see him again, at the market or the library.

Now . . . This is worse. I know a man named Jude. I know the strong power of his grip. I know that I wouldn't have performed at Yamatam's without his goading.

And now I'll never be the same.

It's an unnerving experience to know something so completely, but it's true. I performed for more than a hundred strangers in an unfamiliar club. I opened up a vein and let my lifeblood pour out. And they rewarded me with so much applause and appreciation that I almost felt like doing it again would be worth it.

Only, how much lifeblood do I have to give?

Forget glimpses. Forget fleeting thoughts of seeing Jude again. He was right all along. I've walked away from him, now standing at the bar, but I watch him until my eyes burn. He's flitting through the club, making the rounds. He seems to know everyone. I don't put it past him. He's charming and obviously knows how to make an impression.

I still can't believe he got me onstage. Was that really me? I like knowing where my impulses and emotions come from, but right now, my impulses are absorbing energy from Jude, from watching him, and my emotions come from feeling unbelievably stupid. I'm clueless as hell when it comes to guys. I have no idea how to dodge and weave when in their sights, which hasn't been often.

So I have no idea what to do with this universe-shattering flirt. That nameless librarian had set off a few pleasant imaginings. Jude, by comparison, is an entire symphony that hasn't been written. He's a frustrating masterpiece. Is that why I'm waiting around, as if he might come back to me? Please don't let that be the truth.

"Are you Keeley?"

I turn to see Adelaide Deschamps standing beside me.

"That's me. And you're Adelaide?"

"Yup." She's holding something frothy and pink. At the moment, I don't care so much about her connection to Jude. I'm just grateful to remember why I came to Yamatam's in the first place. It wasn't to hope Jude's spotlight would shine on me again. "So, what was all that up there?"

"What do you mean?" She's a good four inches shorter than me, but I'm immediately on the defensive—my exhausting default reaction to strangers.

I remind myself she's only eighteen. She could've been raised in a sad old trailer park, but that's really unlikely considering that, along with her bohemian clothes, she's wearing a diamond solitaire pendant. With her Blonde Ambition hair and effortless cool, she's unfairly chic. Her eyes are perfectly hazel. She looks priceless. No wonder Jude hasn't been able to keep his eyes off her— between bouts of turning my life inside out in a matter of hours.

"You think it sucked?" I add, when she doesn't reply right away.

The club didn't think so, but Adelaide's opinion will go a long way to defining our mentoring situation.

She twists her hair in an effortless curly messy but not messy style. Bright eyes narrow. She lifts onto her toes and pokes her face within inches of mine. I'm reminded briefly of how close Jude and I sat together, but this is entirely different. Adelaide wears her smirk with an edge of canny humor. She's not that different from the flawless, curtsying megawatt beam of light she'd been onstage. Despite her more petite stature, she stands with the poise of a goddess. She has bearing.

"It was great and I think you know it," she says with that syrup-sweet drawl. Between her and Jude, I'm being given a crash course in the sound of N'awlins suave. "You saw mine, yeah?"

"Yeah."

"And?"

For seeming so composed, her confidence isn't as bullet-proof as I would've guessed.

She probably expects dormouse, after how I slunk away from the stage rather than gather unexpected applause with both arms stretched wide. It's unexpected and reassuring to think she might harbor doubts too.

"You had everyone in your palm until you decided to let them go."

"But my playing? It's . . . I have flaws."

"You want the truth?"

"You're gonna be my mentor, right?"

I nod. But what right do I have to give criticism, when I know how much emotion people put into their art? It seems this girl Adelaide actually wants honest feedback. She's stronger in that regard than me.

"Okay, you're right," I say. "You perform better than you play."

She shakes her head. "I know that's how it is, so don't worry about hurting my feelings or anything. I know that," she says again, then takes a sip of her frothy drink.

I want to ask her all sorts of questions. *When did you start? Where did you study? Who's your favorite composer?* That's the sort of thing a mentor would save for later, over nachos in the student union, maybe. Am I supposed to take the lead on arranging things like that? Crap.

"I wish I could play like you," she adds, setting down the empty glass. "You just *know* the piano, don't you? Up and down and sideways. God, if I practiced more I could be like that, but I guess I get distracted. Too many other things to do. Bartender?"

She signals for another drink to match the other, and the guy hops over to her like he's been summoned by a queen. I don't know how to deal with her. I hate being so unsettled, even though it was freeing to break that plaster mold.

Down from the sky, he'd said.

Because for a few unforgettable moments, I'd been flying.

"You were incredible," I say, sorta lamely.

Adelaide shakes her head. "Jude says that a lot. It's hard to believe sometimes, though. You know?"

She waves across the rectangular bar at the center of Yamatam's and catches the eye of my now familiar stranger. He joins us in a minute. Already, mere hours into the most bizarre night of my college life—because, really, I'd made it through way worse—I recognize Jude's shining hair and easy, lanky yet intent way of moving. A lithe wildcat. In gentleman's clothing. Seeing him isn't necessary, not really, when I feel him moving closer, then closer still. He's a force at my back, like the clouds parting and the sun rising, hot and unrelenting.

I shiver and work to find some calm. It's down in the soles of my shoes. I have to dredge it up and hold on tight.

He hugs Adelaide with an arm around her lower back, then kisses her temple. "Enthralling as always, Addie."

I knew it. It stabs needles under my skin, but I knew it.

Adelaide smiles, but she looks at me with an expression that says, *Toldja.*

Self-preservation isn't about putting up shields to protect one's possessions. It's about having few possessions in the first place. Let the marauders take what they want; they won't find much. Emotions are like that too. So I work on that dissociative thing the court shrinks talked about when I was a teen. Forget about pigeonholing Jude as a player. I lock him in a box and bury it deep.

"So here I find one little cozy duo," he says, eyeing me while leaning his shoulder against hers. "You can teach Addie some discipline, and she can teach you how to get onstage without needing a crowbar."

"Is that it?" Adelaide asks. "You get stage fright? No way."

I shrug.

"Oh, good! I mean, not good, but good that I can do something for you in return. I've never had a problem with the performance part."

Jude rolls his eyes toward the bright lights that line the top rails of the bar. "That's putting it lightly."

"You know." She pushes away from Jude and starts talking a mile a minute. Her hands move as if she's still playing piano. "Franz Liszt used to perform so wildly and with such gusto that he was banned in some cities. He was considered obscene. Women threw underwear at him. Probably big Victorian bloomers. He'd work himself so hard that he only stopped when dehydration got the better of him. That's what we call making an impact." She smiles. "After seeing you tonight, how many people are really going to remember me?"

"Enough so that you leave your lessons aside," Jude says. "The lights are your flame, and you are a moth."

"Butterfly, thank you kindly."

"I stand corrected."

I smile at their lighthearted words and playful smirks. It's like they learned a language of snarky expressions from each other. I laugh, but I want in that circle of two—especially if I can't have him. Can I at least be near them both? Two people so radiant?

Jude kisses her on the temple again. "You girls play nice. I'll see you back at the house."

He turns away, only to stop and glance over his shoulder. "You were good, sugar. *Real* good."

EIGHT

By the time I get back to my dorm, I feel like a cat that's been run over in the rain. My tank top and shirt and hair are a wreck, all damp with sweat and soaked through from the humidity. I smell like the bar. I've lost the echo of Jude's scent. That's the worst of it, because I know it's all I can have of him.

After hours of flirting and taunting me with that arch smile, he winds up attached lip to temple to the girl I'm supposed to mentor. The girl I'm convinced could be of more help to me than I'll be to her. I could think things like, *I've never had a more grueling evening.* But that's not true. Sleeping in a ditch because my parents' Pontiac caught fire on I-40 outside of Tucumcari, New Mexico—that was grueling.

Comparing my past to my college present will never be fair. That was some other life. It still claws at me, but I need to tear loose. Maybe it's time I take another look at my frames of reference. I won't be sleeping in a ditch tonight, but that doesn't mean I'm not drained.

I key the building's main entrance code and walk past the night duty guy, Brandon Dorne. I think he's a junior like me, but he's a few years older. He gets paid to stay up all night and watch *South Park* reruns between handling pressing dorm crises. Last spring, he apparently stood up to frat jackasses who wouldn't take no for an answer when it came to rules about the number of guests after hours. A pair of dumb bunnies on the fourth floor had thought inviting six apiece—and having them bring two cases of Heineken—was A okay. The frat pack was hauled away by campus security after Brandon bloodied three faces pretty bad. The dumb bunnies were given official reprimands and a warning that their next brainless stunt would get them kicked out of campus housing. Brandon walked away with a cut to his right cheek from splintered beer bottle glass. He's practically a legend. Even a transfer like me can recite the tale without having to fake my awe.

Knowing he busted up three guys makes him intimidating even before I talk to him, but I'm trying to be social. He probably doesn't know me from anybody. I guess I feel the need to belong by acting chummy with the night duty superhero.

Plus I'm still buzz, buzz, buzzing. I couldn't sleep now, even if sunrise depended on it.

"Hey, Brandon," I say.

He looks up from the small boxy television on the left side of the wide front desk. "Hey."

He has his feet propped on the scuffed wood. No shoes. Just socks. He's got a cup of ramen in his hands, which is enough to make me break out in a sweat all over again. That he's eating soup in September in New Orleans makes me think he was at least raised in the South. Only in the South would seventy-five degrees at two in the morning still entice anyone toward soup.

Maybe Brandon is a *weird* superhero. Still, none of the other residence halls can claim him.

"It's Keeley, right?" he asks, sitting up, feet back on the ground.

"Yeah."

"Out late." Before I can decide whether that sounded like a condemnation, he smiles. "I need a report on your evening's activities."

I hesitate. "Serious?"

"As a heart attack." He pauses a beat, then flashes his teeth. "It's because I'm bored crapless. Earning a few bucks for my tuition is fine. Missing out on anything exciting is the tradeoff. Help a guy out."

I lean on the desk, happy to engage in a conversation that isn't complicated and doesn't have clumps of drama hanging off it. Considering my night, it's a refreshingly slow change of pace.

"What about the excitement around here?" I ask.

His smile is . . . nice. He has nice teeth and nice lips. His eyes shine in the way eyes are supposed to shine when someone's happy or amused. No taunting to be found. No dares. Just the unspoken invitation to be friendly. I like the simplicity, even though I'm comparing him to Jude, point by point. A buzz of pleasure washes down my whole body at the thought of Jude's galling, frustrating, gorgeous grin.

"Would that excitement have to do with frat guys and this?" He taps a finger to the sliver of white that scars his upper cheek.

"Yeah, that."

His smile broadens. "Yeah, that."

"Kinda hard to miss. The stories, I mean. Not the scar."

Only, that isn't the only scar on his face. A slash angles up from the left side of his jaw, toward his earlobe. His nose has been broken at least once. That he's older, that he has this legendary history—it makes me wonder what else hides in his past. Or maybe that's just me looking for shadows where there aren't any.

"No offense," he says, "but it looks like you've had a helluva time."

"Could say that."

"Just did." He switches off the TV and sets the ramen aside. Once again, I'm the object of a guy's unexpected attention. What is it with tonight? Whatever it is, I could bottle it and make millions. "So, spill it."

"I played piano at Yamatam's. I met the girl I'm supposed to mentor, and then I met her boyfriend."

"Too bad."

"Hm?"

"You sound disappointed that he and your mentor chick are a thing." He ducks his head in an *aw, shucks* way. He's got sweetly floppy black hair that adds softness to brown eyes that never seem to rest. He's agitated.

Suddenly that makes me agitated. I used to watch the world that way. Then again, so do guys high on coke.

I'm being ridiculous. Brandon is just the night watch guy. He's supposed to be on the alert, no matter the cartoons and soup. Plus, he's tall and built and wears his T-shirt like it was modeled to fit his body alone. He's just plain hot.

"It was a teensy disappointment," I say, ducking my head a little. "But there won't be any avoiding him. The girl, Adelaide, is really good. She's like Justin Timberlake onstage. *Owns it.* And I played in public for the first time—well, the first place that wasn't a recital or audition, you know? No profs or families or whatever."

"Just half drunk college kids and rowdy townies who like what they like. Did they like you?"

"Yeah."

He offers a mock salute with an approving nod. "Congrats."

"Thanks."

"But . . ." he says, prompting.

"That same guy followed me around all night."

"I'm good at dealing with assholes who think they can do whatever they want." We've been joking around, so the severity of his tone is a surprise. Total dissonance.

I push a hunk of hair behind my ear. Again I fight the urge to follow his eyes as he scans the faces coming and going through the residence hall foyer.

"It wasn't like that, though," I say, feeling the need to defend Jude. He certainly wasn't some Heineken-swilling frat guy. "All night, it was like a bunch of dares. He sat next to me while she performed. He was the one who goaded me to play. The whole time he skirted this line between sexy stranger and lame player."

Brandon shrugs. "Wish I knew where that line is. I'd stay way clear of the lame player side."

I find myself toying with the spork sticking out of his pot o' ramen. "You do just fine."

"Does that put me on the really sexy side? I could get used to that."

"Pushing it," I say. "Because, really, soup in September?"

"Don't knock it. I wouldn't be working this desk if I had money for real food." Again, he surprises me. There's genuine bitterness behind his words, and that bitterness has turned his wide smile into something closer to what the Joker would show off. "I mean, who can afford Saltines? Too rich for my blood."

I laugh, then chide myself for jumping at threats that aren't there. My adrenaline is doing my thinking for me, and that means not thinking at all.

I hold the cup in both hands and push it toward him like an offering. "Then partake of this delicious yet frugal meal. I wouldn't want your gruel to get cold."

He snickers and takes it from me. Our fingers touch in a half dozen places, and he thanks me. "What's your last name, Keeley? I mean, I could look it up in the resident roster, but . . ."

"Then you're back to creepy guy territory."

"Back to?"

I touch my hair again, feeling caught out. "It's Chambers. Keeley Chambers. Your turn. Where are you from?"

"Pensacola. You?"

"Baton Rouge."

Maybe I hesitate too long, because he tips his head. "Meaning?"

"Nothing. Forget it."

"Army brat?"

"Just brat." As he laughs, I stand away from the desk. His brown eyes follow me. "And now I'm going to get some sleep."

"That wasn't much of a report on the evening," he says, with mock displeasure. He has a sexy voice, sort of . . . messy. It's the Pensacola in him, I guess. I like it. "I expect better next time."

"Yeah. Maybe next time."

"Night, Keeley." His eyes remain fiercely attentive—totally at odds with how he scanned the place during our entire conversation. I take it as interest in me. Has to be, right? He's not Jude, but after all the games at Yamatam's, that's a good thing.

I finally relax enough to smile back without all my psyched-out head games. It's nice. It's a relief. "Night," I say with a little wave.

"By the way," he calls when I'm halfway to the elevator, "who's the girl you're mentoring?"

"Adelaide Deschamps." A frown darkens his expression and raises the hair on my arms. "Why?"

"No reason. Just wondered if I knew her."

I don't like deception, and I can spot it a mile away. There's no place a guy can hide it on his face or in his voice where I won't find it. Roaming eyes, unexpectedly bitter words—and now this?

"Sleep well," he says.

I must be really tired, because the thought of calling Clair and John to tell them about such an earth-shattering night sounds exhausting. I'll tell them in the morning. Instead, I remember only snippets of the short ride up the elevator, and barely anything about collapsing onto my narrow bed. What I *do* remember as I fall asleep is Brandon's frown and the bad feeling he was keeping a secret from me.

What has everyone been missing when they look at Brandon Dorne?

⚈ NINE ⚈

We're just outside Kalamazoo.

The Buick LeSabre that Dad stole from a long-term parking lot at the Indianapolis airport has broken down. We're parked at the side of a small highway. Smoke or steam pours out from the edges of the hood.

I'm . . . nine?

I'm in the backseat, watching semis pass. Their headlights are *so* bright. They leave giant whooshes of air in their wakes, shaking the car. Mom and Dad are outside fighting about who did what wrong. That means neither of them care that I really want my favorite teddy bear, Hammie, from out of the trunk. I'd get it myself if that wouldn't mean attracting their notice.

It doesn't matter when they jerk me out of the smoking car.

"You're gonna help, Rosie girl," my dad says. He looks terrible. His shirt is smudged with fast food grease stains. He's got a goatee that needs cleaning up. Deeper than that, his eyes are wild—not from drugs, but from a lack of them. I know Kalamazoo is where they planned to meet up with some friends. I'm assuming "friends" means dealers or whatever.

Mom's halfway to detox as well. She looks frantic, pacing, tugging at the hem of her too short, red, fake leather skirt. Her hair is platinum blonde and curled like a movie starlet. She could've looked pretty if not for her smudged eye makeup.

"Help?" The word is barely a squeak.

"We're going to hide in there." Dad points to a patch of thick trees. It's summer. The air is humid and full of nighttime bug noises. "Understand? *Hide.* That means you can't tell anyone."

"Tell who?"

"Put these on," she says, half snarling.

I don't look at the clothes she's thrust into my arms and I don't ask if I can get back in the car to change. I already know the answer. So I do my best to hide against its far side, where the headlights can't find me, and wiggle into my best dress. It's my con dress. It's the dress they make me wear when it's time for a cute little girl to become living bait. Covered in lace and swirling patterns of roses . . . I hate it.

Tights.

Shoes.

Then Mom does my hair up in ponytails with bows. I don't complain when she wrenches the rubber bands too tight and snags the tangles. I fight tears. I'm terrified, with a stomach made of cold water.

"Good girl," Mom says, her face drawn tight, like a skeleton wearing skin that's too small. She kneels, with both hands on my upper arms. "Are you hungry, baby?"

I nod.

"Then you'll do this. Stand by the side of the road and wait for someone to stop. Lie your fucking ass off."

"Lie how?"

"Just get them to stop." She glances back at my dad, who's loading a pistol. "We'll take care of the rest."

"You hungry, Rosie girl?"

"Yes, Daddy."

"Me too. We'll get some dinner after this is over. When we get to town. You can have anything you want."

"Cheeseburger and ice cream," I say without hesitation.

"And if you don't do this proper? What will happen?"

I shudder. If I make a mistake, there was no telling what would happen. They do a good job of keeping up appearances. They don't leave bruises people can see.

"I don't know." I'm swallowing the tears now. I heard them say once that I'm a convincing crier. That I pluck heartstrings. I wonder if they think I'm a good con, like them, or if they know how easy it is to wind me up before setting me loose.

"What's that bear you like so much?" Dad asks.

My heart jumps. "Hammie?"

"Yeah, we'll have a Hammie bonfire." He tucks the pistol in the back waistband of his jeans. "And you can forget about dinner."

They disappear into the woods. I'm shaking. My shoes are too small—white patent leather with scuffs on the toes. I look at the scuffs as I force my legs to move.

Standing where headlights will shine on my lace and roses dress, I hop up and down, waving my arms at the traffic. Car after car after semi whizzes past. I couldn't eat a cheeseburger and ice cream now. I'm too sick with worry.

Finally a minivan slows down and parks in front of the Buick. There's a guy driving, and maybe his daughter in the passenger seat. She's probably a few years older than me. I want to climb in through her open window and hide in the back and tell the guy to floor it.

Instead, I wipe away what are real tears. "I need help," I say.

The man unhooks his seat belt and leans toward the passenger window, angling across the girl. "What happened, honey?"

"Dad went for a tow truck. It was a long time ago. I was supposed to stay inside the car. But I'm scared something happened to him."

"Don't worry," the man says. "We'll get this sorted out. What's your name?"

I hesitate. Who am I now? Lila? Sara? I can't remember. *I can't remember!*

"Um . . ."

The man takes a good look at me, at the Sunday school dress I'm wearing on a Thursday night. "Where were you going?"

I hesitate. "Kalamazoo."

"Yeah, but where? To see family? Just passing through?"

I flinch when I hear the cocking of my dad's gun. He'd crept around the other side of the minivan. The muzzle is flush with the man's temple. "Out of the van. The girl too."

It's all over in a few minutes. The girl looks as terrified as I feel when my folks make her and her dad lie facedown in the gravel at the side of the road. Dad searches the guy for a cell phone, then steals it and his wallet.

"Hands behind your back. Don't move. She's driving," Dad says, angling his head toward my mom, "but I'll have this on you the whole time."

Mom transfers our stuff from the LeSabre to the minivan in two trips. She orders me to get in. That's where I'd imagined taking refuge, but not with my parents at the wheel. My legs are shaking. The toes of my shoes pinch. I want to yank the bows out of my hair.

Dad backs up slowly, toward the passenger door. He's got the gun aimed right for the man, whose little girl is crying. I wish I had permission to cry.

"Where's that bear?" he calls to Mom.

"Got it."

I'm already strapped in the minivan's second row of seats. "Did I do good?" I ask tentatively.

Mom glares back at me. "You forgot your name again. If he'd had sense enough to call the police, we'd be screwed. You should know better."

She pulls a lighter from her back pocket and holds it to Hammie's foot. It's amazing how fast fake fur can catch fire, and it's amazing how calm my mom looks when she tosses Hammie on the ground.

I'm screaming, crying, begging.

We're driving within a minute. Dad has the shakes. He puts the pistol in the glove box, and he and Mom start arguing again. I don't hear them over the sobs I swallow with my fist in my mouth. My stomach rumbles, and my neck hurts as I pull and pull against the seat belt until I can't see that little bonfire anymore.

I wake up covered in sweat and my face wet with tears. My stomach rumbles just like it did so long ago. Sometimes I wonder what it'd be like to have a regular bad dream. Mine are just sleeping flashbacks.

I grab my iPhone and tiptoe on unsteady legs to the common room. Luckily, it's empty. Even the night owls have turned in. I swish the home screen and hesitate only a moment before dialing Clair's number.

"Hey," I say when she picks up.

"Baby, you okay?"

"Kinda. I didn't want to wake you, but . . . I had a nightmare and just needed to hear your voice."

"A nightmare?"

"The one about my bear."

I hear her mumble something to John. But there's no recrimination. No anger. Just the wordless sound of his concern. "We're here for you, Keeley."

I soak in the sweet Southern way she says my name. "I know it's late. You probably have lots to do in the morning—"

"No more than you do. I know how hard you work. I'm gonna make a decaf. You tell me everything."

I do. I tell her every gruesome detail, although she's already heard this story a couple times. I curl into myself on the dingy common room couch, wishing for a blanket, cupping the phone to my ear. I've stopped crying, but it takes me a long time to get it all out. We hang up an hour later, with a bunch of *I love you*s and Clair saying softly, "Go get some rest, baby."

I try, but it still takes me hours to go back to sleep.

~ TEN ~

Janissa and I make time to have breakfast together the next morning—breakfast being Pop-Tarts in bed while we read textbooks and aimlessly watch *Lost* on Netflix. She's in her pajamas, per usual. They're cute little shorts and a T-shirt that reads "Frankie Says Relax." Her older stepbrother got it for her. There's twelve years between them, so it's a way of finding common ground with a sibling so much older—the cornier the better. She has yet to wear her set of matching *Magnum, P.I.* sweats, but I know she owns them.

I'm still in my bathrobe with a towel wrapped around my head, because a night at the club meant needing another shower pronto when I dragged myself up from the dead this morning. Between Yamatam's and that nightmare, I feel prickly and unmoored.

Of course Janissa had a host of questions after I recounted the triumphs and tragedies of my night. I don't leave anything out.

"And he just *talked* to you like that? All possessive?" I nod at her. "What an ass!"

"That's the thing," I say. "I really can't tell you why I'm defending him, because he doesn't deserve it, but it didn't feel . . . hostile. It felt like I'd been invited to play a game, but I didn't know the rules."

"I wouldn't defend that."

I close my eyes briefly, then towel dry my wet hair to disguise my wandering thoughts—thoughts that have to do with Jude's buttery rich accent and his lean, capable body. I stand in front of the mirror and spray on some leave-in conditioner. Compared to Janissa's Scottish heroine red and Adelaide's Hollywood blonde, I'm feeling pretty plain this morning.

Maybe I'm just tired, but I suddenly miss Clair and John. Things were easier with them. They knew how to reassure me in ways that weren't patronizing, in ways that made me think they were one miracle short of being eligible for sainthood. Who took on a kid like me and found the patience to turn me into a halfway stable college girl? Clair and John Chambers, quiet heroes.

Before my brain invents new schlocky Hallmark odes, I flip my hair over my shoulders and decide to pop the second pastry in the toaster.

"Brandon would say this is a fire hazard, you know," Janissa says. "I only learned a couple days ago. We're not supposed to have toasters in our rooms."

"Do you think he'll bust us?"

"That could be fun." She giggles. "Maybe we should open the doors and let the smell waft down the hallway."

I start to laugh. "Don't lie. You'd set off the emergency sprinklers. Then he wouldn't have to bust you until after he rescues you."

"Me? Sounds like you have a better chance at getting rescued first." She pillows her chin on her folded hands, lying there on her stomach. "First comes that mystery guy, Jude, and now Brandon? Since when did my quiet musician roomie get boy crazy?"

"Juju in the water, or whatever. Last night. I swear it. *So* weird."

"Are you planning on leaving anyone in New Orleans for me? Pick one and lemme have the other."

"You're being ridiculous." I sit cross-legged on the bed, still wearing my fuzzy pink robe, with a plate of Pop-Tarts on my lap to ensure modesty. "But you should come out with me Thursday. Adelaide already texted this morning that she'll be playing there again. You could come see the circus."

"Are you going to invite Brandon?"

I shake my head. Yamatam's and Brandon? That idea just doesn't work. "No."

"Is Jude going to be there?"

"How should I know? Besides, there's no way. You should've seen him with Adelaide. It's like they spoke a special code language of snark and subtext. They're totally an item. If not now, then in that way exes can be when they're not done with each other."

After a slight cringe, Janissa sits up and goes about cleaning her glasses. "Yeah, I know. There was this guy last year, Kier, who was like that for me. It took him doing a semester someplace in New York for me to get free. When he came back I realized, wow, I didn't want to be postbreakup friends with him. We were never friend material."

I realize there's a lot about Janissa I don't know. "Get free" is a really powerful phrase. I want to ask more, but she already has that closed off, artificial brightness in her eyes, like she never brought up anything at all.

"Just sex, then," I say, nodding sagely, and privately agreeing to drop the subject.

She tosses a pillow at me. My second round of breakfast hits the floor. "I'd dignify that with a response if I didn't think you're a virgin," she says. "Wait, you are a virgin, yeah?"

"Yeah. So?"

"There's no *so* about it. Just glad to know I'm not the only one." Her grin widens. "But don't think we have anything in common. I am not a wannabe slut in the making. You *long* to be corrupted."

I lie back on the bed, laughing. "Is that what I should've said to Jude? Corrupt me! Corrupt me!"

"Or Brandon. Does it matter to a hussy like you?"

"Did you call me a hussy?" I ask, breathless. "Are you from the eighteen hundreds or something?"

"Doesn't matter." She affects a perfectly prim pose. "I shouldn't be anywhere near you Thursday."

"No, you need to save me from my wicked, base impulses. I have these . . . urges. Like . . ." I snatch one of the Pop-Tarts off the industrial carpeting. "Like flagrantly breaking the five-second rule."

Janissa makes a face as I take a big bite out of the frosted strawberry pastry. Strawberry is a fruit. That's healthy enough, right?

"Okay," she says. "Now that's crossing a line. Ew."

We burst into laughter and I smile appreciatively at Janissa.

She's lovely and even tempered, and a slight oddball like me. But I knew that on day one.

Now I'm realizing that she's the best sort of roommate a random computer pairing could've found for me. There's no judgment in anything she does or says, which is a huge plus. Hell, it'd be a huge plus for anybody, but I've come to think of our dorm as a safe haven. I've had so few safe havens that they stand out like bright beacons.

Janissa is ninety percent of what makes it safe. The rest is just white painted cinderblock walls, industrial carpeting, and an illegal toaster. But it's starting to feel more like home.

"So, this Jude guy," she says. "No joke, he's the one you need to stay away from. I mean, he sounds *really* intriguing and all sexy mystery man, but you've got too much on your plate for that drama. Music fellowship, remember?"

I nod. "Is this where you turn on the sensibility faucet and I get a faceful of it?"

"Seriously, you have classes and rehearsals, plus, what's your big campus debut at the end of the semester?"

"The Fall Finish. Part final exam featuring an original composition, part audition for the local music ensembles—including the New Orleans Symphony. I want to compose for a living, but getting established can take years. In the meantime, I'd love to earn my way by playing piano, rather than holding down two jobs that involve serving fries. The university tries to place all of its fellows before we graduate. Now I just need to . . ."

I wiggle into a pair of khaki shorts under my robe, then turn my back to put on my bra and a loose, maroon cotton shirt that I knot at my stomach. "Now I just need to learn how to perform

for people in a way that doesn't make me seem possessed. Or
feel like I'm about to have a panic attack—all those eyes on me. I
need what Adelaide had last night. She was *aware*. Of everything she did and how it would affect all of us."

"You being her mentor doesn't mean the information has to
go one way."

"You're so practical. That's a really good thing . . . normally." I
pull the ends of my hair out from my shirt and give the damp
locks another toss. "But that also means you're right about no
mystery man, doesn't it?"

I don't want her to be right.

Janissa uses her fingers to tick off a list. "He has a young,
cute girlfriend. You have classes, rehearsals, composition,
public performances, and clearly a deep need for avoiding
drama."

I pause in putting on a swish of lip gloss. A fist of icy fear
wraps around my heart. I've never told Janissa about my past.
"What do you mean?"

"You just seem high strung. No offense. I am too. But . . ."
She inhales. "You have bad dreams, don't you?"

"I . . ."

"You don't have to talk about it if you don't want to. Just that
sometimes you sound like you're crying or asking someone to
stop." Her embarrassment is obvious, and I want her to stop
talking, but I'm glad when she doesn't. Because she finds a way
for us to get out of the dark by sharing a laugh. "Whereas I thank
my lucky stars every night that you don't snore."

"You do."

"Do not!" But she smiles around a blush. "So, yeah, from my
perspective, ditching the drama means finding a guy who offers

up less bullshit and more straight-up answers. I learned my lesson. Gimme a nice guy who doesn't go in for head fucks."

"Classy."

"But true."

"Okay, then tell me what happens when I wake up with his voice in my head? *If I want you, sugar, I'll come find you.*"

Janissa's auburn brows shoot upward. "He *said* that? With a straight face?"

"Completely straight face."

"No shit. Because that's *so* unfair. It's USDA grade A crap, but it's also toe curling. Ugh. It's caveman romance. All that stuff we're not supposed to think is dreamy." She shrugs and starts getting dressed too. "But that goes back to the head fuck thing. A guy who has a girlfriend should've never said that to you, then kissed her *in front* of you. Drama city. Take a big detour around it and try out Brandon. He's tall and hot. What else do you need?"

A lot more.

I sigh and stack up a bundle of blank music paper. I haven't had a chance to write down what I improvised at Yamatam's, before notating and plugging it into my Mac. But I have one more question before Janissa retreats to her corner of academia.

"Hey, actually, Brandon said something last night. He asked Adelaide's name and got this strange look on his face. I couldn't make anything of it. Sorta . . . amused? Stunned? But I know he lied when he said it was nothing. Does that mean anything to you?"

"Oh." Janissa practically jumps off her bed and slides into her desk chair, laptop open in a flash. "Oh, no way."

"No way what?"

"Jude and Adelaide. It only clicked now, saying their names close together. His was, what, Jude Villars?"

"How did you know that? I haven't mentioned it."

I feel shaky but why, I don't have a clue. This feels big, because Janissa doesn't normally overreact. She's calm and steady. You can learn that early about a person and trust it. She wouldn't have this gleam in her eye, this on the cusp vibe, if it wasn't really important.

"There," she says, a little triumphant, a little breathless, as she points to the result of her Google search. It's a picture of Jude in a magnificent tuxedo, with Adelaide on his arm in what must be a one of a kind '20s-inspired gold sequin gown. "Jude and Adelaide Deschamps-Villars, the rich as hell heirs to Villars International, this huge paper manufacturing company. Their family practically saved Tulane after Katrina. They were orphaned two years ago when their parents' private jet crashed. Ages sixteen and twenty-four."

"Orphaned by a plane crash? Oh God, that's terrible."

"Yes, but Keeley," Janissa says with a crooked smile, "that means they're brother and sister."

~ ELEVEN ~

Orphans.

Brother and sister.

I'm all manner of idiot. Or the luckiest girl on the planet. Or . . .

There are so many new ways to think about Friday night that I literally *can't* think.

I check in with Clair and John, who's actually the one to pick up this time. "Clair's on rotation today. Sucks," he says, sounding more frustrated than tired. "It's a nice day out. We wanted to go for a bike ride."

"Too bad I'm not there. I'd go with you. Instead I'm in the common room dungeon trying to make sense of a piece I wrote the other night."

I do my best to explain what happened at Yamatam's, even mentioning Jude.

Yes, the *Jude Villars.*

No, I don't mind if you tell Clair, but thanks for asking first.

And finally, *Yes, I'll be careful.*

John's concerns sound a lot like Janissa's, which doesn't surprise me. Clair has always been my go get 'em influence, with John tempering us both and offering quiet caution. He's our rock. They raised me by tag team, which is probably why they've been able to do it so well.

After signing off, I try to get comfy on the floor, with my notebook of music paper open across my knees. The dedicated Saturday afternoon lazies are watching *SpongeBob*. Some of that has to be the brownies someone brought from off campus. I don't want to eavesdrop or watch pineapples under the sea or nibble a little hash with my chocolate. I just like the company of being around genial people, even if I'm the oddball sitting on a beanbag chair against the wall, with my headphones in.

No one notices me. I have that skill—except, apparently, when it comes to Jude Villars. He noticed me. Pursued me. Saw through me.

I duck back to my work. I don't listen to music while I'm composing. Instead, the sounds of distant thunderstorms fill my ears—the Midwest in late spring, when the air is suddenly thick with heat, rain, and the possibility of the static magic that lifts the hairs on my arms and neck. Tornado skies. The whip of fresh, unearthly winds. I live in that world, so to speak, as the music from the night before takes physical form, as scratches and the occasional eraser smudge on stave after stave.

Brother and sister.

I scribble faster, trying to outpace hot and cold flashes of confusion. The worst, though, is anticipation.

Thursday night. Of course Adelaide planned to play again. Would I?

That's a thought to make a girl's skin go numb. Maybe I'm supposed to get charged up about it, but that's not me. I only did it on Friday night because I was dared to within an inch of my sanity.

Will Jude be there?

Janissa is right. I don't need head fuck drama. He played with me so hard that I just about kissed him. Thing is, I only would've proven him right, because no way have I ever wanted to kiss anyone that much.

The music I created on the fly in front of a crowd of bar patrons starts to change, taking on a new motif. As I transcribe the notes in my mind, I'm propelled by the rhythm of those four-four-time words.

Will Jude be there?

I don't like that he's invading so much of my brain space, especially my composition, the only thing I'm usually one hundred percent certain of. A gift by the genetics of my shit for luck parents, like a consolation prize for having been born to those two.

To have Jude influencing my music, after only two encounters and a few hours, is disturbing. My lone consolation is that with every note, I'm remembering even more of how I performed. The music is what does it. If I stop and *try* to remember, it's like trying too hard to remember a dream. Not that I try to remember dreams. Janissa was right about my nightmares.

Each flash of graphite on paper, however, takes me back to Yamatam's. One chord at a time. One note at a time. I can almost see myself at the piano, totally out of body.

I can almost see myself as *he* would've seen me.

Maybe I wasn't as manic as I feared. I was energetic, engrossed, compelled by an unstoppable force. Maybe Adelaide was right about Liszt.

Not that it matters. The music department won't want to see that. They want soul and refinement from their composition students. No hurricanes allowed. I got my fellowship by playing by the rules. I'd play by the rules again when it comes time for the Fall Finish.

I jump out of my skin when someone nudges my shoe. I look *way* up to find Brandon standing there. But for a moment, in my confused mind, he isn't Brandon. He's my father, looming over me.

I used to make blanket forts a lot. I also hid under beds. One time, I found refuge behind a washer and dryer. Dad always found me. Depending on how much he'd drunk, popped, or snorted, his attitude could be anything. Sometimes he was so high and out of it that he almost seemed kind. Even happy. That made the other ninety-nine percent of his moods even harder to take.

So when *he* found me . . . I never knew *who* found me.

I snap free of the memory when Brandon smiles. His mouth moves. I pop out my earbuds and slap my notebook closed a little too quickly.

He stays quiet for a heartbeat, looking at the notebook, then shrugs. "Hey."

"Hey."

"You got dinner plans?"

I about choke on the cough I hold back. "Uh."

Fabulous. I might as well replace my tongue with a row of black and white keys. Sure, I'd pound out a lot of weird music every time I open my mouth, but at least it'd sound better than my oh so eloquent response.

"I don't know," I finally conjure, and it's the truth. "Probably pizza and a stack of textbooks."

He shifts from one foot to the other. It looks a little boyish, but sorta bashful on a guy as built as Brandon. He must've played sports back home in Pensacola. Maybe he still does. Maybe we'd actually have a good time, with plenty to talk about.

But why do I doubt that so much?

"Sounds about as bad as desk duty," he says.

"Nothing sounds as bad as desk duty."

"I'll give you that." He sits on the floor beside me and props his back against the wall, long legs outstretched, ankles crossed. He's wearing loose jeans, Carhartt work boots, and a Black Sabbath T-shirt. Even if his only authentic knowledge of Ozzy Osbourne is from the TV show about their messed-up family, the effect is great. The T-shirt is fitted and just worn enough. Sitting side by side like this, I let myself sink into the idea that he's as nice and cool as he's supposed to be.

"What else are you taking?" he asks.

I really want to get back to my work before I lose my out-of-body feeling. And I still have to feed my notations into the music program on my Mac. But Brandon's too nice to blow off. I'm making too much out of the few little things about him that bug me.

"The sociology of subcultures, the history of early Latin America, and basic biology round out my required classes," I say. "So . . . reading. Research. I have a paper about piercings and tattoos due a week from Tuesday, which has to include firsthand interviews. I haven't even started."

"That shouldn't be too hard."

I want to say, *I bet the people I interview for my paper won't resemble the guys in prison with my dad.* But I don't. I never will.

Janissa can't help hearing when I have nightmares, which makes me want to apologize all over the place. That doesn't mean I'm ready to open up and explain where they come from. I was given a fresh start when Clair and John drove me out of California. That clean slate means no one here gets to know what I've lived through.

I clear my throat. "So, what's your major?"

The question is genuine—the perfect escape route—and he sounds excited about his major. But I'm struck with the idea that I'm using up potential dinner conversation fodder. Again I wonder why talking to him over milkshakes or whatever would be so hard.

No, not *hard*. Just . . . ordinary.

"I'm studying journalism," he says. "Part of my Big Assignment this year is editing a campus news blog, and shadowing a local news crew. So, see? If you need any help on that paper, I'm your guy."

I accept his hand to stand up. His palm is warm but in that pleasant way. Life force. No hint of sticky New Orleans sweat. Thank the heavens above for air conditioning at full blast. I tuck the notebook in front of me like a shield. Against what? Having a life?

"So . . . about dinner?"

I look everywhere but at him, until I call myself a coward and force my chin to lift. "Can I take a rain check until I get a better handle on my schedule? Maybe next week? I know it's asking a lot."

He grins. "Nah, asking was asking a lot. I know everybody's busy." He glances around the room, where co-eds look like they've been hooked up to anesthetic drips. "Well, everybody worth asking out."

"Am I doomed to ramen if I say yes?"

"I save it for the really special girls."

I fake a sigh. "Ninety-nine cents of paradise."

"I buy them in bulk. Ninety-nine cents would be highway robbery."

Slugging him on the shoulder seems perfectly appropriate. He doesn't budge. Smacking him, even playfully, is like trying to make a dent in granite. Suddenly I wonder what it would be like to grab this guy and know he wouldn't let go. To know that kissing him would be solid and safe.

I have to keep wondering, because I can't picture it. At all. Imagining something so domestic with a steady guy like Brandon should be easy. Instead I feel that same agitation.

My imagination is out of control this weekend, which is why I don't trust myself about much of anything—only that Janissa makes me laugh, and that what I'm writing is saving my sanity. Grounding me. It's not the first time I've retreated into deep sonic worlds—places buffeted by echoes of remembered thunderstorms—in order to avoid the real one.

Back in the real world, I'm standing in front of Brandon. His active brown eyes are full of expectation, even though I've already put him off. I like his chin. It's strong without being arrogant. I like his lower lip, just full enough to beg for exploration.

I don't like that I'm imagining someone else.

He smiles again. That particular tilt of his lower lip makes me remember the night before, when he asked Adelaide's name.

He knew.

"So . . ." I shift my weight, as if I'm mimicking the way he'd first approached me. "About last night . . ."

"That already makes it sound like we did more than talk with a five-foot table between us." Maybe my expression stops his jokes, because he blinks and drops to my level of sobriety.

"You knew who I was talking about when I mentioned Adelaide Deschamps. How she and Jude Villars are brother and sister."

He glances toward the 'luded-out television crew, then turns back. The palest pink flush tips his ears, which are revealed by the fall of his black hair. "Yeah. Sorry about that."

I clutch my notebook tighter. "Why not just tell me?"

"You came back looking so supercharged. I liked that you stopped by to say hi." He looks away again. It's making me want to fidget. "Then, to bring up how you'd spent the night with two New Orleans celebs? I guess I didn't want to be overshadowed so fast, you know?"

I take his explanation and roll it around in my head. "Sure."

"Besides." He looks uncomfortable, as if me shooting him down is finally sinking in. But what he has to say, with that bitterness back again, is a surprise. "She has a reputation. Wild girl. Lots of sex and drugs."

"Way to keep the rumor mill in check," I say without hesitation. "Think about what she's been through, then try to think of her behaving like a normal person—if anyone's really normal. I bet it's impossible to muddle past that, even with a truckload of therapy."

"Therapy." The word is clipped and sharp as a blade. "Right. That works wonders."

"Really, I've got work to do." I glance down toward my notebook. Without realizing, I guess I've been edging toward the door, because I'm halfway out of the common room when I say, "I have to finish this sonata before I lose it completely."

He grins—the same one that first grabbed my attention. But it doesn't feel the same now. It feels . . . like trying to gauge my dad's moods.

I shiver.

"Don't worry about it. I was just bored and trying my hand at being spontaneous."

I nod. I don't want to be around him. He's become the human equivalent of rubber cement that I can't entirely pick off my fingertips.

"I'll see ya," I say woodenly.

Later that night, a knock at our dorm door reveals a pizza delivery guy. Janissa and I protest until he says it's already been paid for. By Brandon. A note on top reads:

"I know it's second best to ramen, but I thought you'd be busy working. How about Saturday night?"

~ TWELVE ~

Yamatam's isn't the only club in New Orleans. It isn't the only place with an open mic, frequented by both college students and locals. And it isn't the only jazz bar.

On Thursday night, when I walk up the stairs with Janissa at my back, it might as well be the center of the universe.

It has its own unique scent. Sure it has all the usual smells of a bar and fried food and sticky floors. Lots of bodies, sweat, cologne. Only a few years ago, the whole place would've been overlaid with a fog of smoke too. But there's something else. Earthy? Not damp or musty. No, it's as if part of this place has always been here, wrested from land so close to the possession of the sea, and that it always would fight the Gulf for its right to stand at the intersection of so many cultures and history.

It's sandalwood and mint.

It's potential and fear.

Janissa grabs my arm from behind and utters a quiet "Whoa" in my ear just before we reach the top step.

Thursday night is the unofficial start of the weekend. Plenty of people are here to drink and grab a few hours of entertainment. Still, it takes me only a few moments to find Adelaide. She may as well have a spotlight shining on her all the time. She's at a high two-person table in a far corner, with her feet dangling off the tall bar stool. She's wearing a colorful floral camisole layered over with a bright gold lamé peasant blouse, tucked into black jeans as tight as a parting embrace. Giant gold hoops dangle almost to her shoulders and glitter against her sunshine skin, with her hair pulled up in a '50s-style ponytail, cute bangs and all.

None of it should work. All of it does. She's a performer the moment she steps out of her house each morning.

The guy she's sitting with isn't Jude, but he looks familiar. It takes me a few minutes and covert glances, during which Janissa grabs me a cranberry and soda and a Diet Coke for herself, before I make the connection. Adelaide is having drinks with Dr. Saunders, our music theory prof. He's hot for being in his late thirties, but he's very, very married. Like, so married that his wife's about fourteen seconds from having their first kid.

I manage to tear my gaze away from the duo, although not before I catch the prof slipping his hand up her leg. She giggles and twirls the straw in what looks like the same frothy pink drink she'd had Friday night.

"Is that her?" Janissa asks.

"Yeah."

"But sure as hell not Jude."

"Um, no," I say, rolling my eyes. "This isn't *Game of Thrones*. That is, however, one of our professors."

"With his wedding ring on. Classy. He's a creep for taking advantage of her."

Janissa's comment eases the tension where I store it between my shoulder blades. I feel easier, calmer around her. Maybe one day, she can become a confidant. Until now, I didn't realize how much I want one.

A pair of singers with rough beards and acoustic guitars is warming up for their set. Janissa spots a four-person table to the right of the stage. I make to follow, but she shakes her head. "Go say hi to her at least. Maybe it'll remind that prof to keeps his hands off damaged jailbait."

"Okay." But ever since Janissa and I stayed up past midnight, fitting in another two episodes of *Lost*, I mostly wanted to hang with her. She's familiar and comfortable and happy.

The night has other plans.

"Okay," I say, turning to walk away. "Be right back."

"Or maybe you won't," comes a sleek masculine voice.

The club is warm with so many people. Windows open to the street below don't help circulate air. The idea I can get any hotter—in an instant—should've been absurd. But I know that voice. Or I think I do. The almost week since my Friday night performance accomplished the thankful magic trick of blunting its harmonic power and smooth New Orleans confidence.

But it was just that—a trick. The power is real and stunning all over again, especially now that I know who he is . . . and who *isn't* his girlfriend.

Jude Villars stands with his back against the wall midway between Janissa's table and Adelaide's. They seem like distant female islands, one of refuge, one of drama, but they call to me as being safer than meeting Jude's eyes.

I take up the challenge anyway.

He smiles, then mock salutes with a foreign beer that's mostly full. A drip of condensation rolls down his hand and travels the inside of his forearm. He's wearing another broadcloth shirt, with the sleeves rolled and buttons undone at the throat.

My enthusiasm for the night, which had been building all week, is burnt crispy in moments. Everything has gone wrong in the span of a few heartbeats. First Adelaide, who is supposed to be ready to talk music with me. Then Janissa, who sits alone at a table for four.

Now Jude.

Who is so stunningly magnetic.

How did I manage to downplay his effect since Friday? How did I think I could come here and remain upright while weighed by the curious aloofness of his blue, blue eyes? Maybe it was a self-defense mechanism. Or I've gone temporarily insane.

I hope it's temporary.

I make my feet move forward. Adelaide can wait. She's occupied anyway. Leaving Janissa twists me with guilt. I don't dare look back for fear of seeing a reminder of the truth in her eyes.

Drama. Bad boy. *You don't have time for this.*

"Hello, Mr. Villars." Yeah, there's some bitterness in my greeting. After he made me twist last week, I indulge in one petty comment. There may be more to come if he messes with me again.

"Have I been found out, Miss Chambers?" He takes a sip, looking at me over the lip of the bottle.

"Yes. Now we both have full names. All very civilized."

"I can go back to *sugar* if you want, but I decided to try politeness."

"What about Friday night? That wasn't polite at all."

He pushes away from the wall and presses into my space. I turn, using small steps to slip back and away from his physical presence. I only wind up buffeted by the sturdy bricks.

"Now you've done it," he says.

"Done . . . ?"

"You've let me hide you over here." He touches my cheek so softly, so slowly, that I'm convinced I'm dreaming. "As for last time, I wanted to enjoy teasing you before you found out who I am. Everyone finds out eventually."

I frown at the cynicism in his voice, but he soothes the pinch between my eyebrows. "I thought you and Adelaide were a thing," I say. "Boyfriend, girlfriend."

He drops his hand. His gaze rests on my lower lip. His intensity is even more intimate than touching me. "Creep factor aside, I treat her a lot better than her boyfriends do. I wanted to see if you could keep up with her, because I don't just mean her music."

"You mean her personal life too? I'm not her chaperone."

"No," he says, mouth tight. The only time I've seen him stray from his glib playboy act is when he talks about his sister. "You're not."

"You want me to spy on her for you? Is that it?"

He shakes his head. "You know, I'm already regretting Friday night. I gave you such a bad first impression."

I blink at his words, which almost sound like an apology. I don't know if I'd call his first impression bad. Frustrating. Unique. *Captivating.* But it sure didn't invite involvement in his family problems.

"What would you do differently, if you could go back?"

He doesn't have dimples. Not really. It's more like his smile can get so big and bright that laugh lines bunch together on either side of his enticing lips. Pseudo dimples. I want to kiss each one. To kiss him while he smiles . . . that hits me as way more intimate than fantasies about kissing him in the heat of passion. I already know he doesn't shine that smile at just anyone.

"I'd have told you who I am and used it to tempt you back to my place."

"Liar," I say, returning his smile.

"I'd have asked you out for coffee and beignets."

"I think that's still a lie, but I like it."

He chuckles, then nuzzles my neck until he finds skin. I shiver when his lips touch me. I should protest, shouldn't I? Instead I tilt my head to give him better access.

"I'd have kissed you and called you 'sugar' until you didn't know whether to hit me or kiss me back."

"That's more like it." I'm breathless with anticipation while still trying to hold a conversation. "And you think what you're doing will have an impact on Adelaide and me?"

"Possibly, but they're two different matters. What I'm doing to you is because I want to." He kisses my neck again, inhales deeply, and makes a low, satisfied sound in his chest. "Damn, I was right in calling you *sugar.*"

I want to yell in his ear, *Pick a side!* Good guy or bad boy? Go for it or run away? Instead I let the wall prop up my head as he sweeps his fingers down my throat, between my collarbones.

Then he straightens to his full, impressive height and meets my eyes, his demeanor businesslike. "I don't need a spy, Keeley. I need an ally. She's gifted. You saw that. I don't want that wasted. And I don't want her hurt." He pauses. "She could use a friend."

As if by agreement, we both glance toward Adelaide and the professor. She happens to look up. Her brows lift. She grins like a conspirator who just got found out, but who has enough dirt on her fellow conspirators that she doesn't have to worry. Then she's back to the professor, her hand on his upper arm.

"But everybody loves her."

"That's part of the problem."

"What makes you think I can keep up with her, as you called it?"

"You're keeping up with me just fine," he says, his smile regaining its playfulness. "That's a start."

I want to laugh. That's like saying a girl in a parasailing rig kept up with a speedboat. No choice in the matter.

"And now you're back for more. Are you going to play again tonight?"

"I don't know."

"I've decided, you know. I'm not going to waste my breath one way or the other."

"How do you mean?"

"Either you will, in which case I don't need to say a thing. Or you won't. I've had it up to my eyes with Adelaide today. I don't have the energy to play cat and mouse, luring you toward where you belong."

His arrogance doesn't surprise me, but the contradicting emotions in his voice do. The cat and mouse reference feels like a double entendre from the man who's spent the last ten minutes flirting with me, kissing me. Then, in the same breath, we're back to worrying about his sister. Has he been arguing with Adelaide? About Dr. Saunders? He sounds tired. This is the first crack in the overwhelming, superhuman impact of Jude. Suddenly I realize that yes, he has a life outside of Yamatam's, a life beyond the games he insists on playing with me.

Still . . .

What if all I've needed to get onstage all these years was just the right combination of goading and the urge to impress someone who seems above being impressed? Jude certainly gave me both in spades. He could do it again without a second thought. I don't know if I can muster up the courage to do it on my own. Not yet. It doesn't make any sense, considering what I've seen and done and been. But what I've seen and done and been has taught me that not a lot in life makes sense.

"You don't have the time," I echo. "Then why are you here? Don't you have better things to do than slum it at a college jazz dive?"

"This was my dive once," he says with a return of his terseness. It grinds all of the smooth and charming out of his New Orleans accent, leaving his words a low growl. "But things were different then."

He strokes his thumb up the inside of my wrist. One place of contact. One touch of skin to skin. I try to hide my shiver. He sees it. I can tell, not because of a smile or some tease, but because of his eyes. A gleam of light from the stage has crossed his face. I can see every detail—the length of his lashes, the lines at the corners that seem so harsh and out of place for a man of only twenty-six, and even their hypnotic blue color. They're even darker, more intense, probing, as he pets my skin. He can probably feel every rampaging beat of my blood.

"I came here when I was an undergrad, before the whole city got turned inside out. Before . . ." He stops short and shakes his head. I know that feeling, when I have to swallow words, knowing just how revealing they'll be—more than just facts. But he hasn't looked away, and I *can't*. He leans close and whispers against my cheek, "A whole lot of good memories got swallowed by the bad. But you, sugar . . . You're making it feel brand new."

~• THIRTEEN •~

I chicken out of performing.

Maybe I knew I would even before I left the dorm. I'm almost as disappointed with Jude as I am with myself. If he likes me, and if he liked what I played on Friday, why wouldn't he want to urge me on? But he stays true to his declaration. He doesn't say a word, not even after Adelaide burns the house down again. In fact, rather than watch his sister play, he wanders the club to mingle.

Janissa claps like crazy for Adelaide. "Oh my God, Keeley. You were right. She's *amazing*."

Shortly thereafter, I see Adelaide and Dr. Saunders leave together. My stomach is water, while I'm thirsty as hell. Maybe I should go after her, even just to compliment her performance? Jude watches them go too. His expression is somewhere between thundercloud and sadness.

In the end, I just plop my butt back in my chair. I'm not ready to chase after Adelaide, who's practically a stranger.

Anyway, it's not my responsibility. I'll figure out some way to meet up with her on neutral ground. We'll talk music, not *really* poor choices in guys.

As if I know where that line is.

I make this tumbledown club feel new to Jude? I make him feel anything?

Three musical acts later, Jude puts his hand on one of the chairs at our table. "May I?"

"Oh," Janissa says. "Hi."

Sure, his hand is only resting there, but his demeanor says he's already claimed it like a homesteader. Still, he waits. He stands with grace and the timeless formality of a man who was raised with money. Yet in that odd way of his, he makes it seem perfectly natural, no matter the casual setting.

With amusement in his eyes, he looks between me and Janissa. She had to have been watching when he cornered me against the wall. She has yet to grill me about it, as we each pretended the night was nothing special—or mind bending.

Now she shoots me a look. Well, two looks. One clearly says, *Holy shit.* The other may as well be written in DayGlo paint across her heart-shaped face.

Danger.

Practical girl is practical.

Jude places a tumbler of some golden liquor on the table and joins us. "An introduction, please?"

I can't help but laugh. "That's rich coming from you, Mr. Villars."

"I'm Jude to you or I'm nothing at all," he says, darting me some playful side-eye.

He genuinely seems more interested in meeting Janissa than

in poking my scaredy-cat butt up on stage. He's given up on that being a possibility, just like he said. I'd either do it or I wouldn't. His dares and prodding are off the table. Not that I need him to help make my decisions for me. Not that I need him in order to be strong.

Not that I care.

Except that I do care. *Damn him.*

I decide to play by his stupid rules. At least there seem to be rules right now, based on surface level politeness. We may as well have been making introductions at a country club banquet. I've never been to one. He's probably forgotten the number of country clubs, let alone the times he's played out high-class routines.

A minute ago, a few minutes from now—no telling what his rules will be.

"Janissa Simons," I say. "This is Jude Villars."

They shake hands, all decorum. He offers a smile meant to charm his way into the pants of almost any human being. I want to smack him.

"You guys want a drink?" she asks. "I'm going up for a refill."

"Actually, I just came by to say hello. Keeley and I are getting ready to leave." Jude's certainty is so overwhelming that I check myself. Did he say something? Did we make plans? Maybe I've totally lost my marbles.

"Um, all right." Janissa glances at me.

"I'm not going anywhere," I say, my anger quick and hot. He takes *so* many liberties. That they coincide with desires I can't even articulate makes it worse. "I'm here with Janissa. We're staying."

Jude pins her with what I know to be his impossibly persuasive gaze. "Janissa, I know you two must've been having a good time, so I'll offer my apologies. But I have a proposition for Keeley. Would you mind?"

I expect her to jump in and be as righteously indignant as I'm trying to feel.

She surprises me when she says, "Go ahead."

I don't know whether to hug her or rail at her for letting the wolf in the door. Her expression has slipped toward curiosity, with none of the no go reminders I need. Then again, didn't I just have a similar conversation with Jude about Adelaide? Janissa isn't my keeper. If I want to play with fire . . . well, she's already told me not to.

Although he still seems to be speaking to Janissa, Jude has turned his full-on melty intensity on me. I'm pinned by blue on blue eyes and his casual hint of a smile. The politeness is still there, but it lends an extra wickedness to his words. "I want to take Keeley down to my town car and kiss her. In private. It's either there, or back against that shadowy club wall, or down in an alley like we have something to hide."

My heart stops. Classic cardiac arrest. My mind gives up trying to fight this man, or make sense of why he keeps coming back to me.

The rest of my body screams, *Yes*.

"Wow," Janissa says, her mouth slightly agape. "You really are a caveman in slacks."

Jude arches an eyebrow as he stands. "Caveman?"

"Go ahead. Drag her to your cave."

"I don't drag anyone," he says, grinning, like he can win Janissa to his cause as easily as bribing a kid with candy. "But there are things I want. The question is . . ." He pins me again. "Whether Keeley here wants the same thing."

I'm standing beside him. How that happened, I have no idea. And he's holding my hand. I jerk away as soon as my brain catches up to my greedy nerves. I hold my palm to my chest as if it's been burned. "Is this what you do? Barge through life like this? Tricking people and making them feel foolish?"

"Have I made you feel foolish?"

"Every time we talk. Double that when you talked me into playing." I step away from the table. "Triple that when I had to find out from the Internet who you really are."

"Now you know. My parents died two years ago, and I'm worth more money than anyone without a highly paid team of accountants can determine. If we want to dwell on tragedy or business, I'll move on. I'd rather make good on my proposition."

"You never asked a thing! You might as well have issued a decree. It was all about what you want and whether I'm willing to play along."

Amusement twitches the corners of his mouth. "Do you still think this is a game?"

"Of course! You think I'm something kinda quirky and weird to play with for a night or two."

He looks at me, then takes in the whole of my appearance. "You're . . . novel."

Christ, is that good or bad?

I resist the urge to take in the state of my outfit, to see me as he's seeing me. I made an effort, dressing with that damn sonata in my head. *Will Jude be there?* My jeans feel too tight, and my shirt tugs where it scoops from shoulder to shoulder in a boat neckline. In this heat, I'm thankful it's sleeveless. I paired it with ballet flats and decided against a barely there sweater.

"If she decides to stay with you," Janissa says, "I want your cell phone number and taxi money for me."

Then they both wait. Janissa sips from a straw, her eyebrows raised in expectation. Jude waits, like always, as if the decision has already been made and he only needs to be patient. I wish I could prove him wrong.

I don't want to.

I force myself to look at my friend, already feeling like a royal traitor. "Do you mind?"

"I'm cool with it," she says, although her voice has an edge I recognize as . . . forced. She reminds me of Clair. She's given me her opinion. Now the mistake is mine to make, even if she'll be the one to pick up the pieces when things go all to hell. I hope I can be that good a friend someday. "I got to meet Mr. Mysterio. That's good enough for me."

"Give her your number," I say, still with an edge of anger in my voice. Or is that anticipation? Nervousness? I'm a wreck. My hands are shaking as I reach for my purse. Make two attempts before I'm steady enough to grab the strap. I'm numb, but more sensitive and aware of my body than I've ever been.

Janissa gives me a hug—our first—and a few whispered words. "Call me in a heartbeat. No questions asked. Be careful."

"I think I'm beyond that."

She smiles softly. After saying good night to Janissa, where she shrugs, kinda *que será será*, Jude and I edge to the side of the club nearest the exit.

"Are you sure?"

I think it's the closest I'll ever get from him to an actual request, a real invitation. He's standing intimately close. Such a perfectly beautiful, impeccable jackass of a man.

But for the first time, *I'm* the one determining something of our future.

"Say please," I blurt out of nowhere. "You have to say please."

He laughs. I think it's a full-on Jude Villars laugh, but what do I know? He's not loud. He's expressive. His smile goes super-nova, with bright, straight teeth and eyes so pinched tight that they nearly close into lash tipped crescents. I get the feeling not everyone can catch him off guard.

I can't decide if he's laughing with me or at me. This could be one big taunting joke. This is a dream—part fantasy, part night-mare, waiting in the dark to spring on me and rip my trust to shreds.

But Jude doesn't look like a nightmare. He's confidence, se-crets, and brazen dares pieced together in a tailored shirt and fronted by the world's most enigmatic expression. He has this beautifully frustrating ability to appear on the verge of laughter despite the serious set of his lips and calm, neutral eyes. It's the potential that lures me.

He's told me outright what he wants—to kiss me in his car—but what does he expect? What do *I* expect? I can't ignore this lonely chasm of need in me. Not forever.

I know that Jude Villars is no cure-all. He can't fill the void inside me, because some wounds are too deep to heal. But he's experienced and charismatic, and I'm recklessly in the mood for something dangerous. Danger is something I've avoided ever since I became Keeley Chambers. I did a damn good job up until about . . . six days ago. Jude pulled it open, urged me to share my pain with an eager audience—and made me vulnerable to him.

I tuck my hands behind my back as if he'd see my dirty past still wedged under my fingernails.

At last, he forces his smile into hiding. "You want me to say please? That's it?"

"Yes. And if this isn't a big deal to you, I still have time to catch that cab home with Janissa."

"It is a big deal. Like when you performed last week. I like . . ." He tips my mouth toward his and brushes a soft kiss across my lips. I boil, practically dancing inside my own skin. "I like seeing how far you'll go."

"Maybe too far. You know, I practically ran away from you that morning, alarms and all, because I don't like anyone seeing me practice. It's because of you that I laid my whole self out there."

He looks up to the parti-colored ceiling, exposing the sharp ridges and tendons of his throat. A lock of chocolate brown hair is gilded beneath the lights until it resembles the bonfire in his eyes. He'd watch a comet that way, head tilted back, awed as it streaked across the sky. He's used to looking at the whole universe and seeing exactly what he wants to see.

Except for his family. *My parents died two years ago.* The inflection in his voice was . . . absent, the words stated as plainly as *That table is short.*

"Keeley, would you have come here tonight had I asked? Without Adelaide as your reason?" He pauses. "Just with me."

When he returns his gaze to mine, he appears almost hesitant. Uncertain. A young man who lost his whole world. The expression doesn't last long in his eyes, but it burns into mine and layers over everything that is Jude Villars.

"You didn't ask," I say softly.

"Then . . . please. I'm asking you now."

He watches me, vital and passionate. I'm pinned again. Lost. Trapped. I nod, before every cell in my body changes its mind.

We reach the outdoors. The night is hot and the street is bright. He doesn't take his eyes from the streetlamp, where humidity hangs low and bugs are out in force. Which car is his? Why won't my legs work? I'm left feeling like an actress in a play, but he's not my leading man. He's my director, watching and dictating from afar. I should hate it. Instead I can't wait to see what he has planned.

"You know, Keeley, I don't believe that performance on Friday was all of you," he says. "You haven't shown anyone who you really are."

"No one's proven that they deserve that right."

He extends his hand, as if he has a deal in the making—a deal that could mean anything. "You could show me. A little at a time. Starting tonight. Are you that brave?" His drawl is so low and quiet when he says, "I think you are."

He steps closer and I can't help it. I take his extended hand in mine.

His features explode into a grin. As he tugs me down the street, away from the club, his grip so strong and steady, I suddenly and irrevocably know two things.

One: Jude Villars holds a rare power over me, the girl who's been to hell and back.

Two: Even so, he'll never learn that my real name isn't Sara Dawson or Lila Reuther—or even my favorite alias, Keeley Chambers, the woman I'm still learning to be.

~ FOURTEEN ~

We walk around two corners, with the heavy humidity muffling the nightlife sounds. Laughter and music could be coming from anywhere. We're surrounded by it. Each streetlamp is haloed. The dampness is hot. It's private. Bright daylight would be garish by comparison. Daylight would make what I'm doing seem completely ridiculous. Why did I agree to this? Why did I practically fight to be here?

Because he's astonishing. I would've lived the rest of my days wondering what I missed out on, had I decided to go home with Janissa instead. All of this—every moment spent with Jude—might be that oncoming brick wall or the roller coaster with missing pieces of track, but this was my time. It was *true*. True time. True feelings. These are things happening to me, not to anyone else, not even to some future version of myself. I'll never be twenty-one again, walking nervously, a little too stiffly, on the arm of a man as breathtaking as Jude Villars, while the sounds of New Orleans become our soundtrack. One day I'll be able to compose what I'm feeling and I'll retire happy.

No. That isn't true; I could never retire. The piano is my voice when all others fail.

"You're quiet," he says.

"Nervous."

"I like that you're honest."

"I don't do this. Normally, I mean."

He gives my hand a squeeze, where his body is branding mine. "The thought never crossed my mind, sugar. Innocence is an easy thing to spot."

I snort a really unattractive laugh. "Innocent? Me?"

He doesn't watch me. We're walking, with his face in profile, his nose and brow and chin all so straight and strong. "Tell me I'm wrong."

"I could tell you a lot about me that isn't innocent," I say, although I'm not ready to counter him if he dares me to prove it.

"Then let's start easy. You ever heard of a purity test?"

I laugh uneasily while nodding. "Quizzes people take when they're a little lit and want to prove how badass they are. You notice that? The only ones who really push to play a game like that are the ones who want to show off. 'Oh yeah, I've done it on horseback with Miss June and a banana. Haven't you?'"

He's smiling broadly when we reach the car. With assurance and grace, he turns so that his back leans against the side of the damp metal, then pulls me flush against him. His hands aren't on my ass. They're just above, just a tease. He could grab and hold on tight if he wanted. I feel vulnerable . . . and curious.

"I have nothing to prove. Miss June was a crappy lay, the horse threw us both off, and the banana was mushy."

"I hope that isn't some phallic metaphor."

With eyebrows lifted, his eyes shimmer briefly in the strange, fog-drenched light. "Do you want to talk in metaphor, Keeley?"

I swallow, watching where the throb of his pulse beats at the base of his throat. "No. I said I'm nervous. That was just nerves. I'm . . . There's . . . Okay, purity test. I've kissed guys. Sometimes sloppy. Sometimes gropey. Occasionally decent . . ."

"Nah," he says, that drawl like a fine wine. "We'll skip the metaphors. I'm too old for college games, and you don't want to talk about it. I get it."

"It's not that I don't want to talk." I make a frustrated noise and work up my nerve. "Let's just say I haven't done much. And right now, I'd rather just . . . *do*."

"Make music rather than talk about it?"

I smile despite myself. "Back to metaphors."

He tightens his fingers around my waist, then leans down to brush his lips along my jaw. He finishes the slow, seductive string of touches when he reaches my mouth, until his lips settle briefly against mine. "Then I'll skip straight to my big question. Are you a virgin?"

I drop my forehead against his chest. I could get drunk right there, breathing him in, the sting of salt and the bittersweet magic of sandalwood. It's like he's brought the best of the club out into the night with us, layered over the scent of him. I don't know why I feel compelled to tell him the truth, to expose myself to him like this, but suddenly I'm saying, "Yeah."

He lifts my chin. "Then we do this right."

"This?"

After fishing keys out of his pants pocket, he opens the rear passenger door to the night black Mercedes. It's an astonishing car. It reminds me of expensive watches and golf outings and galas where unflashy rich people—not celebrities, but the invisible elite—bid at silent auctions to support worthy causes. The interior is leather, just warm enough that I don't get goose bumps, just cool enough to give me some relief from the hot, sticky night. Jude follows me inside. The door closes with a definitive sound.

"Here's the thing, sugar," he says, leaning back. We're only touching at the thigh again, like the first time I'd watched Adelaide play. "You're intriguing. I've been with intriguing women before, but they knew exactly what they were doing when they got into my car or came home with me. And that's fine. We played accordingly."

Play.

Play with Jude Villars. Such a harmless word.

"I get the feeling things are different with you." He tilts his head to the side. His grin is at half mast. He appears tired, except for the piercing way he's decided to stare at me, into me. "You're here in the backseat of a car owned by a man you've encountered exactly three times. I'm guessing you're here because you're curious, and because you *are* brave. Backing down from a challenge doesn't fit you."

"Buttering me up?"

"Do I need to?"

"No," I say with more confidence. I even smile. "I'm here. Get to the point, Mr. Villars."

He chuckles. "We went over this, sugar. I'm Jude to you, or I'm nothing."

"Get to the point, *Jude.*"

"So you're here. . . . What do you want?"

"I don't understand."

"Let's pretend you're in charge." At that, he stops and our gazes catch. I can't help but match his teasing grin. "What do we do right now?"

"What do we . . . ?"

He tangles his hand with mine and rests them together on the hard, flat plane of his stomach. "That's a telling squeak. Is it so hard, sugar? To know what you want?"

It's more the fear that I'll never get what I want.

"Knowing what I want isn't the problem," I say quietly. "Telling you is."

"Why?"

"Look." A surge of past anger and nerves whirl together. "I chose to leave the club with you. I chose to get into this car with you."

"Is that all you need? Or should I lock the doors for an extra hit of danger?"

Deliberately, he trails the finger of his free hand along the polished wooden door frame and slides, slides, slides until he presses the door lock. A sharp snick of sound makes me jump. Locked in together. I should be terrified. I should be running out into the streets, not calling for the cops but for terms of surrender. *I'm done. You got me. I'm a scaredy-cat.* I can't say how much I want him to kiss me, because then I won't get it.

If I keep my mouth shut, I won't get it either.

I swallow hard and try to pull my hand away. "You're making fun of me."

He apologizes with his expression. Is a self-respecting woman allowed to let a guy off the hook if he smiles just the right way? "Yeah, a little," he says. "Do you want to get out? For real?"

"No."

He blinks. I would've too, had I been in his place. It's the first firm thing I've said since leaving the club. "Then what does it matter that I've locked the doors?"

Because now things *will* happen. Whatever will happen, I want it more than I'm afraid of it. The fear comes from having it jerked away from me at the last second. But if we're locked in . . . If he really wants to be here with me . . .

If he's *not* doing this as some elaborate joke . . .

I take a deep breath and straighten my shoulders. If I'm going to sit side by side with Jude Villars in the backseat of his Mercedes, I've got to start with my backbone. *Firm the hell up.*

"What happened to *If I want you, sugar, I'll come find you?*"

"This is me finding you." He releases my hand and turns on the seat so that we're face to face. There's a wild light in his eyes that gleams nearly as bright as a swimming pool on a sunny August day. Ours mouths are so close that I can feel his breath, plus mine as it softly ricochets back from his skin. We're sharing secrets in the dark. "I already know you're clever. Learn right now that I hate repeating myself. This is the last time. What do you want, Keeley Chambers?"

"To touch the back of your neck."

Another blink. I like that. He isn't very good at hiding that small reaction. I wonder if anyone else has caught on: how to tell if you've surprised Jude Villars.

"Tell me why," he says.

This is getting easier. I can almost breathe when I speak. "From the night last week when I stood behind you on the stairs. You talked to me."

"Talked down to you."

"Flirted with me? Can we call it that? I don't want to think you were being an asshole on purpose."

"Fine." That bright blue light shines in his eyes. I feel like I'm being soaked into him, dissolving into smaller and smaller pieces until I coat his skin and slip inside every pore.

"You turned away from me," I say. "I was tongue-tied. So I just . . . stared at your nape. Where your hair hits your collar. It's a little long for a businessman, isn't it?" I angle my head to get a better view. Sure enough, the ends of dark hair carelessly curl around the ridge of his collar. "I wanted to run my fingers through it, to see if it's as soft as it looks. . . ."

Explaining is one thing. Running my mouth into absurdville is another. I feel like an idiot for going so far until I see what it's done to him. He's breathing faster. His nostrils flare. "I'm not stopping you," he says, the softest dare.

I reach up and twine a curl around my forefinger. But a hesitant touch isn't what I need. I remember grabbing his collar and practically daring him to kiss me. Practically daring myself.

I lean forward. His upper body supports mine as I slide my hands from his broad, tense shoulders up to his neck, then back around. I dive in. Nails and all. I use his hair to feel deeper—the heat of him. He moans softly. A shudder works up and down his long body.

"You're shaking," I breathe, barely daring to believe it.

"Have you imagined kissing me?" His voice is a Southern gentleman's rasp. It's astonishingly sexy. I have goose bumps fighting to climb over even more goose bumps.

"Not at the time." I shift on the seat. I'm so turned on. Being a virgin at twenty-one doesn't mean I haven't been turned on before, but it's never been this pure. "I hadn't gotten that far in my imagination."

"But now?" He unthreads my ponytail and pushes my hair back from my shoulders. With his lips peppering my skin with kisses, he answers every touch of my fingertips with the touch of his tongue. "You've got more in you," he says. "I want to hear it. Is it because you want to put your mouth on me?"

"Yes," I gasp.

"Where? On *my* mouth?"

I shiver, flashing cold and hot. His lips are already near enough that they brush against mine as he speaks. "Later," I say.

"Then tell me."

"Right where I'm touching. Here, at the back of your neck." I tighten my fingers around his arm, his composed strength—an outlet for my nervous, effervescent tension. "We've come this far. I'm curious. And I want . . . I want to be memorable."

~ FIFTEEN ~

"Memorable?" Jude pulls away and cups my face in his hands. He has long and elegant fingers, as if he were the pianist. "To every guy you're with?"

"I'd hope so. But you in particular."

"Because of who I am?"

I'm made of bubbles. I'm made of TNT. Whatever it is, I burst out laughing. It's not a long laugh, but it's strong enough to buckle me in half. Jude lets go, with distance between us again. I peek up through my lashes and see his features weighed by a heavy scowl.

"You're not used to being laughed at, are you?"

His lips pinch thin. He looks away. "No."

My brain won't keep a straight thought. I should be thinking wholly and exclusively about how strong his muscles are. Only one layer of cotton separates his skin from my touch.

"You said it yourself," I say, "about how easy it is to learn about you. There's no getting around that you're famous and rich, or what everybody knows about your parents. You got away with it for one night, because I was stupid enough to think Adelaide was your girlfriend."

I stop then. His parents. Killed when the cabin of their private jet depressurized. All aboard were already dead when the plane hit the ground somewhere in Iowa. The whole world could learn the gruesome details in three seconds. Every time he's introduced to anyone, he has to wonder what they know of his past. I wouldn't handle it very well, being that exposed.

There's lightning in his eyes. "You do me the favor of telling me why you're laughing."

"I don't do this. Like . . . *ever*. Not with anyone. The back of some guy's car, just because he made an offer I can't refuse?" I take a deep breath and tighten my hold on his upper arm. "But after tonight, I just hope . . . that you'll keep wanting to come find me."

"What did your Google search come up with about my personal life, Keeley? I'm curious."

He must be mowed down by celebrities and debutantes and debutantes' mamas. I keep asking myself, *Why me?* Maybe because he's had the privilege of making a choice, just like I have.

"I read what I needed to, to fill in gaps," I say plainly. "I didn't want to find out the worst."

"What would that be?" His accent is stronger now. He lays his right hand on my thigh and kneads gently. The gentleness is underlain with his lingering tension.

"That you crook your finger at every girl you meet. Equal opportunity playboy. I put on some rose-colored glasses and followed you out here." I shake as if a rocket of cold air just skimmed through the car. "You dared me to get onstage last week. Now I'm in your car and you're Jude Villars, and I want that rush. Because it was a rush, you know. All that applause."

"No matter what we do," he whispers, "there won't be any applause."

I cover my mouth to stifle a giggle. He doesn't give me the chance to hide, pulling my hand down and kissing the inside of my wrist. "You never know. I might be the one to applaud."

"*That* would be memorable."

He kisses me.

It's like he's storming a castle with the gates wide open. I have nothing to defend myself with because his words have stripped me of anything close to resistance. His tongue is hot, softly pebbled, insistent. He dives in as if we've been lovers for months, and this is just another liberty I've permitted. *You, Jude Villars, can plunder my mouth as often and as demandingly as you want. Signed sincerely, Keeley Chambers.*

I cross my arms behind his back and find us pulled flush together. His arms are so strong. Whatever predator I imagine him being, I should've been more specific. He's a sleek panther, all dark hair and lithe muscles. He plunges his tongue into my mouth, taking over, taking *me* over so completely.

"Memorable, sugar," he says against my throat, then kisses my lips, eyelids, forehead. His hand moves to my breast but stops short of touching where I arch toward him. "You brought it up. Make it happen."

I hesitate, as if I'm standing at some dessert buffet and have no idea where to start. His shirt is open at the throat. Maybe I could undo a few more buttons. . . .

I do.

"You have no idea how sexy it is to watch your eyes. You think over every move." He cups my face in his hand once again. "You want to be bold. So do it, sugar."

"You're making fun of me again." I turn my head just enough so that I can gently sink my teeth into the meat of his hand, where his thumb meets his hand—a silent, desperate release for all the things I can't voice.

He hisses. "See? I'm waiting to see which impulse wins out." With his free hand he grabs one of mine and pushes it flat against the hard ridges of muscle that make up his thighs. He's positioned my fingertips within an inch of the bulge I can see deeply shadowed and outlined by his taut slacks. "But I admit to having a preference."

I bite harder on his palm. I'm so tense, so wound up, so utterly outside myself—until it all comes snapping back to me.

"I—I can't do this."

I turn at the waist and reach for the handle of one of the locked doors. He's faster. And so much stronger. My hands are pinned behind my back, with Jude levered above me, before I can even gasp. But rather than turn all date rape, he brings his hand to his mouth and sucks the skin I bit. "Yes, you *can* do this. I've seen how powerful you are when you let go. Here we're alone, and I want to see that power again. Make me feel it." He whispers low and dark. "Give me something to wake up smiling about. To wake up hot and wanting. Shock me, Keeley. I dare you."

~ SIXTEEN ~

"Move," I say—talking, doing, not thinking.

Our body heat has made the smell of leather more potent. More primal. Condensation has turned the Mercedes into a bedroom with the curtains closed. Jude raises quizzical eyebrows and does as I demand. It *feels* like a demand. His grin, however, reinforces what we both know: he's letting me do this. He's no more taking orders from me than I'm forcing him to do something he doesn't want to do. This is him waiting for me to be shocking.

This is me hoping that I can manage.

I scoot around so that I'm behind him. My chest to his broad back. He tries to look over his shoulder. I grab his head in my hands and nip a kiss on one earlobe. Maybe I use too much teeth, because he hisses again.

"Sorry," I whisper, nearly losing my nerve.

"Don't you dare stop. Whatever the hell this is, I want all of it."

"Then you deserve this." I angle his head toward my face, rediscover his earlobe, and suck. I scrape my teeth along that tender skin. His groan rumbles into me, nestling beneath my sternum. That groan wraps around my heart and squeezes, speeding it up, making me breathless.

I roll the palms of my hands around his waist and up, up his fiercely proud chest. He's cut. Ripples in all the right places. From behind, I finish unbuttoning his shirt. I try going slow at first, but my fingers are made of putty and I'm trying to do things in a rush so he won't freak out and decide against the whole deal.

He takes my fingers in his. He doesn't look back at me, just lifts each to his mouth. Kisses each knuckle. Then says, "Deep breath, sugar."

Together, we inhale. It's astonishing. I know it's not sex, and I'll probably laugh one day when I make the comparison, but when we both take a deep breath at the same time, with my nipples so sensitive when pressed against his strong back, breathing as one, I think of it as making love. It's the most intimacy I've never known. Without prompting, we do it again. One long breath in, one long exhale to get rid of the nerves. Nerves are getting in the way of what I yearn to do. I just want to be *able*. Whether it goes well or he likes it or it gets me buzzing—that doesn't matter when I need my hands to cooperate.

Sexual stage fright? Great.

Finally I undo his buttons, one by one. Jude only tries to help out when he reaches for the tails tucked into his slacks. I stay his hands. "Leave it," I say.

He chuckles quietly—more sounds to soak into my marrow. I'll do more than remember them for the rest of my life. I'll *feel* them.

When the shirt is open from neck to navel, I crisscross my hands around his chest, his abdomen, his arching ribs. If he has an ounce of fat on him, I'm made of aluminum foil. He has some hair on his chest, but not much. I like the smooth, hot, inviting textures I explore with each new push of fingers over flesh.

I must've made a noise—a good noise—because he says, "I know. God, I know."

I'm not done. I don't know where "done" is tonight, but I know I haven't reached *my* finale. It's that fascination with the back of his neck. Ever since he mentioned kissing him there, I can't stop thinking about it.

"Bow your head."

He makes a grunting question mark sound. I run my hands under the tucked-in shirt, touching him everywhere I can reach. When I return to the thick, silky thatch at his crown, I push down as encouragement. He complies with another rough chuckle. I tug at the now loose collar and I'm rewarded with the perfect expanse of smooth skin and shining hair.

I edge up on my knees to gain some advantage of height. I need to be above him, at least a little. He catches me when I nearly wobble off the leather seat. He crosses my arms around his chest, then covers them with his own. I'm secure. Safe to explore. He's given me that unexpected gift.

At first I hover over his nape, just inhaling, until my mouth waters and I *need* to kiss him there. I need to taste him. With my nose buried in his hair, I kiss and kiss, lick and nip and kiss. I claim each inch as mine. He'll wear a thousand dress shirts before he retires some distant day. Every time he does, when he secures the top button and wiggles the knot of his tie in place, he'll be covering the skin I've made mine in the backseat of his Mercedes.

After breathless minutes, I melt onto his back. He's still holding my arms in a hug around his upper body. Only then do I realize that I've bracketed his hips with my thighs. My knees press the outside of his. Not only am I flush against him, chest to back, but also pressing groin to ass. My panties are soaked. I have this terrible flash of leaving a wet spot on his slacks and try to pull away.

"Don't stop," he rasps.

"Kissing?"

"No."

He reaches back and grasps my ass. I imagined something like it when we were standing against the outside of the town car, but this is reversed. We aren't facing each other, which adds an extra blare of unimagined thrill. I don't know why. Maybe because it's not conventional. Any frat guy at a party could kiss me to the point where he wanders south and grabs. This, with Jude, with any illusion of my control stripped away, is more deliberate. It's no accident when he smooths his big hands over the outsides of my thighs, grips my ass, tightens his fingers, kneads.

"You were grinding your hips." His voice is so low, his accent so thick, that I almost think my fevered imagination conjured the words.

Was I? No, I couldn't have been.

But it's true, because as soon as he clenches his hands again, I press against him. I'm aching, constrained by my jeans. I'll never get relief from this rough need. I was an idiot. Playing with fire. There's nothing so stupid and ridiculous as a turned-on girl in the backseat of a car with a guy who knows what he's doing.

I pull free. I scamper away until I'm flat on my butt and backed against the car door. Jude whirls. His hair is a gorgeous, snarled mess. *I did that.* His bare chest is heaving. *I did that.* His pants are taut with proof of how much he was enjoying himself. *I did that.*

"Memorable," he says with a beautiful, arrogant smile. "Definitely memorable."

"Don't make fun of me. It was stupid. Forget it."

He turns on the seat and leans over me as if readying to do push-ups while stretched over my body. In fact, he lowers down, down, using only the strength of his arms. I can see each flex and bunch of his chest muscles, and where the caps of his bared shoulders strain. He kisses my throat, then farther down, as much as my boatneck top will permit. "Your turn."

"My turn what? I did the . . . well, the shocking thing."

"Right." He grins widely, all bright teeth and salacious humor. "So if it was shocking for me . . ."

Using one arm—Jesus, how strong is he?—he flips me onto my stomach and holds me in place around my tummy. I don't have any buttons to undo. It's a simple thing for him to sweep my hair away and kiss the back of my neck. He lowers even deeper, so controlled that I'm going to lose my mind, until his chest encompasses my back. Maybe even my whole world. He lowers his groin and nestles his hard-on against my ass. I shudder. I turn my head to find a hunk of muscle: the bicep of the arm he has wrapped around my middle. He thrusts. He kisses. I bite. I cry out against his skin when he thrusts again.

"Like it?" he growls. A deranged part of my mind laughs a little laugh. *I turned this suave businessman into a guy capable of only grunts and single syllables.* "Tell me."

I lick his bicep where I feel the slightest imprint of my teeth. "Love it."

I arch back so that we can kiss. The angle is awkward, and there's so much going on—my whole body sparking and flaming—that it's not the world's most graceful kiss. I don't care. I know Jude doesn't care. We're just lips and heat and *more* until I'm dizzy. He tightens his hold on my waist, then settles even more of his lean body weight against my ass and back, as if to reaffirm that he has me.

He *has* me.

He could've claimed anything from that moment out to eternity. Anything he wanted from me.

Instead he lets out a long, low, frustrated groan and drops his forehead to rest between my shoulder blades. "I can't see straight," he says with a laugh. "Literally. Jesus, Keeley."

Arms still tight around me, he sits up and pulls me with him until I'm sitting on his lap. I curl into him, trembling, my fingers clinging to the bare skin above his ribs, right around his pecs. As good a place as any to hold.

"Gotcha," he says against my hair, smoothing it back from my face. "I gotcha. It's okay. Damn, that was intense."

"I—" I shake my head.

"I'll wait. Find what you want to say, sugar. I've learned it's worth waiting for."

I hide my face against his chest. He's slicked with a slight salty layer of sweat. I can't help but take a taste. He's delicious. He's perfect. At least I keep myself from saying that.

I take deep breath. "I hope I wasn't too frustrating. I mean, I know guys would think I'm being a tease."

"Am I most guys? Seems you've implied that I'm not."

I smile against his neck. "You're not most guys."

"Keeley, would you still be a virgin right now if I hadn't stopped?"

Breathlessness, flirting, nerves, hopes, fears—they all drop away with that question.

"No," I say softly. "I guess . . ." I try to laugh it off, but that's hard to do when I'm sitting in his lap and know exactly how turned on he still is. "I guess I got carried away. Maybe I should go."

He doesn't budge. I'm not going anywhere unless he wants me to, which is an odd thing to realize. I'm glad I trust him or else I'd be terrified. I'm already scared enough of the impulses he pulls out of me. Little inklings become big, huge needs when Jude starts teasing and goading me. Who am I to deserve so much attention?

Oh, great. Hi, crippled self-esteem.

"Where would you go?" he asks.

"Home. Back to the dorm. Unless . . ." I shiver. "This was some big prank. Why did you get me to do all that, then stop?"

"It was fun, wasn't it?" He's all N'awlins slurry cool now, with an artless grin and a flirtatious light in his eyes. "Tell me I'm wrong."

"Yeah," I say, my throat tight. I don't know what he's getting at. I'm still so dizzy, and I can't stop touching him. "But I don't know if I should be pissed at you, or if you're gonna unzip your pants and pressure me into finishing what we started. What— Just, what is this?"

"I don't know."

"No?"

He kisses the top of my head. "I like that you sound disappointed."

"Yeah. Maybe a little. Or . . ." I swallow. "Frustrated."

"I like that even better. Means you aren't done having your wicked way with me."

"My wicked—?"

He tickles me around my waist until I just about scream for mercy. We wind up back on the seat, face to face this time, with Jude's breath hot on my cheek. I shift in his lap, only to realize he's still turned on. His eyes roll back on a groan. "Wicked," he says again, his mouth lax on a teasing smile.

"Most guys tend to look like you do *after* getting what they want."

"Do you know so much, sugar?"

"Not a thing. You gonna teach me?"

I say it flippantly, but his expression sobers. "I'd love to."

Whoa.

"Since you know so much about guys and sex," he says, even when I smack him lightly on the arm, "tell me the stereotypes. About what it'll be like to lose your virginity."

I tick off a list on my fingers. "The guy does all the pressuring. It's over too fast. There's no foreplay. It hurts. It's embarrassing after."

He reaches between our bodies and cups the apex of my thighs. "Jesus," he says roughly. I shake and cry out. He smiles against my mouth and whispers, "Here's the deal, if you're up for it."

I nod. I can't speak. I lace my hand over his.

"I won't pressure you. Memorable, yeah? That's the goal—for both of us. And it sure as hell won't be over too fast. Every look, every word, every touch will be foreplay. And if there's any embarrassment after, it'll be because we want to start again too soon." He kisses my mouth—the barest brush. Electricity shoots from my lips to where our hands clasp with a steady rhythm. "Say yes, sugar. Tell me you want to come play. A whole new game."

"Yes," I gasp. "Yes, Jude. *Please.*"

He settles his thigh between my legs and sets up a hard, quick rhythm. The rough material of the jeans rubs where I'm throbbing and restless. I wiggle and twist. He makes the quietest grunts with each thrust. I want them louder. I want him out of control too, but I'm too far gone for that. I dig my fingernails into his sides and catch sight of his wide, awed eyes just before I kiss him, deep, demanding—just before the entire evening explodes.

I think I just had my first orgasm.

~ SEVENTEEN ~

I don't know how he did it, but Jude didn't make me feel embarrassed after that moment when the sexiest man I've ever met made me feel . . . *womanly*. If he could do that with hot kisses and a hand over my jeans, what could he do with the whole deal? We talked a lot about things that still burn so hot that I can't think about them for long. He was already the sun, too bright, even though I've never seen him in daylight. Now he wants to show me how to have sex, make love, fuck, shag, rut, couple—pick a term—for the first time. Which would it be for us?

I think I'm trying to intentionally shock myself so I'll back out. It doesn't work.

It's not like I've ever been in a rush to lose my virginity. More like it would happen when it'd happen. Maybe that's why Jude's proposition holds so much appeal. I don't like when things *just happen*. That strikes too close to the way I was once forced to live—day to day, place to place, hand to mouth. I enjoyed the predictability of high school, and I'm really getting into my routine here at Tulane.

Mostly I love the beauty of the patterns I find in playing piano. That's all there is to it, really. Find the patterns and the music follows. It has structure, rules, order. Probably the most spontaneous thing I've ever done was perform at Yamatam's. That was *such* a challenge. It's almost made my stage fright worse. But I know what it's like now—terrifying and thrilling and completely unscripted. The "thrilling" part was great. Whether it was enough to overcome the rest . . . I'll have to work on that.

The idea of making love with Jude holds a similar sort of stage fright feeling. It would be terrifying, daring, and *way* beyond thrilling. Only, his proposition has the best of both worlds. We'd have rules and even something as unsexy as a plan, but individual encounters could be spontaneous. Freedom with safety. It's too good to be true, but too good to pass up.

Especially after how amazing he made me feel—like there was a spotlight behind my eyes and hot honey in my veins, until wow, nothing remained but sensation.

He's going to teach me how to make love the Jude Villars way. And I'm going to let him.

Only a few problems stand in the way.

The first is Janissa. She's worried. I get that. She was up till all hours waiting for me to call, which made me feel ridiculous and really uncaring. I floated in at something close to three. She was still half awake, on her bed in her pajamas, with a chem text over her chest as if it constituted a little light evening reading. I had to gloss over too much, which only led to more questions and more worry on her part. I think it would've been easier, in hindsight, to just say, *He gave me my first orgasm and he's taking me out on Monday.*

Eh, hindsight.

The second is Brandon. I'll skip that one for now. The Saturday night date he asked for is still not a done deal, not for me, but I think he thinks it is.

The third is Adelaide. You know, for a girl who never had many friends in high school, and even fewer before then, it's strange to realize that my list is all about people. But how am I going to bond with a girl—or even develop a professional relationship with her—if her brother and I are in the midst of . . . God, I have to come up with a name for it. My initiation?

That's the catch. If I were dating some guy in the tried and true way, we wouldn't talk about sex ahead of time. There wouldn't be a plan of attack or a set of goals. There'd just be moments when things happened, good or bad. How was I supposed to enjoy myself with a grabby guy if it had taken so much effort for Jude to get me to tell him what I wanted?

I don't want to be one of the dozens of girls I've heard say that their first time was terrible or, at best, a disappointment. I want it to be special. And Jude's going to make it special.

Jude had dropped me off at the residence hall wearing a smile that was nearly contented. "You have to promise," he said.

"What's that?"

"You'll do what I say."

"How's that gonna work?"

His grin had deepened. He ran a hand over his nape, then adjusted my wide neckline. "Let's just say there will be plenty of opportunities for you to use your imagination. It's too good to ignore. But you'll have to trust me with the rest. Can you do that?"

So I promised. Spontaneity within the framework of his experience, and now it was a matter of strapping into the roller coaster and enjoying the thrill. I won't think of it as anything more than a great, exciting adventure—one I've never thought of as *me*. Apparently I've been craving this, more than words or even stray feelings would let me admit. I know it's all still a game to him. Forget a one night stand. I'll be a conquest of a kind. He wants exclusive reign over when, where, and all the other details of how a nice little virgin girl like me gives it up for the first time.

What a rush.

Bring it, says one part of me.

Holy shit, says another.

The last and biggest catch is that I can't concentrate worth a damn. I'm in my sociology class when my professor asks, "Miss Chambers? What do you have to add?"

About . . . ?

Crap.

I glance down at my notes. I scratch out where I've written Jude's name. Just his first name. Just once. I feel like the junior high kid I never got to be, with hearts and flowers doodled on single subject notebooks. This was the first time I've gotten to act like a girl with a crush, and it's damn inconvenient. I'm a college junior, about eight years past when acting like a completely smitten idiot is considered cute. Now it's just unprofessional.

And dangerous.

Especially when the bad thoughts creep in, thoughts along the lines of . . . *So, how many other girls has he done this with? Is it his thing? He likes to mold some sweet young thing to his liking, take the final prize, make her grovel in thanks for being treated like a princess for a few weeks . . . and then poof? Bye-bye, Mr. Villars?*

I want to stand out. Back to that again: I want to be *memorable.*

Me, the girl who's done her best to stay hidden for twenty-one years. Memorable to Jude. I have however long this lasts to make sure Jude doesn't forget me.

Why is that so important? I still don't get it.

Does it mean I'm tired of hiding? Because, wow, sometimes I really am.

And I still don't know what Dr. Rivers is talking about.

I take a guess. "I think we're going about it backward. Military cultures have always had 'gang signs,' if you will, that identified them as warriors. Insignias, mottoes, particular songs. Modern gangs with tattoos, and even sexual subcultures with piercings and symbols like cuffs and collars, harken back to tribal times." Because I'm feeling ballsy—or I don't care *at all*—I choose to assume I'm talking something other than complete BS. I raise the finger where I wear the Tulane seal. "We all want to feel like we belong."

"Well stated, Miss Chambers," the professor says, looking as surprised as impressed. "I look forward to your paper next week."

Aw, damn.

That's hours and hours that'll get in the way of me mooning over Jude and blushing over memories of the previous evening or, hell, *practicing.* God, did he make me feel amazing. Daring. Naughty. Protected. I didn't think those things could go together, but I've never known anyone like Jude.

My rumbling stomach means I forgot to eat breakfast. Mooning takes precedence over self-preservation? That has kinda ominous implications.

Great.

I'm sick in the head. I need a way to turn thoughts of him on and off. Like . . . *off*, until my homework's done and I've been a good roommate to Janissa and I've taken care of the basics. Then, once my obligations are done with, I can indulge in every little detail.

The brain doesn't work that way. The body doesn't. The heart *really* doesn't. We're all grown-up kids, demanding pleasure first.

After class, I check my phone and find a text from Adelaide. *Milkshakes @ Duds? 4pm.*

I check the time. I have to hustle to make it from one side of campus to the other, where the union houses a ton of offices, restaurants, computer labs, and shops designed for one of two reasons: to entice the parents of prospective students with sweatshirts and coffee mugs that say they really do belong here in this safe place of learning, and to decorate student dorms. I dash off a text to Janissa, letting her know where I'll be, because I still feel shitty about not checking in last night.

Only, Adelaide isn't alone when I find her in Dudley's, a retro malt and burger joint just off campus. Dr. Saunders is sitting beside her on a red and white–checked bench, but he's waaay too close for anyone to think they're just talking about music. Music is passion, sure, but it's not hand on ass in public. Adelaide has her butt wrapped in a skintight leopard print skirt. The former music director for the Toronto Jazz Orchestra seems to appreciate it. She's laughing and having a good time, apparently, which makes me wonder why she invited me. Showing off? Daring me to tattle to Jude?

More drama!

I blame computers. By random assignment, some computer stuck me in a dorm room with Janissa, in a building where Brandon lives, and assigned me to mentor one half of the very, very famous Villars siblings. But then, the universe is kinda twisted. No matter what pairings some unseen computer conjured for me, there would've been drama. After all, there would've been people involved.

Adelaide sees me coming. Her smile brightens. It's blindingly charming. She uses the same smile on audiences. I'm back to the thought that she's in performance mode twenty-four seven. Makes me wonder who she really is underneath all the glitter and leopard print. If she's half as inquisitive as her brother, she'll wonder the same thing about me.

I reach their table and say hi. Then I extend my hand to the professor. "Hello, Dr. Saunders. Good to see you again."

"Do I . . . ?"

"Keeley Chambers," I say. "I'm in your international tonal theory class."

I know I can be invisible. My skill set, again. That he genuinely doesn't seem to recognize me must come down to two possibilities: Adelaide has him entirely entranced or, despite having made an effort to be more outgoing here at Tulane, I'm failing miserably.

He clears his throat. I notice that his formerly roaming hands are now in plain sight, palms down on the table. *Nothing to see here. I wasn't feeling up a student.*

I'm on Jude's side on this one, although to outwardly smack Adelaide on the head with how stupid she's being—if I had to guess, that's his approach—isn't my style. Sideways moves. Small moves. If not invisible, at least semitransparent. I am just here to chat. Adelaide invited me. That means ditching the creep.

"It's the first week or two," Dr. Saunders says. "New names and faces. You know how it is."

"Sure," I reply, my voice unimpeachably neutral.

"I was just going to head out, Addie. I'll see you . . ." His voice trails off. He adjusts his tie with agitated hands. "I'll see you."

"Yup." Her drawl is stronger than her brother's, and her true meaning is hard to read. That one syllable could mean she never wants to see him again, or that their tryst for later that night is still on. No telling.

We watch the professor walk out.

"Sit, Keeley," Adelaide says, her tone suggesting it wasn't the first time she'd told me as much.

I take the professor's place, where the seat is still warm. That squicks me out. I shift uncomfortably. This wasn't how I pictured meeting her again. There's no predicting her, and I should know better: there's no predicting life. Circumstance has made me into a bit of a control freak, which seems the opposite of what needed to happen. "Nurture" should've made me more adaptable, not the other way around.

After a waitress takes my order, I ask her the obvious. "Why invite me here if he was going to be hanging around?"

"Going to tell Jude?"

"Not my business. That's why I'm asking. I don't want you daring it to become my business."

"Are you seeing him?" Her eyes are sharp; she *is* as perceptive as Jude. I would've been surprised had it been otherwise. "Never mind. Of course you will." She grins. "But as for my brother and me, it goes like this. I'm eighteen years old. He's eight years older. I know him as well as anyone, and I know that he's got his eyes set on you. No offense. I'm sure you're great. But my brother has some serious authority issues—as in, he can't get enough. It's only gotten worse since I started here and I'm not tied in bubble wrap at a boarding school. One drink and one chat with the wrong guy, and suddenly I'm on his shit list. Again."

"Maybe if that guy wasn't one of our profs . . . ?"

"Never mind. I'm not going to let Jude run my life. I'll fight that battle some other time. I've been dying to pick your brain for days."

Maybe it's that deception radar I've honed, but I know that's not entirely the truth. She may have given me a passing thought or two. "Dying" for anything to do with me—I don't think so. I wonder if she's even given a thought to music in the days since her last performance. She expresses herself creatively with every gesture, word, her whole appearance.

"Then let's talk shop," I say.

"Or not." She leans in, her hands lying flat atop each other on the table. "When did you find out who we are?"

"Does that matter?"

"Sure. The sad, tragic, rich as fuck Villars kids. There's a reason I registered using my mom's maiden name. I want to know where I rate on your pity to envy scale."

There's a defensive hostility in her eyes that I hadn't expected. It's really out of nowhere. I decide to counter it the only way I know—other than setting off a fire alarm and running out of the building. I've already done that with one Villars. So honesty it is.

"I was mostly pissed at your brother," I say. "He messed with me all night, and I don't like being tricked, even by omission." I take a sip of my chocolate malt. "But that's not you. I got the formal introduction letter from the department. I just didn't catch on. Mostly I felt bad for you, because I didn't think I had much to offer when it comes to mentoring."

"And now?"

"Now what?"

"You said you *didn't* think you had much to offer. After seeing me perform, have you changed your mind?"

"Yes," I say carefully. "But quid pro quo will probably come into it."

"The Franz Liszt thing?"

"Yeah," I say. "I don't like performing in front of people. Sometimes I get scared that I'll hole up in a studio and compose, and no one will ever see me play, and I'll learn to be fine with that. But that night at Yamatam's took me by surprise."

"You liked it."

I smile. "And now I really want to do well at the Fall Finish, even if it means puking before and after. I wish I could grab a few strands of your extroverted DNA and make that a fun night, not one I spend months dreading."

"Then why did you? Perform, that is," Adelaide says.

"Jude goaded me into it." My voice is rough. All pretense of keeping a nice, even, unreadable tone is toasted. I'm an open book and I know it.

"I'm sure he had some power trip reasons, but that's the best thing he's done in a long time," she says with a smile. "You were amazing."

"You're being generous. I can't get a job with an ensemble if I keep going into trances when I perform."

She shook her head. "I love that you compose on the spot, that you let the music take over and just go with it."

"It's unpredictable. I'm sure employers don't want unpredictable. They want someone to blend in. When I try to do that, I sound like a ten-year-old at her first recital. But you play—"

"Okay, stop there. Either you'll lie outright, which will damage us beyond repair. Or you'll hesitate as you come up with some middle ground near truth. That's what our more astute profs do, just before they ask how many hours a week I practice."

"Or?"

"Hm?"

I swipe a droplet of melted ice cream off my glass and rub it between my thumb and forefinger, then lick it off. "There sounded like a third option there. Outright lies, platitudes, or . . . ?"

"Or blind fawning."

"Lemme guess," I say, smiling more easily now. "That's Jude."

"Most guys. But yeah, Jude."

"Then here's the real deal. You have perfect technique. You probably master everything in a day, then do other stuff, whatever floats your boat. Rinse. Repeat." I'm warming to the topic, because instead of scrunching up her face, all offended, Adelaide's smiling too. She's aggressive and megawatt bright, but she's cheeky too. "Everyone's so floored that you learn so fast that they don't look deeper. So . . ." I take a deep breath. I'm grinning too. This has become less about music. That's gotta be good for both of us. "Fans fawn, as fans do. The profs default to thinking you must not practice enough. They can't see the real problem."

She's laughing now, a wind chime, Tinker Bell sound. Her eyes take on that half moon shape Jude shows off when he laughs. "You're a prodigy. Takes one to know one. Only another prodigy can see past the magic trick. So tell me, Piano Whisperer, what is my real problem?"

I shrug. "Simple. You don't give a shit unless you have an audience."

"My, oh my, Keeley Chambers." She takes my hand and gives it a squeeze. "I hope Jude doesn't break your heart, because I do like you."

Eighteen

There's a lot about people I don't like. If I give myself enough time to dwell, that list can get pretty long. People can be cruel, deadly, heartless, selfish, disrespectful. They can be vice-ridden and lack any basic empathy toward their fellow man.

The tough part is when you have empathy and still wind up behaving like a jerk.

That's me. Tonight. It's Saturday, and I just hit Send on a text to Brandon. *Practicing with Adelaide. Rain check?*

"I'm such a liar," I mutter.

Janissa looks up from where she's set up a sort of indoor picnic. She has this thick, doubled over piece of flannel she uses as a picnic blanket, with her dinner of Eggo waffles and a wedge of cantaloupe arranged on foam plates. There's no chemistry book around. Instead she's holding *Dubliners* by James Joyce. Just like me, just like everyone, we have electives to get through. Maybe someone held a gun to her head when she chose twentieth-century world literature.

Not everything can be tearing down jazz clubs or exploding chem labs.

She nods to my phone. "What'd you do?"

"Blew off Brandon."

"Gotcha."

"I feel like crap." I slump onto my bed and sigh. "But I'm just not up to it."

Janissa looks at me with lifted eyebrows, so damn cute and completely not buying my BS. "Uh huh. You're exhausted, totally spent, ridiculously tired. You're swamped! Just look at all those books," she says, nodding toward the desk I've spent an hour pointlessly rearranging. "I can't believe you're conscious enough to text, you poor thing."

"I didn't know you could talk in one hundred percent sarcasm."

She shrugs. "Gifts are gifts. But, seriously, Keeley. What's wrong with Brandon? And really, what's been up with you lately?"

I don't answer. I only toy with the On/Off button on my phone, watching the screen flash black and then back to a wallpaper of abstract blues and greens.

"It's him, isn't it? Jude?"

No denying that, not even with a mock glare. "Yeah, it's him."

"Look, he might be a great guy. If I wanna give him the benefit of the doubt, I'll even say it. He's a great guy. He and his family did wonders for this city, Tulane in particular, after Katrina. And it sucks about his parents." She grabs a bookmark and sets *Dubliners* aside. "But he's, what, four or five years older than us? That's a thirty-five year age difference in dog years. Take a lesson from the cute little puppies and forget him."

"Forget a gorgeous, melty, mysterious grown-up guy who's decided I'm . . ." I don't know how to finish that. What *does* he think I am? Does it matter? It doesn't now, but it sure as hell will. "That I'm 'intriguing.' That's the word he used."

"Intriguing," Janissa echoes. "You're taking that as a compliment, I'm assuming. I'd have preferred sexy or clever or irresistible."

"How much has he seen of the world? 'Intriguing' is a good thing."

"Or a good way to get into your pants." I must've given something away. An expression? A shift on my bed? Her big, dark eyes widen. "Has he gotten into your pants already?"

"No! Besides, what if he had? I could do a lot worse. Most of female-kind could do a lot worse."

"Okay, it's like this." Janissa stands from her half-assed picnic and sits beside me. "I don't care what you do with your pants. Your choices. Your business. But a lot of the appeal has to be that he is older, and that's super mysterious. It's hot."

"I hear a big 'but' coming on."

"Oh yeah. It's not like he's one of us. We're students. We do boring shit like classes and hideous group project meetings, clubs, Friday night basketball games. Well, maybe not us. My point is, you have no idea what he does when he's not with you. You never will. His real life is like some other planet. Right now you could pop down to Brandon's room and say hi. I bet he even has his door open."

Dorm rooms can feel like hamster cages, so most people do. We make it clear that some company would be welcome. It's more like a cry for help. *We're studying! Come save us!* It's also how we find new music, share Netflix subscriptions, and borrow printers when something's gone wonky. The more open the door, the more open the person—or pair of roommates.

It's funny. In the last couple days, Janissa and I have been leaving ours open more often.

So yeah, I can probably stroll downstairs to where I know Brandon shares room 109 with a short psych major named Gerry, short for Gerard I think. Poor guy.

The problem is, I don't want to.

"Keeley, Jude's out of your league—and I don't mean that as a girl and guy thing. It's a girl and *man* thing."

"Quit."

"Nope. We're in the minors and he's in the major league. The two shouldn't mix. Weren't you saying that about his sister and that professor?"

"Sure," I say, flopping sideways onto my pillow. "Because he's our teacher, and a married expectant father to boot. That's just gross. Jude is not gross. He's . . . I can't stop thinking about him."

"That's probably his intention. Hook, line, and sinker. Oh, and totally in your pants." She kinda frowns. "Not to get too personal, and obviously you don't have to answer, but what happened the other night? I mean, you haven't said a thing. Are you okay?"

"I'm okay." But that's reflex. I shake my head. "No, I'm not. It's . . . Aw, crap. It's complicated."

"I mean, you left the club to go make out with him in his town car. As an aside, who drives a town car? Does that need a chauffeur?"

"It was a really big Mercedes."

"Gotcha. Rich speak for *I paid a ton for this thing.*"

I smile a little. I know she's trying to look out for me, and part of me really wants to confide in her—in anyone. But . . . God, it's so personal. I need to, though. What happened, and this thing I want to have happen between Jude and me, is too big to keep trapped inside me.

"We got sort of hot and heavy."

"Sort of?"

"Not like you'd think. It was . . . Sometimes I wish I could say things with words as well as I can with music." I shake my head. "Anyway, it was sexy. Teasing? Some kissing, touching, and toward the end I was so . . . Ugh. He stopped. He asked if I would still be a virgin if he hadn't."

"I'm guessing not."

My face feels like it's four inches from the sun. "Yup. So we made this . . . I think you could call it a plan. About how to make my first time really good."

"A plan? Keeley, that just sounds weird."

"No, hear me out. That guy you were with last year. Kier. It's my turn to guess. He put a lot of pressure on you to give it up."

Janissa looks away, the first time she's backed down during this grilling. I don't like hurting her.

"Yeah," she says softly. "He did. It's why we broke up. He left me for an ex-girlfriend slut. He made it clear that things would've been different had I loosened up."

"And then there's the rest of the baggage. That it'll hurt or only the guy will like it or that it's over in less than thirty seconds. Jude. Damn." I run my hands over my scrubbed-clean face, but I'm still suffering under the fiercest blush of all time. "He wants to take it slow. A seduction. Like, we know it'll happen, but not by accident in the backseat of his Mercedes. Not on a dorm bunk with the TV on. Not with a guy who doesn't know his dick from his elbow."

"Keeley Chambers, I think that's the first time I've heard you use a cuss word any stronger than 'crap.'"

I grin. "Fuck off."

She laughs and leans over to grab her tumbler of ice water. Her expression is contemplative while she sips. "So . . . you talked about it? You know it'll happen, but . . . ?"

"I won't be in the minor leagues. When it comes to sex, that's gotta be a good thing. I'd rather train under a pro."

Janissa snorts. "Under. On top of. You don't care."

"Quit!" I glance to the door where two passing girls stop short at my shout. "Sorry, nothing to see here," I say with a shooing motion.

"Not true," Janissa says, smiling broadly. "Secretly, the mysterious Keeley Chambers of room 310 is a slut in the making. She's got a mentor and everything."

"Give him my number when class is dismissed," replies a short Korean-American creative writing major named Opal. "I could do with a guy who doesn't think a six pack, nachos, four buddies, and a Saints game means he's gonna get laid."

"See?" I playfully smack Janissa on the arm.

"At least you get beer." That from Opal's roommate, whose name I can never remember, only that she has superhipster horn rimmed glasses and a surprisingly cool bouffant thing going on with her hair. "But please tell me he brushes his teeth after the nachos."

Opal buffs her nails on her shirt, all mock pride. "Damn straight. What kind of girl do you take me for?" She breaks character and laughs. "Mostly he does. God, I need to break up with him."

"Who is he?" Janissa asks. "This needs to be public knowledge to ward us all off."

Opal grins. "What, you think he isn't my forever guy? Besides, he's just Brandon from the front desk."

Janissa flinches. I go completely frozen. I'm glad she's a little more skilled at people stuff than I am. And I'm really glad my face is already half hidden by my pillow.

"Wow," Janissa says plainly. "He's a Saints fan? I thought he was from Florida. Aren't there panthers or gators down there to cheer for?"

Opal shrugs. "I don't know what the deal is. He's a foster kid, so maybe he's been all over."

"Are you two heading out tonight?" Janissa is sly. I'll give her that.

"Yeah," Opal says. "He was able to get out of the desk duty he had tonight. So ta-da, beer and nachos."

"With me as the third wheel," adds her roommate.

Janissa's laugh sounds forced. "I hate that. Happened to me the other night." Although I cringe at the memory, Janissa surprises me. "But it was for the best. Have a good night, ladies."

As soon as Opal and hipster girl are gone, Janissa shoots up from the bed and shuts the door. She leans her back against it. Neither of us speaks for a long time. My heart's beating like crazy, and Janissa is a little pale.

Magic fairies control my life now, apparently, because my phone chimes with two texts, one right after the other.

"You're going to be a good roommate and tell me what those say, right?"

I nod. "The first is from Brandon. *Sorry 2 hear. Will find a way to fill my time. Lunch Tues?*"

"What a shit! You know I'm gonna have to have an intervention with Opal."

"Don't worry about that," I say with surprising calmness. I've felt it before, that calm when faced with a nasty chore and knowing I can handle it. "I'll have lunch with him and take care of things."

"And the other?"

"From Jude. *I don't want to wait until Monday. I'll pick you up at ten.* He spells out all his words. Who does that?"

Janissa pushes away from the door. "Guy's in the major leagues. So . . . what are you going to wear?"

NINETEEN

Right at ten, I exit through the door at the end of the southern hallway. The hall leads to a small convenience store where late-night snacks are always available. The freshman ten or fifteen or whatever—I can totally see how it happens. I've never lived someplace where boredom meets stress meets easy access to junk food so seamlessly. I have a weakness for exotic ice cream flavors and Red Vines, but years of deprivation have trained me to actually savor the special privileges I have now.

The lights of a black car in the parking lot flash high, then low, then high again. I wonder if it might accidentally be Morse code. Likely it's just Jude saying hi with that beast of a luxury car.

I try to be casual as I walk to the car. Janissa let me borrow her little black dress. I'm taller than her, so the crepe-over-satin fabric drapes to only midthigh. It's strappy and has boning along the sides. On Janissa, that boning serves as a built-in Wonder-bra. The girl is stacked underneath her sweats and comfy

T-shirts. On me, the dress isn't nearly so voluptuous. I feel more like a flapper, which Janissa played up by adding a long string of fake pearls. I dug out an old pair of Mary Janes and black stockings. . . .

Walking casually, however, is not an option. I'm so damn nervous.

He opens the lock and I slip inside. "Hey," he says.

Before I can reply, he takes my face between his hands and kisses me. Forget whatever time I spent on doing my lipstick. I should've known better. His fingers delve into my hair, while his tongue pushes into my mouth. I gasp, then moan. He smells incredible, clean with a hint of some elegant aftershave. That smell mingles with the expensive leather, wrapping around me like hallucinogenic incense. He tastes of mint, until we get to really kissing, when he tastes hot, spicy, delicious. I take hold of his wrists, which are solid and thick. I do it to hold his hands in place, then kiss him as hard as he's kissing me. All of the tension of the last few hours, and the uncertainty and sleepless nights before that—I take it out on him.

He pulls my lower lip between his, and nips with gentle teeth. I like the contrast. Soft, hard. Slick, sharp. But I want him to moan too. After sliding tongue against tongue, I suck his into my mouth. He pushes farther into my space, so that he cusses quietly and releases me long enough to undo his seat belt. I'm pressed against the car door, by just his upper body and the force of his kiss. I take his breath into my lungs. I could hold him forever, breathe him forever.

Before I'm ready to let go, he pulls his mouth away. His forehead presses against mine. A slight, low chuckle doesn't break the mood. It enhances the supercharged power between us, because Jude is as unsteady as me. I don't need to do some test, like *hold out your hand and let me see how much you're shaking too.* Part of me still wants to think of him as superhuman. That chuckle is just telling enough. He's having fun. He's surprised. He likes what I'm doing. Pick one, or all three, or whatever.

I just like knowing I can affect him too.

But he's still in charge.

"Well, hello," he says, more formally this time, which makes me laugh. I probably look like I've been through a car wash, while he talks like we just bumped into each other. Or more like *slammed* into each other. "Fancy meeting you here."

"I heard a handsome guy in a big car would be waiting for me. So I dressed up."

"Let me see." He leans back in his seat, against the driver's side door, to take in my appearance.

"No, wait." I grab a package of tissues and a comb from my purse, then flip down the vanity mirror on the visor. It lights up. I do what I can to fix my lipstick and neaten my hair. After a minute, I close up shop and return to facing him. "There."

Jude's eyes are magnets. I already know that. Still, facing him and bearing his appreciative scrutiny takes work. He's limelight personified. I'm reminded then that I've never seen him during the daytime. Janissa was right. He lives in another world. Suits and ties every day. Working lunches. Meetings where he stands at the head of some big boardroom table and owns the room. He's young, but he's arrogant. I bet he gets away with it daily. Men twice his age would shake their heads, wondering how this young prodigy winds up outshining them each time.

So, yeah, his eyes. They're all over me. Blue fire sets me alight. The purr of the car's expensive engine creates white noise between us, but it's not enough to cover how fast I'm breathing.

"I don't like driving anywhere when I don't know where we're going."

The words kinda shoot out of me. I can still taste him on my tongue. I lick my lips and taste him there too.

He narrows his eyes. It's not a threatening gesture—only more assessing. I realize that I interrupted his chance to say that I look nice, and now it'll be awkward to get that back. He'll be wondering why I'm so defensive and tense all of a sudden, when really, on the inside, I want to melt into a puddle of candle wax.

Liar. I want more. This awkwardness needs to take a hike before that can happen.

"You're staring at me."

"In that dress? Damn, sugar. Of course I am."

"You messed up my hair. There's no saving it."

"Do you want me to apologize?"

I try to keep a straight face, but it's impossible. "No. I'll go with tousled. Again. Happens a lot around you."

"Again, do you want me to apologize?"

"Just tell me where we're going?"

He guns the engine, but doesn't pull out of the parking lot. "I have a confession."

My gut drops. "Oh?"

That was an attempt at casual, but it winds up more of a mouse squeak.

"I didn't know where to take you," he says, sounding frustrated with himself. The frustrations tightens up his slow, sloping vowels and turns his drawl choppy, almost unrecognizable.

But I *like* his drawl. "My options were all over the place. Too showy. Too touristy. I couldn't get the right balance. So—and don't kill her—I texted Janissa for ideas."

"Oh no. I'm gonna hurt that girl."

He grins and moves his hand from the gearshift to my knee. It's like I can feel the engine's power transferred through his warm skin and confident grip. "She said something about a sociology paper?"

My brain stutters before I grasp the information. "Tattoos, piercings, sociological subcultures. It's due Tuesday."

"Now I'm *sure* I have the right place picked out." He gives my knee another squeeze, slides his hand just under the hem of my dress, then returns to the gearshift. "I'm glad I asked her, and you shouldn't use homicide to solve your problems."

I'm glad he's not touching me, because I freeze. All that ice water in my gut becomes a glacier. "That's a big word, 'homicide,'" I whisper.

I don't think he hears me, because he's already looking over his shoulder, concentrating on getting out of a parking lot made for much smaller, more affordable cars. He'd meant his words as a joke and couldn't have anticipated my reaction. How many times do people say similar stuff in the course of a day?

I'm gonna kill him for that.

I could kill that moron.

"Hey," comes a voice—a kind, sensual voice from out of the dark. "Keeley?"

"Yeah?" There's a scream in me that I've never let loose. Instead . . . all those poor pianos.

"Are you going to tell me about driving and not knowing where?"

I'm dizzy. Too fizzy headed to pull it together. First the guilt of ditching Brandon, only to find out he's a snake I feel obligated to deal with later. Then telling Janissa about Jude and his mind-shattering kiss. Now, because of an offhanded remark, I'm remembering things from the past I'll never be able to get rid of. I could take a scalpel to my brain, cut out everything that's Rosie, and those memories would still be there.

"It's nothing," I say, trying for lightness. "I didn't stay in one place for long, not until high school."

He doesn't look at me. I get the feeling his strict concentration on the road is his way of giving me some privacy. I'm really grateful for that. He's proving himself more of a gentleman than a playboy—aside from surprise kisses, but I'm really not going to complain about those.

And idiot me, that's when I realize he's not dressed up. For the first time, I see Jude Villars in "normal" clothes. He's wearing a T-shirt with a flannel, jeans, and something like Doc Martens. I'm . . . impressed. I shouldn't be, because every guy on campus could wear the same gear, but maybe that's the appeal. He's in the majors, out living a grown-up life, but he's still in his twenties.

He's not out of my league. I won't let him be.

"We're going to a club called Slink out on Frenchmen Street. It's a little . . . underground." He turns to me for the first time since I had my near freakout. He smiles. "By the end of the night, you'll have all the information you need for your sociology paper. Promise."

"And you keep your promises."

"That I do, sugar."

Eyes back on the road, he takes my hand. Our fingers are laced together in no time. Unlike those terrifying nights when I'd wake up alone in the backseat, driving to hell for all I knew—those nights when they more often than not forgot my blanket or favorite bear or anything comforting—Jude has given me his hand to hold in the dark.

~ TWENTY ~

"You might as well take me to the touristy places," I say. "Not that I'm complaining about a place called Slink. That's too curious to pass up."

"Why act like a tourist?"

We hold hands, walking away from a multistory parking garage. The night is clear, hot, and full of smells I've never found in another city. Each city has a different smell, you know. Depends on the people, the food, the local countryside that creeps in with a stiff breeze, and even the local favorite beer. New Orleans has the perfumed drama I always dreamed about, with hints of old, old histories and the nearby press of the swamps. Stronger winds bring the taste of salt from the Gulf. But there in the lower Marigny, we're closer to Mississippi mud than the sea.

It's exactly as Jude described. Underground. The neighborhood has twenty-four-hour liquor stores and ancient brownstones, all side by side. Doorways harbor secrets I don't want to investigate. Alleys dare the unwary. That he holds my hand now is probably more his idea than mine.

Adelaide called him controlling. Maybe he is. In this part of town, however, I don't mind. There haven't been a lot of times in my life where an overabundance of protection was the norm. Even with Clair and John, they provide security. Stability. They don't pry, and they don't press. I get the feeling Jude would do both if it was important to him. Considering our intimate venture, what's important to him is probably important to me by default.

I've been in worse places, when I was a kid and didn't know any better. Now it's obvious I shouldn't have been in crack dens and run-down bars owned by loan sharks. I'm not too intimidated in accompanying Jude to such a strange part of New Orleans. But what would be wrong with the French Quarter or a stroll down Bourbon Street? I came to Tulane because those were places from my imagination that I'd wanted to make real.

Maybe someday. Maybe someday . . . when I'd see Jude's eyes in the daylight.

Until then, we're still night creatures, moving in shadows from club to club. Is he daring me to keep up?

"I've only been on campus for a few weeks," I reply, with my heels clicking. I take three steps for every two of his. "I haven't seen much of the city. I transferred from the satellite campus outside Baton Rouge. So acting like a tourist is kinda unavoidable."

"Why transfer?"

"My fellowship. And because my parents urged me to come here. They said I'd never get what I needed by staying someplace so small."

"They were right," he says with a nod. The lights of a dozen clubs in a row cast his features in a rainbow animation. He looks like he was standing in front of a movie projector playing a Pixar film. "You'll have to tell me about them."

We reach the end of a line of clubs to what looks like a basement service entrance. He stops there, then circles my waist with his hands. I'm once again the sole focus of his attention.

"Maybe, but do we have to tonight? This is a place called Slink, of all things." I smile up at him. "Besides, from what you've laid out, we're going to spend at least a little more time together."

I want to kiss him again, as a channel for all my intensity and pent-up anticipation. After a slow exhale he leans nearer, so near that I feel his breath and hear his whisper above the chatter of a hundred street voices. "That's right. We'll do some amazing things tonight, Keeley. But we're not even close to the end of this . . . this . . ."

I laugh and kiss his cheek. "Maybe there's hope for me yet."

"Hm?"

"If you'd had a ready word for what this is, then I'd know you do it all the time."

"What do you mean?" He raised his head, staring me down with a deeply furrowed brow. "You think I seek out virgins and set myself up as the center of their world for a few weeks? Then what, scrape them off once they know how to get laid?"

I stiffen. "What am I supposed to think?"

"That you're a special case."

His eyes are shadowed, but I can see his earnestness. And I can see the hurt my self-defensive assumptions caused.

"I have a hard time believing stuff like that," I say with needles in my throat. "I didn't mean anything against you. It's my baggage."

I push deeper into his embrace, so that he has no choice but to wrap his arms around my low back. The fingers of one hand rest just above my ass. All sorts of memories of what we did in his car come rushing back. I'm not wearing jeans today. He'd have . . . access.

"Is this your way of trying to distract me?" His eyebrows are arched, and a small smile has returned to his beautifully sculpted mouth.

"Is it working?"

"Partly." He kisses my forehead. "What would you say if I told you you're the first virgin I've wanted to be with?"

"Um . . . that I hope you know what you're doing?"

He laughs, releasing the tension from between us. "Me too."

"You're doing just fine." I grin, and kiss his jaw. "I've been trying to come up with a name for this. Like I said, what am I supposed to think? Tonight could be step two in *The Jude Villars Handbook to Deflowering the Worshipful and Unsuspecting*."

"It hasn't gone to press yet."

I laugh, ducking fully into his arms and placing my lips against the thin, smooth, musk-scented skin at the base of his throat. "This is seduction, Jude. I don't care where it winds up. I'm having too much fun following your lead."

"I think you're fooling yourself there, Keeley," he says quietly.

"How so?"

"You don't like getting into a car without knowing where it's headed. I don't believe you don't care where this will wind up."

I exhale and shudder. I'm sure he feels me quake. I'm scantily clad, the night is warm, and he's got me pressed against his chest like a second T-shirt. "Okay. Got me. I care. How's that?"

"Perfect. And in return, I'll admit something too. I haven't stopped thinking about you for days."

He could've put his hand down my panties, there, standing on the street, and surprised me less.

"So you have to tell me, Keeley. Can you live with not knowing where this'll lead?"

I pull away, but I still hold his hand. I won't give that up unless forced. "Life's unpredictable."

"Yes," he says, so rough and low. "Life's unpredictable."

I feel like the playfulness of our mood keeps getting overshadowed by, well, shadows. That's not a good sign. Even if he's being completely honest about the *haven't stopped thinking about you for days* thing, which still makes me shiver with the want, the need to believe it, he doesn't have any more control over how this will go than I do. His parents dropped out of the sky and died on a clear January day. My father blew my mom away with a shotgun.

Life is unpredictable.

Maybe that desperation breaks the spell of maudlin. Funky enough. It seems totally backward. But, suddenly, all I want is to prove that past bullshit wrong. I'm holding hands with Jude Villars, about to enter a club called Slink, on what has to be the hottest night in one of the coolest cities in the whole country.

Fuck the past. Tonight I'm living for the here and now.

I link my arm through his. I stand on tiptoe and kiss his jaw. Then, when that isn't enough, I grab his chin and drag him closer. It's my turn to kiss first. He opens to me instantly, as if he was just waiting for the same escape route. *Come this way*, I think. *It's more fun over here.* The future can take a leap too. This is all about making each other feel good, and letting Jude honor the promise he made. I believe his promises.

What I can't believe is what used to be true about myself. In the last week or so, I've performed onstage. I've made friends. I've met an amazing man. These aren't the everyday workings of Keeley Chambers. I like the change. *So much.* It's who I've always wanted to be.

We're still kissing when we reach the entrance. One of his hands is possessively clasped around the base of my skull, while the other roams up and down my ribs. He never brushes a stray finger across my breasts, but he hints at it so often that I hope for it every time. My hands are around his trim waist, beneath his loose flannel, skimming his hot, thin cotton T-shirt. His body is sinuous and strong, pulsing with life. I can't get enough of exploring him. Every new touch makes me want to take another leap. I've felt his bare chest, but what about the rest of him?

A thin, short man at the club's entrance looks at us and rolls his eyes. He has a trio of bar piercings through his left eyebrow and a spike through his lower lip. Several heavy earrings dangle almost to his shoulders, and half his face is marked with abstract black ink. Only half. Exactly half. He's like a comic book villain. Two-Face? From *Batman*? I try not to stare, but honestly, it's impossible not to. Besides, he's the one glaring at us as if kissing is strictly prohibited at a place with a name as suggestive as Slink.

Jude pays the cover charge, and we both get our hands stamped. I don't remember him having a stamp before. Maybe it was the suit. He looked like a Real Grown-Up at Yamatam's. Here, he's just another twentysomething who needs to be carded. Under the light of Slink's neon sign and its brightly lit basement entrance, I see that his T-shirt has an abstract graphic of bold, colorful human figures dancing among cartoon lemons. As we climb down toward the mysteries of the club, I ask him what it's about.

"Keith Haring," he says, with a question in his voice—one asking if I know who he's talking about. Which I don't. "He's a pop artist from the eighties. Big into anti-apartheid and AIDS awareness. Died when he was really young. U2 was a big fan. This T-shirt is from their PopMart tour. I was seventeen when my dad took me to see them. He'd been a fan for years."

"You met them, didn't you? The special Villars backstage pass?"

"Oddly enough, you don't make that sound bitter or insulting."

"Just impressed is all."

"That I met U2?"

"Sure," I say, totally copping out as we push into the club. "Must've been cool."

What I want to say is, *I'm impressed you have anything of your parents that you cherish.*

~ TWENTY-ONE ~

I dodge any probing about that slipup by doing what would come naturally to anyone: I try to absorb the sights and sounds of Slink. It's a circus. Yup, an indoor adult circus where the patrons are the performers. I can't believe the variety of people. Shapes, sizes, colors, clothing, decorations—so many decorations. It's a festival for the eyes, as dubstep blares from a pair of human-sized speakers hanging from the ceiling.

Jude leans in close, nearly shouting. "We won't be able to stay past midnight because we're not members."

"Huh?"

He grins. "After midnight, it becomes a private dungeon club. Sex stuff. Kinky. You know, BDSM?"

I can't help that my eyes are totally wide open and my I think I know everything self gets a kick in the ass. "A sex club?"

"Within limits, but yeah. If you want a drink, they're only served for another few minutes. Then it's water and soda."

"Why?"

"Keeps people safe."

Possibilities reel as my eyes flick across a hundred faces—and their bodies. Because sure enough, lots of people are wearing next to nothing. My little black dress feels like a prom getup by comparison. There's a woman with electrical tape criss-crossed over her nipples and a sheer belly dancer–style skirt offering a tantalizing view of everything else. One man is naked except for tight leather shorts and a hood.

Jude tugs my arm. He plants me on a love seat of sorts and lifts his hand to signal a waiter. The waiter has a chain that drapes from his nostril to a cuff on his right wrist. Jude orders club soda for me and a tonic and lime for himself. With unmistakable invitation, the waiter walks his gaze over Jude's long body, glances at me, then shrugs. He saunters off to collect our drinks.

"He likes you," I say. Well, *say* might be a little tame. The music is loud. We have two volumes: shout face to face, or shout more softly with mouth tucked against ear. I'd do more of the latter if the club wasn't busy sucking up my attention.

"Too bad for him," he replied. "So, do you think you'll be able to get some firsthand information for your paper?"

I laugh, then cover my mouth when he looks nearly disappointed. "Sorry," I say. "But I'm not going to be able to get many firsthand interviews here. I could try, but I'd be hoarse long before midnight."

He shrugs off that boyish look of having gotten it wrong. "Never mind."

"Hey," I say, grabbing his face between my hands. I kiss his nose. "I'm having a blast. And besides, it's a helluva lot more firsthand stuff than most people in my class would dare try to find. I read the textbook. Now I can see it all in person. That's not nothing."

"Textbook?"

"On the sociology of human groupings. People like to be in groups that match internal versions of themselves. You're wearing Docs—well-worn Docs, I might add—because part of you doesn't want to wear suits all the time. You have a vintage U2 shirt, and a flannel like some grunge throwback. You're a mashup. Here, you can do that, where there's no judgment. What would be outrageous for you outside these walls is ho-hum boring inside. You can be daring in your own mind, but otherwise anonymous."

He's staring at me as if I just did a tarot reading. "And your little black dress?"

"Oh, that's just me wanting to look nice for you."

I must've pulled off just the right don't give a care tone, because he smiles and gives a little nod. "You win at that."

"Makes me wonder, though."

"About?"

I tug the knit collar of his T-shirt—not too much, because it's old. "I unbuttoned your shirt the other night, and I touched a lot of skin." I grin, blushing but not caring. "A *lot* of skin. But it was too dark to see if you have any tattoos. Are you hiding more from the world than just a pair of shit-kicker boots?"

"Do you?"

"Nope. Virgin skin."

Virgin? *Really?*

I say it so quickly and so frankly that he busts out laughing. I join in laughing as if balloons have burst inside both of us at the same time. We needed it. Maybe that's what's so intoxicating about being with Jude. We build up and up and up—then something drags us halfway down again. Never all the way down. Every moment with him is building, in unpredictable fits and starts. It's that roller coaster again. More danger.

What's around the corner? How bold can I be? How much will I love it?

"You said that on purpose," he says, wiping his eyes.

"No way. Look at my blush. Are you serious?"

"Then your subconscious is a huge tease."

"You like when I tease back. It's like permission to do your worst. Or best." His grin is positively devilish. He licks his lower lip, deliberately, making me laugh all over again. Only when I catch my breath do I force my voice to work again. "Are you listening, Mr. Villars? I don't like repeating myself."

"You're mocking me with that one."

"Totally. But the question remains. Do you have a tattoo?"

"Yup."

"Oh, c'mon. Now you have to show me." I affect a mock serious expression. "It's for science."

I'm convinced he won't, because doing so would be straightforward, and not too much about us—other than the seduction—has been straightforward. But he lifts the hem of his T-shirt, right above the pronounced, lick-worthy V that dips into the waistband of his jeans. It's a latitude and longitude marker.

"Where my parents died," he says simply.

I swallow back a rush of emotion. I want to say I'm sorry, or even apologize for making it such a flippant, teasing thing. Maybe that's why he was so blunt about revealing it. There's nothing flippant or teasing about it. So I say the only thing that makes sense to me right then. "Thank you for showing me."

"You're welcome. And," he continues with a shrug, pulling his shirt back in place, "I didn't want questions about it later."

"Makes sense." I try to breathe, try to recover the momentum of the easygoing side of us. Looking around Slink is entertaining, but I'm so wrapped up in Jude that I just want *him* back. "So, other than its educational properties, is this where you take girls to shock them?"

"Nope, never been." As if by silent agreement, he goes along with me, returning to the neutral territory of the club and flirting and thick, delicious innuendo. He wiggles his brows and leans close enough to kiss me—but doesn't. "You need to quit assuming I'm running by some playbook. I've never been here. I've never been with a virgin. And before you make another assumption, I haven't been with a college girl since graduating."

"Oh."

"Yeah, *oh*," he says, grinning. "I won't have you thinking the worst of me, sugar. Won't have it."

"You didn't start out that way."

"Eh." He traces my shoulder until one of the dress's straps dangles down my upper arm. "You could've been anyone when we met. I have standards."

"Which include?"

I know it's just a skinny little black strap, but now that it's fallen, my shoulder—that whole side of my body—feels more exposed. He kisses there, licks softly, then nestles his lips just below my earlobe. "Quick recovery when an arrogant asshole gives you shit. The ability to take a dare and fling it right back in that asshole's face. And a body . . ."

"Oh, don't," I say. Even though his words are all the compliments a girl like me could want, I can't let him continue. I like knowing he admires me for how I stood up for myself that first night. I did great. He was an enigmatic weirdo. And here we are at Slink. Yay for us making it past an *intriguing* start, to use his word.

"Don't what?"

"Wax poetic about how I look. Knobby knees and mouse brown hair do not a poet inspire."

"Take that back or I'll drive you home right now." He tugs down the other strap of my dress. "And I don't mean that in the good way, where we'd be alone and on page six of my playbook."

He's grinning so wide that I can't breathe. Or maybe it's because he's practically undressing me in public. Or, more shatteringly, maybe it's because the sudden, smack-me-sideways idea of being seduced by Jude Villars becomes very blunt. It's not a question anymore. It's a fact.

We will have sex.

It had all seemed so theoretical, even when he'd made me explode in the backseat of his car, with just his hand on my jeans. But it's going to get more serious than that, and I'm paralyzed by possibilities, nerves, anticipation.

"Take it back, Keeley," he says, then draws my earlobe between his teeth. I shiver until I feel like my bones will shake apart. "Take it back and let me tell you what I see when I look at you."

"Do I have to believe it?"

"No. But it'll be part of our . . . seduction? You'll believe it before we're through."

I smirk. "Is that on page eleven or something?"

"You've been reading ahead." He toys with one strap, barely nodding to the waiter who deposits our drinks on a little table beside Jude's knee. "I'm waiting."

"Okay," I say. "I take it back. Go ahead."

"You're graceful. You're natural and unpretentious. You're tall—I really like that. You have poise and this air of living in some other world. It sets you apart. And unlike most guys and all the stereotypes we're working against here, I happen to adore small breasts."

"No way."

"I'm totally not bullshitting you." He pulls me close so that he's more my recliner than the love seat is. "Small is exotic. Neat and perfectly formed. Give me that any day."

"You shouldn't be allowed to talk to me this way."

His eyebrows dip. "Why not?"

"Because I like it."

His hand grazes my side. Finally, as if I'd been holding my breath in anticipation of the moment, four long fingers feather over my nipple. The ghostly touch moves on, leaving that sensitive skin aching for more. He's watching, smiling to himself as if he's just performed a magic trick. My libido doesn't argue.

"Should I try that again, sugar?"

"Anyone can see what you're doing."

He leans in closer, moving my hair aside to kiss my throat. One kiss is so intense and deep that I pull away. "Come back here," he says. The club melts into colors behind my eyes and a whirl of distant noises. He talks against my skin, where goose bumps lift to meet his lips. "I'm not finished with you. And you haven't answered my question."

More kisses, until he captures my mouth with his. His hands are back at it, doing that restless dance up and down my ribs. I know he won't go any further until I reply.

"Public. Place." I manage the words in between gasping breaths and his heated kisses.

"There's a guy over there dancing in a cage, wearing gold hot pants and go-go boots. Do you think anyone here cares if I caress your breasts? Or if you let me do even more?"

"*I* care. It's . . ." I remember what he said about waiting for me to finish my thoughts, how they're worth the wait. That's almost as flattering as his compliments about my looks. So I pull it together. "It's like being onstage. Under the spotlight at Yama-tam's, I couldn't see anyone in the crowd. I clung to this idea of a bubble of privacy. Like now. But that doesn't mean we're alone."

"Do you want to be alone?"

"Eventually," I say, feeling kinda powerful. "But for now . . . you can keep doing what you're doing."

He returns his teasing but powerful attention to my breasts. He uses his knuckles this time, softly stroking. My breathing hitches toward warp speed.

"Perfect," he whispers against my throat. "You have no idea what that does to me."

I laugh, needing any release. "I bet I could find out."

"Dare you."

I look around the club, with its party sex vibe craziness, and say, "You got it."

He took me by surprise with slow gentleness. I decide on no holds barred. I don't even bother sliding my hand up his thigh, or running teasing fingers down his abdomen. Instead I just . . . grab. It probably isn't the most graceful move ever managed by a turned on, out of her depth chick, but it has the effect we both want. Jude groans a soft "Fuck" while I grin against the hollow above his collarbone. My fingers are tight at the apex of his jeans where he's hard—but not completely, achingly hard. Apparently that's about thirty seconds later when he nearly doubles in size and he yanks my hand away.

"Don't do that again or I *will* have to take you home."

"Straight ahead to sex?" I ask, not knowing if that's such a bad idea. I'm heady and drunk, just playing with this man, sparring with him, breathing him with every intake of breath. "You've got me in the mind for it, I gotta admit."

"No," he says, his drawl pinched tight. "I'd drop you off at the dorm, then head to my bed. Alone."

"Then when?" I ask, genuinely curious. "What are we waiting for?"

"Not waiting, sugar. *Delaying.* Do you really want to think about what comes after, once we go all the way?"

He's frowning, maybe contemplating what I am. Beyond our first time . . . I don't want to think about it. Taking it slow, with these beautifully frustrating teases, rules, and laughing games, keeps it playful. That's all I want. Being playful with a gorgeous guy who wants to be with me.

When said like that, letting this linger is a really great idea.

"Open your eyes, Keeley." I do as I'm told, which is damn easy when it comes to Jude. It's his power over me. I suspect he's got a lot of power over a lot of people. "Tell me where you're at."

"Delay away."

Just before delving deep for an intense kiss, I wind up sitting on his lap. I don't know how. It just seems like the place to be when he kisses me. I like the tartness of the tonic and lime on his tongue, and the way his arms crisscross my back. He knows what he wants from me, how he wants me. That's so damn hot. "So, for the foreseeable future, you're mine."

"Yours?"

"Mine to teach, flatter, surprise. Having power over you is keeping me up at night . . . as much as the idea of your first time."

"Even if I've given you that power?"

"Especially that." He pulls me close. "Hostile takeovers are for boardrooms, where I wear a suit and a scowl and nobody likes me very much."

I go still at those words. I touch his cheeks with unsteady fingers. "I can't imagine that."

He grins, all showy arrogance. "You would've that first night at Yamatam's."

"We're at a *way* different club, and you're not wearing a suit." I kiss his nose, then his mouth, then his chin. "And I like you very much."

"This is give and take," he says, bathing me in the hot molasses of his drawl. "This is what I've been missing. Believe what you will, Keeley, but you're seducing me just as much in return."

⟿ TWENTY-TWO ⟾

Midnight arrives like Cinderella's closing bell. Sure enough, people who are wearing next to nothing congregate around a distant door. I wonder what's behind it, those mysteries, but no way am I ready. My head would probably pop off. I've been doing my best to keep up with Jude.

He has me so worked up. Private words. Kisses and touches—some as slight as a brush of fingers down my throat, some as suggestive as running his hands up the back of my dress, cupping and squeezing my ass. In full view.

"Tell me when I go too far," he'd said.

"You assume you'll go too far."

With a chuckle, he smiled against my breastbone, where cleavage would've awaited him had he been with some other girl. "Okay, how about, tell me when I go too far too fast."

"That sounds just about perfect."

I can't get enough of his skin. Even as we exit the club, with me casting one last glance toward the dungeon door, I'm clinging to his bare upper arm. He's tied the flannel around his waist.

He follows my gaze, with a last look of his own. "You curious?" he asked, his eyebrows high.

I laugh and lean into him as we reach the top step and exit back onto the street. "Dungeons are for another lifetime."

I shudder unexpectedly.

He pulls me closer, a questioning expression marring the sweeping wonder of his lower lip. "What was that for?"

"I . . ." I swallow my uncertainties and how the word "dungeon" doesn't do a damn thing for me. "I think you're intimidating enough."

"Intimidating? I don't know if I like that."

"You are," I say softly.

Something has happened tonight, between us, that has a lot to do with seduction and not so much to do with actual sex. We've wrapped each other in a spell. It's so beautiful and hypnotic that I can put away my fatalism. I lean into him even more closely, letting myself pretend, if only for the length of our walk back to his car, that our future is a pretty one.

Our agreement that we're not ready to take the next step tonight continues to be a relief. We'll have more walks. I don't have to pretend those.

We continue in silence. Part of me wishes I could just think what I want to confess and he'll hear it. My past by osmosis. Just . . . get it out in the open. Most of me wants to close it all away so he'll know me as Keeley, kiss me and hold me and care for me as Keeley. No one else, because that old life keeps tripping up the good things I have now.

"I'm sure the people in Slink are having a good time doing dungeon-y things, but they're some jump in evolution compared to me. I can't imagine past kissing, and maybe getting naked." I laugh, a little hysterical at the edges. "Don't worry. I diligently read the high school health textbook. I know how it all works."

"Noted," he says with a slight grin. I love his grins. That's all I'll admit about loving pieces of him, for now, because it's been about eleven minutes since I met him and I'm not a completely idiotic fool. Just a *mostly* idiotic fool. He could smile at me and I'd do anything. If he ever finds that out, I'm in real trouble.

Thing is, the whole nature of our agreement means he probably already knows that. He's experienced. He's smart. He knows just where to touch me. Maybe that means he knows how to read me too.

"But," I force myself to say. "I can't imagine it for me, even after . . . after how we've been . . . playing. I can get it, you know—people liking what people like. I like . . ."

He stops beneath the lights of a quiet bar with outdoor seating. Light halos him. The sheen of his hair becomes angelic around his shadowed face. I see the top of his nose and the set of his chin and the deep hollows beneath his high cheekbones. "What do you like, Keeley?"

"Being safe." The words jump out of me so quickly that I follow them with something close to a hiccup.

"Being onstage isn't safe," he says. "Being exposed that way." I nod.

He folds me into his arms. He's dressed to blend in with every other twentysomething in New Orleans. He could be some grad assistant and no one would blink an eye. I like that he's revealed himself to me this way, and I can't help but adore how tightly he holds me. I feel like he's holding me earthbound when I could float away on bad memories—no, be carried away by them, hoisted by a monstrous murder of crows.

"You're here with me," he says. "And we have some evening left. Let's get a drink, if you're up to it. Or anything else . . ."

I kiss the underside of his chin, feel him swallow. "I can imagine a lot. But a soda would be great."

We find a table next to the sidewalk, where we become just another couple, just another pair of voices among dozens. My eyes are lazy, sleepy feeling, although I'm charged up like lightning ready to strike. It's early October. I'm a late Midwestern thunderstorm—that last gasp before the cold comes. I don't want to be cold. I want to sizzle. Jude's doing a damn good job of making that happen.

"I want a couple less mysteries," I say after taking a sip of Sprite. "Can we do that? A little at a time?"

Sitting close, he strokes the hair back from my face. "That's the plan, remember? Loose as it is, the plan is a little at a time. Do you know what's so good about it?"

"Hm?"

"It could happen at any time. Tonight. Weeks from now. There's no telling how the moment will happen. That's . . ." He shakes his head, then kisses me, hard, swift, without holding back. "That's sexy as fuck."

I shiver with want. I'm as wet as I can remember being, even more than when we were in the backseat of his car. Everything about me is humming, like an orchestra warming up. Nothing's in tune yet, but it will be.

"So . . . we could go to your place?"

He hesitates, then takes a drink from whatever he ordered—scotch, I think. "Would you mind if we went to a hotel?"

The heat inside me dims. *Be honest.* Even about the hard stuff. "Are there things at home you don't want me to see?"

"No, more like a person I don't want you to see. Adelaide comes and goes when she wants. I don't care if she knows about us—"

"She already does."

"Ah." He circles his forefinger around the rim of the tumbler of scotch. "She's always been nosy when it comes to my personal life."

"Pot, kettle, black?"

"Yeah, except I'm twenty-six. Eight years is a big difference. I don't feel like turning on the lights at home and finding what's his fuck's coat in the foyer."

"Dr. Saunders."

"If you want to give him a different name, then yeah. Him."

"You could text her? See what's she doing?"

"If she gets in a mood, she won't reply. It's worse than not having asked in the first place." He shakes his head vehemently. "She's not going to screw with me tonight. Damn stubborn girl. You'd think—" He bites his molars together so hard that I hear them click. "Forget it, sugar. I didn't mean to put all that out there."

"It's okay," I say, glad my voice is steady. "Family can be tricky."

He holds one of my wrists, there on the table, with the bar's ambient lighting turning my paler skin and his tan skin into something symbiotic. A joining of sorts. It's almost more intimate than how he touched me in the club. It's possessive. I love that too.

Ugh. I really need to find a thesaurus and get a stronger vocabulary going. A girl who says "love" too much in her head starts to get ideas. I don't need any more ideas than I already have.

"You hide it really well," he says. "How nervous you are."

"If I hide it so well, how do you know I'm nervous?"

He thumbs my wrist again. "Pulse like a butterfly in flight."

I drag in a gulp of heavy nighttime air. "I think it's been building in me for a long time. It's harder to loosen up than I can explain. Harder than just willing it to happen. But it's different with you."

"So apparently I intimidate you, make your pulse race, and inspire you to set off fire alarms?"

I laugh, which feels good. "You're impossible, you know that?"

"That's a step up from arrogant asshole."

"Oh no. You're not out of that doghouse yet."

"Jude Villars?"

I flinch and turn to find a couple standing on the sidewalk, within a few feet of our little table. The guy is middle-aged, maybe in his forties. The woman is way younger, although I think she's already had collagen work on her lips. I take an instant disliking to both of them, not based on anything they've done—but because Jude snatches his hand away from my wrist. He picks up the tumbler and downs the scotch in a single gulp.

"Wes Templeton," he says, standing quickly. "It's been a while."

They exchange handshakes. Jude angles his body so that I no longer have a view of the man's face. The woman has knowing eyes, jaded eyes. She keeps looking between me and Jude with this itty bitty smirk on her fat lips.

I stare at my glass of Sprite. What I already drank is bubbling and sour in my stomach. I'd been so sure Jude's suggestion about a hotel room was to keep me hidden. He convinced me otherwise, because Adelaide was an explanation that makes sense. But how can I believe any of it when he and this Templeton guy keep talking and Jude still has his back to me? I was hoping, in some secret garden of hope I didn't know I tended, that if given the chance . . . he'd want to show me off.

Or at least introduce me.

The guy Templeton made sure his trophy wife got an introduction. Eve was her name. I don't have a name right now. I have a glass of soda and a basket empty of expectations. I feel lower than low when he says his farewells and offers a masculine wave goodbye.

"I haven't seen him in a year at least," Jude says when he retakes his seat. "He was a consulting lawyer on a tricky merger. Nice guy."

"Seemed that way." My tongue feels like a swollen sponge. Then I shake my head with a sick little laugh. "And I thought the hotel was the bad part."

"What does that mean?" His jaw is tight. I can see it in his eyes, that he knows what he did and he isn't going to apologize. Our evening, my hopes, his seduction—they're all in splinters now.

That doesn't make me shrink back, thank God. My voice is quiet but strong when I meet his stare head-on. "You said the eight years between you and Adelaide was a lot. I'm barely three years older than her." I wave a hand toward where Templeton and his wife had walked into the night. "Apparently that means I'm not worthy of the courtesy of an introduction to some company guy."

"That's my daytime," he says tersely. "My *life*. It doesn't have anything to do with you and me."

"Why not?" I cross my arms. My thunderstorm power is ebbing away like clouds clearing. We're whipping up a storm of a different kind—a tornado bearing down. "Guys like that *are* your daytime. They're your real life. I don't even know what you look like in sunlight. Okay, so you're not hiding me from some person back at your house, but could you take me to a cocktail party with your colleagues? Could you handle how they'd look at you, with a student on your arm? You didn't even have the guts to do it right here."

"I do what I want," he said stonily. I've never heard that tone of voice from him. He's pissed off. That much is loud and clear. "I've done what I wanted since my parents died because no one's allowed to contradict me. The legal paperwork says as much. I've had to earn the rest of my authority by impressing guys like Templeton and making sure they know who's in charge."

I'm numb all over. "And being seen with me would put an end to all that?"

"Now, you listen up, sugar."

I rub my arms with the return of that word. *Sugar*. No, not the word itself. He's turned it into an endearment. I hate the return of that tone. I'm lost all of a sudden, reminded that I'm just a small, disposable part of his big, important life. I'm treading water with no land in sight and sharks rubbing against my legs as they circle.

"What?" I ask.

I sound like my old self. My scared self. Because I *am* scared. Jude Villars has reminded me, loud and clear, of what I've tried telling myself over and over. It's easier to leave possessions

behind, rather than have them, cherish them, and see them
taken away.

"First, you're right about our ages. Five years doesn't seem
like much, but it's huge. You don't know what it's like to live in
the real world and make the decisions I've been forced to make."

"Stop right there," I say, as angry as he is. "You don't know
shit about my life. And this is exactly what I didn't want. You
might as well have a family at home that you're hiding me from,
like how that creep professor hides Adelaide from his wife.
You're not ready to tell a colleague my name, let alone take me
out on a date, just to get some burgers."

He clenches his jaw. He doesn't look at me. "That's the other
thing, sugar. Who ever said we're dating?"

~ TWENTY-THREE ~

I don't sleep that night.

Jude drove me home in silence, but I heard his words, over and over, like an out of tune piano repeating the same song.

Who ever said we're dating?

I didn't even change out of Janissa's dress when I snuck in— just crawled under the covers and hoped six hours before dawn would be enough time for me to pull it together. I lie in the dark with tears leaking down to wet my hair and my pillow. I don't make a sound. Crying is something I learned to keep to myself a long time ago, and I don't want to wake Janissa. She's sleeping soundly across our little room, making quiet, indelicate snoring noises.

I don't think I hate Jude. He turned out to be just what I'd been so wary of, and just what Janissa warned against. Mostly, I hate that I was right. A sad, fatalistic ending is the safest bet.

I gave him more trust, more of myself, more quickly than I have to anyone else. I got my hopes up that the time between us, no matter how brief, could be amazing—that he could show *me* how to be amazing. Instead he showed me what I'd already been wary enough to suspect. I had no chance of protecting myself against such a smooth, aggressive man. He'd held me the right way and told me what I needed to hear, and had it not been for that guy Templeton and his plastic surgery gone wrong wife, Jude would've taken me for all I'm worth. That meant my virginity, sure, but also my self-esteem and my stupid, eager, *please love me* heart.

I was a fool to look for more. I was a fool for thinking the thrill ride would be enough—and it had been, *in the moment*. I was a fool for hoping it would never end.

I relive so many of those moments as tears keep trickling down my cheeks.

I'm sure I'll be memorable now. I'll be that girl who got so starry eyed that I couldn't tell night from day, seduction from dating, player from gentleman.

Dawn slowly changes the color of the ceiling from charcoal gray to stuff that's way too bright and cheery. I'm no closer to pulling myself together than when I stood on trembling legs and forced myself to walk with Jude away from that bar. Side by side. A wall between us.

End of story.

Only, my epilogue is still in the making. I find a new refrain to drive myself crazy with.

Now what?

When Janissa wakes up, she smiles over at me. "Hey, you. How'd it go?"

I've held it together long enough. I can't answer her. I just double over and hug the pillow to my face, letting hours' worth of sobs take over. She's perched on the edge of my bed in no time, her arms around both me and the pillow.

There's really no telling how long I cry. It feels like a week before I'm finally able to tell Janissa what happened. She helps me out of the dress and into some pj's, then makes me my favorite peppermint tea.

"You told me so," I whisper over the rim of the mug I clutch like a lifeline. I'm propped up in bed, where Janissa stacked some extra pillows against the wall. She even closed the curtains halfway so the sun doesn't hit me full in the face. "You said he was too dangerous."

Janissa is sitting cross-legged on the floor, holding her mug of hot chocolate. "Yeah, but what I never told you is that a little part of me was jealous. I'd have done just what you did. In a heartbeat. You'd be the one popping open a second box of Kleenex for me."

"I'm glad that isn't how it went. You've been so good to me."

"You're my friend," she says simply.

I start to cry again, but softly. "Thank you, Janey."

"Did you just call me Janey?"

My cheeks heat up. "Sorry."

"No, I like it." She sips her cocoa. "I've always thought Janissa was too formal, but I didn't want to be the dork who starts insisting on a nickname. You just gave me one spontaneously."

"I goofed. That's all."

"Too late. I'm Janey to you. Maybe it'll catch on." After standing up, she stretches. "So here's what's going to happen. I'm going to get dressed and go work at the chem lab. You're going to take a Unisom and sleep until dinner. I'll bring us back a bunch of stuff, from crackers to chocolate bars. Then more sleep. If he doesn't call to apologize by then, fuck him."

I feel my eyes go wide, but she stands even more resolutely.

"I mean it, Keeley. No one has the right to treat you that way." She gathers a change of clothes and starts getting dressed. "Next chance we get, we'll stay in like hermits. You'll work on your sonata and store up more strength. We'll eat too much, refuse to get dressed, and pretend the Internet was created just for Twitter."

"You're so bossy," I say with a little smile.

"It's my way of coping. I really want to make fliers and post them all around campus. 'Beware This Handsome Dickweed.'"

I nod to my mug. "Peppermint tea and Unisom are a lot better."

"Mission accomplished."

Janey is great, and so is the familiar pattern of my classes, but I need my parents. When I'm this desperate for some safety and affection, I stop thinking of them as Clair and John. They're my parents, way more than the two people who shot me into the world. That doesn't mean it's easy to ask John to drive down and get me. I don't have a car, and it's three hours round trip down I-10. Guilt about being treated how they insist I deserve being treated is a hard thing to get over. Six years, and I'm still trying.

He makes it easier by showing up late after his shift at the supply company, where he manages a company that imports and distributes things that make things: sheet metal, ball bearings, rivets, screws, rebar. Stuff comes in from China, and then gets shipped out to all the places across the planet that need the basics for their own manufacturing. His job is mostly about people and keeping them happy and productive—more of that *he's our rock* personality—but it's always been a job that helped me make sense of a crazy world. I mean, who thinks of where hinges come from? How they get to houses so that doors can open and close? The little details are cool. They ground me.

It's late when he bundles me and my duffel in his ten-year-old Accord. He and Clair are frugal and they work hard. They just couldn't ever have kids of their own. A few tries at adoption, and even fostering babies, had broken their hearts. Instead they wound up with me. I guess it was a good tradeoff, no matter how hard I was to handle in the early years, because I sure as hell wasn't going to leave them.

"You planning on telling me what this is about?" John asks, about ten minutes out of the city. We're surrounded by green and green and more green. I'm convinced Louisiana is about fifty percent water and fifty percent blinding foliage. "Clair and I made a lot of guesses, but we'd rather hear it from you."

"Can we talk about it when we get home? I don't . . ." I swallow an unexpected sob and look back out the window. "I don't think I want to say it more than once."

"Sure."

He says it so plainly, and he means it. No offense taken. Instead he turns on the radio and listens to the sports recap before turning it over to a classical station that lulls me to sleep.

We arrive in Denham Springs just after ten. Clair is swinging softly on the porch and has the light on above the front door, as well as the one over the one-car garage. Gravel crunches beneath the tires as John pulls up. Bugs think the light is the best thing ever, but they're fewer in number now. I'd never seen so many bugs before moving to Louisiana. You can't have that much water and greenery without the inevitable result.

Clair darts off the porch and squeezes me into a big hug. She looks the same as when I left for Tulane in September. Maybe because I've changed so much, I expected the same from her and John. But her hair is still coppery red and wiry, a holdover from her Cajun roots, and her skin smooth and freckled. She's only forty-five and sometimes acts about half her age. Her vivaciousness reminds me of Adelaide—or vice versa. No wonder I've tried so hard to get along with the girl. It's not wildness so much as sucking up life with every breath.

John kisses Clair and gets my bag. Soon I'm slouched on the sectional in the living room, where a big wall of books and a flat-screen TV take up the whole thing. The windows are open a little and the ceiling fan is a gentle whirr of sound. Everything is pinewood, from the ceiling panels to the floors, except for the marble-wrapped fireplace they barely use except during the holidays, when crackling flames add to the hominess. It even smells like home, with lemon wood polish and the remnants of what must've been a roast. I bet if I sneak into the kitchen later, I'll find homemade cornbread. Cornbread plus honey equals comfort-food heaven. I feel tension leak out of me, down into the couch upholstery, down into the marrow of the wood.

Clair brings me sweet tea and settles in beside me. John sits on his recliner, a little distant, but still all ears.

I tell them what happened. Well, almost all of it. A rehash of Yamatam's. How I didn't play the second time I went. Jude. Janissa. Adelaide. More Jude. Not a word about our seduction plans. My classes.

And finally, the nondate that ended with me in tears.

John only shakes his head, mumbling something about a shotgun. Clair, though, has bright green eyes full of sympathy.

"Oh, baby, you didn't deserve that! To have him just . . . dismiss you? If he was anything like you've described, he should've stood you up and put your arm through his and introduced you with a smile on his face—lawyer be damned. Has he called?"

"No."

"Nothing?"

"Nothing."

"Then I have to say it, even if you can't, but screw him. He doesn't get to treat you like something to be ashamed of."

She's got her full tiger going, which means there's no room for me to break in and defend Jude. I shouldn't. There's no reason to. But the urge is there. I think it's because I'm still in shock and disbelief, hoping what happened is a misunderstanding. I tried playing that game. Maybe he was just startled because of the area of town we were in, or because he was wearing such casual clothes. I never win at guessing. If the lawyer was in that area of town, then he had no reason to judge Jude for it, and I was dressed in that pretty black dress I'd borrowed from Janissa.

No reason to defend him. Just a lot of reasons to be heartsick.

"I know that," I say. "I haven't done anything to be ashamed of." *Not even what we did in his Mercedes and what we'd planned on doing.* "But it almost felt like he could tell about . . . about the old stuff. I've been struggling with it a lot lately. The nightmares and all. The change from here has been harder than I thought. More pressure. New friends to try and make. My music. And now this. It's stirring up a whole bunch of crazy. I thought I could handle it, and I was doing good. But that was because things were going good." I wipe my eyes. "Now, not so much."

"You still have all that," John says quietly. "Your studies and music, even the new friends."

"We've been concerned." Clair gives my hand a quick squeeze. "Jude Villars? Really? It's so impossible to believe. And I'm not saying you don't deserve a guy who's practically Louisiana royalty, baby. That'd suit you just fine. But he's not stable. He can't be, with all that's happened to him and his family business. Now he's proved he *can't* handle it. Otherwise he'd have stood up and been a man about you two."

"So that's it," I whisper to myself. My throat is parched. Not even the tea helps. Hearing it from Clair is like shutting it all down. No more me and Jude. Clair hands me a box of Kleenex and hugs me when I start crying again.

"How long can you stay?" she asks.

"I emailed my profs that I had a family emergency," I reply between sniffs.

"Good. A little R and R." She touches what must be huge bags under my eyes. "I think you could use it. And maybe you can play us the sonata you've been working on."

"Maybe." But I know I'll dodge that like flying bullets. Too much of it is bound up and tangled with and inspired by the man I can't have.

~ TWENTY-FOUR ~

The following Sunday, sometime in the early afternoon, I finally catch up on the classwork I missed and get around to putting away the clothes Clair washed. I even drag together enough energy to fire up my Mac. Janissa's hard at work at her desk. I try to get up my nerve twice before finally tapping her on the shoulder. She's jumps, then yanks out her earbuds.

"Sorry," I say. "You got a minute?"

She spins on her desk chair, then stirs a half eaten yogurt, giving it a sniff as if it might've spoiled since she got it out for breakfast. She must decide it's okay, because she spoons some into her mouth. "You're going to distract me, aren't you?"

"Yup."

"Thank God. Go for it."

My hands shake as I click the track pad to hit Play. The Sibelius program is awesome because it plays back the music you feed it. Out from the Bose speakers Clair and John gave me as a

September going away present comes the music I made—music that originated that night onstage.

Janissa takes her glasses off. Her eyes go soft as she listens. She's barefoot, wearing a gold striped tank top from PINK and a pair of capris. Her hair is barely brushed and loose. It looks great on her, all wavy and auburn. She's too pretty to hide behind her glasses, but she tries.

Faces give away a lot. It's like how I watched Brandon, feeling a little off about him. A hint of something beneath the surface. And damn it all, I was right. Too bad I wasn't able to read Jude that way. Especially after how things turned out, I would've been happy to have Brandon as a nice, good-looking fallback. He clearly isn't.

Two disillusionments for the price of one. Only, the way Jude disillusioned me hurts a helluva lot worse, like having my eyes burned out. Crying for most of a week will do that to a girl.

So I watch my roommate's face. After a few minutes, I know she loves my budding sonata.

A soft smile tips her full lips. She's tapping a gentle rhythm on the armrest. Her posture has relaxed. Then the music picks up tempo where I launched straight into a legato-on-speed section, full of fast minor chords and a restless melancholy that moves me even more than Janissa's wide, bright eyes. When I get goose bumps about my own music, it makes me feel pretty silly.

The computer goes silent. Janissa blinks. "Wow."

"Wow?"

"Yeah." She blinks again and shakes her head, then runs her fingers through her hair.

I duck away, save the work, then close the program.

"Is it going to be your December recital piece?" she asks.

I shrug, wanting to fold into myself. I'm so tired. "Maybe? I like it, but something's still missing. It's just not there yet, and even when it is, it won't be pretty. Too wild. I'm trying to get a job, not blow their hair back."

"That sounds exactly how to get a job." She tosses the empty yogurt container in a bin. "You're really gifted, Keeley. I hope you realize that."

My impulse is to take a nap, but it's not even lunchtime. The day is hot as hell, even though it's the second week of October. The whole residence hall is keeping fans on and praying the air conditioning keeps going. The heat adds to the fever in my brain. I want to be magically clearheaded about all I have to do and all I'm scared of and all I'm working toward . . . and free of Jude Villars.

Who ever said we're dating?

"So, look at us," Janey says. "Sunday and stuck in here."

"All work and no play . . ."

". . . makes Jack Nicholson put an ax through a door."

"Sounds about right," I say with a thick sigh. "I'd rather scream in terror than cry anymore."

Her face is overwhelmed with sympathy, but—*thank you, thank you, thank you, Janey*—she doesn't say anything. She blinks and puts on a cheeky smile. "We reinforce each other's negative habits, you know."

My head feels thick and cottony. "How's that?"

"I stay in to work, so you stay in. Or vice versa. We eat left-over takeout and barely leave the room. The best we do at socializing is leaving the door open and hoping for a bit of gossip to walk past."

"Look how well that turned out the other night."

Janissa makes a sour face. "Yeah, that wasn't cool. But now

the door's shut. We don't even get the chance to hear more reasons why we should be disappointed with the male species."

"I don't want another reason."

She slumps heavily onto her bunk. "Yeah, but I want a life."

"You sure? It's not all it's cracked up to be."

"I'm a junior taking eighteen credits plus lab hours. I work four nights a week at the student outreach center, just to keep my loans down. You sure I can't have a *little* bit of a life?"

Her expression becomes more imploring. My heart heats up, knowing she's trusting me with this personal talk. It feels good to know things aren't totally one-way with us. She's put up with a lot from me since waking up to me curled into sobs.

"When does the fun stuff happen?" she asks. "I've had one disastrous relationship, a few friends, and one roommate who wouldn't stop eating goddamn cheese. I'm surprised she could take a shit."

"Oh my God. Did you just say all that?"

She nods emphatically. "Freshman year. I thought everybody went through that hazing stuff, you know? Getting lost and feeling overwhelmed. Or bad luck with roommates. Eventually she moved off campus when she was dumb enough to get pregnant by her grad assistant. We don't have much 'let's get out of here' between us, and then with you meeting Jude . . ."

"You don't need to worry about that so much anymore."

She stares at our industrial walls and sighs. "We need posters. Mine got ruined this summer when my parents' basement flooded. You?"

"I have one of . . ." *Ah, screw it.* She won't judge—especially as long as I keep it on my side of the room. "I have one of *Doctor Who.*"

She actually gives a little clap. "Which Doctor?"

"Number Ten. I love David Tennant."

"And you've been hiding him in the closet? You're mean and terrible."

So I dig out the poster and we hang it at the head of my bunk.

"He's like a dream catcher," Janissa says. "For good dreams."

"I wish."

"You know what this means." She nods at the Doctor, then grabs her purse and heads to the door. "We need to hit the union. Our room needs personality."

"The union? You think they have anything other than LOL Cats and Imagine Dragons?"

"*We. Have. To.* Then we'll keep walking 'til we find something worthy of our discerning eyes." She makes toodle-oo fingers at the Doctor and then waves me along to follow.

Possessions. Things I can lose in a heartbeat. That meltdown with Jude took only a moment or two. A reactor core gone critical.

That I'd eventually make love with Jude had been a certainty that night. A scary, wonderful certainty. Now it was gone. How could any experience with a gropey, inexperienced coed be any more disappointing?

I shove my pain—because, damn it all, I am in pain—away to a distant place. Following Janey is self-preservation.

We spend three minutes in the union gift shop, about forty in the university bookstore, and two hours in a chill out dive that sells LPs and proudly proclaims that it refurbishes turntables. Janissa surprises me by picking out a framed eight by ten of John Lennon. It's the iconic picture of him with a sleeveless New York

City T-shirt and long hair, with round sunglasses and a magically enigmatic expression.

"I didn't know you were a fan," I say.

"Not really. I just think he's cute. And that the world lost a
cool soul when he was killed."

"He can come live in our dorm any day," I say. "It's perfect,
Janey."

By the time we finish with the collector's place next door, I
find a print of one of Alphonse Mucha's renditions of the four
seasons depicted as women. Don't ask me which foursome, because he did about eighty sets of them. Talk about a guy who
stuck with what he liked. I also slip in a three by two stretched
canvas painting of the Chicago skyline. I only shrug when Janey
asks me why.

"Because I've always wanted to visit," I say, hating to lie to
her.

We move on to a trendy boutique that's ten minutes from
closing. Janey finds a bedspread quilted with the entire periodic
table in neon colors. She has this look of stupidly cute longing
across her wide cheeks and soulful eyes. I know what it is to
want things that are frivolous and silly, then have to walk away
with a tiny hole in my heart, leaving them behind, cussing at
myself for being so petty. I don't want that for her.

I force money on her so she can buy it. I literally *shove* bills
into her hands. "It'll make the room incredibly ironic-nerd. My
stuff's just purple. This'll help balance the purple infestation."

"You do have a lot of the damn stuff," she says, her hands
closing around forty bucks.

Then, ta-da, she owns a periodic table for her bed.

One more shop, and I give in to a picture of a piano.

It's not just any piano.

The room looks like a restored Victorian ballroom. The baby grand is impeccably beautiful. Beneath it is a couple huddled together, legs artfully posed in the most amazingly passionate embrace. He's practically devouring her, but with a steadying finger beneath her chin. I imagine that the kiss started light enough. Maybe just a taste, but it exploded before they could stop themselves—that moment Jude talked about, when all the planning in the world doesn't prepare you for when magic happens.

I shouldn't be buying it. It'll hurt to look at it.

Only, this couple . . . They're enveloped within one another. Some touch of wishful thinking says they'd have a happy ending.

I need to believe that's possible.

TWENTY-FIVE

Jude hasn't called.

Brandon hasn't stopped texting.

I'm fed up with nine days of both.

On Wednesday, I wind up having lunch with our so-called residence hall hero. Jude's been a thorn in my brain, and to see Opal so misguidedly happy—I want to smack Brandon in the face. He's not Jude. I don't have to be a psych major to understand displaced anger. But seriously? Brandon watches me whenever he's sitting at the front desk. If I make eye contact, I get double the texts for the rest of the night. It's creeping me out.

It's such a shame. He's got a great jaw and a strong chin, like Superman. We sit together at Dudley's, where Adelaide and I had milkshakes. He's busy noshing away on a burger with bacon and barbecue sauce. I'm picking at a Greek salad. Mostly I just like the olives.

"I heard you have foster parents." I could just open up a hard core grilling, but I don't have it in me. Mostly I want to fill dead air.

"You heard that?"

The restaurant is crowded. Students are everywhere, some socializing, some with their noses buried in books and their eyes glued to glowing screens. I want to be in the practice room. I'm supposed to meet Adelaide for a tricks of the trade session tomorrow night. I'm worried she and Jude talk about things. I'm worried the whole rest of the year is going to be as awkward and disappointing and agonizing as the last few stupid, endless days. Maybe if things don't go well for Adelaide and me, I can ask to be assigned as a mentor to someone else—the music department's version of irreconcilable differences.

"You know how fast rumors move through tight spaces," I say.

"Can't get tighter than our rabbit warren of a dorm." He smiles. I could be totally taken in by him, if I didn't know any better. Besides, one run at playing the fool for a good-looking guy was way more than enough.

But I was a complete moron to think Jude was just another good-looking guy. What we'd done. What we'd talked about doing . . .

He was so much more.

And he never called.

"Anyway, yeah," I say, clearing my throat. "So was I. Foster parents. State custody. The whole deal."

Great. I should be grilling him, being all badass. Instead I'm ready to spill my life story in ways I'd been too embarrassed to with Jude. I spear a chunk of feta and chew it down, not saying anything more. Let him fill the quiet.

"Sucks, don't it? The whole system. How many did you have?"

"How many what?"

"Foster families?"

"Just one."

He snorts derisively. "One? You're shitting me."

"No. They were good to me." I don't mention that they're my legal guardians, not just temporary foster parents anymore. No one deserves to know that much about my past. It was dangerous back then, anyway. I was warned repeatedly that even with my dad locked up, he could hire someone to come after me. Sometimes I have nightmares about that too, but they feel more speculative. Unrealistic. After all, why would I tell *anyone*? The bad stuff I've already lived through is fodder enough for bad dreams.

Yet, I must feel the need to connect on some level. Or to find a reason to think Brandon isn't a complete dick for how he's been treating me and Opal.

"I know I got lucky," I say, leaving my words vague—the exact opposite of my thoughts.

"Lucky?" He sets the burger down, wipes his hands. The forceful way he smacks the napkin back down makes the utensils rattle. "That's a helluva understatement, Keeley. You got a winning lotto ticket. Congrats."

"Hey, don't get so upset. You asked."

"Yeah, well, now you get the truth too." The handsome face turns twisted and mean—but sad too, felled by Kryptonite for reasons he's about to lay on me. I *really* don't want to be here anymore. "I had six foster families, from age eight on. Mom had a side business that consisted of collecting baby daddies. My bio dad left after my younger brother turned out half black. Fast forward, and I was out of school more often than I was in it. Then, hey, say goodbye to Mom, kid."

"Brandon—"

"Six families. They shuffled me around. I was a paycheck and a pain in the ass. You probably know I'm older than other juniors, but do you know why?"

I shake my head. Beneath the table, I'm shredding a paper napkin.

"I had to take my GED twice. There's a reason I work the damn front desk to make ends meet. If I don't depend on myself, there's no one to depend on." He scowls hard. I'm getting really nervous, and I'm glad we're in a public place. People turning to watch as his voice gets louder and louder—that's bad enough. "So, yeah, we were both in the foster system. You think we have something in common because of that, don't you?"

"I thought we might. I was wrong."

I could come back at him with worse tales of woe is me, but no way. This was already skating on thin ice. He seems so . . . placid on the outside. Maybe that's his way of coping, like I have my ways. The truth is way different. And kinda scary.

"Yeah, you were wrong. You got here on, what, a fellowship? Little Miss Prodigy. Did brand-new mommy and daddy buy you a pony as well as a piano?"

"Keep your bullshit to yourself," I snarl. Forget scared. I've been storing up eleven days of pissed off. He's got about as much right to talk to me that way as I have to throw plates and glasses around the restaurant. "I admitted it. I got lucky. That's something I won't ever deny. But it doesn't mean you get to shit on me and make assumptions."

"I can think what I want, like how I got it way wrong when I asked you out. I didn't know you were some brainwashed little princess."

"Brainwashed? You have some nerve. And you sure as hell got it wrong by asking me out. Does Opal know about that? Does she know you text me on the nights you take her out? Is she your backup plan, or am I?"

"Shut up. You know what, just shut up." He stands abruptly and glares at me. I'm transported to that morning when he stood over me, when he reminded me for a split second of my dad. Maybe my subconscious was onto something. "I like Opal," he says, sneering. "If you say a word about this to her . . ."

"What? What will you do, Brandon?"

He smiles in a way that sends chills up across my scalp. "I was in juvie when I finally passed my GED. Assault and battery charges. I can't smack you around, princess, but I can find ways to make you regret getting up in my shit."

My heart is slamming. The heavy flavors of my salad are pressing up on the back of my tongue. I'm frozen and freaked, and, crap, do I wish I'd told Janey about seeing him today. She'd have come with me, and I'd at least have a witness. But her being here wouldn't have changed that Brandon is so totally not what he seems. In fact, it might've delayed finding out the truth.

"You can pick up the check," he says just before he turns tail and storms out. Curious eyes follow his exit. Then I bet some of them shift to look at me. But I'm frozen, looking at what's left of his cheeseburger. The grease is congealed and cold now.

My hands are numb with shock, but I manage to dig my phone out of my purse without dropping either. I don't call Janey. I call Adelaide.

"Hey," I say, grateful that she picks up.

"Hey. Shit, did I mess up? Are we supposed to meet today?"

"No, we said tomorrow. But I wonder if you could meet me anyway?"

"Um, hold on." I hear the muffled sound of her hand over the phone's mic. And, oh shit, the voice that answers her is Jude. I'd know that low, rumbling accent anywhere, even with Adelaide trying for some half assed privacy. She couldn't have hit mute? Then again, maybe he's kept his mouth shut. She might not know there's any reason to keep Jude and me apart.

Which would be worse? Her knowing everything, or us having to go day by day through the rest of the year with *What happened between you and Jude?* as an unspoken question between us? Again that idea of getting reassigned jumps to mind. It's sounding damn reassuring right now.

Yet I called her in a crisis. I don't understand it, but I go with it.

A rustle and rasp, then she's back. "Sure. How about an hour? You'll have to reserve a rehearsal room, though."

"Why?"

"Because I keep forgetting to show up when I do. They don't trust me anymore."

"That's why you have a mentor," I say, trying for a joke despite the icy lances in my throat.

"Same reason Jude has a secretary. So he won't forget his head when he goes into meetings, let alone his notes."

"I don't believe that." My voice is quiet.

"No?" Her curiosity is like a megaphone in my ear. She shushes someone—obviously Jude. "Why do you say that?"

"Because he knows exactly what he's doing. All the time."

Adelaide's laugh is that Tinker Bell sound again. It's so pretty and light despite the burdens that life has layered underneath her outward playfulness. "Oh, honey," she says, her drawl an extra layer of thick. "You've got it *so* wrong. I'll see you in sixty. Text me the room number, 'kay?"

Then she's gone. Brandon's half eaten cheeseburger looks even worse, if that's possible. I gather my things and try not to think about Adelaide's words. I try not to make sense of them or read into them, but isn't that what we do? We're here in college, trapped in a bubble that looks like real life until you stroll off campus and see how people really live. I keep forgetting, although Jude never did.

Maybe Brandon had that much right. I'm not brainwashed, and I know I've been really lucky with my foster parents, but I'm losing perspective here. I don't go home at night to eat dinner with Clair and John. I don't see how tired Clair is after being on her feet all day, working as a pediatric nurse at a children's hospital. I don't see how John's hair is turning gray, slowly, as he nears his thirtieth year with a manufacturing supply company. Those things used to ground me. I was constantly in touch with the outside world, even while I devoted myself to my music at the satellite campus.

Now I'm in a fish tank. The biggest financial decision I've made since being here was helping Janey buy that quilt. I'll probably talk to Opal tonight—she sure as hell needs to know who she's dealing with—then relive that drama by filling Janey in with all the details.

No wonder Jude made such a distinction between his life and mine. He's out there every day, earning God knows how much money because of his decisions—and he risks losing just as much with those same decisions. My big choice this morning? Whether it was going to rain and should I bring an umbrella. It's pouring outside, so I called that one wrong. For Jude to make a wrong call could mean lost jobs and angry shareholders and negative press.

There was no way he and I could ever be together. Dating. Or whatever fanciful notions I'd let creep into my head and heart. He was right to keep me in the dark. The literal dark.

But could he have been right without it hurting so much?

I need to vent. I need piano keys beneath my fingers and pedals beneath my feet. I shoulder my bag, wipe a surprising sheen of tears off my cheeks, and leave the restaurant.

Jude and I . . .

We could've had a really amazing time. If I'd been able to keep it simple, I could've walked away smiling, knowing he'd treated me to an experience few women ever knew: how to be slowly, surely, completely seduced.

That was the problem. His version of seduction had felt too real. He'd made it way too easy to imagine becoming his one and only.

~ TWENTY-SIX ~

Some things, you have to wait for. In this case, Adelaide and I are sitting on the floor in Dixon Hall, outside the line of rehearsal rooms. A few are free on the floor below, but they're not equipped with pianos.

"I guess trying to reserve a room at a moment's notice is easier said than done," Adelaide said, smiling amiably. She's filing her nails although her manicure looks perfect. She's wearing so many bangles that I wonder if she'll take them off when she plays. Or if she even plans to play. This was my idea, after all. "It seems pretty spontaneous for you. No offense."

I don't say anything. Maybe she takes that as a reason to elaborate.

"I mean, you don't come across as a spontaneous person. I bet that night you played at Yamatam's is the most outrageous thing you've ever done."

"Outrageous? Was that it?"

I smile at the word to hide what I'm really thinking. I've done a lot worse, and a lot bolder. What happened between me and Jude in his car—*that* was outrageous. If someone put a gun to my temple and made me choose which was more life changing, I'd wind up headless.

"Sounded outrageous, anyway. You floored the room. Is that what you'll perform for the Fall Finish?"

"Maybe," I say, obviously hedging. "That was all improv. I'm still trying to make sense of it."

And try to expunge Jude from every note.

That isn't working.

"Well, you should. It'll blow away the stodgies."

"That's part of the problem. The stodgies. My music isn't for everyone."

"Bull puckey," she says, laughing. "Your music is for anyone who has ears. It's not *polite*, but who wants to sit through eighteen half-assed variations on the fourth movement of Beethoven's Fifth? That's as bold as the boldest of them will be. And every stodgy will see right through it. You're going to hit them with a baseball bat and they'll love it."

"I really don't think so." I shake my head. "People like polite. And refined."

"That's the thing, girly." She tucks her nail file away, leans her head against the shellacked cinderblock wall, and turns to eye me. "People think they want refined until they jerk out of a stupor with a bit of drool on their chin. If you get hired by one of these ensembles someday, sure, you'll be playing Beethoven's Fifth. But that won't be what catches their attention in an audition."

I try to believe her words. I do. But something about me is so encased in Teflon that they're just sounds. The melody of her drawling accent is what gets through, not her advice. Playing it safe is the safest thing. Besides, if I rip myself open and show people what I've been hiding all these years . . . then what? I'll get a smattering of applause but still be ripped open. The best I can hope for then is a polite rejection and the strength to hold it together until I find someplace private to cry.

I'm feeling edgy and awkward. After the encounter with Brandon, I'm still in a mild state of shock. Now, talking shop with Adelaide, I'm constantly sorting her from Jude, Jude from her. They look similar, with wide smiles that can come out of nowhere. Adelaide's bleach-blonde locks look great on her, which adds a welcome contrast to his caramel-tipped dark brown hair. Although hazel, she has the intensity of his eyes— dark and unflinching in how she looks at the world. Privilege, maybe? Or just the way she's processed the loss of her parents?

"Ugh," she says with a sigh. "We've been waiting so *long*. How long does it normally take?"

"Blocks of one hour. We have ten minutes left. You *do* practice, don't you? Or will I have to take sides with the professors and chastise you?"

She sticks her tongue out. "Don't you start. Normally I practice at Jude's house."

"Oh?"

"He's got the best piano *ever*. It's on the top floor of the mansion. I don't know how they got it up there. I was stuck at boarding school."

That's a lot for me to take in at once. Mansion. Boarding school. Playing piano in Jude's house.

"Where did you go for school?"

"Here in New Orleans. I was barely sixteen when my parents . . ." She looks away. "You know."

"Yeah." I restrain the urge to touch her, somehow, just to say that I *do* know. It's not just a platitude from me.

"Anyway, I started running wild. It was messy. I'm . . ." Pausing again, she stops to dig a lip gloss out of her purse. It smells of marshmallow cream. "I'm lucky I made it through without needing rehab or hiring a nanny. Although Jude would say I'm still playing Russian roulette."

"I think that's an exaggeration." I decline to mention Dr. Saunders. "What turned you around?"

"More like *who*. I hated him for him, sorta for the same reason I hate how nosy he is now. Not that I can blame him sometimes. But I blame him plenty when I want to have fun. That's college, right? The freedom to have a little fun?"

She exhales shakily, in a way that takes the gusto out of her challenging words. "When our parents died, Jude had just finished business school. Dad left him in charge—some shareholder thing built into the works when he incorporated. If Jude had finished business school, and the worst happened, he'd take over. Twenty-four years old and boom, suddenly he was head of a multibillion-dollar company. I don't know how he did it and stayed sane. Well, relatively. And with me, to boot."

To take on that burden at such a young age . . . I shiver with the need to apologize to Jude, although I can't figure out what for. Doesn't that just suck when it comes to arguments? I can't remember when he and I went from *Let's go get a hotel room* to *The end*.

"He decided I needed stability," she continues. "And that I needed a keeper. Instead of moving the company headquarters to New York like all the board members wanted—really, we were kinda oddballs for still being based in Louisiana—he said no. Kept it right here. Fought for it. That way he and I could still be home. I didn't need to change schools. He didn't need to leave the mansion, although I've been telling him to sell that place for years. It's like living in a crypt with our parents."

She shudders, then rubs her hands together. "Anyway, enough sad sack Addie. Now you can tell me about you. I'm super curious." With that conspiratorial smile of hers, she bumps my shoulder. "Jude is too. I swear, other than how to rein me in, I can't remember seeing him this worked up over a puzzle that wasn't based on opportunity costs and PE ratios."

He's been talking about me to Adelaide? Before or after how things ended?

"Nothing to tell," I say evenly.

If I was inclined to tell her anything, I'd only be playing a game of telephone with her and Jude. I don't want him to know anything more about me than he's already pried out. And if I thought our age difference was a barrier to being more serious, I can't imagine what my past would do to any second chance with him.

Jude's parents: paragons, lost too soon.

My parents: menaces, not gone soon enough.

"All right, fine." Adelaide stands and offers me a hand. "I'm only letting you off the hook because we're up."

A slim boned young man with slightly hunched shoulders is clutching his portfolio, leaving rehearsal room number one. He hurries past us without looking. God, do I look that with-drawn and scared? What's scary is to realize that might be the case.

If so, why did Jude notice me in the first place? A jest, maybe, to begin with. Not later, though. I know he'd been perfectly serious about making that deal with me. What I couldn't know then—and knew now—is what craving more of his attention would do to me.

Thinking about him too much, with no relief.

The piano room is cool, as always. I'm gratified to see Adelaide strip down. She means business too. She takes off her hundred thousand bangles and even her four-hoops-in-one earrings. She ties her hair back and sheds a knee length sweater that isn't missing a single color from the rainbow. In fact, I think it made up a few colors no one's ever seen before. I do the same, getting rid of my purple jacket and opening my portfolio.

"Ooh, wait," she says. "I forgot to ask. What do you listen to? You know, in your off hours?"

I list a few singers, mostly Florence and Ellie Goulding and Sara Bareilles.

"I thought so. No offense, but you're just the type. Crazy creative on your own, but a little stuck in a rut."

"How can you tell that?"

"Just a guess. Plus, I like showing off my diverse tastes. Jude says it's pretentious, but he still listens to The Killers." She fishes through her giant tote. How she could find an elephant in that giant thing is beyond me, let alone a little flash drive. "This is for you. The Dead Weather, Santigold, Lana Del Rey, Flyleaf, Bastille, Purity Ring, Billie Holiday, Skrillex. Even some old school Reba McEntire and Johnny Cash."

"Country music?"

"Don't knock 'em. Great performers. So . . . listen and take it all in."

I shrug and pocket the drive before spreading my sheaves into place. Unlike that time with Brandon, when I reflexively hid my work, I don't do it now. Not because I want to be open, but because for a few delusional seconds, I forget Adelaide can read every note as easily as a junior high kid reading a baby's board book.

"Whoa," she whispers over my shoulder. "That's come a long way. I'm impressed. But I wanna do something different. I get the feeling you wouldn't have called me if you wanted to practice this. You sounded . . . flustered."

I shrug to readjust the tension between my shoulder blades. "Yeah. A run-in at lunch with a guy I don't like much."

"Tell me who he is and he won't bother you again."

"Is this some *If I tell you, I'd have to kill you* thing?"

"Totally." With a giggle, she looks down at her flowing skirt and unfurls its colors. "I'm *so* the secret-service type."

"He's just a jerk in my building and he's been trying to play me and this other girl at once." I shrug some of the tension out of my shoulders and roll my neck. "Turns out he's a bit psycho. I mean, he got *really* defensive and angry when I called him on it."

"You expected something else?"

I smile to myself, amused by the idea that, yes, I'd expected something else, something better from Brandon. Do I think that of everyone . . . without even realizing it?

"Now," she says, her voice surprisingly no-nonsense. "You wanted performance tricks? I have them for you." She sets my sonata aside and replaces it with a single sheet of music. On it is a basic melody and harmony, only twenty-four bars long. Thirty seconds of music, tops. "That's your assignment."

It's elementary. It's something I could've played when I was three. Had my parents realized what a whiz I am with the piano, they'd have used me for stuff other than luring potential marks. Instead my moment of discovery came by chance with a music teacher when I was twelve. Some junior high. Some town. Her name was Mrs. Krevitz and she must've seen what no one else could. She kept me after class one day and sat me at the piano.

"Play," she said.

I was only scared that getting home late would get me in trouble. An hour later, I didn't care. I had a gift . . . and a secret. Being raised by two people who knew what it was to keep secrets, I hid mine well. I only spent a few months with Mrs. Krevitz before I was jerked away again, but they were profoundly formative months.

I saw a glimmer of who I could be. Sometimes it was empowering when my secret gave me strength. Sometimes it was this heavy *thing* in my head. My living with my folks would've been like Mozart working in a coal mine.

"It's for kids," I say, my throat rusted. "Besides, who's the mentor here?"

"It's for kids." Adelaide nods, fake earnest. "You're the mentor and doing a great job. I'm serious! Here I am giving a damn about music, without a bar-sized audience and no spotlight. I'd have only asked you to do this tomorrow."

"Play this?"

"Yup."

She sits on a chair she pulls close to the bench, wearing a satisfied expression I don't get. Whatever. Let the Villars sister get what she wants. I glance at the sheet music, then press the appropriate keys. The end.

Adelaide grins unexpectedly. "That's our starting point," she says. "What is—shit, that intro science class I'm in. What's that called?"

"The control group?"

Snapping her fingers, Adelaide says, "That's the one. That was your control. That was you playing twenty-four boring bars as boringly as possible. Nice job." She leans back in her chair. "But that's not your problem, remember?"

"I have a problem?" It's a token reply.

"Yeah, Miss Stage Fright. You don't know how to work a crowd. You know how to *move* people, but you don't know how to harness that skill—like an untrained superhero or something."

"That sounds just like me."

"You're a goosey," Adelaide says. "Now play it again, but do it trying to make me laugh."

"No way." I shake my head. It's all defensive. I know it even as I do it, but I don't want to try any sort of playacting with Adelaide, when we're just getting to know each other—and in the neutral ground of a rehearsal room. "That's . . ."

She leans forward on her chair and props her chin in her hands. "That's what? Childish? Silly? Or . . . No, I got it. You think it's a waste of time."

I look down at the keys. With my hair pinned up, she can probably see my blush. The bright rehearsal room isn't as brightly lit as a stage, but I feel that exposed. Only, I'm not a performer; I'm being interrogated.

"That's all you want? Just to make you laugh?"

Before Adelaide even answers, I think of Jude's smile. Nothing about him was simple, and I sure as hell didn't know how to make him laugh. Otherwise I would've done it every minute we were together, just to see his full-on smile and hear that rich, full timbre. He'd look at me with affection and surprise. . . .

And I'm playing. Those—yes, childish; yes, silly—notes tinkle out from my fingers. Without Adelaide needing to say so, I try again. I try again. I know it's not right yet. I'm still too stiff. I wrestle with those scant few bars. I want to beat them. Win against them.

That idea makes me laugh. *Me.* Sitting on the bench. The idea of me wanting to win against a few scratches of ink on paper, and the absurdity of this situation, and the three of us locked like mental patients in a padded cell, and just . . . God, all of it.

Adelaide giggles, but that's like saying a twister is a light breeze. She's her own whirlwind of pure energy. Her drawl is the only part of her that's syrupy slow by comparison.

I gust out an exhale that feels like expelling fire. Then I suck in something very near to . . . success. Her reaction is great, but I want more. I want the hard-core junkie stuff. She seems to know it, just like she knew I needed this ridiculous exercise.

"Try again," Adelaide urges, smiling brightly. "Do it intentionally."

She's right. The first time was me being caught by the surprise of my own thoughts. As if practicing scales rather than performance technique, I do as she says and play the piece one more time. I do it with gusto, a bit of cheekiness, some saucy bubbles in my blood. This time Adelaide laughs and gives a little clap. His eyes have tipped into half moons that remind me so much of Jude that it nearly kills my sense of triumph.

"Okay." Adelaide's all business again. "Make me cry. Same notes. Be *sure* this time. Don't guess. You know this piece inside out now. Know it well enough to find the cracks. The places that'll twist my heart."

I do. Intentionally. I own these twenty-four bars. They're mine to mold. I think about the bad kind of crying—my mother's face the night before she died, her haggard features, her sunken eyes. But I don't let those memories overwhelm the pressure of each finger against each key. Then there's the good kind of crying, and how happy I was the night of the Joshua Bell concert. Clair and John looked so fine and lovely in their dress clothes. My own personal angels.

I'm in charge now. I play it three times, each slower, each more like a funeral procession walking toward a gravesite in the rain, with shoes soaking wet to match tearful faces.

When I finish, Adelaide wipes her eyes, looking at the back corner of the room, completely distant—but not unaffected. This is . . . guarding herself.

"Wow," she says at last. She stands and shakes her fingers out, like getting blood back to frozen limbs. "You're forbidden from doing that again. But are you feeling it now? Control? How to work us both?"

I nod, speechless at what's happening.

"Believe me," she continues, "it's easier with an audience. Then emotions feed off each other. Make one person laugh, and others follow. One sniffle turns another person's sniffle into tears. You just gotta pry inside and the whole thing ripples out."

I swallow thickly, my legs restless until I stop tapping my toes against the pedals. "That's what you did at Yamatam's."

"Sure. Just a trick." She smiles, almost self-deprecating. "That's all it is."

"What did you say earlier? *Bull puckey*. I'll play real mentor later and talk you down from that pity-party ledge." I grin to match hers. "Okay, what next?"

From behind me comes the voice I've heard through dark nights of dreaming. "How about Adelaide lets us have a few moments alone?"

Whirling, I find Jude standing in the doorway.

Oh God.

Adelaide smiles at us both, watching, as if she's expecting romantic music to swell out of nowhere. When Jude and I remain rooted, she shrugs slightly, then skips over to give him a hug.

"Hi!"

I start to gather my papers. Although Adelaide appears genuinely surprised by her brother's arrival, she shoots me a warning look. "Don't even think about the fire-alarm thing again," she says.

I glare at Jude. "You told?"

"It was too much fun to keep to myself," he says without apology.

"And I won't tell," Adelaide adds. "You were completely justified after he sneak-attacked you like that."

"Like now?" I'm surprised by the strength in my voice. This was supposed to be my refuge. Now it would always have Jude's impression here, lingering, like how he's become such an integral part of my sonata.

"It was my fault," Jude says casually.

"Honest." Adelaide's words are a whisper near my ear as she gathers her papers. "I didn't invite him. But . . . maybe it's a good thing?" She glances at Jude over her shoulder, where he's standing woodenly. She huffs out a breath. "Or not. Keeley, I hope you don't let him off the hook as easily as I have to."

"You don't have to go," I say.

You're leaving me? He's your brother, but I'm swimming in the deep end here.

"It'll give me more time to get ready for my date tonight."

Jude stiffens. "Not with that professor again."

Adelaide shrugs. She collects her bangles by throwing them in her purse, then slings her sweater over her shoulder. "Don't do anything I wouldn't do!"

She's gone as quickly as I was the first day Jude and I met, out in that same hallway.

~ TWENTY-SEVEN ~

Not looking at him is impossible now.

He's wearing a business suit and carrying a briefcase. He holds himself with the bearing of a young prince. Wide stance. Shoulders braced against the strongest wind. His hair is neatly combed and his expression is flat. I imagine that more than a few lawyers and accountants have stared at that impassive expression and given up. Jude is too powerful. He takes up too much air. Too much space in my head. I can barely feel Middle C beneath my fingertip. I get frustrated, as if the piano is what's abandoned me.

He's there in the full light of the rehearsal room, but I can't see his eyes. He has his head lowered, his arms crossed. Lights that should've lit every feature are angled in such a way that his face is more hidden than exposed. His top lip is highlighted, with the dip at the peak. The end of his nose is visible. How the end of a nose can signal distance—I don't know.

He's a businessman. Almost anonymous.

Yet he's the one who stood up to his board of directors just to keep Adelaide in a stable home and school. He's the one who took on the impossible challenge of heading a multibillion-dollar company—fresh out of business school, his parents barely buried—exceeding all expectations.

That's when I see him as if for the first time, all over again. The night we split, he wore a faded U2 T-shirt and a battered pair of Docs. That was Jude as an average twenty-six-year-old.

This is Jude Deschamps-Villars, CEO.

With Adelaide gone, I have plenty of room to combust privately and not take her down with him. Suddenly, our gazes lock. *Now* I can see his eyes, so dark, so fierce. I can't read his emotions, only his intensity. He's there, but why? To berate me? To tease me? To unnerve me?

He walks to stand at my back. I can smell the wool of his suit, a suit warmed by his body—the body I barely learned to touch and kiss . . . and why is it I can't have more?

Too young.

Too starry-eyed.

Too damaged to hold it together.

Damn. I haven't had a wrong-brain thought that powerful in a long time. It rings true in every corner of my mind and every place in my body—except in my heart.

I am a good person.

I deserve good things.

He leans near, an unconscious echo of how Adelaide stood over me while I waited rigidly on the bench. I can smell more of him now, that hint of expensive cologne and the fresh, masculine fragrance that is simply Jude. The smell of his skin.

"We were working," I manage to say.

"I didn't say the lesson was over." He strokes my hair back from my temple. I'm wordless, motionless, breathless. "Will you play it for me?"

"Do you need a laugh? Some angst? Do you want me to make you angry?"

"No," he says quietly, still petting my temples. "I want you to turn me on."

I'm trying to remember what breathing was like. It must've been nice. "And how am I supposed to do that?"

"I'm not the performer," he says softly.

"Do you want me to perform? Or be truthful?"

He stops touching me and sits on a chair against the wall. His posture remains intimidatingly upright, all powerful grace, but if I knew him better . . . If I knew him better, I'd say he looked exhausted. Under his sunny midday blue eyes are deep circles of fatigue. Because of work?

"Turn me on, sugar," he says, smoldering and daring. "Just you and that piano."

I close the key cover. "I came here to vent to someone who's becoming a friend. And I was here to practice, for real. I'm not playing games. Besides . . ." I shake my head and turn away. I gather my music to keep from trying to read the tea leaves of his expression.

"Besides . . . ?"

"If I'd had any clue what turns you on, I'd have done it already. We'd have gone to a hotel that night, and . . . Never mind. I don't know what you want from me. I haven't from the start." I'm like an opera singer stretching a note too thin, running out of air. "I'm not going to make a worse fool of myself."

The silence between us is a thin sheet of glass. I don't want to move for fear of smashing it. Glass would rain down around us both, but I don't think any would land on Jude Villars.

"Keeley?"

I flinch. He doesn't use my name often. I always notice when he does. It's like a code. *I'm being serious now.* I wish the rest of him were that easy to decipher.

"What?"

"I'm sorry," he says, words low and rumbling. "About our argument. And about how I ended it. It wasn't fair of me."

Spinning faster than thought, I face him dead on. "Then why did you say it? Do you know how something like that sticks? Words last a lot longer than bruises and broken bones."

He frowns, that classic drawing together of masculine brows. His mouth pinches tight.

I'm *so* not finished with him. "You seem to think that just because I'm a virgin and I can't keep up with your head games that I don't know *anything*. Do you want someone fragile, Jude? Keep touching me, jerking me around, telling me to turn you on—then, sure, you'll have a fragile girl at your beck and call. Because I can't keep up." I wipe surprising tears away. "But I don't want to be fragile. If that's the price for being around you, then you need to leave."

With the subtle grace of a big cat predator, he stands. Three strides later, he's beside me on the piano bench, where I'm both numb and raw. He takes my upper arms in his big hands. "I don't want you fragile."

"I feel that way when you're with me. You're in charge. Your pace. I've been so amped up about some of it, and good-terrified about some of it. But there's no way to catch my breath."

I find the strength to look up at him. His eyes are stormy and dangerous, but deep inside, I see a shelter. If I can only run fast enough to reach it . . .

"I want to be your first," he says plainly. My heart jumps, my belly turns to fire, and I know he can feel another flinch. "Before the other night, I never thought about the consequences. About how you'd take it. Or how *I* would. I do have responsibilities in my life, and I wasn't prepared for how you'd fit in that way. I took my mistake in judgment out on you."

He soothes his hands up and down my arms, which are covered in goose bumps.

"I can't trust you," I reply. "Do you see that? I stumbled after you like a blind puppy because I didn't have reason not to. Now I do. You have to know what you're doing. You're overwhelming!"

He barks out a sharp, bitter laugh.

I fling my arms to get free of him. "Start talking, Jude, because you've got a lot of ground to make up. What's so special about me? Forget the piano and all the other pretty words. *Why me?*"

"Same question back to you," he says, his words clipped. "Forget my damn money and my tragic headline life. Why me? Why were you willing to follow me like that? Why did I deserve your trust?"

"I don't know anymore."

Hands in his pockets, he radiates that sexy, so-unfair combination of confident, powerful man and lonely, lost soul. I want to touch him and say it's okay, that I'm sure it was just a miscommunication. Then I can turn myself over to his care and command again. All will be fine and thrilling again. But I can't unlock my jaw to form the words.

I won't.

"You want to know why you?" he asks quietly. "Why you stood out to me like one of those spotlights at the club?"

"Yes."

"Because there's *always* a spotlight on you. You may as well have a neon sign above your head flashing 'Over Here.'"

"You have me confused with someone like your sister."

"Don't tell me my mind, sugar. You're just the opposite of Adelaide. You're so closed off that I want to pry you open and find out what no one else ever has. That's intoxicating." He stops pacing and returns to my home turf—stitting on the piano bench. "You told me that you showed the club all you have. All you are. What did I say?"

"That you didn't believe it."

"Because I don't. I've kissed your lips, but I don't think I've kissed *you*. I could get you stark naked and we could be lovers for months, and it wouldn't matter." He's within inches of me. He brushes his lips across mine. I tingle and jump. "Do you know the biggest fight I've had since my parents died?"

"Adelaide?"

His smile is rueful. "With her? Always. But about her."

"She told me about keeping the headquarters here in New Orleans."

"I figured she'd say something about that. You're turning into the friend I hoped she'd find." Before I can process the pride that blooms beneath my breastbone, he blows a long exhale through his nose. His shoulders are bunched, with his hands fisted on his thighs. "I took a huge chance as a fresh from school kid, and I won. No one has dared go up against me since, except you—you, like a bolt of lightning out of nowhere. From everyone else, it's bow and scrape and *Yes, sir*."

"You won't ever hear me call you sir."

His rueful smile takes on a salacious edge. My body prickles and heats in response. "Good. I don't want you fragile. I want Keeley Chambers." He clears his throat. "I just didn't know how to answer questions about anything outside of . . . the seduction. Not to you. Myself. Anyone. If someone on the board asked me what I'm doing with a college student? *Oh, I'm teaching her how to fuck.* Can you imagine?"

"I don't have to. I'm not anyone on the board." I stare at him—stare and wait. I feel a surge of power when I realize that I'm in charge now. I'm the one to say yes or no. That power burns in my blood, but it doesn't point me to the right answer. "I'm just me. I'm the one you need to convince."

My hands are clasped together at my waist. He takes them in his and tugs them apart. Slowly—God, so slowly—he pulls them up, up, to circle behind his neck. There he lets them rest as he undoes his tie and unfastens two buttons of his dress shirt. "Touch me there. At my nape."

I'm a melty puddle of *guh* before I take my next breath. He's all around me, invading every sense, seeping into my pores and turning all my thoughts toward sex. I could be with him in the way I've never been with a man. His voice is so inviting, so riveting. It's deep swamp voodoo, the way he can bind me without even touching me.

I sink my fingers into his hair and tighten them until my nails scrape his scalp. His arms crisscross my back. I'm pulled flush against his chest. So close now, I can reach even more of his hair, and the skin of his back and his shoulders. He cups my head and angles my mouth to meet his. I'm shocked by taste and heat. My thoughts are burned away like fall leaves in a bonfire.

There's nothing but the feel of Jude beneath my palms, and how masterfully he uses my body against me.

His tongue sweeps over mine, pebbled and sweet as if he's been chewing cinnamon gum. I can't get enough. I need more, tipping my head, fighting his hand to find the angle *I* need. He lets up just enough, smiling briefly, until we're kissing again. I swirl. I clutch. He's got me. I know that somewhere—somewhere deep and in charge of protecting me from danger. He has me in his arms, and despite all good sense, I feel safe there. I go practically limp. Only with my mouth and hands do I keep questing, keep searching for more of what he can give me.

He slides one hand down toward my ass, but pauses at the waistband of my jeans. I moan and nod my approval. But instead of simply grabbing my ass, he forces his fingers between skin and denim, pushing, hooking my lace thong. Even that isn't enough. He undoes the top button of my jeans and dives again. I'm filled with the hot, pulsing taste of him and trapped by curiosity—his and mine—as he finds the bare skin of my ass. I gasp into his mouth. He returns my gasp with a moan.

"I—"

That was me. One syllable. At least it's a start, because there's no more to say.

"You're still content with just the back of my neck," he whispers against my mouth.

I blink, then flex my fingers. Sure enough, they haven't strayed beyond what I can reach behind his head—nape, hairline, the muscles along the base and column of his throat. "Seems a shame," I manage to squeak.

"So that's *not* all you want?"

I shake my head. He gives my ass another long, languorous squeeze, pulling up, fitting me against his pelvis, testing me. Now I know how ready he is. If he reached down a few more inches, between my legs, he'd know I'm turned on too.

"That's not all I want."

"Then tell me," he says. "Tell me, Keeley."

"I want to forget how that night ended, because I want to trust you again. Fresh and new. I want to know that if you take me home right now, you'll be amazing to me. But that won't be enough."

"So we're not talking about a onetime deal here."

"No," I say, my tongue tingling, feeling thick and hard to manage. Too much of me is screaming, *More, more, more. All of you. As long as you'll have me.*

No, that's not right. I'm screaming, *Forever.*

Little-girl fantasies. Fantasies of never being afraid.

I try to veer my thoughts back to the physical. When it comes to Jude and losing my virginity, I know I'll be protected. He'll do exactly what he promised.

"You have to give me an answer, sugar. We have to be clear."

I find the courage to say what I need to, because he's right. I need to know going in just how much I'm putting on the line. "You're the one who said we aren't dating."

He finds my stiff knuckles and kisses them. His earnest eyes hold mine, still and calm. "I should've introduced you to that lawyer and his wife. I'm sorry I hurt you. And what I said—hell, I didn't mean it."

"Thank you," I whisper.

"As for dating, I think we got it all backward. We agreed on a seduction, but not how to share a beer in public. I'm supposedly the big bad grown-up." He shrugs, then smiles the most self-deprecating smile of all time. "Instead, I was an ass. I was probably a coward. Until I screwed up the ending, that was one of the best nights out I've ever had. Kissing, teasing, talking, laughing—you gave me a little of everything, and I never knew where I stood."

"*You* didn't?"

"I'm floundering too, sugar." He rakes his hands through his hair, way more angrily than I'd done when stroking his nape. "Every day, I put on one of these damn suits and see a fraud in the mirror. I'm blustering my way through, trying not to fuck up Adelaide's life and lose everything our parents worked toward. You called me overwhelming. It's more like *overwhelmed.*"

"I don't believe that."

"Then I met you," he continues. "I've been thinking about you, sleepless over you. I made something complicated out of something pure and full of potential." He draws in a breath. "I never know what to expect with you. You have me so tied in knots. And for the first time in a very long time, that feels like a good thing."

Protest bubbles on my tongue, but I'm too busy reveling in the idea that I tie this amazing man in knots.

We're in this together.

"So call it seduction," he says. "Call it dating. Call it spending as much time together as we can and seeing what happens. All I know is . . . I want no regrets."

When I finally speak, it's with a throaty voice I don't recognize as my own. But it's true—the only truth I'm one hundred percent certain I believe. "No regrets."

~ TWENTY-EIGHT ~

Apparently "no regrets" starts in a horse-drawn carriage through the Garden District. We're wrapped up in each other, emotionally and physically, as a new sort of tension builds between us. One storm has passed. A new one is gathering, despite clear early evening skies.

"Tonight's the night, isn't it?"

I don't know where I get the courage to say it out loud, but I do and the look on his face reminds me of the power I have. *That's* why I said it. His eyebrows shoot up, and he clears his throat. "If you want it to be."

"Of course I do."

"Believe me, sugar. There's no 'of course' with you."

I grin, then kiss the hollow under his jaw. Soon we're kissing for real, with the rustling willows and the steady clop-clop of horse hooves as our soundtrack. I make him ditch his suit coat. He dares me to reciprocate by taking off the sheer black blouse I wear over a strappy camisole, which I flat-out refuse. Instead, I shed my purple jacket while he takes way too many liberties over my leggings, with his hands roving beneath my houndstooth skirt. Not that I stop him. The driver does his job, guiding us through the most picturesque streets of New Orleans and keeping his eyes front and center.

We wind up at a nondescript corner, where what must've once been mansions push right up to the slim sidewalks. Now they're hotels and restaurants.

"Your choice," he says. "Cheap authenticity, medium-priced touristy stuff, or damn expensive?"

I laugh. "Who's paying?"

"*Moi*. No Dutch dates for us. If tonight's the night, I want to treat you like a princess."

"And if tonight doesn't happen to be the night, mister?"

He grins and nuzzles where my sheer top brushes my collarbones. "What, the carriage ride isn't enough for you?"

"Not when I'm starving and you can't keep your hands off me."

His smile is out in full force—the one I can't resist. I can't even resist touching it. With light fingertips, I trace his lips and the near-dimples that dot the smile lines that dig into his narrow cheeks.

"Don't move," I say. "And keep smiling."

"So bossy."

"That's what my roommate says."

That only makes him chuckle a little more, smile a little more. I lean up to kiss those teasing dimples, one on each side, before diving in for a completely mind-warping war of tongues and lips and even a nip of gentle teeth. We break away laughing. I think it's a release. Still a release. We came so close to losing everything, but

Jude made it right and I was brave enough to trust him again. This is how it's supposed to be.

I shoot down all of the protests that come to mind. This *isn't* how it's supposed to be. He's supposed to know who I am. I can't ever let that happen, or magical rides and beautiful kisses will disappear. *He'll* disappear. Jude Villars could have his pick of just about anyone. Why would he stay with a girl whose past is as shady as these tree-dappled streets?

Taking his head in my hands, I kiss him even harder, until he moans. The driver could've heard that one. I don't care. I want to get lost with Jude as my only guide. He thinks I'm wonderful, and nothing will jeopardize that—not when I'm finally beginning to believe it. Parts of me *are* wonderful. The rest can stay hidden deep down. They don't deserve the fading light of sunset.

We wind up disheveled and grinning like cats in the cream by the time we reach our destination. Apparently he'd already decided on "damn expensive," because the combo restaurant/hotel is absolutely gorgeous. Only when I inhale the amazing scents coming from inside do I realize I haven't eaten since that disastrous lunch with Brandon. *Ugh.* I need a meal do-over. This looks like the perfect place.

He helps me down from the carriage and discreetly pays the driver, who winks. I dip my head to hide a blush, then smooth the ends of my hair. I hope I look okay. I've been practicing all afternoon. Jude, by contrast—despite how tired he appears—is a god come down from on high to dine with us commoners. He has the jacket slung over one shoulder. His tie and collar are artfully mussed, and his hair just a little wild. His expression is what pulls it all together. He's amused, confident, and strides with my

111111111

111111111

arm tucked in his, as if the whole city belongs to him. No, the whole world.

I'm intoxicated.

"Stop fidgeting," he says under his breath. I realize I'm tugging at my skirt and still fussing with my hair. "You look fantastic."

"I like the sound of that."

He leans in closer. "You look like you've been doing some very heavy petting with a guy you can't get enough of."

"God, I forgot how arrogant you can be." But we're both grinning. Once upon a jazz club, I took that attitude seriously. Now I know the difference between the ego he hurls at other people like a hundred-mile-an-hour fastball, and the teasing he uses against me. He's making me so excited. I could pace with how much energy he's stoking in me—a close second to my nerves.

"But here's the deal," he says as we follow a tuxedoed maître d'. "You have to try everything I order."

"I know Louisiana food. You're not going to scare me off with jambalaya."

"I don't even think jambalaya is on the menu here."

The maître d' seats me, then hands over menus and the wine list. What drink Jude chooses for us—no clue. It's in French, which rolls off his tongue like honey. The maître d' nods, appearing impressed, and leaves us to ourselves.

"Do you speak French?"

Jude shakes his head. "I can pronounce it N'awlins style. But the lessons never stuck. Addie's good, though. She claims it's like learning piano, just patterns and rules."

"What did you say to that?"

He leans in, where candlelight from the little floating votive at the center of the table adds depth and drama to his features. "That I don't play piano either."

"She's wonderful, you know. Adelaide."

"Sure she is. Been playing since she was two or three."

"No," I say, spreading the napkin over my lap. "As a person. I'm really glad she and I were partnered."

An easiness settles over his expression, and a placid smile over his mouth. "Good. I'm glad." Then he huffs out a tight breath. Bouncing from one side to the other is a little disorienting. "Now if only I could get her away from that damn pervert of a professor."

"She'll come around."

"Before it's too late? I don't know about that."

It's my turn to shrug. "Maybe you're not giving her enough credit. I think she's hypnotized by him. I know what that's like."

"I'm not married with a kid on the way."

"No, but I don't think that matters when hearts get involved."

"Can we talk about something else?" he asks, voice tense.

I take his hand—which has curled into a fist—and unlock his fingers until he twines them with mine. "No problem. You can go back to telling me how great I look."

"Mouthwatering, sugar."

"That's just your stomach talking." I finally open the menu, only to be confronted with about a hundred French words. "Let me guess. You're doing the ordering?"

"Yup," he says with a smile that banishes his brief flirtation with darkness.

"And I have to try everything, even if I don't know what it is."

"Yup."

The restaurant is high end, for sure. Chandeliers that I bet are made from real crystal hang over sets of four tables. Grecian statues stand watch over wide, wide windows that overlook the lush Garden District street below. Fresh flowers are probably wasted, because the smells from the kitchen are overpowering, especially when I'm ready to taste everything, try everything.

That means Jude too. He looks at me like *I'm* the main course. He promised foreplay, and this feels like part of it. He's seducing me in the slowest, most courtly way possible. He's making me laugh and making me wait and making me adore him in ways that are dangerous to think about. So I don't. I enjoy the moment, especially when a waiter comes to take our order. More of that delicious French. I have no idea what I'll be eating, but I'm convinced it'll be mind-blowing. And if it's not, I get to watch Jude when his eyes roll closed over flavor that leaves him floored.

I want to affect him that way.

"So . . . what do we get?"

"Let's call it an assortment," he says playfully. "Get used to that, sugar. Has anything changed? About tonight?"

"Full steam ahead."

A dangerous grin shapes his mouth into playful wickedness. "You want to kiss me again, don't you?" He laughs. "Oh, but your blush is precious, Keeley."

"Quit."

"No way. Admit it. You're racking your brain to think of some way to set me on edge too." He lifts my hand and brushes his lips across my knuckles. "You hide so much from so many people, but you want to be memorable to me. That's gotta be quite a contradiction in your head. A constant war. I wonder which will win the day . . . and the night."

"You think you're so badass." Laughing, I untuck my sheer chiffon shirt and, there in front of whoever's watching, I whip it over my head. I ruffle my hair before smoothing it back into place, then hand the shirt to Jude. I'm chilly, which probably explains why he's trying really hard to be inconspicuous about splitting his attention between my eyes and my chest. "You said you like small breasts," I whisper.

"Mean, mean woman."

"No. Generous, generous woman."

"Mmm, very much so."

I tilt my head. "This is a pretty posh place, Jude. What would happen if you met one of your business colleagues here, and here I am, all sweat-cooled from practice and wearing this camisole?"

"I'd introduce you, but I wouldn't stand up to do it."

A little part of me shrinks down, surprised that after the foul air we cleared, he would still hold something back. "Okay."

"Keeley? Look at me."

I do. His Caribbean blue eyes are shining with mischief and secrets. "I wouldn't stand up because I don't want the whole restaurant to know how turned on I am."

I sputter into my napkin. Not the most graceful. Then I grin at him from the top edge of the starched cotton. "You're mean too."

"Just following your lead, sugar."

The food arrives, but it seems like a complete distraction. The waiter is polite. He keeps his reaction to my change of attire down to a minimum. One appetizer is some sort of dome that has oysters and bacon, along with—to my surprise—absinthe from Switzerland, all under a pastry crust. Oh my God, it's amazing. Then there's gumbo, but not like the gumbo they serve on campus. That's like saying a steak from a waffle house is the same as a filet mignon. This is flavorful, not just hot. There's turtle soup too, which is the one dish where I hesitate.

Jude shakes his head. "Everything. An assortment, remember?"

"You're not just talking about the food."

"No way. If you're giving me the whole night, sugar, you're getting everything I have."

I shiver. "Can I be honest and say that sounds a little scary?"

"I made you promises. I intend to keep each one." He nods to the bowl in front of me. "Now give it a try."

"And what, I'll thank you for it afterward?"

"Absolutely." He's the most handsome, most infuriating, most incredible man I've ever seen when he unleashes his smile—all amazement and sensuality. "And I'll thank you."

~ TWENTY-NINE ~

We don't go to the hotel adjacent to the restaurant. I'm glad, even though he didn't bring it up and I didn't say anything one way or the other. Is he so good at reading what I need? That's the best of daunting and wonderful, both.

Besides, I really want to see where he lives. I want to sink beneath his weight, onto a bed and into thick blankets that smell of him. A hotel for my first time sounded bold and even exciting when he brought it up before, although I'd been wary of him hiding things. Maybe we both need this to be . . . intimate. As private as possible.

That's not an issue when he pulls the Mercedes into a crescent driveway that fronts a Victorian era mansion. I force my mouth closed. The façade is draped in ivy, and two great willows sway on either side of a massive wraparound porch. Twin columns stretch up from the top step to a second-story veranda that looks like it borders only one room. One *big* room. French doors lead out to it. I assume it must be his room. The view over a quarter mile of sweeping grounds would be magnificent. It seems like we drove forever to get here, but the grand old house is probably only ten minutes outside of New Orleans proper. Getting here is like driving back in time. Arriving is like lighting dynamite.

No more waiting. No more holding his free hand as he drove casually, confidently away from the city.

Lots of things are coming together now, although I can't honestly say, *No more time to back out.* Something deep and trusting tells me I could change my mind and, in an instant, Jude would take it like a gentleman. Tonight, I'm willing to believe he'll give me whatever I want. That's heady. It's probably un-healthy.

I'm thinking too much.

He takes the keys from the ignition and meets me on my side of the car. He's still wearing that astonishing suit. I can hardly stand it. That the collar is scrunched up and his slight curls are tangled at his hairline makes my insides giddy and hot. We've done a lot, compared to what I've ever dared.

We've done hardly anything at all.

"I can't keep up," I whisper, knowing I said it in the practice room and I'll probably think it another thousand times.

He bends his knees a little, so that he's standing at my height. "We're here with no regrets."

Not a question. And I have no doubts when I reply. "You're right. No regrets."

"Do you trust me with this? I need to know, Keeley."

"Why is it so important to you?"

"Because when you say you can't keep up, I don't know how to behave. Slow down? Press on and think you're just psyching yourself out?" He presses against me, enfolds me, breathes against the hollow beneath my jaw. "If you try to catalog everything and make sense of it all as it's happening—I know you'll try—you won't be able to relax. If you can't relax . . ." He shrugs slightly. "It's just better if you can. That means trusting me."

"But . . ." I swallow when burying my face against his chest. I find a bare place revealed by the open buttons and nuzzle. "How will you know what I want or like or . . . anything?"

"I enjoy making women happy. You probably don't want to hear that right now, because it means there've been women before you, but it's true. I already know the sound of your breathing when you're getting turned on. I know how you forget to touch me when I'm touching you. That tells me you're engrossed in what I'm doing."

"I don't mean to, you know, *neglect* you."

He pulls back. The lone wrought-iron lamp that hangs from the second story, down toward the front door, spreads warm golden light from one side of his face to another. He's light and shadow this time, except I can see every delicate lash and the purely masculine confidence of his smile. "Believe me, sugar, I won't let you. Come on."

He leads me up the steps and into the foyer. The mansion's subtle fragrance reminds me of him—mint, sandalwood, cinnamon, lemon oil. There's a deeper musk too, as if the swamps out back refuse to be polite and hide away. This is a wild place, briefly tamed. I glance at Jude's angular profile. He's the same way.

I expect he'll take me up to the room with the veranda and the astonishing view, but we veer softly to the left of the massive

front staircase. It looks like something out of a movie set. It's
not. He *lives* here. Like seeing the suit, I'm hit again with the differences between us. I live in half a shoe box with Janey.

But it must get lonely here.

The room we enter—there's no mistaking it's Jude's. The bed
is an heirloom four-poster with a hunter green comforter. A pair
of leather recliners take up space against the right wall, with a
wrought iron and glass table between them. A low dresser of
dark oak stands opposite, with a flat screen hanging just above
it. Wood paneling adds to the richness of texture and scent, and
keeps the room dark and intimate even when he turns on his
nightstand light. This is a space for a man to rest.

The nightstand is that same wrought iron and glass, covered
to toppling with business magazines and notebooks with
creased pages and red ink scrawls. He lifts the whole bundle and
flops it onto one of the recliners. He stops moving, his neck
angled toward the bed.

I don't know what to do. He said to trust him, so I do. I wait.
I wait, even though it's one of the strongest tests of willpower
I've ever managed. I want to jump on him and follow him
straight down onto the bed.

"Undress," he says quietly.

I must've made a noise—God, I can't tell anymore—because
he lifts his eyes. Our gazes meet. He's not haunted. I wouldn't go
that far. He's in a deep place. Only then, idiot me, do I realize the
truth. What I'm seeing is pure lust.

It's happened to me before, but this is the first time I've felt it
so suddenly, so purely: I go wet. Totally. The hotness in my belly
turns liquid and slides down, down. I'm stunned, really. I didn't
know it could happen that quickly, especially with just a look. He

could shove me against the wall and take me, right now, and I'd be ready.

I'm so *not* ready, in my head, but my body is saying, *Bring it on.*

"If I repeat myself, sugar, I won't give you a choice about how to do it. I'll strip you how I want." He looks me up and down, devouring me as surely as if he used his mouth. "Undress."

Part of me is terrified. *Tell me I shouldn't be!* This is Jude, with his intensity on steroids. Maybe he's thought about throwing me back on the bed too, and this is his way of keeping it . . . calm?

Completely not the right word.

Gentle. He's trying to be gentle. My first time. He's trying to honor his promises.

My hands are shaking as I pull the camisole up over my head. I grab my ponytail holder in the same move and shake my hair loose.

I reach to undo my jeans, but he cuts his jaw to the side. "No. Your bra."

I'll have regrets if I let this stay totally one-sided. So I ask why.

"There's something so damn sexy about a topless woman still wearing jeans."

I reach behind my back and grab the hook-and-eye closure. "You're a guy," I say, smiling some. "You're going to have to explain that one."

"Bra and panties." His gravelly words are softened by his accent. It's getting thicker with everyone sentence. "Might as well be a bikini. That's not so special. But half dressed? Clothes coming off? That's intimate."

I think I get his meaning and decide to brave it out. I drop the bra to the floor. It *is* intimate. I'm bared from the waist up,

for him alone—his relentless eyes. I arch my back, feeling languorous and sexy.

My tiny surge of confidence grows when I take off my jeans,
then my panties. He stares at me like I'm a goddess. I could be
one, for him.

He undresses without fanfare, but I take in every move as if
he's a man in slow motion. Tie slips free. Buttons unfasten.
Zipper slides low. I'm burning up with each newly exposed inch
of smooth, golden skin. The nightstand light accentuates his
masculine curves and planes. High, strong muscles gleam. The
shadows between them are deeper.

He slides his hand into his briefs and slips the waistband
over his erection. The briefs slip to the floor.

I can't breathe. Speak. Swallow.

But I can stare.

He's . . . big. I'm liquid, eager, but the last scraps of fear won't
fly away.

"Come here."

I obey without hesitation, when I would've sworn movement was beyond me. He's a vortex, or a planet with its own
powerful orbit. He's gravity and the tide. There's no denying any
force of nature that powerful. Jude is one of them.

He stops me with hands on my hips. I flinch, then laugh—a
bubble of release. He smiles indulgently. I love that grin. It's
nearly the smirk I first saw on his thin, perfectly shaped lips, but
there's no malice behind it. Just a shared moment. I can feel it.
He's sharing this amazement with me.

Surely, confidently, he pulls me nearer by slow degrees until
his erection presses flat against my stomach. Oh my God, it's so
hot. And hard. It juts between our bodies in a way that almost

makes me panic. My heart freaks out and starts some crazy rhythm that *isn't* rhythm. He loops an arm around my low back, holding me there, forcing me to feel his pulse where it radiates from our exquisite contact.

He tips my chin up to meet his eyes. "Now you have proof. How much I want you. Are you still nervous?"

"Yes."

"And you still trust me—here at least?"

"Yes."

He places his hand flat between my breasts and presses, urging me to bow back against his supporting arm. He finds one nipple with his mouth. I gasp as wet heat circles and flicks. I never knew I could be so sensitive. Every nerve is made of electricity—especially there, where he sucks deeper. My other nipple is just as sensitive, as are the slight swells under each breast and the hollows above both collarbones. He plays my upper body like an instrument made for his firm lips.

I'm moving now. Shaking. Trying to get closer. He tightens his hold on my lower back, then slips down to cup my ass. His hand is almost big enough to span both cheeks in one firm grip.

"I could slide into you," he rasps against my throat. "Any other time, any other moment, like this—and I will. Do you believe I could hold on to you? That we wouldn't even need a bed?"

"Yes." I'm surprised at my calm, no matter the fireworks his words set off in my imagination. "But tonight I want the bed."

"Yes, ma'am." He turns me in his arms and lowers me down. Just like I'd pictured, I'm surrounded by the scent of his linens, even as he hovers over me. "You're going to drive me crazy."

"That's a good thing."

"A very good thing." He tosses me a crooked grin. "Now open your knees."

I'm beyond shock, and beyond being shocked. Or so I think. The light in his eyes is as electric as I feel. His face is surrounded by ruffled hair, with each strand gilded by lamplight. I give in completely. My body goes limp on a sweet exhale of pure relief. I let my knees part so that Jude Villars can have his way with me.

~ THIRTY ~

How can anything feel this amazing? How do I still have brains enough to notice tiny details? His nails are blunt, and the left side of his mouth quirks higher when he smiles at me. Maybe because I'm so overheated and sensitive that each detail blazes across my senses with hyperclarity. I'm being tattooed. There's no place he'll leave untouched, and that touch will be permanent.

This particular smile is new to me. He grins up from where he's kneeling between my legs, with his lips hovering over my inner thigh. He licks. He kisses. I'm immobilized by the slightest touches of wet to trembling, hot to steaming. My gasps make him smile even wider. *Yes.* Just like he said. He's learning me. I'm a gasping, writhing road map, and the man does love to explore.

When Jude nuzzles up to meet the center of my need with his firm, determined lips, I sit half up off the bed. "Wait" is what I say. And I know how the world works. When a woman says no, a guy stops. I didn't think any different of Jude. But I catch myself. I find myself on my elbows, watching where his face is so . . . very . . . close.

He angles a look toward my face, then raises his eyebrows. "Let me," he says. "Promises, remember?"

"And I'm going to love it."

"Hell yes, sugar."

"Okay."

"Has anyone else touched you here?" He traces his forefinger down, down, down. . . .

"Jude. God, please. Do you want me to talk or just melt?"

"Talk a little?" His smile is changing again. Dares and wickedness. I recognize the dares from the night he got me onstage. He's speaking a whole new language—almost literally. "You didn't answer."

"No one's touched me there."

He drags his head up and grins. His hair lays across his brow, as if an artist drew outside the lines. I slide trembling hands back along his temples. I love touching his hair and I love seeing his face. Double win.

"How about a cock?" He wiggles his eyebrows. "And yeah, I said that on purpose."

My face is on fire. Pure flame. "What about one?"

"Have you ever touched a naked one? Aroused, like I am?"

"When you pressed our bodies together."

"But not with your hands?"

I shake my head.

"Here," he says, even more gently now. He moves up my body until he's lying nearly parallel. "Like this."

Covering my hand with his own, he starts with the easy stuff. The familiar stuff. Our fingers are twined as he guides me to touch his face. We're locked eye to eye as we flutter across his temples, brows, nose, smiling lips, and cut-granite chin. His throat is tight and corded, although he keeps his guiding hand light on mine. It's like he can read just when he's taken me as far as I can stand, then brings me back to a place where I still have relatively firm footing.

I take a deep breath. "More," I say against his cheek. "I'm ready."

Still guiding, he strokes our hands down his body. I feel the shifting strength of his biceps. The hair along his forearms tickles my palm. I let myself laugh because this is heady and scary and just . . . *us*.

His breathing picks up, outpacing even mine, when we reach his defined pecs and abs. Below his navel, his rougher body hair tapers. What has yet to happen is still a drumbeat, but the journey—this exploration together—is just as exciting.

"I like foreplay," I say just before I kiss him. I don't remember if I've kissed him like this, some mix of needy and sweet. We're still lip to lip when he takes my hand down those last few inches. He closes my fingers around his shaft. Of course he knew what would happen—he made it happen, after all—but he hisses in a sharp breath anyway. *My* grin feels wicked now. "In fact, I like foreplay *a lot*."

He rolls me onto my back, and for a brief, panicky moment, I think, *This is it.* Instead, he just kisses the hell out of me. It's like he's taking out all his pent-up, gentlemanly restraint out on my mouth. I haven't let go of his thick erection. In fact, I'm caressing him, learning him, still marveling that this was really happening.

"Okay, enough," he says roughly. He grabs my hands and pushes them flat against the bed. "There. That's safer."

"For you."

"Yeah." He grins. "Because you're in trouble now."

He takes hold of my thighs. His hands are so strong, but I'm not going anywhere. He opens me, then dips his head. My spinning craziness becomes a whirlwind as he licks and nuzzles my . . . Maybe one day I'll be able to think the same daring way he talks. Right now I just *feel*. I grab the sheets, but they're not Jude. I grab the muscles of his back, but he's slippery with sweat. Finally I grab his hair and pull.

He releases one of my legs and slows the rhythm of his mouth. Two fingers. That's it. In the whole scheme of the planet, how important are two fingers? Jude's are stunningly, blindingly important as he traces me and glides inside.

I cry out. There's a sharp bite of pain, but then there's Jude's mouth to soothe and tease. I don't know what he's going to do next. The lack of control threatens to rob me of how good it feels. I force my mind back to the present. To Jude. To the gentle, almost lulling way he's stroking with those two insanely talented fingers. His tongue is more insistent. He's seeking out every gasp. It's like he's after me, chasing down my pleasure as his prize.

I shake, call his name, thrust my hips. He presses his fingers deeper as I clench around him. I'm sweating and I probably look like a wild animal, but that doesn't freak me out when I can't describe the hot-cold electricity coursing through my body. I don't have to be anything else for him. His self-satisfied smile is as beautifully smug as any a guy's ever worn. I'm crying or panting or something, until—

I freak the fuck out.

I don't know what happens. I really don't. It's confusing and scary all at once when I sit up and take his face between my hands. I kiss him. Hard. I reach for any part of him I can get at. He's so solid. Everywhere. Arms and pecs, shoulders and abs. Even his firm backside.

"Keeley, shit." He tries to peel me off him. "I can't go slow if you—"

I find his cock. Two hands. Fingers all the way around. He cusses until I can't understand what's a growl and what's a word.

"That was the pain, wasn't it?" I ask, just before biting his earlobe. "You did it with your fingers."

"Yeah."

"Then it won't hurt now?"

"It will if you keep this up. Sugar, good Christ, *stop*."

I let go of him completely, because, oh, his voice. When he *means it*. I don't remember hearing that before. My bones seize and my whole body becomes his marionette. I flop back on the bed. "Stopped."

"You wanted this to last. You— You're acting like you know what you're doing."

My hair rasps against the pillow when I shake my head. "I can't help myself."

I take a deep breath. I won't be able to live with myself if it's all because of what Jude makes me feel. I've wanted to be memorable to him. Now I can be memorable *with* him.

That means I want to be an active participant.

He matches my moves as I climb to my knees. We're facing each other on the bed, stomach to stomach again, with his stern face looking down at mine with an expression near to pain. "I'm trying to keep my promises, Keeley. Help me out here. You're making it so I can't think."

"You remember what you said?" I scrape my fingers down his chest, every line and graceful arc and stubborn ridge. "We knew it was going to happen. We just didn't know how."

"I remember."

"You've kept your promises, Jude. Slow. Foreplay. I came and it barely hurt. Now . . . this is us doing it how we want. No more rules."

I'd thought his eyes were filled with lust before. I'd thought his body tense and ready—so ready. I was wrong. *No more rules* blows his mind. I swear I see sparks shoot across his irises. He bares his teeth and settles back on his haunches. His cock is like a spear aiming up from between his thighs. He grabs a condom off the nightstand and rolls it on.

"Right there," he says past gritted teeth. He nods to his lap. "You belong right there."

God, God, God . . .

I'm frozen and racing at a thousand miles an hour. His hands on my hips break my paralyzed spell. He lifts. I lift. With my arms around his neck and his around my low back, I sink down his stiff length.

I throw my head back on a dizzy, giddy cry. He bows his forehead low, between my breasts, groaning, already thrusting up. I catch his rhythm and hold on. Who knew it would wind up this way? Here's where I have to trust him again. No more rules. *Sure.* But he's still Jude, and his pride is a fierce thing. I remember Yamatam's, knowing he'd be watching me all night, waiting to see if I'd seek him out. He's a man used to winning.

To finish this without me? I can't imagine it, even as he drives harder and holds me so tight—down, on, around him. I find the place where his neck meets his shoulder and nibble tense flesh.

"You're . . . Jesus, so beautiful. Pink skin all flushed. Your lips plump from our kisses. I've wanted to kiss your lips from the beginning." He groaned. "I wish the light was brighter. I want to see your eyes. Such brilliant green. And your body—Keeley, sugar, you're so fucking perfect. Perfect for me."

"Tonight," I whisper in his ear, "I believe you."

His grin is tight, almost pained, but it's still teasing enough to flip my heart. "Good."

"Show me the rest now. Please, Jude."

He bends me back against the bed. I catch my heels together at his low back. There's nothing gentle left between us, except maybe the distant knowledge that yes, we both want the other to come. I want him to. I want him—

He changes the angle of our bodies and hits . . . *something* deep inside me. I rocket into pieces. Fingernails become claws up his back. I see black and red and fireworks. There's a moment when sleep and ecstasy seem to blend. Dreams on top of reality. Utter relaxation—totally lost in him—layered over a pleasure so great that I'm dizzy.

Jude buries his face beside mine on the pillow and drives deep. He's saying my name and I wish that it had always been my real name, so that when he says it with such reverence and passion, he won't be chanting a lie.

He knows how to make himself feel good now that he's blown me to bits. His hips are—just, *damn*, where does all that strength come from? He's amazing and beautiful and sweating, growling, grinding, and I come again without even thinking about it. Pleasure sneaks up on me and crashes down, almost as heavy as Jude when he stiffens, then collapses across my body.

We're panting and he's wiping my cheeks. "Tell me these are good tears."

I start to laugh like a maniac let out of the asylum too soon. I wrap my arms and legs around him so tight.

Never let me go.

"Good tears," I choke out, rather than say what my heart is shouting. "So good. Words all gone-gone good."

"Christ, sugar."

He eases off of me, ditches the condom, and folds me against his hot skin. We'd be steaming if the air was any cooler. As it is, we add ten degrees to the room's thick mood. I can't remember it being this heavy and perfumed when we walked in. It's all us. The smell of sex and satisfaction.

"Getting up on your knees like that," he says against the top of my head. "Was that trying to be memorable again?"

"It crossed my mind." I stretch so hard that I can almost reach his toes with mine. "But I didn't do it on purpose. It's just . . . how I needed to do it."

He rolls me onto my back and lounges beside me, with his head propped on his hand. "Passion. Pure passion. I should've known. And there's your answer again."

"What answer?"

"To the question of *Why you?*" His breath is a gorgeous shudder, while his smile is as slinky as when we started. "Why I wanted you. Why I still do."

I lift my head, just enough to brush my lips against his. "Tell me?"

"I thought I had you all figured out, that first night. Not even close." He wipes away one last tear, then touches it to his tongue. His eyes roll closed as if he's just tasted the most exquisite dessert. It's beautiful to watch. "I wonder if I ever will."

THIRTY-ONE

I'm obsessed with him.

Anyone inside my head or feeling the beat of my heart for the last three weeks would know that. I should be used to it by now, right? But no. I listen to music, where every lyric is my cliché. I watch the sky, where hazy clouds remind me of how contented and dark Jude's eyes get after we make love. I look to the future—and feel as terrified as always.

It was hard to tell Clair and John that we got back together. I could hear the concern in every word, but in the end, they did what they've always done. They gave their advice, then backed off with the promise they'll be there if I need them.

I'm warmed by their constancy, but I don't want to imagine needing them like I did when I took that spontaneous trip home to Baton Rouge. After all, Jude and I having an amazing time. My version of amazing has the word "always" attached. His probably runs more toward, *Wow, I have a great time with this girl. Isn't that a nice way to spend the fall?* No talk of always. But lots of sex. The man is a master and a very, very patient teacher. I've learned what a freak occurrence our first time was—that I surprised him. Now he has agendas that blow my mind. I learn something new whenever he touches me.

No matter what happens to my heart, I'm going to be spoiled for life when it comes to sex. The idea of a lover other than Jude is powerful enough to wake me from a sound sleep. How many eyes are on me in class when I fidget and can't stop watching the clock? Probably only a pair or two. I feel like everyone should be able to see through my fake workaday calm.

Whatever professor is babbling in the background should use his mic to make an announcement. "This daughter of murdering druggie convicts has fallen for Jude Villars. She's five years younger and a wannabe piano player. He's a CEO. Go on, look at her. She's about to barf. Of course she is!"

There's nothing I can do but hold on. Every kiss. Every night spent in his arms. Every whispered word. His drawl is like honey in my blood, overcoming all the old bitterness until only sweetness remains.

I know that's what would happen if he was really mine. Instead, I'm just borrowing him.

Adelaide makes it difficult to remember that. She and I have been practicing like crazy for the Fall Finish. We exchange snarky texts about the classes we're forced to take, because they get in the way of meeting at Dixon. I'm still working on controlling my emotions and channeling them when I play. Adelaide is fighting to find the same fire in a lowly practice room as she can when surrounded by a hooting audience.

She finishes a really awesome rendition of "Seasons of Love" from *Rent*. The song really suits her, because her voice has enough power to rival a song intended for an entire cast. "Five hundred twenty-five thousand six hundred minutes . . ." She's stripped what would've been human harmonies, replacing them with piano accents.

Basically, she reimagined the whole damn thing. I'm stunned and awed.

But I don't clap when she finishes.

She looks up at me, eyes expectant. I keep my expression passive, although it's really hard. "Keeley?"

"How do you think you did?"

Today she's wearing a shapeless '60s throwback floral shirt that has billowing sleeves, a deep V neck, and yellow rickrack trim. It flows over a pair of beige cords. A kerchief that picks up the blues of the floral print holds her hair back, but a few sweaty bleach blonde strands poke out by her ears, where three inch strings of opaque stones hang from her lobes.

On top of all that, she's wearing an expression of helplessness. It doesn't suit her.

"I don't know," she says tentatively. "Good enough. I was flat through the chorus." She shrugs. "The ostinato is hard to keep even when I just wanna boogie away, but maybe that's okay. My own spin . . . ?"

I stand and meet her at the bench. "You're still waiting for my opinion."

"Wouldn't you be?"

"Of course," I say, smiling. "Which is why I'll put you out of your misery and say you blew my mind. The ostinato got a little out of control, yeah. It's the backbone rhythm, not the thing to tamper with. But you've turned a song meant for an entire cast into a one-woman show. Tell me you're not impressed with yourself, even without the applause."

Bright red lips—the color clashes with the maroon trim, but on Adelaide, it doesn't matter—smile wider and wider. "Yeah, I did good."

She turns back to the piano and tinkers with a few keys. They're still pieces of the melody, but just playing with sound. She sighs.

"Are things okay with us?" I ask. "You don't seem like your-self."

Her grin is lopsided. She hasn't looked up from the keys. "What do you think it means for me to be myself?"

"Megawatt. Wild and not giving a damn."

"Oh, I give a damn," she says softly. "Hey, can I ask you a question?"

I sit with her on the bench. "Sure."

"You and Jude. Doing fine?"

"We're having a good time. That's the best I can describe it right now."

"That's not bad. And—please answer this with full awareness that he's my brother and I don't feel like getting squicked out—he treats you good, yeah?"

I can't help how my face heats up. If she can't handle that re-action to my thoughts about her brother, she shouldn't have asked. It's not like I'm giving her a blow-by-blow of the last few weeks. I'm just blushing. "He does. It was kinda rocky, and I didn't know what to do sometimes, but now it's . . . it's . . ."

She rolls her eyes. "Okay, fine. Just spit it out."

"Compulsive. I'm fixated on him. I like it, but it's annoying too. It's music turned up *way* too loud, you know?"

I'm shocked when Adelaide closes the key cover, crosses her forearms over the gleaming wood, and drops her head. She's crying.

"Hey." I turn to hug across her shoulders. "What's this?"

"I . . ."

There's a lot of hiccupping and sniffles. I fetch a minipack of tissues from my purse. She uses most of the pack. Aside from that bright lipstick, she hadn't been wearing any makeup, which is a good thing. Her eyes are rimmed with red by the time she catches her breath.

"I broke it off with David." She must read the confusion on my face, because she adds, "Dr. Saunders."

"Oh. Wow."

"I just couldn't take it anymore." She turns on the bench, then drops down onto the floor, where she sits with her elbows over her knees. Her head hides in that retreat. Everything she says is muffled, but I get this hot glow of pleasure that she's confiding in me. Even with Janey, I wonder sometimes if our friendship is one sided, if I'm too clingy, if it's really okay to share my thoughts and confusing emotions.

I'd been even less sure of my footing with Adelaide. Not anymore.

"I was finally going to go through with it. He'd been after me for . . . well, since we started. He said his wife resented him because he wasn't more excited about having a baby. It was a whoopsy pregnancy. He gave up going on tour with the Boston Philharmonic to stay home with her. So she's been all cold and distant from him, yada, yada, and wasn't it nice that he finally found someone to talk to him and make him feel like a man again? I liked being that someone special, like I'd won against this faceless woman I know nothing about."

She wipes her nose, this time with the back of her sleeve. I hand her another Kleenex and she looks chagrined.

"Anyway, he took me out to dinner, roses, the works. He had champagne waiting in the hotel room. I've faked my way into clubs before, drunk when I wasn't supposed to, but this was the first time a grown-up bought me booze. It felt wrong, but I was flattered too. He thought I was mature enough to handle it."

This whole time, my mind is doing triple duty. I'm hating Dr. David Saunders, I'm hoping against hope that her story turns out at least mostly okay, and I'm comparing her experience to mine with Jude. Mine could've turned out so badly, had Jude really been the player I'd thought he was, or had he been any less true to his word. I was *so* fortunate. I rub Adelaide's back, soothing, waiting to see if she at least got out of that hotel room on her terms.

"It was all bullshit," she says, suddenly angry. Head up, eyes fierce, she kicks her feet so hard that the strap on one of her wedge sandals snaps. The sandal flies off. "I was half undressed and he had me working him, you know, with my hand. Then his cell phone rings. His wife was having contractions. He jumped off me like I was a pit of vipers he needed to escape. He lied through his teeth to his wife, that he was at a buddy's house or some shit, and then he turned on *me!*"

"How?"

"He said I was a stupid, naïve kid, and didn't I know any better?" She shakes her head violently. "But the topper was, he looked me up and down. His pants were kinda unbuckled, and I swear he got even more turned on. It was sick. I got really scared, because he could've done anything to me. Instead he just zipped up his pants and gave himself a little rub, smiling, and said he'd see me in class."

I'm furious, and I'm glad she's furious, although I know she must be hurting. "You mean he wants to see you again?"

"No, it sounded more like a threat. He's still my professor! What am I supposed to do, go tattle? I'll be the Lolita whore people thought I was in high school. I ran wild, but I wasn't stupid and I wasn't this naïve. It was easy to play with boys my age. They lag, you know? Then suddenly it's like, *boom.* They turn into older men who're hot and say all the prettiest things, and if it hadn't been for that phone call, I'd be some virgin kid he got to roll around on for a night."

"You've never . . . ?"

She laughs, which sounds bitter and frayed. "Never. Although I bet even Jude would have a hard time believing that."

I exhale slowly. This isn't my business anymore. She's vented. I should step away from sibling drama. But I don't want to lose either from my life, and I certainly don't want them in pain. "I think you're underestimating him," I say quietly. "I know I do sometimes."

"That's because you're you and he likes you so much. Geez, Keeley, you wouldn't believe how much he talks about you. It'd be annoying if I thought you were a bitch, not worth his time. Instead it's adorable. I'm really happy for you, and I'm *so* glad he's finally loosening up. It's like . . ." She blows her nose. "It's like having him back."

"Then why not tell him about this?"

"Because his rules for you and his rules for me are way different. There's no chance, *ever*, that he'd let me off about this without a lecture. I don't feel like being hammered with *I told you so*. Even if I deserve it."

"Now, wait." I stand up and forcefully drag her to her feet. "How old is Dr. Saunders? Thirty-something? He's the one to blame for this. He's the one who lied and blew off his pregnant wife to get you in bed. It's impossible to keep perspective when it's so much fun and so exciting." I catch her eyes. "Not to squick you out, like you said, but I know what that part's like. Only, Jude's a good guy. He takes care of me. Dr. Saunders was only going to use you. Don't you *dare* think you deserve that, no matter how blinded you were."

She starts crying again. I hug her and she hugs back. "I told him to fuck off," she says against my shoulder. "I told him, yeah, I'd see him in class, but I'd wear a turtleneck in August before he got another look at me naked. He didn't even have his shoes back on before I grabbed my things and left. I couldn't stand the idea of him leaving first, and me sitting there on the bed we'd messed up together. *I* did the leaving."

I hug her harder. "You bet your ass you did."

Adelaide uses a tissue instead of her sleeve—or the shoulder of my plain lime green T-shirt—and wipes her eyes. "Thanks," she whispers.

"I'm glad I was here. I mean that."

"Will you tell Jude?"

I hold her upper arms and make sure she doesn't look away. "Only what you give me permission to."

She shrugs. "Just that we broke up. Nothing more, please."

"You got it. Cross my heart. But Addie—"

She smiles.

"What?" I ask.

"That's the first time you've called me that, Miss Priss," she says, her smile more genuine now.

I stick my tongue out. "Addie . . . consider telling Jude yourself. Will you? He loves you so much, and I know you think it's smothering . . . but trust me, *not* having someone to smother you is a lot worse."

Her hazel eyes turn canny. "There's a story behind that line, isn't there?"

"Yeah. But no more stories for today. We need another milkshake."

~ THIRTY-TWO ~

My promise to Addie is put to the test the next time I see Jude, when he takes me to the annual Po'Boy festival on Oak Street. It was so much fun, and we even stay for the awards. He rooted for some overflowing oyster concoction from a place called Mama's, while I liked my Louisiana spicy sausage, served "hot" with Cajun mustard. He didn't think I could eat something that flaming, but the burn was as good as the sandwich was tasty. In the end neither of our favorites won. That didn't matter when we shared a piece of crème brûlée cheesecake that had been caramelized with molasses.

I'm getting really uneasy, though, about balancing time with him against my goals for the semester. Yes, I'm obsessed with him, but I've been obsessed with my music for a lot longer. Maybe the urge to spend as many hours as possible with him comes from that: my music will always be there for me. Jude, no matter how good he is and how much fun we're having, is not a sure thing.

Neither is doing well at the Fall Finish. . . .

Around and around and around goes my head.

He and I are curled on his giant sectional. We're naked, with a blanket covering us. I've been texting Adelaide for the last half hour, missing the end of whatever action movie Jude is streaming.

He teases me, trying to grab my phone. "Keeley, what is going on?"

"Nothing. Everything's fine."

"Wait," he says, sobering. The blanket slips when he sits up, revealing his bare chest. I've seen him in daylight plenty of times now, but I still like him best when wrapped in nighttime. It's where we met. It's where we can hide away from shitty things like reality. "That wasn't a flippant answer. Something *is* going on."

"I shouldn't—"

"It's Addie, isn't it? She's been acting so weird the last two days and she won't return my calls."

He eyes me with an expression I've decided he must use in boardrooms. It used to intimidate the hell out of me. He looks so *serious* and scary-powerful. That was weeks ago. Now I know he can try it on me, but there's nothing he can do to threaten me . . . short of breaking up.

The nuclear option, I suppose.

"What happened? She told you, didn't she? Whatever's been going on? Maybe you two don't think it's a big deal to keep secrets, but she worries me sick."

I touch his face, palm to cheek. He leans against it as his eyes roll closed. "I'm sorry. I know you worry," I say. "My bond with her isn't as strong as yours, obviously, but she's becoming really special to me. I'd be worried too, if she didn't text or return my calls."

He nods to my phone. "Apparently that isn't a problem."

"Because she's not scared of what I'll say." I take a deep breath. "She's scared of what *you'll* say."

Agitated now, he pulls out of my arms and stands. Before I can blink—blinded by the stark beauty of him naked—he tugs on his briefs and jeans. Maybe he thinks that's being modest when we talk, but that means he doesn't have a very high opinion of his chest. Then again, with his hair gilded by lamplight and his eyes flaming, I'll have a hard time concentrating no matter what he wears.

Yet he looks sickened by his burdens, which calls to me on such a deep level. I want to stand and hold him and take away his cares until his stark frown disappears.

"Keeley, please," he says harshly. "Give me a clue here."

I sit up too, because there's no way I can get through this conversation without being strong. Really strong. I have to protect two people I care about—by protecting them from each other. I grab my tank top where it got tossed to the floor, and shrug into it.

"No, Jude. I can't."

"What?"

"I said no. I'm not telling you anything."

"Keeley—"

"What would happen if I told you and Adelaide found out I'd betrayed her confidence?"

"I'm her brother!" His shout is unexpected. I flinch and draw back. He's never shown any sort of temper toward me. I know this is just his frustration cracking through, but I don't like being on the receiving end of *anyone's* temper. "I'm all she has and I deserve to know."

"You're her *brother*. Do you think she wants to tell you the nitty-gritty of her personal life if she's embarrassed, or if she thinks she'll get railed at? I wouldn't open my mouth, and I sure as hell wouldn't trust the person who'd blabbed." I meet him where he's pacing. The muscles of his forearm jump beneath my hand, before he exhales. That gives me permission of a sort. I start to pet the hair on his arm, so silky, when it gives him such a rough, masculine appearance. "You'll lose her forever if you make me do this. We both know you could. You could figure out a way to get me to talk."

He looks at his hand I'm holding and seems to force his fist to unclench. "Probably."

"Then for all of us, I'm asking that you don't try."

With suddenness, he takes both of my hands in his. He kisses my knuckles in that endearing way of his. "Would you tell me . . . Dammit, Keeley . . . Would you tell me if she needed the police?"

My heart skips. Ouch. That was painful, as a reminder of my own past, but also as a look into Jude's worst nightmare. His sister—hurt, alone, and too embarrassed and alienated to ask him for help. I can give him relief from that particular fear. "Yes, I would tell you that. She doesn't, though. And maybe one day, she'll tell you stuff on her own."

"How? How do you know that?"

"Because I asked her to try confiding in you. And . . . because of my parents."

I have to tell him *something*. Jude has been a patient teacher when it comes to physical intimacy, but he can't help me with this. When will I finally feel okay about opening up about my life? For Jude, for Adelaide, and maybe even for me, I have to try.

"Clair and John have held on to me even when I was at my teenaged worst," I continue tentatively. "I don't know why they didn't just throw up their hands sometimes. But they kept a schedule, expected me to do my part and pull good grades. I never stopped wanting to impress them, and I never wanted to disappoint them." I lean nearer to him, needing his hands on me, his security layered over bits and pieces of my train-wreck past. "They didn't have to say a word. They didn't need to ask a ton of questions. They just needed to . . . be there. They held my hand until I trusted they'd never let go."

My voice catches on that last. I want the hand I hold to be Jude's. Clair and John have been amazing. They saved me when no one else thought to. Is it really ridiculously selfish that I want Jude to take over that role in my life now?

"She's so damn stubborn, Keeley. I've done . . ." He runs his hands through his hair before curling me against him again. "Christ, what I've done for her. All that I could. I've tried too hard, haven't I? Driven her away?"

"You've done the best you possibly could. You rearranged your entire life to give her stability. But . . ." I look up to kiss him. "You're used to knowing everything and being in charge of hundreds of people. Her keeping secrets must seem like an insult. Or heartbreaking."

"How did you know that?"

"I see you better than you think," I say with a smile meant to soften his hard jaw. "You have to trust me. Can you do that?"

He nods and leans his forehead against my crown. I don't think he realizes how hard he's squeezing our twined fingers. "I can try. Will you tell her that? I'll try."

"I already did. But . . ." I lift our hands in front of me, clasping them tightly to my chest. "She gave me permission to tell you one thing. She isn't seeing that creep Saunders anymore. She walked out on him. That's enough for now, right?"

"Thank fuck," he says under his breath. "But she really won't talk to me about it? Hell, about anything?"

"Now? I don't think so. You have to get her to believe you won't let go, even when she makes mistakes."

He exhales so heavily. "She'll be expecting an inquisition. How do I not?"

"Tomorrow's Friday night. She'll be at Yamatam's, of course. Give her a hug and ask what she'll be playing. She never tells me." I turn to catch his eye, smiling. "Did you know that? She shares all her tips and tricks, but not what's coming up the next time she takes the stage. Where your talk goes from there is up to her."

He looks so bewildered. I'm reminded again of how much he had to take on, on such short notice, and under such tragic circumstances. That Adelaide is in college and doing as well as she is—that's Jude's gift to her. Do either of them realize what a special bond they have? How lucky they are to have each other?

I wonder briefly what it would've been like to have a brother or sister when dealing with my parents. I'm envious of Jude and Adelaide, but I'd refuse a sibling in a heartbeat. I could never be that selfish, to force my upbringing on someone else, just so I would've had company through the bad times.

"Have you ever asked her? What she'll play?"

"No," he says with a slow shake of his head.

"You'll shock her so much that maybe she'll tell. And that would be something special?"

For a long time, he just rubs my upper back. Between that and the beat of his heart, I sway on my feet. He must realize, because he scoops me into his strong arms and walks me to his bedroom. Only when we're nestled together under the covers does he speak again, in a whisper. "Keeley, she's really all right?"

"She's really all right," I say, turning over to lie atop his chest. "And she'll be better tomorrow, and the day after that."

His smile is as tentative as I've ever seen. "Thank you, sugar."

Okay, this deep, serious mood has got to go. Adelaide is rid of that creep. And I'm mostly naked and draped across a man who continually awes me. "Sugar again?" I tease him with a wink and the walk of my fingers up his ribs—his guaranteed tickle spot. "Now I know you're back to yourself."

"I haven't felt like myself since I met you." His voice is low and calm, his blue eyes are darkly earnest.

No fair.

So very, *very* not fair.

I was trying to liven things up, and he pulls out a phrase so melancholy romantic that I can't take a steady breath. I close my eyes. I'm surrounded by him, and the image of his intent expression follows me into the dark behind my lids. I can't look at him when I ask, "Good or bad thing?"

"Good thing." He pauses long enough for me to risk peeking up at him. I should've known better. Jude Villars is a complicated man—and he's still watching me. "A good thing and a hard thing."

"Gee, thanks," I force out.

"What do you need to hear from me right now?" He frames my face and kisses me so sweetly that a tear works out from the corner of each eye. "This isn't you telling someone else's secrets. But you can give me one of yours. Something you want but haven't been able to say."

I swallow. I force myself to meet his eyes. It's a risk. He's a smart, perceptive man. All he has to do is look deeply enough to see how hard I've fallen. "Just to hear that I'm your girl."

For a moment, we're suspended in space, time, air, gravity, forward, backward. None of it matters. We're held by whatever is between us and all the things we can't or won't say. All the things we're too afraid to say. I hope that's what he feels, anyway. I hope I'm not the only one with a tender heart to protect.

"*Just?*" he says at last. His cocky smile is almost up to snuff. It's forced, but I'm willing to take anything. "C'mon, sugar. Being my girl is a privilege."

"Pig."

"But you are, you know. You're mine."

He kisses me for what seems like forever, or a promise of forever. I'm his in every way, so I pretend he means it—really means it. But sometimes make believe isn't strong enough to conceal reality, no matter how much I want it to. I kiss him back, forever and ever, while the voices in my head turn sweetness to ash on my tongue.

I'm yours. But for how long?

God, Jude, for how long?

~ THIRTY-THREE ~

It's Halloween. I'm wearing cat ears sticking up from a head-band. My hair is loose and poofy a la Anne Hathaway, although I don't fill out my rented Catwoman suit the way she does in the movies. I don't know what Jude's going to be. We agreed to surprise each other, after he asked me to go to the on-campus Halloween dance Adelaide told him about. So goofy. Off the charts lame. But I'm bouncing on my toes, waiting for him to pick me up.

To my surprise, Janey is getting dressed up too. She slips into a long white nylon dress that's been splattered with red paint. A blood-covered blonde wig and tiara complete her *Carrie* ensemble.

"You didn't tell me you were going out," I say.

She smiles a little. "You've been kinda preoccupied."

"Crap. I'm sorry." I slump into the bed. "Did you tell me and I missed it, or have I been so checked out that you didn't bother?"

"Didn't bother."

"Janey—"

"Look, it's okay. Really. I'm just going out with some other geeky chem chicks. There's only about four of us. Like, *total.*" She grins as she sits on her bed. "We're going to the Mortuary Haunted House over on Canal Street. The place is supposed to be actually haunted, so maybe they'll try harder to keep it from being lame. Not that it matters. I need to get out more." She shrugs. "I'm really glad we're roommates. You're the best friend I have on campus. But . . ." Here, her grin turns a little naughty, a little sad. "Sometimes you have other places to be."

"Tell me I shouldn't feel bad about this. Wait, only if you mean it."

"I mean it. Don't feel bad. Just do what I've said from the start, okay? Be careful."

She likes Jude well enough, although I think she still holds out reservations about him. I can't blame her, because I do too— when I let make myself climb down from the clouds for a few moments of critical thinking. She always seems surprised when he keeps proving to be a good guy.

There's a knock at our open dorm door. Janey and I turn to find Jude standing there in a fantastic 1920s pinstripe suit, from fedora to spats. I should've worn a flapper costume instead of trying to be a superhero. I don't have the tits for Gotham City, but definitely for the Jazz Age.

"Well, hell," he says, sweeping off his hat. "I think we'll skip the dance."

"What?"

"I need to get you home and out of that. Pronto."

Janey snickers and leans back in her chair to watch. "That doesn't sound very Gatsby."

"Okay," he says. "Hey, doll, let's blow this popsicle stand."

"I have *no* idea what that's from," I say, laughing.

He extends his arm. "C'mon. We have a super awesome university dance to get to."

I flutter my hands. "It's like prom!"

"I never went to prom," Janey says.

"Eh, neither did I." I loop my arm through Jude's and smile. "I guess I'll have to make do."

"I dare you to tell me straight up that you're just making do," he whispers.

I shake my head, then give my hair a fluff. "Not a dare I care to take, Mr. Villars."

"It's Jude," he says, teasing.

"Not when you're dressed like that, gangsta boy."

Janey waves us good night. The air is finally starting to get a little cooler in the evenings, but anywhere up north, they'd already be taking parkas out of storage and getting cars winterized. I've considered telling Jude about Chicago, about seasons, but then I'd have to tell him why.

Part of me insists on holding on to those far-back memories, when I've had better experiences in Baton Rouge and even here. Maybe . . . Maybe it's because we'd been normal once—my folks and I. They might have started their bad shit there, but I didn't know about it. Only when we hit the road did things become too bad to overlook, even for a kid.

So yeah, there it is. Answer found, finally. I still can't tell him. There are too many details that might come spilling out. Unless I'm ready to hit the self-destruct button on Keeley Chambers, I can't do much other than sketch out the big picture.

The dance is just what I need to get that crap out of my head.

He finds a table and orders us a few sodas while I hit the bathroom. Catsuit + public stall = a circle of hell. But the best thing
happens when I finish reprimping. I step into the ballroom used
for ceremonies and welcome orientations. Now it's decked out
with orange and black crepe ribbon, a really great strobe light, and
every cheesy fake spider and shriveled plastic corpse to be had in
the city. "Poker Face" comes on just as I start walking.

I love strut songs. Songs where, if given enough space—for
example, a long stretch of sidewalk between classes—you can
walk in perfect time with the beat. I keep a playlist just for those
walks, now that I know where I'm going ninety percent of the
time. "Poker Face" is a little too high school for me, but it's definitely a strut song. I swing my hips, work my three inch stiletto
boots, and fasten my gaze on Jude. He watches me the whole
way. I feel radiant and beautiful. Then I feel like a queen when a
few guys part ways to let me through. Jude's shifting eyes tell me
the guys haven't stopped watching me saunter away. He has the
sexiest possessive streak. It's what gets on Adelaide's nerves, but
I'd get down on my knees for him to wrap that protectiveness
around me for the rest of my life.

I would never be scared again.

I shake off that thought in favor of the desire written across
Jude's expression. "Damn," he whispers. "Can you wear that
every day?"

"Nope. One time only."

He catches me by the hips. The latex ripples and creaks
under his intense squeezes. "Then we'll have to make the most
of it."

"Later," I say, catching his tie. He's just too damn handsome
for words. "I want to dance."

There are a lot of things I've gotten used to, living in Louisiana. The best is that the guys can dance. Not only that, but they
like to. It's a way of life in New Orleans, and it's a rare person
who doesn't know the basics. Jude can *move*. He's sexy as hell in
his suit, his fedora tipped low so that his eyes are almost entirely
shaded. Only when I slink up his chest toward the underside of
his jaw, seeking out his gaze, does he look down at me and wink.
Then he laughs, and those shaded eyes turn to half moons that
make my heart pinch.

It's so weird when "American Pie" comes on. That line about
being in love with him, dancing there in the gym . . . it hits like a
hammer. Decked out with crepe, and after our cracks about
going to prom, the ballroom could double as an overdressed
gym. And I adore Jude Villars. When he turns me in a two-step
spin, I swear I'm going to fall. I can see it. Falling. In slow
motion. All my saunter and sexy Catwoman vibe sprawled
across the parquet. But that's not how Jude operates. He catches
me under the arms, gives me another spin, and suddenly we're
facing one another again. I'm secure in his arms. We're still
dancing bye-bye, Miss American Pie, and he's still laughing.

"I gotcha," he says close to my ear. "Can't have you break an
ankle. We'd have to spend the night in the ER. No good."

"Because I'd be in screaming pain?"

"No, because I have a meeting at seven in the morning.
Sucks balls."

"So gallant."

He lets out an exaggerated sigh. "I'll just have to make do
with you sucking—"

I stand on tiptoes and kiss him before he can say it. But
that's just asking for trouble. I'm still on a whirligig ride with

only Jude to hold. I cling to his middle, with my hands under his pinstripe coat. He clings to my ass.

"Let's get out of here." His voice is dripping with sex. He angles one of my wrists down his body. He's pulsing and hard. I give him a squeeze, just to watch his eyes roll shut and his lips part. "I'm serious, Keeley."

We're out of the gym in no time, me strutting, Jude dragging me. I like being caught, but hard to get is fun too. Not that I can keep up the pretense for long. We reach his car, which is parked in a darkened student lot. He's managed to find the only parking spot in the place where lamplight doesn't follow us. "I would've called for one of those walk me home guys if I had to go through here to get back to the dorm."

"Lucky for us, you have me. Get in, Catwoman."

He ducks me into the backseat. I'm made of champagne and nitroglycerin when he finds the zipper that runs down the back of the latex suit. Within seconds, he bares my back and my ass. He covers me with the drape of his undone suit coat. The sound of his zipper is next, followed by the foil of a condom wrapper. I'm on my hands and knees and, oh, damn, he's got his hands everywhere. I'm already moaning when he pushes deep.

Jude bows over me. His breathing is quick and sharp. "You never fail to surprise me, sugar."

"I'm surprising me too."

He helps get my arms out of the suit. I don't think it's altruistic. He just wants access to my bare body. Fine with me. I arch into his hands, then balance when he guides my hand between my legs. "I'm not doing all the work here," he says with a brilliant smile in his voice.

I wiggle so that my nipples bead against his palms. "At least do your half."

"Can do."

Sometimes we can take hours making love—a night in, when dinner is just pretext, although I love talking and laughing with him. Most times I can forget my own head and live in his world. The world we build together. Then we take as much time as we want, like the first time, where every movement was deliberate, slow, aching.

This isn't one of those times.

"You're gonna get us caught," he whispers against my nape. He scrapes his teeth there, making me shudder from head to heel. "I'm being good, holding off. You're taking forever, just to tease me. You want someone to see us. Sure, I've got this coat over you, but would anyone mistake what's going on in here if they walked past?"

"No."

"What would they think?"

"That you're talking too much. Shut up and let me—"

He nibbles my nape, which—oh my God—it's become one of my favorite things. There's nothing more possessive. You can think what you like about different positions and vows and promises and all that pretty stuff, but the deep, primal, gut, *scary* part of me loves it when he uses his teeth there, his kiss claiming me. It's never deep. It never hurts. It's just a reminder that he's over and around me.

I shoot into the sky on an orgasm that makes my throat hurt. He's poised with his mouth on my skin when he follows me over the edge. I'm still zinging and floating when he gives me one last forceful drive. His moan is pure music—the most erotic music. I take it into myself and store it away. A hundred new memories a day.

"I should've known. Setting off that fire alarm was only the beginning."

He's an animal at times like this, which I love. It's thrilling and so bizarre to think, *This is me. This is who I am now.*

But then Jude, my gentleman, comes back to me in a few blinks and a few rasping breaths. He takes off the costume coat. I use it as concealment as he zips me up. I'm back to normal— well, normal for Catwoman—when he brushes the hair away from my neck. Softly, he kisses my nape. It's almost an apology, although I want to tell him it's so very not necessary.

"I imagine sometimes . . ." he says, before breaking off. I have to pinch the back of his hand where it rests at my waist. "Sometimes I imagine you keep those deep kisses with you. That if anyone lifted your hair, they'd see that I'd taken you."

I shudder and dive into his arms. I'm not going to let go. I think that every time, but something always happens to end it. No embrace can last forever.

"I need to take you home. That meeting of mine. I'm sorry."

"It's okay. This was . . ." Laughing, I give him a kiss. "This was perfect."

Although the nitroglycerin feeling has eased—blown apart when we came—I'm still filled with champagne bubbles when he drops me off at the residence hall. After ten minutes of kisses and good nights, I wave at the Mercedes's taillights and turn to head inside.

Brandon is behind the desk. My blood goes cold. He looks freakish in his own Halloween costume: an undertaker who looks as dead as the stiffs he'd bury. Thick black paint rings beneath his eyes accentuate the hollows of his cheeks. Otherwise he's chalk white.

"Another lotto ticket to cash in, Keeley?"

"None of your business." I flip my hair back, accidentally grazing my fingers over where Jude claimed me. I leave my hand there. Clasping. Taking strength from Jude's intimate words.

They'd see that I'd taken you.

"Just watching to see if I can get any pointers," Brandon says. "You seem to be a pro when it comes to moving up in the world. That's a pro's outfit, all right."

"How's Opal these days?" I ask with a sneer.

Because of course I told the poor girl. She didn't speak to me for a few weeks, which hurt, but I guess she needed to put the blame somewhere. Only after she caught him with another girl on the fourth floor did she shove him to the curb—and apologize to me. She didn't need to, but it made me feel like there was some justice in the world.

"Wouldn't know," he says with a tight shrug. "You did your best to make sure of that."

"I protected a friend."

"And when you piss off the wrong person, who's going to protect you? It sure won't be him."

He stands when I begin to walk toward the elevator. God, don't let him get in with me. He takes his desk duty stuff seriously. *Just . . . stay there.* His smile—I used to think it so friendly and handsome. It's macabre now, twisted in ways I can't understand. Have I really treated him so badly that I deserve this?

He doesn't need to follow me physically, not when his words hit me so hard.

"Jude Villars won't be around to protect you forever." His smile deepens. "One of these days he'll find out who you really are. Trash knows trash, Keeley. That means I know it when I see it."

THIRTY-FOUR

I'm in tears in the elevator. The mascara I put on to become Cat-woman is coming off in streaks on my fingers as I wipe my eyes.

My name was Rosie Nyman.

I haven't been called that for years. I can handle thinking occasionally about the fake names that came after, but Rosie is so much harder. That girl was innocent. That girl didn't know what it was like to sleep in a car or listen to prostitutes and their johns through paper thin walls of seedy hotels. That girl had something approaching a normal life in Chicago. The names that came after—Sara and Lila—had it rougher. At hotels, I stopped sleeping on rollaway cots, always feeling too exposed. I slept under nightstands and desks and upholstered chairs, tight in a ball, hands over my ears. Eventually Mom and Dad stopped giving me crap about it. "Let her sleep where she wants. At least she's quiet."

Now, with Brandon. I was an idiot for revealing as much as I did, hoping to find a bit of humanity when, apparently, there wasn't much to be had. I genuinely feel for him, because I knew how iffy the foster system could be. With Clair and John, I got luckier than my talent at the piano will ever eclipse. But he has a grudge against me. Worse, he has connections in the world of journalism. The two put together . . . What if he's hell bent on digging up dirt on me? Following the right trail, he could've found a whole compost heap of it.

My blood is running sprints through my veins. I can't breathe. I'd already been breathless with my pulse racing only an hour alone, with Jude, being daring and exquisite. Now this . . .

I don't want the elevator doors to open. I actually look up at the ceiling ventilation cover and imagine the dozens of films where people escape through air ducts. They're usually on a secret mission or on the run from bad guys. What if Brandon learns my real name, my history, and tells people? My dad never forgave me for testifying against him. *I'll find you if you do.* I've felt safe and protected in Louisiana, swathed in my new name and my new life. I don't feel safe anymore, and bad guys most certainly exist.

Would Dad send someone to get me? Could he hold a grudge that long?

Yes.

I'm dressed as Catwoman, but I'm not a girl in a movie. I'm terrified. And elevator rides don't last forever.

The doors part to reveal the third floor. I stand there with my feet frozen. Janey will be distressed to see me like this. We're friends. I have *friends.* It's a beautiful thing, but I don't know how to lean on them when the hard stuff comes along. Will it in-convenience them? But I'd be upset to learn Janey felt this way and didn't turn to me for help, or at least to be a shoulder to smudge with mascara and tears.

I lean against the elevator door to keep it from closing.

If she's home from the haunted house already, Janey will listen to me all night. But I'd have to explain why I'm so upset. I've been able to keep most of this haunted bullshit in a deep, deep pit for years. Now it's a guillotine over my head. People could find out.

Jude could find out.

Tonight was just breathtaking. We were everything a couple should be, from funny to sexy to heartfelt. I ran through a thousand emotions in just a few hours, but looking back, each of those hours meant holding myself slightly apart from Jude. It felt like we were intimate—as close as two people could hope to be—but he didn't know who he was dancing with. How would I feel if he kept something this huge from me?

How would I feel if I heard it secondhand?

But there's no guarantee Brandon will do anything. He's a stupid coward, like he was with Opal and me. He was just poking a raw place so he can feel important, using what he knows to make me freak out. Yeah, I'm scared as all hell about what he'll do and how far he'll go, but I can't think about it. I can't think about much of anything.

I want to play. I want to compose. I want to use black and white keys when my brain is too overloaded to speak.

Dixon is closed, though. Too late tonight.

But what Adelaide said . . . Jude, with a piano in the ballroom of the Villars mansion . . .

No way.

I step back into the elevator, my heart pounding even harder. I've been to Jude's house by invitation, many times now. To show up in the middle of the night, though . . . ? Will he be as welcoming as I know Janey would be?

Trust.

Back down in the lobby, my knees a wobbling mess, I force myself to strut. I play "Poker Face" in my head and grapple for some Gaga attitude, despite what must be the world's worst raccoon eyes. Brandon stares. He looks like a moron, dressed as a dead undertaker condemned for all eternity to swallow bitterness and salty noodles. In that garb, the ramen looks like he's shoveling in a mouthful of worms.

"Running crying to your sugar daddy?"

"Fuck off, Brandon," I say sweetly, then stride outdoors.

One Google search for cab service and a phone call later, I'm in a taxi on the way to Jude's place. Funny thing. I don't know his address. I could've done another search, but I take a chance and simply tell the driver, "The Villars mansion, please."

It's starting to rain. Wonderful. The cab navigates up the quarter-mile road to the mansion, which I can't see until we're almost there. I never noticed the gate outside. "You'll have to buzz in," the driver says.

I hop out of the busted up old Taurus and push the intercom button. Does he have a camera as part of his security? Can he watch me standing there in the streaming water, looking for him, dying to find him? Does he see *me*?

Of course not. I haven't told him who I am yet.

Moment of truth. Moment of sheer, sluicing panic.

"Adelaide, if you've forgotten your damn keys again," comes his voice past the slight crackle of static.

"Jude? Can you let me in, please?"

"Keeley? Jesus."

The gate clicks open right away. Maybe his invitation, that his doors are always open, is true. And he's not hiding some secret double life. Why am I so convinced he's got one? My parents, maybe? I've answered to four names in my life. There's a lingering feeling of Doesn't everybody?

I go back to pay the driver. My heart sinks when I realize I have my phone but not my purse. What the hell?

I buzz the intercom again. "Jude, I don't have money for the cab. I . . ." I start crying. "I don't know where my purse is."

"It's here in the house. You left it in the car. I'll be right there."

It turns out that five minutes in the rain with a head full of buzzing anger and fear and foreboding is a *really* long time. Jude emerges from the streaking sheets of rain. He wraps me in a blanket and unfolds an umbrella over my head before paying the cabbie. He's wearing an overcoat, but the shirt beneath is soaked. So's his hair. Droplets of rain cling to his lashes when he comes back, hands on my shoulders, his expression concerned.

"You're still in costume? What happened? Keeley, you're scaring me."

"Inside? Please?"

"Yeah, inside."

I let him shuffle me into the mansion, mostly because my strength is gone. He towels me off. Without more than one or two stray touches, he unzips me from the catsuit for the second time that night. This is one hundred and eighty degrees around from stealing a quickie in his car. He bundles me in a robe and makes me a decaf. Sugar and cream. I don't even have to tell him anymore. I've been spending as many waking hours and as many

BLUE NOTES   287

hot nights with a man so damn wonderful that I'll cry again if I think about it too hard.

I've been with a wonderful man. He's been living with my lies.

It's gone. It's *so* far gone. I've been Keeley Chambers for more than six years. That doesn't mean I'm any less shaky.

Jude sits beside me on the sectional, where we snuggle under a fresh blanket. "I'm getting your new shirt wet with my hair."

"You think that's top of my list? It's two in the morning and you show up on my doorstep. Start talking."

"Oh, shit! You have that meeting this morning! I shouldn't be here. You didn't invite me and—"

I try to push away, nearly spilling my coffee. My whole body is trembling. I'm a robot on self-destruct.

He calmly takes the cup of coffee and sets it aside, then drags me back onto his lap. "I can sleepwalk through the meeting. You're always welcome. Don't you know that by now?"

"I know now." I let out a breath I didn't know I'd been holding. Then I blurt out what I want but won't be able to explain. "Can I play your piano?"

His unapologetically aristocratic features warp into a frown I wish I could erase. "Of course." He pauses. God, I knew he would. "But you gotta tell me what's going on."

I stroke the bare, slightly damp hair on his forearms and clasp his fingers with mine. "You remember what I said about you and Adelaide? How sometimes you have to trust that everything's okay and just hold on?"

"Keeley, sugar, you're going to ask that of me? About you?"

We're wrapped up together. I'm naked under his borrowed robe. He's wearing nothing but a T-shirt and boxer briefs. I feel his every reaction, including his flinch. I'm hurting him. I'm test-ing him. I'm keeping things from him. But that's an old life. It's not *my* life. How would he look at me if he knew? It's already taken me this long to have faith when he gazes at me as if I'm something truly, amazingly special. I believe him now when he says I'm fascinating and beautiful.

Don't I deserve time to enjoy that a little longer?

I can't bear thinking about the alternative.

"That's what I'm asking." I shake my head, not knowing what else to say but "Please."

He takes a deep breath. There's so much vitality in the chest that supports my trembling body. I want to dive into his strength and live there forever. Protected and . . . hiding.

Jesus.

I call myself all manner of coward, but I still wait. I want too much: his permission, no questions asked.

I see the war on his face. His brows are furrowed first. That was a given when he frowned. Then twin muscles bunch on either side of his jaw. His nostrils flare. He squeezes my hand, nearly to the point of pain. I can feel him trying to accept what he can't change. How often has he had to fight like this? That he's doing it for me is terrible on my conscience, but I need it so badly. I need *him*.

And I need that damn piano.

With one last shuddering exhale, he nods. "C'mon."

We stand, and he cinches up my borrowed robe. He grabs a pair of jeans on the way past his bedroom. His bedroom . . . I want to be in there almost as much as I want to bang away on a keyboard, but it isn't the time. I don't have the energy to be inti-mate in that way. It's only been a handful of weeks since Jude and I first slept together, but in the time since, I know that fears and anxiety would steal the pleasure of indulging and being indulged.

We climb one more flight of steps and enter the ballroom. He flicks on a light that illuminates nothing but the piano. The concert grand sits dead center, as if onstage. The way the light strikes its gleaming black surface and blocks out the ballroom's other features adds to that impression. I only know the place is huge because my footsteps echo as I walk forward, and because of the slight draft from what must be the storm lashing against windows.

I approach in a trance and sit on the bench of matching black lacquer. There's no audience here, other than Jude. After I touch Middle C—no matter how much I need him—even he disappears.

Minor chords are a given. There's no need for perky major chords, with their fresh vibrancy. I start off more tentatively than I would've expected, but the acoustics and the rain get under my skin. My pulse picks up the pace, as does the swift dance of my fingers and the thump of my feet on the pedals. I don't think I'm crying, not with my body anyway. This is the release I needed—even more than sex. This is confession and salvation in one, even if I can't admit to one and accept the other.

For once, while composing, I'm not insensate and possessed. I'm telling tales about being scared and in pain. About being lonely. About rain drenched nights and being welcomed into a shelter from the storm. I'm crying with parts of my soul, and screaming, and shaking from fears that I'll never be able to say with words. Who needs words when eighty-eight keys are more eloquent and far more beautiful?

When I finish, I'm surprised to hear that the sweet gum trees are still creaking beneath the strength of relentless winds.

"That sounds . . . familiar," Jude says after otherwise silent minutes. Even the little hitches in my breathing have eased.

"Did I copy something? I didn't mean to."

"No, not like plagiarism." He pushes away from the wall, out of the darkness, and sits beside me on the bench. I close the exquisite wood over the keyboard, where he promptly rests his elbows and tunnels agitated hands through his hair. It's still a little wet from the rain. "I've *felt* that music before." A warped smile doesn't do anything to ease his tension. "I guess Addie's tricks about making people react a certain way are paying off."

I'm still pulled into myself physically, but I dare to rub his back. "I wasn't using any tricks. I just needed to do that."

"I don't know where you pulled it out of, but maybe that's why you didn't want me to ask." He exhales and straightens. "I get it. I do. Because there are some things about my life I'd stonewall too. You make it hard not to, though."

I don't know what to say to that, so I keep quiet. Maybe he'll tell me. Maybe he won't. I hadn't realized my music could be *that* powerful.

"You reminded me of people," he says roughly. "Good people. And people who chose to save themselves first. The breadth of humanity, really. It's a rough thing to take in all at once." He looks toward where light reflects off a bank of windows. "This thunderstorm isn't helping either."

I go still. "Katrina?"

He nods, and takes a long time to compose himself.

"I was eighteen. Adelaide's age. I thought I was pretty hot shit. Top of my class. Full ride to Tulane. Maybe that's why I'm so hard on her, because she thinks the same thing now. But then . . ." He chuffs a dazed sound. "Then there was no Tulane. The storm swallowed the city I loved. Some folks climbed on top of one another for canned goods and blankets, while others took the shirts off their backs so babies would have cloth for diapers. My parents opened this whole place to refugees. I think at our max, we had about seventy-five people sleeping on the floors. We did what we could, but stories coming out of the Astrodome—God, none of it felt like enough."

His breathing is rougher than mine, mostly because I'm holding all the air in my lungs. "I wound up taking classes at Louisiana State while my family and FEMA and all the other government misfires tried to dry out the Big Easy and put her back on her feet."

He closes his eyes, shakes his head. I take his shudder into my body.

"I can feel it," I say very quietly. "That's not the end of your story."

"I lost two of my best friends in the storm. They were on scholarship to my boarding school, but they lived down in the lowlands. Their houses, just . . . gone. Them too. I was humbled and scared. Everybody kept asking me why. *Why haven't people come to help? Why haven't we been rescued?* Or even, *Why is Jude Villars down here?* At least I could answer that one." He kisses my forehead. "Because I didn't know who I was anymore. Rebuilding a house was easier than dealing with how much had changed. Some rich kid with a future laid out like a red carpet— that'd been me. Not after the storm . . . and not after the crash."

I swallow hard, but there's no getting air past the lump in my throat.

"I'd finished my last exam at Vanderbilt an hour before the call came in. I was celebrating in a campus bar with my friends. We'd done it. Top honors MBA, here I come. Mom and Dad were supposed to come back the following week for the graduation ceremony. They'd finally decided to take time off and were flying to Banff for some Canadian sightseeing thing. Addie and I laughed at the idea of them both hiking, but they were excited, beaming like little kids. That's how I remember them last." He exhales heavily. "I guess that's a good thing."

"I think so," I whisper, still stroking his back.

"I didn't change my name because, hell, I couldn't. I was trapped. I was too young. I'd fuck everything up. What had my parents been thinking, leaving me in charge of Adelaide and the business? I knew pieces of what Dad did, his responsibilities, but not enough to run the whole show. So I got thrown a new batch of questions. *Why is Jude Villars here? Who does he think he is?* One or two had the balls to ask me to my face. But . . . it got easier. I got stronger. Some would say I got pigheaded and arrogant. At least I stopped thinking I was trapped. Instead, I made it my own. Mostly because I didn't have a choice. Move forward. Build again."

"Take charge of a multinational corporation and pound a few dozen pianos into dust. That's us?"

"Yeah, something like that." He turns me to face him. I wipe a lone tear off his cheek, my heart breaking for him, my own fears subsumed by his confessions. My heart's too big, too full of the bad *and* the good. "Do you see me?" he asks. "The real me?"

There's no hiding from those eyes. No one would suspect by looking at us from the outside, and I didn't understand it either, but we share a bond of loss and resurrection. The clubs and dances and sex, even the teasing laughter and life-changing dares, don't connect this deeply. We're being tied together by stronger forces—forces he doesn't even realize—while the storm keeps raging outside. Here, we can take shelter in each other's arms.

"Yes, Jude, I see you."

He kisses me softly at first, then hauls me across his lap on the piano bench. His mouth finds everywhere he can reach. I inhale his rain-drenched scent and can't stop touching him. Roughly, against my neck, he whispers, "In that, you're *my* first."

It's then, kissing him, hearing those hoarse words, that my heart makes the big leap. I'm completely, terribly, beautifully in love with Jude Villars.

THIRTY-FIVE

"It's smaller than my dorm!"

Jude laughs and nuzzles my neck. "I'm glad that's the only time you've mentioned small in relation to me."

We push through the small door of the "roomette," as Amtrak calls their sleeping cars. Early afternoon sunshine streams in through the large pane window. Two berths are folded into regular chairs, and a table between them is tucked flush against the outside wall. There's enough room to wiggle in together, then stow our luggage. Just three nights' clothing. It's an adventure.

At least, that's how Jude proposed it to me. "It'll be an adventure. My treat. My surprise."

But we've been together now for almost two months. He's a smart guy and knows me as well as almost anyone ever has. So he'd nodded. "Never mind. No surprises when it comes to travel. I'm taking you to Chicago."

My heart had stuttered. "Chicago?"

"Because of that poster on your wall. Janey told me what you said, about how you've always wanted to go. And for a right Southern boy like me," he said, laying his accent on thick, "here's our chance."

"You in Chicago in November? No way."

"As if Little Miss Baton Rouge will fare any better."

I didn't bother correcting him. Let this be the first time. Let this be a trip that rewrites history.

He'd already bought the tickets and reserved the hotel room for the Thanksgiving holiday. But I wasn't going to make the same mistake I made at Halloween. I didn't agree to go with him until I found out what Janey and Adelaide were doing. I couldn't leave them alone. Turns out Janey was driving the five hours to Tupelo, Mississippi, where the whole Simons clan gathers at her eighty-year-old grandma's house.

Clair and John agreed, with more reservations, but I think it was mostly because they have to recognize that Jude and I are together. Like, *really* together. This is the first serious relationship they've had to navigate along with me. I got the feeling there was a lot of worry behind the moment when they finally agreed that, yes, it would be an amazing adventure. They told me to have a good time, even though they know what Chicago means to me—the good and the bad. Maybe they understand too, that this is a chance to new, prettier memories. They decide to head over to the DePraus' house for Thanksgiving. They've known Jean-Marc and Deb DePrau since grade school, and the four regularly beat the snot out of one another at bridge. The friendliest grudge match in Baton Rouge.

Addie knew about her brother's plans, so she arranged to eat turkey and probably caviar with the twin daughters of a New

Orleans city councilman. They'd been besties at boarding school and hadn't seen each other since summer. That she'd be with friends made me happy. Jude smiled when he told me. I think he knew our escape wouldn't be right if we left our friends and family hanging.

I've never been on a plane, so that prospect was exciting, but I wasn't surprised when he mentioned faux-offhandedly that the tickets were for an overnight Amtrak. He flies when he needs to for business, but I bet he white-knuckles it the whole time. My slight disappointment was quickly replaced by empathy and a really fierce need to kiss him. I did. He kissed back. And we didn't get out of bed until late, late on Sunday morning.

Now it's the Tuesday before Thanksgiving. I spent about thirty-six hours working my butt off to get all my assignments done before the four-day break. Our train travel is going to extend it by two extra days. He wants to be in Chicago on Thanksgiving morning, first thing, and won't tell me why. That, at least, can remain a secret. I'll have him to hold as we speed north on the rails.

I've never been on a train either. So I hug him and squeeze with such a burst of excited energy that he steadies himself against the window. "Hey, now. What's that for?"

"I'm stoked. And you're amazing."

"I am. Now let's get naked."

I'm giggling fiercely when the train pulls out of the station and, yes, he has me stripped bare. We're lying on one of the berths; the other is useless because they stack one atop the other like bunk beds when unfolded. "This is going to be a tight sleep. You're used to that big four-poster."

"You're getting pretty used to that monster," he says, tracing circles around my navel. "Besides . . ." He dips low to circle his tongue in the same pattern. His eyes are illuminated by the slanting sunshine, which turns dark brown hair into caramel and chocolate and other irresistible things. "Who said anything about sleeping?"

"These are sleeping berths. It's in the name."

Stretching up to nestle his mouth against my ear, he whispers, "That's because 'private place to fuck on a train' didn't go down well with marketing."

We spend the trip exploring each other, in daylight and in darkness, as the countryside clatters by at beautifully dizzying speed. At one point, while curled against him, as he filled me so deeply, I was watching the lights of some anonymous town speed by in a rush of color when I came. I kept my eyes open, which I never do. The color and the sensation of being filled and satisfied so completely was so dazzling, so perfectly blended. I'll never forget it.

Morning finds us in Chicago. Unreal. I clutch Jude's arm as we file out of Union Station. A limo whizzes us to Hotel Burnham. I've never heard of it, and it has in-room spa services, so I keep my curiosity to myself about how much all of this is costing.

"Is it what you expected?" he asks. "I hope it is."

I sit heavily on the bed, which has much more in common with his bed in New Orleans. "I don't know, to be honest. We need to see more than a hotel room," I say, keeping my voice light.

"Damn. I thought I had you tricked." He grins with a naughty glint in his eyes. "I thought I had you trapped."

I look up at him, staring, only just realizing what I've done. I was only seven when we left. And for those seven years, we certainly didn't live in a high rise downtown. How much did I really know about the city I'd practically mythologized in my head, the way I'd made New Orleans an exotic mystery too?

I think I needed a place to call home, so I made this home. Willfully. I couldn't just be a wandering girl with too many names. I had to *be* from somewhere. So I was from Chicago. And then I was from Baton Rouge. It kept people from asking questions. Now I have to be a tourist, which isn't hard because, well, I'll be seeing it with entirely new eyes.

"We could've saved the trouble and just stayed home."

"Are you sorry to be here?"

"No."

"Then I did just perfect." He puffs out his chest with a flare of mock arrogance. I don't tease him that it's not that far off from his usual arrogance. "As usual. So, dinner tonight. And the parade tomorrow."

"The parade?"

He frowns. "What do you sound like? Disappointed? Because I also have tickets to *Tosca* and to the Chicago Symphony's first holiday concert of the season."

"All of that? For one day?"

"No. Contingency plans."

"You're adorable," I say, kissing between his brows until the frown goes away. "I like the idea of the parade. Adelaide and I have been practicing so much for the Fall Finish that I don't think I'd appreciate a concert. Too much pressure to see the pros when I'm on the verge of having to go through that."

"You're going to play piano, make a hundred people fall in love with you, and walk off the stage into my arms. That's not something to *get through*. Applause at the Fall Finish will be the cherry on top of a damn good semester."

I giggle. "Not walking offstage and into your arms?"

"I don't mind being second to rabid cheering." He waves a negligent hand at the hotel window. "So, the parade it is. I have seats in a booth next to where NBC broadcasts."

"What, no standing in the wind with the peons?"

"Hell, no. I bought us coats especially."

He glares at two brand-new ski jackets. His is a rich sapphire color that will look amazing with his dark hair. Oh, who am I kidding? I think he looks amazing in anything from battered boots and ripped jeans to a three-piece suit and woolen overcoat. Mine is a graceful fawn peacoat with oversized tortoiseshell buttons and these cool corset-like ties at the low back. It's *gorgeous*.

"You're going to laugh at me, aren't you?"

I grin as he stands and walks to the huge window. Already a flurry of fresh snow is streaking the sky. "Because you're going to freeze your hot as hell N'awlins tushie off? Yeah. But you'll laugh at me too. Tell me that wasn't part of the present. Laughing."

He returns my grin, looking wicked and breathtaking. His hair is careless, but his button-down immaculate. "Keeley, sugar, I'm here for your satisfaction and entertainment."

We do all the usual tourist stuff, including a trip to the top of Sears—I mean, *Willis*—Tower, a vintage theater showing of the Thanksgiving classic *Home for the Holidays*, and an absolutely frozen walk along Navy Pier. Even hot chocolate and cuddling doesn't ward off the chilly breeze when I insist on a ride on the little Ferris wheel.

"The water is so different," he says, his voice distant, as if he's standing on the coastline overlooking the Gulf of Mexico. "Lake Michigan just looks frigid. You can't mistake it for anything but kill you instantly cold."

"It must be different in summer," I say, making hypotheticals out of a real memory. "The beaches down by Lake Shore. Have you seen pictures? Some people can walk there."

We'd been able to. It was a *long* walk, but we did once. The water was like getting into a bath. There were so many people. I take a sip of the cooling chocolate and veer my gaze to the south, where that day would've taken place so long ago.

I shake my head. I'm feeling raw and charged up all at once. Maybe it's a good thing he's distracted by the view, because I remember losing sight of Mom. I wasn't afraid. I just sat there with my toes in the surf and the sun on my face, happy. I looked around to see which family I'd pick if I could walk up to one and join right in.

Jude pulls me close and kisses me. We taste of chocolate, which makes the kiss that much sweeter. I'm surprised when I find frozen tears on my cheeks. His lips warm my skin, all over my face, banishing the worst of that old, forgotten pain.

"You crying?"

"It's the cold!" My voice is shaky. Maybe it'll cover the worst of what I push to one side.

"I shouldn't have brought you here."

I shake my head vigorously and grab him into my arms so quickly that his chocolate spills on his new coat. I cuss. He laughs. I slug him on the arm. "Take it back," I say. "Don't ever say this is less than the perfect adventure."

"See?" he replies, still laughing. "Me and perfect. We go together."

"What does that make me?"

He stills, his gaze intense on my face. His skin stippled by lights from the rides along the pier. He brushes his lips whisper-soft against my jaw, then one kiss lower to my throat. "We go together." His words are low and intense, shooting straight to my heart and then low into my belly.

We take a taxi back to the hotel because the snow is really coming down. "I have a confession to make," he says. "It seems especially appropriate now that my new jacket is a walking chocolate stain."

Although I fill with trepidation at phrases like "I have a confession to make," I force my breathing to remain even. This is Jude. He's treating me like a princess, making me feel special and beautiful in ways I've never experienced. "What's that?"

"I don't really have tickets to a booth for the parade."

"No?"

"Ah, there it is." He touches my hair, smiling. "I guessed you'd be disappointed if I said that, and that's how you sound. I'm learning you, Keeley."

I shiver, but it has nothing to do with the cold or his gentling touch. Learning me? Is that worth the hassle? Apparently trust comes easier when it has nothing to do with the pokey parts of my self-esteem. He'd wanted me to see him. *Really* see him. I don't think I'm strong enough to be that open. It's one part beautiful and one much bigger part scarier.

"I requested them too late," he goes on, still watching me with that enigmatic smile. "Instead we have this here." He lifts his arms to encompass our room. "Hotel Burnham, which just happens to look out on State Street."

I exhale with a tentative bubble of happiness. "Over the parade route?"

"Exactly. So if you want to head down and mingle with the commoners for an hour or two, fine. I'll have this fluffy blue monstrosity cleaned overnight and we'll brave the cold." He makes a face before laughing. "Again."

"And if not?"

"The parade starts at eight. I can't remember the last time we slept together when we got up in time for an eight o'clock anything."

My shadows are gone. How can they stay for long when he's looking at me with such boyish, unbelievably sexy playfulness? I slip my hand under his coat. He hisses when my chilly fingers meet the bare skin of his stomach. He tries to fight me off, but not too hard. I love the feel of his muscles bunching beneath my hand. I love the feel of him.

"What would we do instead?"

"I'm very strong," he says, still laughing as I grab more of his flexing muscles.

"I know."

"With some help, we could probably shove that bed against the window and order Thanksgiving brunch." He leans back, not fighting me now as I pet and grasp beneath his stained jacket. "So how would you like to watch the Chicago Thanksgiving parade naked in bed with me?"

~ THIRTY-SIX ~

That was the happiest weekend of my life.

This week is karma biting a chunk out of my ass.

I'm sitting in sociology class. I got an A on that paper on tattooed subcultures. The professor was impressed how I took an approach unlike my fellow students. I used Jude's tattoo as inspiration to look at body modification as a form of mourning and commemoration. Goodie for me. . . .

Until two men enter the classroom and ask for me.

Me.

They're detectives. Or maybe lawyers. I don't *know* . . . but I know. I remember how men like that carry themselves. Not like Jude, with all his confidence and ambition. No, they stand with legs braced and arms at their sides, as if the world is a place full of people who strike first. Why would they believe any different?

I sure as hell don't stand that way when I manage to make my legs work. "I'm Keeley Chambers," I reply. My voice sounds like I've just shouted across the Grand Canyon. Might as well have. The entire class of sixty students and my professor can see and hear everything.

No one realizes yet what a fool I've made of myself. Keeley Chambers is a joke. Being in love with Jude Villars is a joke. Because these men are real, and they're here to rip my life back into pieces.

I blindly shove my textbook and my A paper in my purple messenger bag and stand. I walk slowly, deliberately, until I reach the top of the shallow amphitheater-style classroom.

"Do you have any weapons on you, ma'am?"

"No, sir," I reply, feeling fourteen all over again. The paramedics asked me that when they found me in the kitchen, leaning against the counter and staring at my mother's lifeless eyes. "But you can carry my bag."

I hand it to him and lead them out of the classroom. I lead by floating. I don't have feet anymore. I'm not even sure I have nerves.

The early December chill in New Orleans isn't anything like Chicago, but I still shiver when I step outside. The two men face me. "Miss Chambers, we're from the local DA's office. We've been contacted by law enforcement agents in California. We'd like you to come with us. Completely voluntary, of course."

"Of course," I say woodenly. Only then do I realize they were already subtly herding me toward an unmarked car.

I manage to convince myself that the next three hours are the toughest I've faced since I was fifteen. With my limbs numb, my insides a completely liquefied mess, the DAs lay everything out for me like a dingy carpet. What my father did in prison . . . and the choice I face. By the time they're finished, I'm a wrung-out rag. I shakily step out of the car, but even Dixon Hall doesn't offer me the peace of mind I need. It's only a place to come in from the cold.

An hour later, I hear banging on the rehearsal room door. "Keeley! I know you're here!"

Jude.

Jude finds me.

He slams into the room like a Viking in an Armani suit, there to save me from beasts and pirates. His expression, however, is just for me. It shifts from relief to frustration to anger in the span of two heartbeats.

"Christ, Keeley." He shuts the door with a fierce bang, then strides to kneel before me.

I can hear him through a long, echoing distance. My mouth tastes like mushrooms. Everything about me hurts.

"What the hell is happening?"

I curl into a tighter ball. My head is pounding. I notice piano pedals for the first time. I've taken refuge beneath the rehearsal piano, like I did as a little girl, hiding under anything that might shelter me.

"I was about to call the police." Unyielding hands haul me out from under the piano. I'm on his lap, where I love to be. "Do you know how worried we've been?"

I come to rest with my head against his chest. "We?" I croak.

"Yes. *We.* Didn't you get our texts?"

With cold, numb fingers, I find my phone in my sweater pocket. It's a litany of worry that twists my stomach.

From Janey: *Thot we were on 4 lunch? U OK?*

From Clair: *Janey says it's all blown to hell. I'm on shift. Call John pronto?*

From Adelaide: *Reporters ambushed me at the union. WTF? Call me!*

From Jude: *We need to talk.*

Oh God.

Jude strokes my hair back from my face, although his voice is still tight and brittle. "I got home as soon as I could after Addie got worried and found a half dozen reporters around the house. So start talking. What the hell is going on?"

"Nothing."

"Bull." He pushes me away, although not hard enough to bounce me off the floor. "When did you become such a coward? You, of all people?"

"I'm always afraid!"

"You had me fooled," he says bitterly. "About a lot of things, apparently."

"I didn't want to . . ."

"To what? Lie to me? Because it seems you've done a lot of that. Do you want me to know the reporters' version of things, or do you wanna weigh in? Act like a goddamn grown-up and *trust me*, Keeley."

"See, that's just it."

I scamper up from the floor and find no refuge. The best I can do is find a wall. Just a wall. *Prop me up while I let him go.* I tuck my hands behind my back. My head feels so heavy.

"I'm not Keeley Chambers. I'm Rosie Nyman. Or, I was. When I was born in a slummy part of Chicago."

Jude is sitting with his knees up, his fists resting on either one. He's only a few feet away, but by his expression, it might as well be miles. His frown deepens—not with anger. With sadness.

"You lied to me? I tried to do something wonderful for us and you were, what, revisiting old times?"

"It wasn't like that. I only lived there for seven years. Then I was Sara Dawson and Lila Reuther . . . all because of my birth parents."

"Birth parents?"

"Clair and John Chambers were my foster parents until they adopted me. But for most of my childhood, I lived on the run."

"When did you choose to be Keeley? When they made you pick a new alias?"

"They never let me choose a damn thing," I say, my throat burning. "*I* picked it when I was placed with Clair and John. We moved to Baton Rouge just after my father was sentenced. They got me out of the state and nearer her family. Keeley Chambers is fiction."

"Go back." His voice is quiet, but there's steel beneath the easy drawl. "When your dad was sentenced. Sentenced for what?"

"Second degree murder. He killed my mom."

He jerks. I'm so calm it's scary, like I can take refuge from the present by telling the bare facts of the past.

"I found her body in our kitchen in some backwater trailer park in San Joaquin. He'd stabbed her." There's a scuff mark on the floor, so I fix my eyes on that and don't look away. "A woman has roughly eight pints of blood running through her veins. That's a whole gallon. Imagine a gallon of milk busting on the kitchen floor. Then imagine that gush completely red with a body in the middle of it all. That was her. The cops had already caught Dad, staked out in a nearby vineyard. I'd just gotten off the school bus before they cordoned off the crime scene. They took me away in a different ambulance from hers."

There's craziness in me. I don't realize just how much until I start laughing. I'm hysterical. Jude's joined me against the wall, and I'm smacking his chest and thrashing my head. "She was going to give it up, go to the police. Turn state's evidence. She'd threatened it before, but maybe he really thought she meant it that time. I don't believe it. She was dead on the ground holding her open switchblade. She could've just gotten away. She could've just *rescued me.*"

Jude holds me. I don't know how long I cry, but there's not much left inside me when I finally quiet. My eyes sting. My chest aches. I've worn raw crescents in my palms—my fingernails clenched too tight.

"Then what is all this? The reporters?"

"He's been accused of killing two inmates." I hiccup in some air. "The case is pretty solid, but they still need to prove it to a jury. That means physical evidence, but also establishing character stuff. They want me to go to California and make a statement."

"Will he be there?"

"They didn't know policy out there." I shiver. "He could be."

"Christ, sugar. No way. The police will have enough evidence or they won't. The prosecution won't be able to submit a character statement unless the defense brings up the issue first."

"They could," I say. "What if he's been a model prisoner all this time? No history of violence? Lots of people could come forward and say that, even guards and cops. What if there's no one to say he's a murdering bastard? I have to be that person! Again!"

He frames my face in his hands, which are—I'm really surprised—shaking as badly as I am. "You will *not* sit in the same
room as that man."

"You just don't want me to leave."

"Because you've suffered enough! You're actually considering
this? Your recital is in less than two weeks. Leave that monster
in the past, where he belongs."

"If he's done two more murders, he'll rot in prison forever." I
speak with more certainty. Each passing word is stronger and
clearer. My brain is stitching together again. Too bad about the
rest of my life. "He was only convicted of second degree murder
because Mom fought back. I didn't realize when I testified back
then how short twenty-five years can be, in the scheme of
things."

He goes still. "You testified against him? How old were you?"

"Fifteen." I shrug stiffly. "See? I've faced him down before."

"And you've hidden this? That's one of the bravest things I've
ever heard."

"I had to! No stranger has known who I am since then.
Now what if he learns my new name and where I live? Jude, I
plan on playing piano for a living, and the press will eat it up
about us. He'll find out eventually! I have to make sure he
never gets out!"

He grabs my wrists in one of his big hands, then catches my
chin with his other. "Sugar, the company I run just edged to a net
worth of over two billion dollars. Do you think I'd ever let anything happen to you? *Ever?*"

"Are you saying you can protect me forever? One day, I'll be
forty. I'll have a family and a life well earned, and that motherfucker could be released. I can keep that from happening. I can

help make sure he's three strikes and out, that he'll never be able to come after me. I won't need to look over my shoulder ever again. I won't have to *keep hiding*."

He shoves me away. "What's to say you'll stop hiding? You have one incredible fucktard of a dad, but talent, support, and *very* worried friends. Friends you let down tonight." He huffs air out of his nose. "You were the one to help Adelaide through the bullshit with that professor. What would you think if she'd gone quiet rather than come to you?"

I swallow a roll of nausea. "Be disappointed."

"Back at'cha, sugar."

"I needed to get away from what I knew was coming. The stares. Questions. Pity."

"Not pity." He jabs a finger at me. "*Not* pity. Sympathy—and there's a big difference. Do you think I wanted pity after my parents died? Did Adelaide? Did everyone in this city whose life was smashed to dust by Katrina? We didn't want pity. We wanted help to get through it. You haven't even given us a chance to help. You haven't given *me* a chance."

"I love you," I whisper. "I'd give you anything . . . if I could."

His eyes are unfathomable—so dark and hostile, and still layered with that hurt I caused. "Anything? Define that."

"I'd have been perfect for you. Like you said. You and perfect go together. I'm not. I tried not to live in fear, but there was always that chance. Someday I'd get found out and everyone would judge me for it."

"They didn't need to," he says harshly. "You've already judged yourself. Since you're so big on making choices for yourself, is this the punishment you chose?"

"I didn't—"

"You chose your name and your hometown. You chose to be with me—although apparently with conditions. You chose to be a friend to my sister. You helped Janissa choose that quilt she loves. But you don't get to choose how other people respond to things. That's not your right. I get a say in this too."

"I bet Addie would have something to say about that—your reactions to her life."

"She did, in fact. She and I had a long talk when we were waiting for you to call, or waiting to call the police—whatever we debated doing. And you were right. She confided in me. It felt amazing. I kept thinking . . . I held her hand and she finally came to me, just like Keeley said. So forgive me for being over-protective. I have a history that makes it a little hard not to be." He scowls at me, when I should be stroking away the pain etched at the corners of his eyes, or celebrating the connection he's made with Adelaide.

"And if you think you're the only one walking around pretending," he says, "then that cloud around you is pretty thick. I pretend every day I sit in my dead father's chair. But somewhere between then and now, my faking it became real." He shakes his head and looks away. "I can't believe I trusted you with all that—the night you came to play piano. I told you everything. You didn't think it was time to open up and give me something in return? Jesus, did you ever think you could hurt other people this much?"

Ow. Just . . . *fuck.*

He waits. I know he wants me to say something, but my words are all used up. I can't think. All I know is that Jude and I are hurting—that I've hurt *him*—but I'm not in his arms and I'm not begging his forgiveness. Is that how it's come to be between us? I'm supposed to snuggle deep in his embrace, happy and loved and safe.

Instead he's got barbed wire and Do Not Cross signs all around him.

"Next time you need some distance," he says so quietly, "a text or two would keep your nearest and dearest from tearing their hair out. But . . ." He looks at me with his intensely probing eyes. "You don't believe that, do you? Not really. You try, but you don't believe there are people in this world who give a shit what happens to you."

"I know it so much that I don't want anyone else tainted by my father. He's poison. You seem to think I'm some sort of masochist for doing this, but I'm not. I need rid of him. For good. I'm . . . I'm sorry, Jude." If I'm going to do this alone, I might as well start now. I step away from the wall on knees made of steam. "So . . . that's it."

"That's it? Are you high? Do you think I'd be here if I didn't love you?"

"You love me?" I about gag on the words. "It took my asshole of a father to bring you to say it?"

"It took a bunch of reporters to get *you* to say it?" he counters. "So, yeah, the timing is shit, but that doesn't make it less real. It doesn't mean I haven't been thinking it and feeling it for weeks."

He's so tall, like a god above scared supplicants. He looks ravaged, with dark circles beneath his lids and his mouth set in a grim line. His suit has disintegrated down to a pair of slacks and a half done up shirt.

He's even wearing running shoes.

Tears prick behind my eyelids. He put on comfy shoes to come look for me.

"But what will your company say about all this?"

"The company?" His voice booms. "*I'm* the company, sugar."

"Then you should go."

"What? Why?"

"Because you need to meet with your lawyers. Damage control. Isn't that right?" My gut shrivels into a pebble when he looks away. "Come up with something that saves what you've worked for. You owe it to the people who depend on you."

"That doesn't get to include you?"

"It *can't* include me. This is my horror show." I touch his face. He presses my fingers against his skin, warming us both, but I pull away. "I have to . . . go."

"You don't just mean California, do you?"

"You'll see," I say, my soul shriveling into dust. "It was always going to end this way."

"You know . . ." He punches his hands into his pants pockets with a curse. "I thought you were somebody different."

"I told you who—"

"I heard what you've said, but I also know who I fell in love with." He gives me a harsh look, up and down. "What's that called in music when it sounds all wrong?"

"Dissonance."

"That's the word for it."

My body vibrates from the effort of *not* grabbing hold of him and begging him to take me home. To his home. To the place that feels like it could be my home forever.

He calms some, then shakes his head. "You were so angry, asking why your mom didn't try to rescue you." He spreads his hands. "I've been right here, Keeley. And from what you've told me, Clair and John did a pretty damn good job of saving you too. I don't think this is what they wanted for you. This . . . self-pity."

"This is self-pity because I have to say goodbye to you. It's the hardest thing I'll ever have to do."

For a moment he looks confused, maybe even sympathetic. "Face your father?"

"No, that'll be number two." The pain in my chest—it's a screaming, flaming pain that refuses to end. I have to let it burn. For his sake. "I won't ruin your life by clinging to a romance that never had a future. We might have imagined one, privately. I know I did. But how likely was that ever gonna be? Time for us to bow out before it gets any worse."

I can't look at him anymore. That's when I leave my heart behind, with Jude still standing there, hands in his pockets, head bowed. I need to forget that he ever said he loves me, although I already know that'll be impossible.

Nothing that happens between my father and me will ever be this hard.

~ THIRTY-SEVEN ~

I wish I could've taken the train.

I wish I could stop thinking like that, searching for Jude in everything as I fly west to some strange destiny I can't escape.

The economy cabin is cramped, just like my stomach. I'm crunched into a ball of fear. Not all of it has to do with facing my father again. I'm afraid, so afraid that I've thrown away the best thing to come into my life since my foster parents. Jude Villars. I adore him. I hurt him because fear has been a part of me for longer than my deepest memories.

I was stronger with him than I've ever been. Now I'm alone and I still have to be strong.

I lock my seatback table as the plane begins to descend. It would be so easy to let him do it—just make it go away. Clair and John did that for me. They gave me a stable, safe place to come into my own, sheltering me from the worst as I struggled to find my feet. They even offered to fly out with me, to wait in a hotel while I made my statement, just like all those years ago. I ask them to understand why I need to go alone. I've grown up, and this is a fight I need to take on by myself.

This was supposed to be the year I set out on my own, for real this time. But who did I find within weeks on campus? Only one of the richest guys in Louisiana, maybe even the country.

And he fell in love with me.

Me.

He was right to think that he's never met the real me. I don't think I've met her yet. All those niches I've constructed to lock the bad, the really bad, and the unimaginable—they're bursting open. What will be left of me when I've got Pandora's open box slicing holes in my soul? Nothing Jude would want. I already feel like a husk filled with other people's ideas of who I am. I go to Tulane. I play the piano. Is that enough to define a whole person? Is that enough to love?

The man next to me on the plane folds a copy of the *Times-Picayune* and shoves it into the accordion thingie on his seatback. I catch sight of "Villars." My heart becomes a Thoroughbred jolting out of the gates.

"May I?" I ask, pointing to the paper.

He shrugs and hands it over. "Keep it. I'm finished."

My ears are popping from the cabin pressure. I catch streaks of scenery out the window to my left, but the bulk of my attention is on the front page article.

"Jude Villars Convict Scandal."

Could they have concocted a more ridiculous sham of a headline? But isn't that how I'd framed it in my head—as if he was dating a real con, not the innocent daughter of one? There's a photo of me fleeing in the taxi outside Dixon, my face contorted with the best sort of newsworthy angst.

Only then do I notice the photo credit. Brandon Dorne? Seriously? Did he tip off the press about my real name, maybe even let them have a copy of my schedule? I wouldn't put it past him to keep track of my comings and goings. This must've been his personal lotto ticket—and some personal revenge, all in one.

I'm going to throw up. Maybe explode.

But I don't. That doesn't mean I torture myself with the article. I shove it in the passing stewardess's bag as she collects the last of the trash.

There's a man in a black suit and sunglasses waiting beside the baggage claim with "Chambers" on a sign. At least they're using my real name.

I'm whisked away by a secret ops–style black cruiser to a prison facility. I've never seen it. I only ever saw the inside of the courtroom, and that was intimidating enough. Being admitted past the barbed wire and armed guards is enough to make my skin try to slough off. I want to be a puddle of leftover parts that'll slink onto the floor of the anonymous car, waiting like gum to get stuck to the bottom of a shoe.

I'm met by DAs and lawyers whose names I forget as soon as we're introduced. All I force myself to remember is that these are the good guys, like Ursula was a long time ago. I memorize their faces. There's about six of them by the time we walk through a secure hallway and down a flight of stairs. Each possible throughway is locked, with a guard to permit us passage. The basement hall is austere and lined with a series of doors. In some weird way, it reminds me of the rehearsal rooms at Dixon. Plain spaces. Very different purposes.

I pinch and pull at my clothes. They fit just fine a few minutes ago. Now everything is two sizes too small. Black dress slacks. A raging purple dress shirt. A looped silver necklace Janey made me take. I remember her concern, her parting hug, and how heavily she collapsed onto her periodic chart quilt just before I closed the door. I remember Adelaide meeting me downstairs, telling off the cabbie when he honked. "Gimme a minute, asshole!"

More hugs.

"Come back to us, y'hear?" she'd said. "You don't belong in California. We got work to do here, you and me."

And I remember Clair's and John's worried voices when they talked on speakerphone earlier that morning. "You sure you don't want us to come with you?" Clair had asked.

"No. Just me. I don't want you to worry too much."

"We have your back, Keeley. No matter what." That from John. He wasn't a man of many words, but I soaked up each one. Their love still felt so incredible, even after all this time.

But just before I stepped into the room to face my father, Jude's was the love I craved the most. I don't care anymore why he loves me or that it doesn't seem possible. If he loves me, he'll take me back when I'm through with this nightmare. Right? I'll grovel. I'll beg. I'll hold out my hand and hope he takes it. I'll hope he never lets go, because I won't be able to walk away from him again.

I was a fool to do it at all.

"Miss Chambers? Take a seat."

I'm flanked by the six lawyers or DAs or Martians. Whoever. The good guys. At the head of the wide oval conference table is a man in a black suit, with a stenographer beside him and a digital recorder by his pad of notepaper. My words are that important.

A door on the other side of the room opens. Greg Peter Nyman is ushered in. He's flanked too, but by armed guards.

He's wearing prison orange and looks like hell warmed over—not at all like the spiffed-up version who once glared at me in court. Chains connect handcuffs to a pair of manacles around his ankles.

It's been six years.

He looks like he's aged twenty.

If anyone held up a picture and said, *This is your bio dad*, I'd have denied it. No way. My dad was tall, robust, intimidating. He had full jowls and dark blond hair. This man is slightly stooped, weighs twenty pounds less, and is half bald. What remains is going gray. He was young when I was born. Only seventeen. He's no more than thirty-eight now. I'd have denied that too.

"Rosie girl. Been a while."

I shiver. His voice is nearly the same—just rougher and fiercer, if that's possible. And his eyes . . . His eyes haven't changed a bit. He stares at me with contempt and so much anger. Snakes' eyes look more human. His expression is as dangerous as venom. The manacles and armed guards are all that keep him from lunging across the table and twisting my neck until it snaps.

He killed one woman in our sick little family. Maybe he killed two other people. I don't care right now. I only want to say my piece and get the fuck out of that room.

"Quite the woman now," he says. Guards shove him by both shoulders onto a chair across the table from mine.

"That'll be enough," says the man at the head of the table. He introduces himself as something something, independent arbiter. There are lawyers on the other side of the table, but I class them as enemy combatants. I suppose it's their job. That doesn't mean I have to like them. There are shrinks on both sides—more independent parties, but from Social Services. That I might need a shrink to get through this seems laughable. Don't they know counseling was as much a part of my youth as high school classes? The woman at my side, though, sitting next to me, takes my hand beneath the table and gives it a squeeze.

I'm not alone. Not here, not in Louisiana. No matter the people paid to represent him, the shriveled man in front of me is very much alone.

Speaking to me, the arbiter asks, "Would you please state for the record your name and occupation?"

"My name is Keeley Chambers. I'm a pianist and junior at Tulane University."

"Your name is Rosie Nyman and you're my daughter," comes that goose bump–inducing growl.

"Mr. Nyman, you will refrain from comment or you will be removed from these proceedings. A judge would hold him in contempt," he says. "My authority extends to confining him to a cell where he can watch and listen via video monitor. Keep him quiet, or that's the next step."

I like that he's so blunt on my behalf, but I want to tell him that it isn't necessary. *That man is a liar*, I want to say. *I'm not Rosie Nyman, and he gave up any right to call me his daughter a long time ago.* In fact, staring at him across that wide table, I feel the fear soak down through my new dress flats into the concrete floor.

This man is nothing. He has nothing. He'll be nothing for the rest of his miserable life.

By contrast, I have an amazing life yet to lead. It's waiting for me in New Orleans. And I have a man—a wonderful man—who dearly deserves my apology.

"Continue, please, Miss Chambers. How do you know the defendant?"

"He *was* my father," I say with strength enough to make Greg Peter Nyman flinch. "And he was convicted of killing my mother."

~ THIRTY-EIGHT ~

I sit in Clair and John's living room, having talked to Janey and Adelaide several times since returning from California. Two days of TLC from the people I consider my real parents—my forever parents, from this day forward parents—have done me a world of good. I talked and talked, cried and cried, and in the end, now I'm okay. This was the safest place for me to return to after the torturous hours I spent in that room, which kept getting smaller and smaller no matter how confident my words sounded. I *was* confident. But it's unnerving to be stared down by so much hatred for so long.

I've missed four days of classes. I need to head back. The Fall Finish is Friday night. Sure, it might seem like just another public performance open to the whole campus. Those of us in the department know what rides on the night. Basically, our futures as musicians.

I could put my hopes on a second chance next year. Seniors

are going to perform too, after all. But I'm not in the mood to put off anything important.

Not ever again.

Clair and I had a heart to heart about my split with Jude. After another gentle grilling that echoed a lot of her concerns from a few months before, she said what I already know. That he sounds one in a million. That he's just the right man to have in my life.

Only, he isn't in my life anymore.

I have to fix that. If it's not too late.

I return to campus and a flurry of hugs from Janey. More crying and talking, but less frantic this time. I'm tired of the topic. I've purged what I needed to.

Working up my courage, I text Jude. *Will you be at the Finish?*

He doesn't reply. I check my phone about seven hundred times in two days. I even reset it and do that thing where you take the battery out and blow on it. I don't know if it helps, but I'm willing to start talking to voodoo priestesses if it means hearing just a word from Jude. I've been tempted a thousand times to use Adelaide as a go-between—and I know she'd do it— but it feels unfair to her and completely cowardly of me. I either deserve him, or I don't. I have to find a way to reach him that doesn't mean dragging his sister into the mix.

The night of the Fall Finish, I'm a shaky wreck until my friends get hold of me.

Janey is dressed in the most figure-hugging gown I've ever seen her wear. It's bombshell red, about a hundred and eighty degrees from her usual sweats and T-shirts. I keep trying not to stare, but that's out of politeness. I bet any guy who sees her that night won't be so reserved.

She's eager to go, partly because of the music and partly because I need her *so much*. Adelaide arrives just as we're getting ready to leave. She's gorgeous in a little black taffeta and toile cocktail dress that looks like something from an '80s prom. Even her hair is teased out, New Wave style. I don't get it, but as always she pulls it off.

"Addie," I say, just before we hug. "Meet Janissa."

I'm a little bewildered when they embrace too. "Janey, I'm glad you're coming."

I must be letting flies in. They're both staring at me where I stand, mouth agape. I've never introduced them.

My nerves take on an extra dose of puke worthy when I realize what happened. They met when they gathered in our room, worried sick over me.

"I'm so sorry," I whisper. I've said it to them each before, in the hours before I flew to California, but this feels stronger and more devastating. "What if I can't do this? What if I used up everything when I faced off against my dad? I'll freeze and that'll be it."

"Don't talk shit," Addie says. "You told me once that you worried about the people in the audience who might be watching. Did you ever freak yourself out and think he might be there?"

I nod, feeling pried open. "There at Yamatam's."

"Is that possible now?"

"No," I say with more strength.

She smiles, crooked and cocky. "And if you pull any punches, I'll know and I'll give you hell for it. Worse yet, I'll threaten to blow off this whole thing. I'll behave like it's a big joke. What would you think of me if I behaved like a bratty little show off tonight?"

"That you'd wasted the chance to be awesome."

"If you can't see the flipside of that, then you're playing dumb on purpose." She looks me up and down. "And you're about a million miles from dumb."

I sniffle, but Janey practically assaults me with a tissue. "If you cry, you'll ruin an hour's worth of my best makeup skills. And Opal will be pissed too. Those fake eyelashes took *forever.*"

The primping had seemed like forever, at least. I was hella nervous already, but it was good to have a mini swarm of fashionistas keeping my mind off things. They'd bickered about eye shadow colors and whether I should wear nude or black stockings. I wound up in a long black evening gown made of heavy jersey that drapes elegantly to the floor. The bodice has wide straps and a deep V-neck that plunges even lower to the base of my spine—that flapper look I'd second-guessed at Halloween.

"Yeah, don't mess it up," Addie tells me. "You look like a model, all willowy and elegant."

I can't help but beam and pull her into another fierce hug.

"I tried to drag him along," she whispers. "Seems I'm about as good at herding him as he is at tempering me. I mean, we're still siblings. Bickering and power games come with the territory." She lets me go, briefly adjusting a black velvet bow nestled in her bleach blonde updo. "But he'll be there. I know it."

I'm not so confident as we step out of the elevator. The night is cold. I'm wearing a floor length coat of delicate velvet to complement the dress. I'm glad I have it when we face off against Brandon in the lobby. I'd feel on display without it, when the last thing I want is his eyes on me.

He starts to speak. I don't know what. I don't care.

"I didn't know you had a knack for photography," I say. "You couldn't have captured that moment any better. Good thing you were there right when it happened. Lucky, I guess."

His ears turn pink and he crosses his arms. He's built. I should be intimidated. I sure as hell am not. "What are you saying, Keeley?"

"Oh, I thought it would've been Rosie to you." I take Janey's hand. I take Addie's hand. "But never mind. Bygones and all that. I hope you spend whatever cash you made on something other than ramen."

"Peanut butter and jelly," Janey says. "Live a little."

Adelaide nods earnestly. "In the meantime, we have places to be."

"He won't have you," Brandon calls as we walk toward the exit. "No one would."

His words cut right to my most sensitive, fearful place. But I'm dressed to the nines and flanked by my two best friends. I laugh when they both flip him the bird over their shoulders.

The recital hall is on the ground floor of Dixon. It's a theater in the round, with a harp, piano, organ, and other big-ass instruments set up for the docket of performers. The program list looks like the entire department, plus another couple dozen they dragged off the street. I count forty in all. Adelaide is number six. I'm number twenty-two.

She and I are backstage, with Janey somewhere out in the audience, meeting up with her friends from the haunted house night. Clair and John are out there too. God, so many people I want to impress. I want to show them who they've known—but haven't known—all this time.

"Number twenty-two," I mutter. "Just enough time to work

myself into a tizzy. Is the middle good or bad? Will everybody be ready to go home by then?"

"Quit talking." Addie cracks her knuckles. "You're making me nervous. And I never get nervous."

"Liar," I say with a smile.

"Yeah, totally. C'mon now. Air kisses. I gotta go get ready." She looks at me, her hazel eyes bright and hopeful. "It'll all work out. And in case I forget to say it, you've been one helluva mentor."

I snort with laughter. "That can mean so many things."

"I know!"

Watching her head toward the lineup where other performers wait, I wish I could be in the audience when she wows them flat on their asses. But I don't have to be. I've seen her come into her own throughout the semester. She adores the spotlight and soaks it up, but she can play to an empty room now and be happy with the results. She *can*, but lucky for the world, empty rooms aren't her style.

I wring my hands backstage as performer after performer does their thing. It's such an eclectic mix. I've been so wrapped up in my own drama and anxieties that it's a treat to hear what the rest of the department has been working on. There's Dixieland, stripped-down Philip Glass–style minimalism, a *really* amazing soprano, and some stuff that sounds remarkably rockabilly. I wonder if the crowd is loosened up enough to boogie in their seats, at the very least.

I'm still nervous, but it feels . . . bearable. It's the kind of nervous that happens when I deliver a presentation in front of a class or meet a stranger for the first time. I'm not drowning in it, and it's not going to change anything about what I do onstage. I'm bolstered with happiness and cheer like mad when Addie brings down the house. "She's only a freshman," I hear people whisper, and my heart swells with pride.

That's right, I think. *You just wait. She hasn't gotten started.*

When my name is announced, a strange, welcome calm washes over me, as if I've just stepped into a hot shower. Tension eases out of that spot between my shoulder blades. My fingers don't feel numb, but nimble and eager. The last minute changes I made to the sonata feel so very right. I'm going to perform a piece about a woman who's lost two men from her life—one for the best, and one for the heartbreaking worst.

The extent of control I feel over my own body is astonishing. I'm charged up like the moments when Jude and I are just starting to get serious, naked, playful, at ease with one another during such intimacies. Despite the heartache those memories cause, I think that ease has helped me.

God, I wish he was here.

But he's not. He's gone, and this is what I've been working for a lot longer than I've loved Jude Villars.

The spotlight that had been so intimidating and blinding at Yamatam's is like sunlight. It even *feels* like sunlight, shining on the skin bared by my gown and making me feel like summer has arrived for me alone. I hear the clicking of my heels and the welcoming applause as I cross the gleaming parquet floor. The piano at center stage is magnificent, like the one in Jude's mansion—a concert grand, polished to such a radiant black shine that I can see my reflection in the wood.

I don't recognize the woman I see, but she's lovely and strong. She's me.

The ache in my heart and the happy memories and . . . everything. It's all there, ready to burst out. Keeley Chambers, whoever she's becoming. Unlike some comforting figment I made up in the backseat of a stolen car, just trying to get myself through another night, I *am* real. I'm not a scared, hurt rabbit. I'm ready to play to a crowd of several hundred, to open up and show them my soul. My music won't be pretty or coy. I'd be a fraud if I tried to pass off something so tame. This will be a raging storm, but *I* won't be.

Sharps, flats, blue notes and all . . . I'll control every moment.

Middle C. I stroke it once.

Hello.

And then it's me and my music.

At its heart, the sonata owes a lot to the improv that began on that long ago night, under Jude's watchful, brazen gaze at Yamatam's. I'd busted out something wickedly unrestrained—the product of that night's confusion and excitement. Now it's an introduction. It's the start of something great, with the underlying backbone of the changes yet to come.

I increase the tempo. My heart is beating fast and hard, out of rhythm with what I'm playing, but I'm aware of every intake of breath. I don't just play the notes. I glance toward the crowd, I sway, I let myself be transported by the music while still keeping my enthusiasm in check—like letting a horse run free, knowing full well that I hold the reins.

With the increased tempo, I weave in my first motif. It's simple, really. Only four words, but so full of uncertainty. This is anticipation in E major, lively and edgy: *Will Jude Be There?*

Another motif follows, slowing to an adagio, taking place of the first. In the days following our first argument, I layered in darker notes into the sonata: *Whoever Said We're Dating?* It's the sound of my near silent sobs and what it felt like to have my heart broken for the first time. Rather than cry myself, I put all that emotion into the press of key and pedal. I want the audience to feel that pain, to be moved by what changed me forever. It feels right as I play. It feels like the whole auditorium is breathing with me.

The third motif is brief. *Do I love him?* Of course I do. But that feeling, that bubbling sense of belonging to him, there in Chicago, or as simply as sleeping in his bedroom, is only a bridge to the finale. It's an interlude, like the moments before jumping off a platform diving board.

The final draft—my finishing touches—drained more out of me than I thought possible. I dredged it up from the bottom of my heart while flying back from California, scared shitless, but no longer about my dad. The work had been powerful and hard to face, but it is also some of the most flawless music I've ever written. It came to me, flowing, a gushing waterfall of all I kept inside. The motif . . . That was obvious.

Can You Forgive Me?

I didn't notice they were all questions until I launch into the final few measures. Then again, what is a relationship if not questions? They're the blue notes that hover between yes and no, maybe and definitely, the present and the future. So many doubts. It took missing Jude so badly and facing the man who'd warped my life to realize I possess the power to answer those questions. I possess the power to shape my own life, and to inflict hurt on others. That's pretty hard to admit.

I've said I'm sorry to the people I love. I give them another apology, this time using the instrument that was once my only voice. Now the piano is *part* of my voice. It's part of me too, but it's not all I am or all I have to offer.

The last note fades into silence.

I'm sweating and shaking, but I think it's relief mingled with the triumph of hundreds of clapping hands. I touch Middle C and thank the piano. I've done enough apologizing. It's time to start living and laughing again.

I straighten and fill my lungs with all I've accomplished. My knees are firm, my legs steady, as I stand and walk to the edge of the stage. I'm dead center now, not buffeted or hidden by the beautiful instrument at my back, not defined by anyone but myself. I'm the one they're cheering for.

I bow, with my hand over my heart, where it's full to bursting with pride and accomplishment. *I did it.*

Somewhere deep inside, I always knew I could.

~ THIRTY-NINE ~

After another few bows I make my way backstage. My ears still ring and my pulse is through the roof. Already, a flautist is readying for her big moment. I don't hear her, the poor thing. I wish for a moment that I could have been in the audience, listening impartially to so many great musicians, but I wouldn't give up what I just did for anything.

Adelaide nearly attacks me with hugs—hysterically but nearly silent so as not to disturb the current performer. "Breathtaking," she whispers over and over.

She takes my hand and drags me deeper back toward the dressing rooms, where we can talk with more freedom. I still haven't caught my breath.

"Tell me how it felt." Her grin is a mile wide, so effervescent.

"Indescribable. But I bet you felt something similar," I say, clasping her hands.

With surprising acuity, she tips her head. "I don't think so. I was performing—but screw the audience, like we practiced.

I think you were speaking to everyone. And you knew it, didn't you? You were there in every moment. I saw it. I *felt* it, honey."

I sigh with the relief I didn't know I needed. "We need to call this something different from a mentorship. You've taught me just as much in return."

She grabs my upper arms and pulls me near. "It's called friendship and trust."

"I didn't trust you with the truth."

"No, but if fate had given me the chance to keep my pain a secret the way you did, I would've taken it, no questions asked." We meet gazes filled with tears made from a whole host of emotions. "But you look free now, Keeley."

"I feel free."

"Hey, I forgot to give you something." She hands me a newspaper—the same one that nauseated me so badly on the plane. "I didn't know if you saw it when you left for California. But I think you should."

"Addie, I can't. You know . . . that whole freedom thing."

"There's being free, and there's being happy."

"She's right about the paper," comes a deep, masculine voice that makes me shiver all over.

I go cold.

I didn't need to hear his voice to know Jude was backstage with us. My skin had already prickled with the static charge of being near a man so electric and vital that I'll never know his like again. I turn because I'm bound to him in ways that transcend my five senses.

He's leaning against a pillar, so unfairly regal and wearing an immaculate tuxedo. I have to think it's because of Adelaide, but I want to think it's for me. His luxuriously dark hair is swept back from his forehead, which accentuates the sharp beauty of his features. Who says there's no such thing as royalty in America? He's a prince among men.

Adelaide gives us both a quick, hopeful smile before she shoves the paper in my hands and bids us a quick "Catch ya later, right? Dinner after the show?"

"Yeah," I say with more calm. "Clair and John insist. Gather everybody up and meet in the lobby."

"By the will call window or we'll never find each other."

I look her '80s prom dress up and down. "I doubt that," I say, smiling.

She dashes off, met only ten feet later by another musician she hugs and congratulates. The girl knows everyone. No matter how far I poke out of my shell—or, like tonight, stand exposed and good because of it—I'll never be the butterfly Addie is. I don't need to be.

But I need to apologize to Jude. He's the only person I haven't spoken to since getting back from California.

I want him back. I *need* him back. I'm jittery and numb, like I thought I'd feel onstage. That didn't happen when I was in my new, liberating element. Now I stand before the man I have so much to give. So much to make up for. And so much to lose.

"Hi," I say, completely lame. I force myself to keep my eyes on him, this overwhelmingly handsome stranger, rather than seek out some distraction.

"Read it." Nothing more by way of greeting. No change to his impassive expression. "Aloud, please."

My heart, lungs, and every other organ crush into my throat. It wasn't supposed to be this way. I was supposed to cling to this joyous success for the rest of my life and be content with it. That wasn't going to happen, knowing things are unfinished between

Jude and me. I'm ready to go down on hands and knees and beg, but . . . no.

Not like that.

He never wanted me fragile.

He only wants me to read the paper, which is hard to do through pending tears and the fake eyelashes Opal meticulously applied. I give him one more glance. My heart pinches. He's so damn beautiful. I want him. I *miss* him.

Hands shaking, I open the paper I've unconsciously crumpled and I recite details about me, from my worst days on through my current studies at Tulane. They sound so stark and soulless in print. *That's not me*, I want to scream. I'm not just a few paragraphs of grim details.

There are details about Jude, too—a summary of the worst, and a subtle judgment about his obstinate behavior ever since. There's a quote from some member of the board of directors, re-hashing Jude's decision to keep the headquarters of Villars International in New Orleans. "He has a history of putting personal relationships above his obligations to his family legacy. It's further proof of his youth and inexperience."

As if Adelaide and Jude himself aren't the most important parts of his parents' legacy. Don't they know what he did, and how hard it was? How much of that weight he still carries? My heart burns with indignation.

About his flat refusal to step down as CEO, Jude is further tarnished by people he must see and work with on a regular basis. How many turned on him when given this chance? One is quoted as saying, "Mr. Villars made us aware of his romantic relationship with a college-aged woman. Her obvious personal issues have turned concern into genuine distress. I don't speak for the entire board, but I fear this may affect his ability to make the best decisions on behalf of our shareholders."

That's when I come to the scary soul of the article: Jude's official statement. That crunching knot in my stomach? All those vital organs choking off my air? I didn't think they could get any worse until I read what he issued to the press.

"'Keeley Chambers and I have been involved in a serious relationship for nearly three months, and I made that relationship clear to the Board when the time came.'" I stop and try to swallow. "They've known for months," I whisper.

"Yes."

How long has he struggled to prove himself in the face of so many doubts, even mine? Mine above all. He'd given his heart into my safekeeping, but I haven't kept it very safe.

Me, the girl who's always wanted to be safe.

His face is so damn impassive. *Give me something? Please?*

No. It's not his turn to give. It's mine.

I dare to approach him. Both of us flinch with the first click of my heels. I smell his cologne and the warm richness of skin wrapped in that spectacular tuxedo. My voice is shaking when I keep reading, although the words twist a knife between my ribs.

"'My sister and I intend to support her however we can during this difficult time. Her biological father has already been convicted of one heinous crime. I'm sure that with Keeley's aid, the prosecutors in California will ensure that justice is served yet again. In the meantime, I ask that she be left to continue her studies at Tulane as she recovers from what will be a trying time.'"

It's supportive but . . . impersonal. It's lawyer speak. He had to come up with something ambiguous and calm. What did I expect? Some declaration of his love to the *Times-Picayune*?

"No one understands you," I say softly. "You're a public figure, but such a private person. That you've invited me into your life without reservation . . . Jude . . ." I'm fighting for my life here. Feeling more daring with each second, I look up to meet eyes made unrelentingly blue in the backstage shadows. "You've given me everything, when I've only given you half a person."

"And lies. Even by omission."

I cringe, but there's no denying it. "I have," I say simply. "I regret each one of them."

"Did you do what you needed to in California?" I could melt into his accent, so rough now. His stare is intense—searching, yet still distant.

"What I could, yeah. He goes to trial in February. But me . . . I'm done with him. Done with a lot of things."

Jude stiffens. "Is that so?"

I force my stubborn, refusing-to-do-its-job mouth to open. "I sent you a text."

"I got it."

"Oh." I take a deep breath, made dizzy all over again by the masculine perfume of him and how much I want to sink into his embrace. Instead, I'm grounded by the pain of what it is to stand before this man and not have him. "I had another text in mind, but I didn't send it."

"Why not?"

"Because some things need to be said in person. What I wanted to type was, *Will you forgive that I've been a coward? That I've had no stomach for what it takes to love and be loved. Will you trust that I'm as brave as you've always said I am?*" I try to reach out for him, just the crisp fabric of his white shirt cuff, but I pull my hands back. He's not mine to touch. "You've been brave for both of us. I thought I was running to catch up. I just didn't know it was about the emotional stuff too. I'm young and naïve and you were right to think that was a big difference between us."

His assessing gaze narrows. The set of his shoulders is defensive, which doesn't suit him at all. "And now?"

"I let go of everything up there. Were you there? Did you hear me?" I deliberately echo what he asked in his rain-lashed ballroom. "Do you *see* who I really am?"

"I haven't always." For the first time, he looks away. His Adam's apple bobs. "But you were . . ." He not only returns his magnetic gaze to me, but he takes my face in his assured hands. "You took my breath away. I could feel it, Keeley. You were playing for yourself and completely in control for the first time."

"I was. I was free of my father and—this is the part that surprised me—I was free of you. I've been thinking my strength over the last few months, and even the strength to risk losing you by going to California, was because I love you." I angled my head back toward the stage. "Up there, I had nothing left to depend on but myself."

"How did it feel?"

"Like conquering the world." I *do* touch him then, just where I imagined. I slide my finger over his shirt cuff. "I never need to see my father again. But I remember what you told me in Chicago. You made me smile until my cheeks hurt."

"What was that?"

"'You're going to play piano, make a hundred people fall in love with you, and walk off the stage into my arms.' I didn't believe it. And I've screwed up so badly that I don't dare believe it now."

Looking down at where I'm tentatively stroking his sleeve, I see a lock of hair loosen across his forehead. I want to push it back in place. "Why keep it from me? All of it?"

"Scared," I choke out.

"I'm gonna need more than that, sugar."

"I love being who I've become over the last six years, but I only really believed it tonight. I did that for myself, just like I went to California. *For myself.* To get rid of all the shit that made me so blind to what you mean to me. It's time I grew up. It's time I deserve you—and I believe that I do." I tip my chin to find him staring. In his eyes, I see my same yearning: for all of this to be over, for all of this to be good again.

Please, let that be what I'm seeing.

"I can be strong and fight battles on my own," I say, "but I can't really conquer the world without you. I'm so sorry I didn't give you the trust you deserve. I'm sorry I hid so much, when I had nothing to fear from you. And if you give me the chance, I'll do everything I can to make sure you can trust me for as long as we're together."

"How long do you want that to be?" His voice is surprisingly tight and thick.

"Forever," I whisper. Then, with more force, I repeat myself. "I want forever. I have for a long time. Because, Jude, I love you so much."

Before my eyes, his tense posture loosens. He inhales and extends a hand toward me. "Hi, I'm Jude Villars. You may have heard of me, but I'm more than what you've read in the papers. I'm flawed and I make mistakes and I want someone to love me for who I am."

Smiling the wobbliest smile in the history of smiles, I take his hand. I kiss his knuckles in that endearing way he's always done to me. "I'm Keeley Chambers. I had a shitty time growing up. But now I have friends and true parents who adore me. And I screwed up by pushing away an amazing man—one who made me realize I'm worth loving."

"Come here, Keeley."

I do just that. He holds on tight, saying my name over and over. I love the sound of it. *My* man saying *my* name as if I'm the answer to his prayers. His heart is pounding almost as fast as mine. My eyes go dizzy with black spots.

Only when he whispers against my ear do I find the presence of mind to wake the hell up and enjoy the moment. "You were astonishing, sugar."

I'm so amped. I touch his mouth, then his high, sculpted cheekbones. "That's one of the best things I've ever heard."

"Is this enough now?" He pulls back. Lines of tension bracket the lips I long to kiss. "I'm glad you got through what you needed to. But I . . ." His eyes are stormy and full of need— the sort of need I wouldn't have been brave enough to handle a few months ago. "I can't do this halfway anymore. I want forever too. If we're going to be together, you're stuck with me. Just like Adelaide is. We lost our parents so suddenly that, yeah, I tend to keep a pretty close hold on what I consider mine. I won't ever regret that, or my life, or loving you. If you're with me, you're with me."

"That sounds even better," I say, happily keeping my shit together. "I'm not perfect, you know."

"Of course you're not." He brushes his fingers along the bare length of my throat. "But it's not because of your parents, or because you blew off people who care for you. I was hard on you because I haven't felt that kind of hurt in a really long time. It caught me by surprise, like a bruise from a punch I suffered years ago. I took it out on you." His smile is a more manly version of my wobbly one. "We're not perfect because we're people. It's a fine line, I think—being in love. There's the risk of idolizing an ordinary person, just because she rings every bell and knocks me over with the force of a hurricane."

"That's me?"

"Yes. I thought you were naïve and needed protecting. I thought you ungrateful, especially when you talked about how you'd wondered what it would be like to be rescued. I wanted to be that person. It was easier to get defensive than to give you time." He exhales heavily, his brow tight. "After all that's happened in my life, I feel too old to play games. But until a few days ago, I thought I was too young to say *I love you* and mean it."

I cup his hands in my face, then lift on tiptoes to softly brush my lips against his. He sweeps me into his arms and turns the kiss into a firestorm. I think briefly of Janey and Addie getting on me for ruining my makeup, but I don't care. I kiss him with all my heart.

"I was too lost to hear you."

"You play your music *really* loud," he says, with a kiss beneath my jaw. "It's making you go deaf. But you hear me now? Do you hear how much I need you in my life?"

"I hear you. And I mean it right back. I love you, Jude. So much."

His eyes sparkle. "It was the promise of really good sex, wasn't it? That's what did it."

I give him a wry smile. "Long before that."

He kisses me so softly. "I know you were playing for yourself, and that the whole audience heard you, but I sat on the edge of my seat. I heard our whole time together, the rocky and the wonderful. I thought you were playing just for me." He grins and gives me a secret pinch to my backside. "I already thought you wore this dress just for me."

I let out a relieved burst of laughter. "It was all in there, Jude. In every note, back to when you first dared me. How could I write about anything other than how obsessed I am with you?"

"Obsessed?" he asks, his eyebrows lifted, teasing me.

"Totally."

"I like having that effect on women, sugar."

"Women?"

"Just one," he whispers against my cheek. "Just you."

An invisible weight—the weight of so much worry and sorrow—is gone. It hasn't vanished so much as become a part of me, rather than something to hold me down. "It's *us* now, right? Us together."

"I promise."

I fight off tears, even as I bubble and smile. "I've always liked your promises." Jude kisses my forehead, my nose, then settles on my lips. I've never felt more heat, more pure joy. I wrap my arms around him, taking all he'll give me, giving back all I am. That's the best I can do, right? Keep holding on, living for love and air and magic and the most beautiful, beautiful music.

ACKNOWLEDGMENTS

I offer many, many thanks to my usual suspects, who help me just keep swimming. Love and adoration to my darling Keven, Juliette and Ilsa, my dearest Cathleen, my youthful partner in crime, Casey, and my original, unflagging cheerleaders, Dennis and Kathy Stone. I also want to express gratitude and respect to Lauren McKenna, Alexandra Lewis, Elana Cohen, and my fantastic agent, Kevan Lyon. I could not do this without all of you.